GREEN RATH: A CAIT REAGAN NOVEL

GREEN RATH

BOSTON PRETERNATURAL
INVESTIGATIONS UNIT

AOIBH WOOD

ISBN-13:979-8-9885694-4-2

Cover Art By Rebecca Frank

To the librarians, teachers, and good people who understand that no one should be able to take away your right to read any book you wish.

To the parents of queer children everywhere, may Mother Morrigan protect them.

And for Eva and Calvin, without whom, I would not be here.

Rath (IPA: /ɹɑːθ/) (pr.: ră)

Definition: (n.) (historical) A walled fort, especially in Ireland, typically built during the Iron Age.

CHAPTER ONE

Aoife

I took in a deep breath of the frozen air as I stepped out of the terminal, watching my crystalline breath fume. I wanted to say that there was something distinctive about Logan Airport or Boston, that there was a scent of the city that was unique. But there wasn't. It was just jet exhaust and diesel and the whiff of cigarette smoke from people in the petting zoo. I considered going and asking for one even though I'd quit eight years ago. *I could certainly use one now,* I thought.

The weather echoed my bleak mood. A shroud of overcast lingered overhead, a gray and dismal sheet. It reflected the grimy brown of the city lights along with my dour emotions and mood. My heart thumped in a slow, leaden pace of grief that made my chest ache.

I had always been firmly convinced that if my sister died, I would know. Given my experiences over the years, it wasn't such a far-fetched thought. And I hadn't felt nothing. There had certainly been something, but Liz's voice bearing the news over the phone had still left me bereft and collapsed my world around me. By all measures, it was the worst day of my life. And now, here I was, slogging through the ice and oil-strewn lanes of Logan, looking for Liz.

A parade of buses adorned with a mosaic of logos and names swept past me. From the rainbow hues of car rental shuttles to the demure browns and grays of long-distance passenger lines to the city's Silver Line, marked by its robust T emblem. I felt, for a fleeting moment, more akin to a disoriented stranger than a returning offspring of this city, scanning the ceaseless flow.

"Aoife!" Liz called from the pickup lane. She looked as she always did, never aging, forever twenty-whatever, blonde and perfect, dressed in a brown wool long coat, black blouse, leggings, and riding boots.

I clenched my eyes shut, steeling myself against the encroaching shadow of dread that gnawed relentlessly at the edges of my consciousness. A potent cocktail of resentment and frustration surged within me, leaving bitter emotions in its wake.

I took a deep breath, steadying myself, and opened my eyes once more.

Liz, who, for a fleeting span after Marcella's divisive machinations, had played the part of a surrogate mother, loving and caring, only to abandon me at the brink of adulthood. She'd left me alone to grapple with Uncle Donny and his whiskey-soaked incompetence, hard to do from Trinity, Oxford, Sandhurst, or any of the dozen other places I'd been between school and the military, including Afghanistan. On top of that, the prospect of confronting Ma after an abyss of nearly two years was a daunting beast in itself. Had time trickled by so relentlessly?

"Hey. Good to see you," Liz's voice broke through my musings. Her arms unfolded, an offering for what seemed a heartfelt hug that I chose to disregard.

Good to see you? The phrase hung in the air, a strange welcome for someone freshly grieving a sister's loss. Surely, an 'I'm sorry' or an 'I wish it were better circumstances' would have been a more fitting sentiment. *Gods.*

"Let's just go, okay? I want to get this over with."

Liz frowned in annoyance and slid behind the wheel of the Audi while I took the passenger seat.

We sidled right into a lane headed for the Sumner Tunnel, forcing our way between a beater of a Honda and a new-ish Ford redneck F-150, complete with a gunrack and Georgia plates. She was taking us down past the Science Center. It made sense this time of night. Traffic would be light, though I had no idea where we were headed. I couldn't remember if Cait had mentioned where they lived.

"This your car?" I asked absently, the question serving more as a distraction, an attempt to fill the enveloping silence and stifle the rising depression in my chest. Besides, I didn't know what else to say. What I wanted was comfort, but clearly, Liz wouldn't be bearing any. I was doing my best not to drown in the raging tide of sorrow over the last words that Cait and I had shared—angry words, enraged even. We'd both been upset. And now, she was gone. I'd never be able to say, 'I'm sorry' or 'I love you.'

"No, it's Marcella's."

My chest tightened further with a deep swell of rage at the mention of her name. "Will she be there?"

"Of course, Cait and I live with her. Now, I know— "

"It's fine," I interrupted, cutting her off. "It'll be fine." *It's not fine,* my thoughts screamed at me. *It's not fine at all. It'll never be fine.* But I said nothing, keeping my eyes forward and my mouth shut.

"Look, before we get to the house, I wanted you to know that there's no funeral."

I snapped my head around and stared at her, the sudden declaration bringing another boiling surge of rage and a deeper ache to my chest and stomach. Tears and sobs of grief finally burst forward and threatened to overwhelm me as I snapped, losing my temper. "No! You're not sweeping this under the carpet! I won't let you erase her like you erased me! Cait deserves a proper memorial."

Liz's hand darted towards the glove compartment, retrieving a handkerchief and throwing it in my direction. Her fingers then tightened around the steering wheel, pale against the dark leather. Her ruby lips pressed into a firm line, a silent declaration of her irritation. "Aoife, it's not like that. I—" A weary sigh tumbled from her lips, hanging between us for a long moment.

Her words, when they finally came, held the crisp, firm tone she'd often employed during my tumultuous teenage years. A

4

remnant of a past that seemed lifetimes away, each syllable felt sharp and precise. "Listen, it's not what you think. Not in the slightest."

"How could you know what I think? You called me and told me that my sister had died. That she was shot. And you sounded pretty fucking distraught. If she's not dead, it was a hell of an acting job. Where is she?"

A profound loathing churned within me, not for Boston itself, not really, but for the specter of Da's funeral. It seemed to cling to every corner of the city, every crosswalk, the different, and yet still familiar, skyline, even the airport, the place where I'd been whisked away on a one-way ticket to a world of chaos and turmoil, first to London and then to Ireland, stuck for two and a half years with me Ma's booze-addled friend and the pain-in-the-ass vampire surrogate mother sitting right next to me.

Now, here I was, back in the place where it all happened, where my life had been turned upside down. I wouldn't say ruined. I'd made an okay life for myself. But it had never been the same, never right. I'd lost my twin, the other half of my soul. No, not lost, abandoned. I could have found her later. There had been nothing stopping me. In a dark corner of my thoughts, I acknowledged a haunting truth. I had forsaken her, driven by my own distorted quest for selfhood. I had wanted to be uniquely me without the comparisons of a mirror image that always seemed just a little brighter, a little smarter, a little better. And in my selfishness, I had sown the seeds of my own bitterness, and now, here I was, reaping the fruit, rife with thorns, that I'd laid in my own path. It was karma.

"It's not that I know what you think," Liz replied, an old, familiar restrained agitation tightening her jawline. "It's that you can't imagine the situation. Now please, just wait until we get there. It'll only be a few minutes."

"Fine," I huffed in a verbal sigh and crossed my arms, letting the silence drop between us, thick with furious frustration for the remainder of the ride.

She wasn't wrong about the trip, as it turned out. It was, in fact, brief, and we arrived only about fifteen minutes later, the car practically overflowing with a suffocating and icy quiet that felt almost physical, as if we'd brought the cold weather into the car with us.

Liz pulled us into the underground garage of a posh-looking four-story house. An old BMW 3-series lurked quietly in one corner like some dusty, undead beast, its spectral gaze following us as we pulled in. Three of the half-dozen or so parking spots were filled with two Honda Civics and a police cruiser. *They must have guests,* I thought.

"The gym is through there," Liz said, jabbing a finger at a door to my right as we disembarked. "The lift is over there. That stairwell," she motioned toward another door, "leads up into the house as well as the sub-basement."

I glanced around, taking in the exits and the stairs she mentioned, also noting the location of the garage door control panel. "You live here? This place is pretty posh."

"Your sister and I do. We raise our daughter here," she said, and I thought for a moment she cringed a bit.

"Katie? The little vampire girl? Cait said it was a long story, only that she was taking care of her. She was short on details, I guess."

"She didn't mention we were together?"

I raised an eyebrow at that. "No, but we only spoke a few times in the last couple of months, and it was—" I sighed. "It was awkward." Could this day get any weirder? The vampire who'd practically raised me for two years was dating my sister. Eww.

"Come on. I'll take you to Cait."

Liz ushered me into the lift, unlocking and pressing B-2. The lift descended with a mild hum as we stood in silence. I half-expected Muzak.

"Christ, how far down is this sub-basement?" I asked after a minute or so.

"Nearly a hundred feet into the bedrock," Liz replied with a mischievous curve to her lips. "Consider yourself fortunate we chose not to brave the stairwell."

I didn't have anything else to say, so I shut up and waited.

Eventually, the doors opened into a compact corridor, and

we stepped out, turning right. At the far end ahead of us, flush into the sealed concrete, sat a water-tight steel hatch, wheel lock and all. To our rear lay the door to the aforementioned stairwell. Just the thought of climbing it made me feel tired.

In between, nestled halfway down the right-hand side, was a door of striking red wood with a knob at its center, a beautiful anomaly in this subterranean environment. The etched wheel of runes with which Marcella had a fondness for embellishing her notepads and other possessions was also embossed on the door at about eye level. "Oh, look, it's Cruella's little magic circle," I said snidely. "Is she around? Looking for puppies to drown?"

I was almost convinced that the ghost of a grin threatened to crack Liz's grim facade for a fleeting moment. But it rapidly solidified back into her stern glower as she ushered the door open, signaling for me to enter ahead of her. "Marcella is at work."

The sight within stole my breath. Cait lay in repose, garbed in a sheer gown of pure white silk, a picture of gentle sleep on a polished wooden table. Bathed in the pure light of the overhead, she seemed more a serene specter of a woman than the sister I once knew. Her gangly arms and legs were filled out with corded muscle. The stark alabaster of her skin lay over those muscles in a flawless expanse, a vivid contrast to her crimson lips. She looked like an auburn-haired Snow White lost in perpetual slumber, missing only a glass casket and seven short blokes with pick-axes. The moment was surreal, like looking into some dark, magically distorted-looking glass.

"Mirror, Mirror on the wall," I muttered to myself wryly.

We were roughly the same size and build, and similarly fit, but even if I hadn't known already, there was no doubt, gazing at her, that my sister was a vampire. The scene was breathtaking in a macabre way, like something out of a twisted Brothers Grimm tale. I chuckled to myself at my odd thoughts, though, as a weird part of me was glad she'd been hitting the weights before she'd been turned. At least she'd be buff for eternity.

"Is she—" I glanced at Liz.

"Alive? Oh, yes. I mean, in so far as any vampire is. But, Aoife, her soul is missing."

CHAPTER TWO

Weyna

"Weyna, blossom, wake up."   The tender prodding of a delicate hand elicited an ungraceful grunt from my throat, and I rolled over, seeking refuge in just a bit more sleep. The nudge shifted to an insistent jostling of my shoulder. "Weyna, you have to wake up! We've overslept."

One eyelid lifted reluctantly, revealing Boudka's stunning face, framed in the halo of her untamed mass of golden hair. Her lips, generously full and ripe for stealing kisses, were drawn into as fine a line as they might manage, and her striking ice-blue eyes glared at me in a mild annoyance that was teetering dangerously on the edge of disgust and irritation.

"Damnit, Weyna! Wake up," she barked, her voice edged with anger and disapproval. "I've already filled the bath water, but you owe me. Nemhain will be here any minute, and I need to leave."

I stuffed my head under my goose-down pillow to ward off the ambient light filtering through the tent walls. "Just a few more minutes, Boudka. Please?" I was whining now, but I'd been having the most vivid dream, even up to the violent and terrifying end.

"Maybe you can lay about, but I work to earn my keep." She blew out an exasperated breath and thumped my bed. "I have a dozen duties, and you are not going to make me late. If you get into trouble, that'll be on your head."

I cringed and sat up, a ready retort on my tongue, but she was gone. I ran a hand through my hair, then shook my head to clear the fog of the far too-lifelike dream. It had been so real and immersive; it took me a moment to figure out where I was, even *who* I was.

"What the hell?" I murmured softly, but it came out strange, in a language I both understood and spoke but seemed alien in my ears, much like tasting a strange fruit whose flavor contains familiar notes but is still foreign.

Boudka pulled back the flap to the tent's confines, ushering in an accompanying breeze that held both a bitter chill and the sweet perfume of the nearby grasslands. The resonant whispers of the ancient trees that grew beneath the high ridge upon which the fort stood sounded in the distance, providing a soothing undercurrent to the bustling morning activity outside.

I let a playful smile curve the corners of my lips as I gazed at her through my mop of black hair and danced my eyebrows at her. "Couldn't stay away?"

She smirked, maybe a tad taken in by my childish grin, and shook her head. "Brat."

In my youth, I had never been one for blondes. They just never tugged my fancy, probably because there were so few in my village. The few that lived there often wed swiftly. Not that I hadn't stolen a memorable moment with a few, maybe even married, but I'd never tell. Yet, Boudka, who seemed to radiate the morning's glow, entranced me from the moment our lives intertwined.

In the early morning light, her hair danced like a field of wheat interwoven with gilded rosé threads, and the fingers of dawn streaming among the clouds anointed her head in a soft pink and purple halo. Her skin glistened with the dew-laden droplets that descended from the canvas overhead, which seemed to shimmer as they fell and traversed her skin, giving her a glow that rivaled the best of Fae glamour. She was truly stunning.

I took a deep breath, appreciating the light balm of the early spring air. I felt as if it cleansed me of the lingering frost of my dream, which had been biting and cold, the ground, the trees, the streets, all but the gaping maw at the end of the damp tunnels, which had blown hot with the desolate breezes of my mother's shattered home. This was so much nicer, bewitching even in some ways. And between the crisp morning air and Boudka's beauty, I found myself thoroughly distracted.

I glanced up at her again, finding her eyeing me once more with tolerant irritation. "What?"

"I *said* you are such a brat," Boudka laughed. Then she raised an eyebrow, and her annoyed smirk turned to devilish delight. "Uh oh. I see your mother tromping through the camp, and she looks to be in a foul mood. You probably want to make yourself presentable because I'm leaving before she sees me and I have to look at her sullen puss of a face. And I don't want her dressing me down. I'm late enough as it is."

Snatching my tunic from the floor, I chuckled, but when I looked back, the flap was vacant once more, though she'd left it pinned back, giving anyone who might happen to walk by a full view of my skinny childlike body. Boudka called it willowy, but she was just being kind.

Great, I thought wryly. *Thanks for that.* Then I snorted in amusement. *Sullen puss. That was a good one.*

"I'm on it," I grunted to the empty air as I pulled myself from my bed and pulled on the robe.

I still felt groggy, as if my mind were gummed in a barrel of sticky syrup. My thoughts diverted down the strange avenues of the dream that felt more like memories than constructs of my subconscious. But now, at least, I had a firm grasp of where I was, here in my mother's bathing tent, my home for the last four years.

The waxed canvas walls wafted like sails in the wind, their tympanic rhythm tempting me back toward my cot, but I resisted, instead pulling my waist-length hair into a ragged bun and readying myself for the day's chores. Straightening the rugs that covered the dusty ground and making my bed somewhat haphazardly, I prepped the tent and adjusted the stand that held a large depiction of Shaddani at its apex. The painting didn't really need to be moved, but it gave me a moment to admire the exotic image within. Of everything in the tent, it was the one thing I truly appreciated, the only thing that sparked some sense of wonder.

Within its gilded frame, the massive painting showed The Vermillion Palace, blood red and glowing, the centerpiece of the capital city. Great Black Dragons and vast murders of crows circled its heights. Shaddani's three moons floated in the backdrop of the night sky.

A few feet from my bed, beneath the wide painting, a large wooden tub lay recessed into the ground and surrounded by a circle of flagstones, and within it rested slightly undulating crystal-clear water, the breeze giving it a slight flutter as eddies and currents of air created small whorls and ripples across its surface.

Bless you, Boudka. I'd have to thank her later for filling it. Nemhain finding it empty ahead of her morning bath would have been the last thing I needed right now. Not after yesterday. Not after what everyone was calling "the sheep incident." I drew in an exasperated breath as a flush of embarrassment swept through my thoughts, and I relived the same vivid mortification I'd felt only the night before, bringing on a sensation of being a simple and complete failure.

Thickly woven towels of Fae watercloth, dyed in black and emblazoned with the emblem of our clan, sat draped across their stand, their ends perfectly even. Boudka again. She was such a sweetheart.

My thoughts drifted back to the long, bizarre, and frightening dream, still pulled as if drawn by some gravity. Though, if I was honest, some parts had been less than terrifying. I suppressed a hot-cheeked smile at the more prurient aspects of the reminiscence.

Slices of the dream had been positively scandalous, and every sparkling detail was still shining in the theatre of my memory, haunting, uncanny, and bewildering, as if I'd been living another life entirely, one I honestly did not understand. What was worse, an altered state of being hovered about me. My head was weirdly muddled, swaddled with thick emotions, and though my thoughts felt more directed and precise than they'd been in years, trembling rage nested somewhere, burrowed deep within me. It squeezed at my chest. I took a few deep breaths to quell it. And it helped— some. But the ember still remained smoldering in my chest like a poorly extinguished flame.

The Dark Lady's unique timbre wafted in from outside, just over the noise of the flapping canvas. It sounded as if she was scolding someone for something, and her sharp tone interrupted my uncomfortable musings. Then I heard Boudka. Nemhain had spotted her hurrying from the tent and was laying into her. The only thing I could make out was Nemhain saying, "Unless you'd rather be down in the village."

I hurried to the bathwater. It was, of course, still ice cold. Boudka hadn't had time to place heating stones in the water. How could she have? She didn't have access to the Bethadi stores. *Fuck,* I swore to myself again. *Fuck, fuck, fuck.* I'd have to heat it myself.

In the strictest sense, my mother's edict had unequivocally forbidden me to dabble in the mystical arts until I acquired a more robust command of its intricacies. Yesterday's fiasco had only served to cement this decree. Nevertheless, the prospect of her arrival to chilly bathwater threatened to stoke a slightly more incendiary wrath.

As I drew in a lungful of air, an involuntary prayer fluttered in my mind, pleading not to blow up myself, the tent, or the whole damn camp with my magical meddling. The incantation, "Tednia," was no more than a simple utterance, a mere ripple in the vast ocean of spells. Yet, the resulting surge of arcane energy coursed potently through my veins, raw and untamed like a vast current.

It demanded a brief, anxiety-stricken duel to tame this elemental tempest into some semblance of order. My inner sight honed in, splitting the world into myriad threads of 'tarzhi,' the lifelines through which the blood of magic pulsed. They appeared as vine-like striations, their spectral luminescence denoting their origins — radiant white, sterling silver, and gleaming gold represented the ethereal Bethadi, verdant green and oceanic turquoise bore the essence of Earth magic, and a palette of cosmic purple, deep blue, and bloodied vermillion stood for our own, for the Shaddani's mystical lineage.

With a desperate resolve, I swept aside the intrusive tendrils of distractions and focused my entire being on the task at hand, perception wide open to the intricate dance of magical strands before me.

They were wild things, following my nervous system somewhat but fraying and braiding in chaotic, random chains. Slowly, with effort, I coaxed them into a semblance of structure, directing each strand into an orderly direction in-line with the whole, sending them lancing to my fingertips.

Once I felt I had the energy under some air of control, I dipped my hand into the water, holding the magic just long enough to bring the water to a pleasant, comfortable temperature, only satisfied when a soft waft of steam floated up from the bath. I breathed a sigh of relief. My control had been less than stellar as of late. But then again, this was a minor spell, and I suspected my body wouldn't let me boil my hand. At least, I hoped it wouldn't.

The tent flap flew back just as I withdrew my hand and stood. I bowed my head in mock obeisance to the royal pain-in-the-ass, Nemhain, the most high and mighty, obnoxious, annoying, and capricious hero of Mother Danu's army. She was also, unfortunately, my mother. Ugh.

"Oh, lovely," she said, her voice tinkling like glass in critical irritation despite her words. "Thankfully, you didn't cook yourself while heating the water."

I froze, still staring at the rug-strewn ground. *Why does she always have to rub it in?* I thought. I knew I was an awful witch, but I didn't need a reminder. Nor did I need her to scold me either, but that was how she was, never satisfied or happy with me or my efforts.

"Weyna, I am the Goddess of Magic," she declared as she stripped off her clothes. "Did you think I wouldn't know immediately when you used magic to warm the tub?"

"No, ma'am. I mean, Yes, ma'am," I said, cursing silently under my breath. "I didn't want you to miss your morning bath ritual."

A long, thin finger crooked under my chin, pulling my eyes to hers. "You seem different today. Something about you is—" She paused, a thoughtful expression on her face. "Nevermind. It would be best if you had a bath yourself. Why don't you join me?"

"Mother—I mean, ma'am?" I almost stuttered. "It's forbidden. I'm supposed to be your servant."

"And I am the Queen of Shaddan, and though I have few subjects left, you are my daughter. I can do as I see fit. Now, take off that tunic, step into the bath, and get the smell of yesterday's chores and last night's fiasco off that body, girl."

I sniffed at myself. I didn't smell fantastic, but I didn't stink, not really. Still, I stripped out of my tunic and took my mother's hand, letting her lead me into the tub.

The warm heat conjured an errant memory from my dream. I was sitting in a pool, my head against milk-white breasts, feeling almost drunk as hands roamed over my body, washing off dried skin and cleaning my hair. I pushed the thought aside quickly and suppressed the shiver running down my back. Best to be bathed and out.

"Nemhain, I'd like a word—What is going on here?" A harsh raspy voice called from the tent flap. "Planning on seducing my slaves now, too, are we, Nemhain?"

My mother turned, sloshing a bit of water over the edge onto the flagstones. "Saya! If you recall, this is my daughter, so I won't be seducing anyone. And if you try to take my daughter in place of that stupid boy, I will place my foot less than delicately in your fabulous gray arse. We came here to save these people from the Kaushkari, not enslave them. Now get out!"

Saya squinted at my mother, then turned her spiteful gaze on me as if I'd done something to her personally. I quickly looked down at the water, and after a moment of seething, Saya threw down the flap and left.

My mother scowled at the tent entrance, waving slightly in the morning wind. "Obnoxious bitch," she muttered. "As if I'd let her take you. Honestly, Weyna, that woman is going to push me too far one day."

I said nothing, choosing instead to finish washing.

Saya and my mother had been feuding for months now. It had something to do with a servant boy Saya had captured trying to sneak a peek into her tent one night. In response, Saya had claimed him as a slave. I didn't really know the rest of the story.

From what I did know, though, I thought it too harsh a punishment. He was young and stupid, and it didn't excuse the indiscretion, but sometimes kids did stupid things. I had done plenty.

Truthfully, though, Saya had only been trying to get a rise out of my mother. Of course, I didn't see why. It was about as hard as stabbing a dead goose.

"How was your rest, Weyna?" My mother asked, abruptly pulling me from my thoughts.

"I rested well, ma'am." *As if she was really interested,* I thought bitterly.

I looked up briefly into her eyes, expecting the usual cold calculation I saw there, but this time they crinkled at the edges with a bit of humor.

"Is something funny, ma'am?" I scooped up a bucket full of water and rinsed off the body soap, and began washing my matted hair with her champi bar. If I was going to break the rules, it seemed a shame not to do it all the way, but if my mother found the use of her personal supplies irritating, she certainly didn't show it.

"Funny? No," she replied and grabbed the sponge off of the small squat tray next to the bath. Then, as she scrubbed under an armpit, she sighed. "Weyna, daughter, why do you think so ill of me? I'm simply trying to teach you some responsibility. Why can't you take Badb's or Macha's example if not mine?"

I pursed my lips in aggravation, and my mouth ran away, my brain in tow. "What kind of mother are you? Why are you like this?" I snapped hotly, voice shrill and loud. "All you do is criticize my every effort. Never once have you given me a kind word. You insist on having me call you ma'am or your majesty or a hundred other weird appellations, but never just mother or, heaven forbid, ma." My hand flew to my mouth, sending water into her face.

My mother's hands went still as her expression turned hard, eyes drilling into me like motes of reflected crystal light. "I am the kind of mother that wants her child to survive. Remember when I found you, your father's body pulled over you, stinking and rotting, trying to hide from the emisai? Did it occur to you that I might not want to see you dead with him?"

I scowled. "If you cared so much, where were you when the Fomori came? Where were you when those things slaughtered everyone in the village? Where were you when—"

"I was coming for you!" She shouted back, her voice echoing throughout the tent and probably beyond. She took a deep breath, calming herself. "The Fomori invasion was unexpected. But I felt it when your father died. We were connected. I winged it straight back to save you. Then I brought you up here to protect you and to try to teach you something, anything really, to protect yourself because I realized I couldn't be there all the time." Her voice rose again, and the tent darkened around us, the shadows lengthening as her temper began to falter. "We are at war! But all you do is complain and shirk your responsibilities and chase that wench's skirt."

My eyebrows rose at her rather ignominious description of Boudka, and I opened my mouth to say something about it, but she held up her hand.

"Stop and listen for once, Weyna. Everything north and east of here is in ruins, everyone dead at the hands of the Fomori or fed to the maw of Mother Darkness as raw material to make more of them. You have a purpose here, and you will learn to use your magic and defend your people. One day you will have to take my place! I can't live forever. Even the Shaddani die."

"They're not my people," I shot back hotly, pulling myself from the tub now that my hair was rinsed.

"If not them, then who? Who is like us, child? Besides, your father was human, and those humans are the only people we have."

"And they would see me burned alive if they knew what I could do!" I had no people, only her. We weren't of Mother Danu's people, the people that humans called the 'Light-Fae.' Nor were we of the Óşeni or the Kylr, but we certainly weren't human. We were of Shadden, and that home was gone now, destroyed by the Kaushkari and claimed, at least in part, by Mother Darkness, a land irredeemable from my mothers telling.

"It doesn't matter, Weyna! They're all we have, and we'll not see this world turned to ash like our own. Don't you want Boudka to have a home?"

Ouch. That was a cheap shot. "Of course I do. But couldn't she come to live with us in Bethad? I thought when this was over, we would be going there."

"No, child, she can't. The magic there would twist her into something unrecognizable, and even if it didn't, she'd be at the mercy of even the weakest of them. Boudka has magic in her, for sure, but I've yet to figure out how to unlock it. And given all the interest you've shown in developing your own skills, you'd be at the mercy of those flippant dimwits, too."

I blanched. The Bethadi were capricious creatures. They had a code of honor and a religion of sorts, which is why they were following Mother Danu at all, but they had no morals as humans saw it, and many of them thought humans were nothing but sport or playthings.

My mother read my expression. "Now you see the reality."

I grabbed one of the towels and began to dry myself. "Well, then, Óşen, why not there?"

"Óşen is a miserable place. Just look at the Swasari. Do you think they earned their reputation as battle-hardened warriors by sitting at a summer lake eating grapes? Óşen is cold and too dark for any human long term, drifting around a dim red star. She would be miserable and looking to leave for Centrus within a week, and I wouldn't blame her. This is her home— *our* home. Besides, getting to Óşen means going through Shadden, which means winning this accursed war with Mother Darkness and at least pushing back her forces so we can cut a path there. Though, given how quickly she is massing forces and creating new Fomori, we may have to just close the gate. Or would you like to try sneaking her through Kaushkar and Centrus? There's no direct gate to Óşen here or in Bethad."

"But— " I tried to protest, but my mother shut me down.

"Even we can't go home. And even if we could, where would we go? The old palace is all that remains of our once-great civilization. It's livable, yes. My sisters and I stayed there, trying everything we knew to stop Mother Darkness until even we had to flee. It's barely thirteen leagues from the current gate, but she'd find us eventually.

"No, Weyna. This is our home. This is where we stay. Maybe, one day," her voice softened, and she stepped from the tub and grabbed a towel, giving me a pitying look. "Maybe one day, someone, maybe even someone like you, will bring back the trees and the stars and the moons. But we don't know how to wrest control of Shaddan from Mother Darkness, save for sending her somewhere else, to be someone else's problem. As long as she controls the magic of Shaddan, we're stuck here."

"Send her to Kaushkar," I murmured. "It's where she belongs anyway. It's where she wants to be, isn't it?"

"We can't do that. I made a promise as queen to protect her from Dyeuspater, and part of that pact was not to send her back. An agreement among the Fae, light or dark, is sacrosanct. I couldn't break it if I wanted to, and for any Shaddani to try would be to court death and ruin worse than we have already faced. I have explained this to you. It's why the Fae are so," she paused, then settled on a politic word, "particular about their agreements."

"Ruthless, you mean," I muttered.

But she wasn't listening now. Her entire demeanor had shifted like a summer breeze, turning contemplative. "Now, that would be something to have."

"What's that?" I asked, still scowling at her.

"The agreement between the Shaddani and Hel."

I raised an eyebrow. "Hel?"

She waved a dismissive hand and paced. "Mother Darkness.

It's her true name." Then once again, she was scowling at me. "It doesn't matter. The agreement was lost with the vault. There's nowhere else to go, Weyna. We're stuck here. We have to make this work."

I pulled on a fresh tunic and cast my eyes toward the tent flap, defeated. She was right. This was the only home we had if I wanted to be anywhere near Boudka. I wasn't ready to concede the point but nor did I have another good argument, so I pulled my hair into a loose braid and stomped from the tent to attend to my chores. Obviously, Ma had never been in love. *Yes, she has. Don't be stupid.*

I stopped and shook my head just outside the tent. My internal monologue was definitely taking on a much cheekier tone.

CHAPTER THREE

Aoife

Liz guided me upstairs, the weight of Cait's condition settling in my stomach. As we waited for the lift, Liz explained that Cait had remained unresponsive for the most part since being shot, leaving them uncertain of how to pull her out of it. They had even run an EEG to confirm there was brain activity, and surprisingly, there was far more than expected for a human in her condition, let alone a slumbering vampire.

The sight of Cait in her current state shook me to my core, leaving me withdrawn as the lift rumbled to the third floor in a way that seemed off. Liz led me to Cait's room, where I would be staying, at least for the night. I envisioned a room filled with colorful posters and peculiar trinkets reminiscent of our childhood. However, the reality before me was starkly different.

When we'd been kids, Cait had put up posters and collected weird things. She had this clock-lamp thing shaped like a panda that sang happy birthday and a penguin-shaped music box that played the Imperial March from Star Wars. It seemed like everything she bought for our room sang or played or tapped out some tune. And they were all colorful and bright. This place was dreary by comparison. There was a polished cherry wardrobe along one wall. It was nice, elegant even, probably antique from the look of it. Two nightstands flanked the queen-sized bed, covered in a tasteful solid blue duvet with a grey throw blanket, and a gorgeous pen shell lamp sat on one nightstand next to her badge and a small gun safe.

"God, sis," I whispered with a snort. "You've gotten old."

On the bed, a fat orange tabby meowed at me, and I walked over to stroke him. He sniffed at me, then looked at me through narrowed eyes, then sniffed at me again. I'd say he jumped off the bed then, but it was more of a plummet. Once on the floor, he collected himself and sauntered away, looking extremely put out.

"That's Jabba," Liz chuckled. "Cait's—our cat. He's probably hella confused right now."

Liz opened a small chest in the corner, constructed from gray-painted wood. "I picked up clothes in your size. I wasn't sure of your preferences, so I sized them for your sister and hoped." She paused, her eyes scanning the contents. "Mostly jeans, t-shirts, and sweaters. There's a Canada Goose jacket hanging up in the closet downstairs. I bought it for Cait, but she won't be needing it anytime soon, so you're welcome to it."

I nodded. "I'm sure it'll all be fine." *Nothing like hand-me-downs for the afterthought sister.* I turned back to Liz. "Umm. . thanks. I'm sorry I was so grumpy. I just—"

I blinked back hot tears before a high-pitched voice squeaked, "Auntie Aoife!" from the doorway.

I turned and found a pretty girl of maybe seventeen with long black hair and big grey eyes staring at me. If you discounted the cute stuffed vampire bat in her arms, the pair of wide-legged jeans and white t-shirt hocking 'Girl in Red' would have been right at home with about a quarter of the girls in Galway. She was definitely in the current mode. Given that she was a vampire, I'd expected a mini-mosher. And something in her expression and demeanor reminded me of Cait when she was young. Adopted or not, the apple had fallen pretty close to the tree.

"So, you must be Katie," I said, a hint of a smile forming on my lips.

"Yup." The girl barged forward into the room and threw her arms around me. "I'm so glad you're here. Wow, you really do look just like Mama."

"Mama." The word felt foreign on my tongue. I struggled to

find the right words, feeling a strange mix of familiarity and uncertainty. She was my foster niece, after all, but the lack of a shared history made me feel like an outsider.

I returned the embrace, then took a step back, unsure of how to navigate this new relationship. *Say something, Aoife.* But my mind was blank, and the silence stretched longer than I'd have liked.

Sensing my discomfort, Liz intervened, rescuing me from my awkwardness. "Katie, come on. Let's let Aoife get settled. She's had a long trip, and I'm sure she's tired." Liz gently shooed Katie out of the room. "We'll let your aunt get settled, and then we can chat. Aoife, there's a lot you need to know." She closed the door behind them.

Shite, I thought. *What the absolute fuck in an arsehole am I doing here?*

I let out a sigh, momentarily feeling a weight lift off my shoulders. But then, fatigue tugged at my body, reminding me of the long flight. Opening my bag, I glanced at the medications and medical file inside and sighed once more.

A deep melancholy settled in my heart as I thought about Cait, Liz, and Katie. It was a twisted kind of family, but it was still a family—a family I'd never have.

I shook off the somber thoughts, undressed, and wandered into the bathroom.

"Well, Cait, not short on the comforts that matter," I mused, taking in the luxurious shower before me. It was bloody glorious, with multiple heads and wall jets. I just about had an orgasm on the spot. I'd spent the last God only knew how long with one of those fucking pump showers we all had in Tourmekeady. It beat the alternatives, and they weren't awful, but still. Honestly, any place with a regularly working shower was great after Afghanistan, but this place was the good of it, and I didn't waste any time diving in.

It was heavenly. The warm water jetted out at all angles when I turned in the shower, and I let it hit every part of me—every part. I tried to remember when I'd ever had a shower like this. The water was instantly hot. As I bathed, the scent of smelly soap and shampoo filled the air, and I thoroughly enjoyed myself until the door opened.

"Who the fuck is it?" I blurted out, then cringed, my initial irritation giving way to a sudden self-consciousness as if it could be Katie at the door for some unfathomable reason.

"Hello?" A woman's voice, soft and low like melted chocolate, echoed through the bathroom.

I peeked around the frosted glass and was confronted with the most beautiful woman I'd ever seen, carrying a pair of white bath towels. She was six-foot-two if she was an inch with short red hair, porcelain skin, and captivatingly huge green eyes that sparkled in the light. A scar ran down the left side of her face, breaking at her neck and continuing past her collarbone and under her t-shirt. And, Christ, she was fit.

"Well, I can see why my sister lives here," I remarked, turning on a little Irish charm and stepping out from behind the glass. "Is there something I can do for ya?"

She spun around, putting her back to me. "Oh, God, Sorry. Sorry. I just brought you some towels."

"Oh, well, fair play, then." I moved back behind the glass, grinning mischievously like the Cheshire Cat. "I'm Aoife, by the way. And you are?"

She snorted a laugh. "I know who you are. I'm Morgan. Your sister and I work together."

"Go or stay, but close the door; you're lettin' the steam out."

"Uh, yeah. I'll be going. It was nice to meet you."

"Oh, aye!" I called out, peeking again to confirm her departure. With a quick bite to my bottom lip and a shake of my head, I returned my attention to the shower, the warm water now accompanied by a shiver of anticipation. Perhaps Boston wouldn't be so bad. *Sweet Mother Mary and Joseph, Sis,* I thought. *How did you manage to stay away from that one?*

The chest in the corner had several pairs of black pants and blue jeans, and I silently cursed my sister's lack of style. There was also a pair of brown cargo pants, so I took those. A little further digging about uncovered a green t-shirt that said, 'Kiss

Me, I'm Feckin' Irish.' I laughed, unable to decide if I should be amused or offended that Liz bought it, and stuffed that to the bottom, instead grabbing a plain grey tank top and a green jumper. I also snatched up a pair of woolly socks. I didn't bother with a bra. I wasn't planning to go anywhere.

Glancing at Cait's shoes in the closet, I silently hoped she wouldn't mind me borrowing a cute pair of heeled Timberland boots. Finally dressed in something comfortable, I located my medication, swallowing a dose of Keppra with a prayer that no seizures would interrupt my stay. Ready to face the world —or at least the kitchen—I left the room behind.

"Hello?" I called softly, and Katie poked her head out of a doorway further down the hall.

"Are you feeling better?" She asked, then looked back. "Come on. It'll be fine." She reached over and towed a young girl out of the doorway, obviously Katie's sister by the look of her. The younger girl was maybe eleven or twelve with soft gray eyes and black hair in a long braid.

"Oh, hi. Who are you?" I asked, adopting a kind tone and a warm smile.

"I'm Leah." She practically hid behind Katie.

"Well, I'm Aoife, Cait's sister."

"You don't call her Cáitlín like grandma does?" Leah observed.

"Grandma?"

"The snake lady. That's what we call her. Cait's mama."

I shook my head, completely befuddled, but who knew what twelve-year-olds thought? "Only when I'm upset with her. When we were growing up, Cait hated being called Cáitlín, and I'm sure she still does."

I took a step forward. Leah took a step back, her haunted grey eyes wary and her posture suggesting she was about to bolt, though Katie had a firm hand on her arm. It was an expression I'd seen on a few kids back home who'd been the victim of domestic violence.

I knelt down to her level and gave her a warm expression. "I'm about to make a sandwich. Are you hungry?"

Leah nodded, and I held out my hand. "Come on, then.

Let's get you something to eat." Then I added, "Don't worry. I don't bite."

A split second later, my hand shot to my mouth in embarrassment. "Oh, Gods, I'm so sorry. I didn't mean—"

Katie just beamed a wide grin and started laughing. Then Leah and I joined in, and just like that, we were grand. Leah took my hand, and we made our way downstairs.

As the lift doors banged and jerked open, we entered the kitchen to find Liz, Morgan, and two other women seated around the table. The sound of their conversation stopped abruptly as they turned their attention toward us.

"Here five minutes, and you broke the fucking elevator?" Morgan said with her back to me. For a moment, I thought she was serious, but then she twisted in her seat and flashed me a dazzling, if terrifying, smile, complete with fangs.

My face fell. *Another fucking vampire,* I thought. *I should have known.*

Morgan's grin vanished as her face screwed up in anger, and she shot to her feet, placing her hands on her hips in indignation. "You know, you don't have to make that face. I didn't choose this. Almost none of us did, not even your sister. So don't be a bigoted asshole."

Leah flinched and hid behind me.

My eyebrows shot up in surprise, and I sputtered for an apology. "Fuck. I mean, fuck, I'm sorry. I just haven't—" I clamped a hand over my mouth, realizing I'd sworn in front of Leah.

"We clear?" Morgan demanded.

I looked around at the others at the table. They all looked non-plussed, but only Morgan looked angry.

"Crystal," I mumbled and looked back at Katie apologetically, who was likewise looking at me with a disappointed expression.

I cringed. *Way to put your foot in it, Aoife.*

"Good." Morgan sat back down amid snickers from everyone else.

"Damn, Morg, really?" One of the women said, a woman in a grey suit.

"I had enough grief in life for being a lesbian. I'm not taking it for being the walking dead. I intend to confront this shit when I see it. You can't back down in the face of bigotry, or it never goes away."

"Mouth Morgan," Liz said sharply.

Leah gave her an incredulous look. "Dad says way worse than that every day, Auntie Liz." Then she turned sullen and quiet.

Sheepishly, and feeling about as bad as Leah now looked, I led her over to the island and grabbed a seat on what looked to be a brand-new barstool. I noted she grasped onto the edges of the countertop.

I opened the commercial refrigerator that dominated one corner of the room. Blinked. Then closed it and blinked again, as if I couldn't believe what I'd seen. Then I opened it once more. One whole column of shelves was filled with bags of blood. The rest had human food, enough for a few people.

Turning back to Leah, I couldn't help but wonder how she perceived this unusual arrangement. The contrast between the bags of blood and the human food displayed the delicate balance this household maintained—a balance between their innate nature and their connection to humanity.

The lady in the plain gray suit jerked me from my musings when she called for a Sprite, which I handed to her.

"I'm Angela Schaeffer, Bureau," she said perfunctorily, rising and offering her hand, which I took.

"Aoife. Aoife Reagan, Garda Síochána, Tacaíochta Faoi Arm." At her puzzled expression, I added, "Sorry. Irish Police, Armed Response Unit."

"Ah." She sat back down. I immediately recognized the type, a seasoned veteran with a no-nonsense attitude, and I thought it odd she was sitting around the table with a bunch of vampires, but everyone here seemed like proper mates. It was weird and, oddly, a bit encouraging. I realized how unfair it was to picture my sister as some blood-bound floosie clad in ridiculous attire. Glancing at Katie, who watched me intently with those earnest eyes, I saw a good-natured kid. Cait had made it abundantly clear how much she loved her. It was really becoming obvious that I needed to shed my biases and reevaluate my views.

Shrugging nervously at Katie's scrutiny, I pulled out some luncheon meats and set about making sandwiches for Leah and me.

"I hope you don't mind, Liz. I'm starving."

Liz nodded, but her attention was fixed on the raven-haired vampire seated to her left. She possessed an air of mystery, accentuated by her dark brown eyes and a cocky smirk that danced on her lips as she observed me with unnerving intensity, her gaze piercing through me. Finally, after a few moments, she stood up and began making her way toward me, but before she could reach me, Katie stepped in.

"Nope!" She said, placing a firm hand on the older woman's chest. "You just go back to the table, Nastasia. Leave her alone."

Nastasia gently pushed Katie aside, her determination unwavering. "Move aside, child. I was just going to introduce myself. I promise," she assured, her voice tinged with a hint of a Russian accent.

Unlike Cait, I inherited my mother's talent for languages and had once thought I might follow in Ma's footsteps. So, seizing the moment, I switched to Russian, breaking the tension that hung in the air. "Are you Russian-American or Russian-born? You don't have much of an accent."

Morgan looked up at me then, her face a mixture of astonishment and, maybe, a bit of grudging admiration. Nastasia, however, remained unfazed, responding in kind. "Russian born. Your Russian is very good. Do you speak any other languages?"

Switching to French, I replied, "Oui." Yes. Then seamlessly transitioning to German, I added, "Ich spreche mehrere." I speak several. Finally, in Japanese, a language I had been studying for a couple of years, I uttered, "Dakara, reigi tadashiku."

Nastasia's laughter filled the room, a melodic sound that seemed to hold a touch of mischief, and her amusement offered a revealing glimpse of a vibrant personality. Switching back to English, she said. "I understood the French and the German, but I don't speak Japanese."

"I said," also switching back to English, "to make sure you mind your manners—especially when talking about me behind my back. I speak some Chinese as well, Mandarin and Cantonese."

She tapped her lip thoughtfully. "It's interesting that you don't seem afraid of us."

"Should I be?" I asked flatly, giving her a defiant stare.

A wide, wicked-looking grin spread across Nastasia's face, drawing my attention like a moth to a flame. It was a grin that exuded an undeniable allure, carrying with it a heady charm that sent unexpected shivers down my spine. As she laughed, the sound wrapped around the room, all silk and seduction, weaving a web of temptation that ensnared my senses.

"I'm Nastasia Volkova," she announced, stepping gracefully around Katie to close the gap between us. "I think I like you better than Cait."

With a certain audacity, she extended her hand in invitation. My instinct was to reciprocate the gesture with a handshake. However, she intercepted my hand, bringing it to her lips in a tender, lingering kiss. The tip of her tongue tantalizingly brushed against my skin, leaving a trail of lingering sensation. Her words reached my ears like a seductive whisper, igniting a flicker of anticipation. "Oh, yes," she breathed, her voice dripping with suggestion. "Much better."

"Nastasia," Liz warned.

I fought to suppress the sudden surge of desire that threatened to consume me. I licked my lips, attempting to regain composure as I found myself entranced by Nastasia's liquid brown eyes, which sparkled with delight beneath the cascading strands of her dark hair. The interplay between her captivating gaze and her enticing demeanor left me yearning for more while a mix of curiosity and trepidation coursed through my veins. I felt smitten, needful, and full of longing.

"Don't—Don't do that," I whispered, my voice barely audible as Nastasia inched closer, her magnetic presence enveloping me.

Her innocent façade played out perfectly as she questioned, "Do what?"

My breath hitched as I struggled to find the right words. "The glamour," I managed to breathe out, my voice laced with a mixture of trepidation and vulnerability.

In response, Nastasia adopted a cute pout, effortlessly shifting gears from seductive to playful. She gently booped my nose, an unexpected touch that sent a jolt of electricity through me. "Maybe later," she whispered, teasingly hinting at the potential for something more. With that, she gracefully retreated, allowing the veil of glamour to dissipate.

I clenched my jaw and tightened my fists, attempting to conceal the surge of fear that welled up within me. Words eluded me, and I remained silent.

So much for proper mates, I thought.

The encounter left me questioning the boundaries between desire and apprehension, unable to ignore the lingering sense of both intrigue and terror that pulsed through my veins and left me shivering.

"Now, what were we talking about?" Nastasia inquired, settling into her seat with a soft smile that exuded sin and sensuality.

I realized Leah was speaking to me and used the moment to shift my attention away from the vampires at the table. "Sorry, Leah. What were you saying?"

"No mayo, please. Mustard."

"Of course," I acknowledged, completing her ham and cheese sandwich. After deftly cutting it into small, triangular pieces, I slid the plate over to her. Spotting some roast beef and a bottle of HP sauce, I swiftly assembled my own sandwich before settling down beside her. "There you go, one hang sandwich," I declared with a playful grin.

Leah giggled at my choice of words, and I responded with a cheeky wink, fostering the connection between us.

Seizing the opportunity for a quiet conversation, I leaned in and spoke softly. "So, Leah, how do you like living here?"

"It's way better than home. Everyone here is nice to me, even Nastasia, and she hates everyone."

"I heard that, you little brat," Nastasia chided with a sweet smirk that looked completely out of place on her.

"Oh, yeah," Katie interrupted. "Everyone just loves Leah. I'm the one they make do all the work."

"That's not true," Leah shot back. "I help. I take out the trash and clean your bathroom."

"Well, you should clean the bathroom," Katie answered with a laugh. "I don't use it."

"Do too! You shower and get toothpaste all over the mirror. And you leave empty blood bags in the trash."

Liz piped up, clearly hearing magical words that indicated food in the bedroom. "Katie! What have I told you about taking blood to your room?"

"Thanks a lot, you little squealer."

I suppressed a giggle. *How many times had Ma read us the riot act over bringing food into our room,* I wondered. Kids will be kids, even vampire kids.

I turned back to Leah. "You said it was better than home?"

Liz watched us intently, waiting for Leah's response. "Yeah, Mom and Dad used to hit me a lot. But Dad's dead, and Mom is in the hospital. She's not doing well," Leah confided, her voice tinged with sorrow. "Ms. Colewort came by and said we could stay here for now. But that was before—" Leah's voice trailed off, her eyes welling up with tears. Overwhelmed by emotion, she clung to me, seeking solace as she buried her face in my chest. "You won't let her take us away, will you?"

I shushed her, stroking her hair. "There, there, love. It'll be alright." It was weird how she'd glommed onto me almost instantly. I looked at Liz, who waved her hand, obviously wanting me to comfort her more, so I lowered myself to Leah's level and looked her in the eye. "Over my dead body, love. No one's goin' to take you away. You hear me?" She threw her arms around me again and began to bawl once more. I just held on and kept stroking her hair.

After a few minutes, Leah dried her eyes and said, "I'm not hungry anymore. I'm going to go back to my room."

I nodded. "Okay, sweetie, if you're sure." I didn't know what else to say. I wasn't great with kids.

After Leah was gone, Liz spoke up. "That's the first time she's cried since the attack. She must feel very comfortable around you."

"Yeah, I was wondering about that."

"You look like Cait; she was the only one Leah would talk to. I'm sorry if it made you uncomfortable."

"Yeah, sure, but what can I do? Kids need to cry when bad things happen."

Liz gave me the same smile she always had when I'd done something she appreciated, and for a second, I was sixteen again, feeling that old swell of pride.

The front door opened, and a crisp British voice called from the foyer. "I'm home. What a shit show at the office. Did Aoife arrive yet?"

I recognized the voice immediately, and every muscle in my body heaved with tension as Marcella strode into the room. *Fuck.*

CHAPTER FOUR

Aoife

"Oh, Good! You're here. We can get started!" Marcella said as she blew into the kitchen, poured herself a glass of blood, and took the seat next to me. "Angela, dear, do we have any leads?"

I stared at Marcella. "What, not even a hello? Well, you made bags of your manners in the last sixteen years," I said. "We're not old mates from school, Marcella. I'm here for Cait, not for whatever this little gathering is. Oh, and nice buzz cut. It definitely brings out your inner dyke."

Angela shot me a nasty glare as Marcella turned toward me, touched her hair briefly in an uncharacteristic show of insecurity, then schooled her face into a mask of indifference.

"My apologies, Aoife. I was certain you held a bit of a grudge, so I didn't want to say anything to set you off. Since that offended your sensibilities, tell me, are you alright?"

My jaw worked with uncertainty as I tried to figure out how to respond. Her voice had been flat, but the words had been cutting. Finally, I settled on, "Yeah, sure, I'm grand. But before you get started, I'd like to know what this is supposed to be."

Marcella opened her mouth, but Katie beat her to it, launching off at ninety miles an hour to enlighten me.

"Right, so, here's the deal, Auntie Aoife. You're here because we thought Mama was dead, but thanks to Angela, who somehow managed to get some of her own blood into her at the last minute, she turned instead of dying. Because all Mama needed at that point was a little bit of someone's soul. Right? You follow?"

Schaeffer raised a languid hand and dropped it, not bothering to turn around. "Don't forget it almost killed me."

Katie didn't even slow down. "Right, so Mama came to for a few seconds at the morgue, and it totally freaked out the coroner. Fortunately, Liz was there to identify the body, and Nastasia was called in to glamour him within an inch of his sanity to forget she was there, but Nastasia's the best. And when I say the best, I mean she can make you want her so bad it hurts. So it worked, okay. Yeah, Auntie Aoife, she wasn't really trying a few minutes ago."

Nastasia nodded and winked at me.

"Meanwhile, Mama's soul's gone on holiday. Carol, Mama's witch friend, is convinced she'll be back, but they're," she pointed at the crowd around the table, "not so sure, except Auntie Liz, who's my other Mama, but she doesn't want me to call her that on account of her kids, which she still blames Marcella for, even though she says she doesn't. And Mama and Liz are a couple, so be nice to her.

"Liz wanted you to be here when Mama woke up, and she knows you're a cop, so she wants you to help us find Mama's killer. Marcella wanted to see you so you two could bury the hatchet, preferably not in her skull. Nastasia wants to get into your pants because you're Mama's twin, and she wants the matched set. Eww."

"Katie!" Liz shrieked, but Nastasia just kept staring at me with alarming intensity until I flushed, then she waggled her eyebrows, and Katie kept going, clearly still on quite the roll.

"And Morgan's just here right now, trying to figure out how to be a vampire, but she knows you think she's hot because she heard your heartbeat quicken upstairs and doesn't know how to feel about it because she and Mama were in love in Iraq. She does think your cute, though."

"Hey, private thoughts, Katie!" Morgan protested and blushed more than I ever thought any vampire would. For that matter, I was suddenly feeling pretty pink myself, among other things.

"She's also waiting for Carol to tell her whether her sister, Caileigh, is still alive. If not, she hopes Carol can tell her where her body is, so she can take her home to bury her. But to do that, Carol has to have something personal of Caileigh's, which is being shipped from East Bumblefuck, Montana. So she just waits and scowls all the time."

"Oh, and you're my family, so I just wanted to see you," Katie finished and sat back with a wicked, wicked grin.

Schaeffer barked a laugh. "Did you catch all that?"

Everyone was staring at Katie, but no one protested or said anything, so I figured she had it spot on. The kid was fucking brilliant, that was for sure. "Katie, love, you're my wingman from now on," I crowed. "We're best mates as of right now."

"Goody!" She chirped. "We'll have to hit the bars!"

I raised an eyebrow. "The bars?"

Katie gave me a fang-laden grin that was both adorable and terrifying and rose to leave.

"Katie," Liz warned, and Katie turned, sucking the last of the blood from the bag in her hand before making a show of putting it in the trash. Then she was gone down the hall.

I just laughed. "Is she always that precocious?"

No one answered. They were all still stunned, it seemed, and there was a lot of shifting around uncomfortably.

Nastasia spoke first, which I somehow expected. "Well, now that everyone's up to speed, can we begin?"

Again, silence. So I took another bite of my sandwich and then grabbed a Coke from the refrigerator to wash it down.

When I came here, I hadn't known what to expect, but this definitely wasn't it. And, even though I'd wanted to get right back on the plane and go home as soon as I got off, I realized this lot was way too entertaining to pass up, and I wanted to see what happened next. Katie's explanation alone, and the aftermath of discomfort that had followed, made the entire trip worth every second.

Marcella finally composed herself. "She's not wrong."

"About which part?" I asked, still trying to digest it all.

"All of it, I assume. Though I didn't know you found Morgan attractive, nor that it might have bothered her in some way. And I knew that Liz still blamed me for—"

"Marcella," Liz interjected. "Now is not the time to discuss it."

"Quite right," Marcella answered her. "In any event, here we all are. Your sister was shot, point blank, in the chest with a shotgun. She's the only one who saw the man. And he peeled out in a late model Dodge Charger or Challenger. Liz and Katie were too busy trying to save Cait to get a good look at it. We suspect it was someone in one of the hunter families we've been contending with lately, but we have no idea who.

"Carlos caught the perp's scent on the envelope the man gave Cait before he shot her, but we have no leads, and the envelope had only a smudged partial print, unusable. Our best guess is a man named Matthew Reynolds, who used to work for the FBI. Cait glamoured him a few months ago, and he had a psychotic break. We think he may be part of the same hunter family as Carter Reese, Schaeffer's former boss, who is now dead."

I raised an eyebrow. "Look, I'm not at my best, but I'll do what I can. But over here, I'm just a civilian. I can't do much. And who is Carlos?"

"Cait's supervisor at the police department. He's also a werewolf and a total bore." Nastasia chimed in. "You look just like Cait, and no one knows she's downstairs in the basement except her squad and Detective Freyer. We have kept her condition very quiet.

"Those are all people we trust, and they've all agreed to keep mum. As far as the rest of the department knows, she was shot, but she was wearing a vest, and she's on leave to recover. I had to glamour a few people to make that work, but —"

"Oh," I muttered. Then, rather abruptly, understanding dawned. "Oh!" I didn't like this at all. "You want me to *be* Cait. You want me to be the bait for the killer."

"And there we have it," Nastasia said with a wink and a broad, spectacular smile. "Now we know which one is smart and which one is pretty."

I shot her a dubious look. "I don't know anything about

Cait's life past the age of sixteen. I can't just pretend to be her. What am I supposed to do when someone asks me something personal? I'll fuck it up."

Marcella turned toward me. "No one's going to know, Aoife. Almost no one knows she has a sister at all except those same people we mentioned, and people believe what is right in front of their eyes. Right now, the bad guys believe Cait is alive and well. We need to find out who they are. We need the killer to come after her, or rather, you, again. Besides, Morgan will be there to help you through it."

"Me?" Morgan blurted. "I'm barely under control as it is."

"Pish. You'll be fine." Marcella waved her off, then gestured to Liz. "I'm going to have Liz keep you feeding properly for a couple of weeks until you get the hang of things, and—"

Morgan scoffed. "Oh, no. I'm not doing that. You want Liz to be my minder? I don't think so."

"Would you prefer me?" Nastasia said with a nasty smile. "I'm sure we'll find each other's company entertaining."

Morgan sat down. "This is insane. I have to feed way too often."

"Well, we have a full two weeks before Cait is expected back at work. If we're lucky, she'll wake up before then. If not, this is the best plan we have."

I laughed. "I'm with Morgan. This is insane. You're asking me to impersonate a Boston Police Officer. If I'm caught, they'll put me in jail and then likely deport me back to Ireland."

"Don't be silly, Aoife, they can't deport you," Liz said. "You're still a US citizen, or did you forget you were born here? They'll just send you to prison."

"Great," I muttered wryly and ran a hand down my face. This kept getting better and better.

Liz continued, smiling in amusement at my discomfort. "Besides, no one is asking you to pretend to be a cop. Carlos will make sure you're not breaking any laws. You just need to learn Boston Police procedure, re-learn to speak with an American accent, learn about all Cait's friends, and catch up on everything you've missed in the last fifteen years. With two weeks, all of that should be easy for someone with a Doctorate in Linguistics."

"Fuck me," I said and sighed. *How did I get roped into this shite?*

I stared balefully at the little leprechaun on the box as I muddled my way through a bowl of kid's cereal with Leah the next morning. "Lucky charms, indeed," I muttered, and Leah laughed.

"You're funny," she said with a grin.

I grinned back. "Am I?"

"Are you ready to get started?" Marcella asked from the doorway.

I shifted my gaze to Leah, who just shrugged.

Then I looked up at the blond vampire, and my breath caught in my throat. Marcella was standing there in what I assumed was her usual business attire, a white blouse, black skirt, and patent leather court shoes. Unlike the night before, when she'd looked a bit haggard from work, she was absolutely smashing.

I firmly pressed my lips into a thin frown. But it was probably too late. Marcella's entire face lit up with a wide smile that crinkled the corners of those fabulous eyes, though she didn't say anything, waiting for an answer to her question.

I hesitated, just knowing that if I opened my mouth to speak, I'd smile in spite of myself. *I don't like this lady.* I professed internally. *She fucked up my entire life. Damnit.* Hell, I didn't like any of these ladies except Katie and Leah. Katie was a little terrifying in a ruthless child sort of way, but her adorable attitude was thoroughly endearing. And then there was Morgan, but that was my twat talking, and I couldn't trust that.

I schooled my face as best I could. "I haven't agreed to anything yet."

Marcella nodded thoughtfully. "That's true. You haven't, and if it's not something you want to do, I won't push you." Then her voice turned gentle and pleading. "But we really could use your help. If we don't find this guy, we might all be in danger, including Katie and Leah."

I sighed. That was rude, bringing the kids into it, but it was a fair point. "Fine, but I'll only agree if Morgan agrees to help. She knew Cait in Iraq, and her knowledge would help me sell it. I'll get a more complete picture." I was almost definitely not asking because I thought Morgan was hot—almost.

Marcella squinted with a playful smirk. "Uh-huh. Okay. I don't see a problem with that, given that we were going to have you stay at her place anyway. There's more room, and—"

"No," Morgan said, crossing the threshold from the foyer. "We're not. She's not staying with me. Come on, Marcella. There is literally no room. You know that. My apartment is a shoe box."

"Morgan, we've talked about this. It's not a request." Marcella said firmly, eyes flashing. "If she stays here, she's unlikely to draw out Cait's attacker. I want it to appear that Cait is isolated from everyone here."

"Then go rent her an apartment back in the North End," Morgan argued. "I have a tiny efficiency. Where's she supposed to sleep? And what if I lose control?"

"You won't. Like I said yesterday, Liz will be taking you out to feed every two days. We've worked all this out. And as I said, it's not a request."

I watched them stare at each other. Morgan crossed her arms defiantly, and she looked like she wouldn't budge. But then something passed between them, some unspoken thing that clearly scared Morgan, and she capitulated, dropping into a chair.

"Fine."

"Excellent," Marcella said and hustled off with Leah to get her ready for school.

"Did I do something?" I asked as I went to wash out my bowl. "I mean, I know that it's not ideal, and I made it pretty plain that my experience with vampires hasn't been all that great, but you seem like you hate me."

"No," Morgan said morosely. "It's nothing you did. I— Nevermind. It doesn't matter. I'm not being given a choice. I like my head attached to my body."

I barked a laugh, but Morgan just glowered even more, and it took me a moment to realize it wasn't a joke. "Wait. Marcella would kill you?"

"So it would seem." Morgan crossed her arms and watched me as I put my breakfast dishes in the dishwasher.

"That's barbaric."

She shook her head. "No. Of everyone here, I probably get it the most. It's what's required. Marcella is taking control, and I'm not really upset about that. We need a firm hand with some of the others, but I didn't expect her to turn that on me, what with my friendship with Cait. And this seems like such a small thing."

"It's wrong," I said flatly. "She shouldn't force you. If you don't want me there—"

"Aoife, it's not that. Like I said, let's just forget about it and make the best of it."

I blew out a breath. This was going to be fun. Morgan was gorgeous, scar and all, but Gods, she had an attitude. Then again, all vampires did, except Liz, of course. She was always the exception.

I set my bowl on the counter to dry, then turned my attention back to Morgan, my voice quiet and probably sounding a little petulant. "It's my sister, isn't it."

"No, Aoife, it has nothing to do with Cait. But you won't leave this alone, will you? I had a really bad experience a couple of years ago." She scooted her chair in and glared at me with hard exasperated eyes. "Having someone living in my personal space scares the shit out of me, okay? Is that enough of an explanation?"

I jerked as if she'd slapped me. I'd struck a really raw nerve. I hadn't meant to, and I said, "I'm sorry. I shouldn't have pried."

"No, you shouldn't have." She pressed her lips together, then ran her hand through her short hair.

I scowled back at her, reminding myself that her sister was missing and she had a whole bunch of shit going on, then blew out an exasperated breath. "Okay, so can we start with police procedure?"

She shook her head. "Not here. Go upstairs and pack. I'm sure Marcella has a suitcase for you. Carlos will meet us at my place in two hours with everything you need."

"So you already knew this was the way it was going to go."

She nodded.

"Then why argue?"

"For my dignity and sanity," she sighed, though I could see the hint of a rueful smile tugging at one corner of her mouth. "Just go get your stuff."

I rolled my eyes and headed upstairs. *Well, this is a great start.*

CHAPTER FIVE

Weyna

The sun rose and fell with dreary regularity several times before my mother, accompanied by her coterie of sister deities, once again departed the fort. As always, their destination and purpose lay veiled in obscurity. Such departures were common and always kept secret, steadfastly guarded against my curious inquiries. But that didn't stop me from speculating as my imagination wandered down multiple paths of scouting expeditions, spying on our adversary, or even battles. Any of which seemed logical. Yet how does one understand the comings and goings of goddesses?

Without my mother, I had no one to stave off the jabs made at me by Saya, but there was a silver lining. With her departure came an absolution of some of my responsibilities, my mother's daily bath, for instance. As luck would have it, this coincided with a rest day for the Ọṣeni as well, further liberating me from afternoon duty carrying water for the women.

It was during this afternoon respite that I found myself locked in mortal combat with my magic lessons and the cryptic tome Mehada, one of Aine's finest witches, had provided me. I had reached an impasse. My fingers skimmed the soft parchment, tracing the ink lines that denoted a complex equation. I had tried everything, but the numbers seemed to run together. I understood the concept, but the implementation eluded me, and I resorted to keeping my fingers placed on various symbols to make sure I didn't lose them in my math-stupid brain. It was like having a puzzle whose interlocking pieces moved as I tried to place the next one. Finally, I threw my head back and howled in frustration, ready to toss the book into the morning bathwater, which I'd neglected to drain.

Boudka appeared in the doorway with a gleaning bag under one arm and a pack on her back. "You busy?"

I shook my head in disgust. "Not really. I'm trying to get this, but I just can't make sense of it."

Boudka peered over my shoulder. "Well, that looks like it describes a limit. You see, as this number here," she pointed at a symbol, "gets closer together with this number, " she pointed at another symbol, "they reach a limit of how close they can actually get. That's represented by this line. But, there is a point where they enter a synchronicity that keeps the magic stable."

I turned my head and looked up slowly from my sitting position on the floor. "Where did you learn that?"

Boudka scoffed. "To read Bethadi? It was the first thing I learned when I got up here three years ago. I got one of the Bethadi knights to teach me as soon as I realized the squiggles on a page meant something."

"No, the maths. And how did you know this was a magical stability equation?"

She shrugged. "I've always had a head for counting and understanding numbers. Until I got here, I just never understood how to express it. As for the magic, I've read a couple of books on it. I had hoped that I might have some aptitude. That," she pointed to the page I was struggling with, "is an addition that applies to spells with long-lasting effects to give them a greater level of permanency."

"I know that, but I can't follow the equation. It would be so much easier if my mother would just show me." I sagged and then lay back on the floor. "I must be stupid or something. I can't get it. I keep trying, but I just lose it."

Boudka knelt down and tugged at my upper arm and spoke to me gently. "You're not stupid, blossom. Maybe you just

AOIBH WOOD

need to rest your brain. I think I smell the peat burning in there."

I let out a laugh, the sound vanishing into the gently flapping fabric of the tent walls. "Is that what that is?"

She smirked evilly, then. "Come away with me for a bit. I have to go pick herbs, and I don't want to go out alone. Besides, you just said that you're struggling with it. A break might help."

I gave her a skeptical look. "It won't be any easier when I get back."

"Perhaps," she acknowledged, her voice a warm whisper, "Perhaps not. But we might find a nice secluded spot for lunch." With a practiced nonchalance, Boudka let one fold of her robe slip aside, revealing a hint of her toned leg, and a playful wink graced her features.

"Well, fuck this then," I said and slammed the book closed and stuffed it into my footlocker, then followed Boudka out of the tent. Twenty minutes later, we were outside the grounds and tromping into the forest on the northern side of the ring fort.

"Did you get in much trouble the other day?" I asked as we stepped out of the tall grasses and into the undergrowth.

Boudka didn't answer, but her face grew dark at the question. "It's fine."

It certainly didn't feel fine. And we walked a bit further in silence until a small murder of hooded crows began chattering in a nearby tree before winging off, and I glowered at them with suspicion.

Boudka laughed and tugged at my elbow. "Hey, come on, not every blackbird is a spy for your mother."

I frowned at the now absent birds but continued walking. "Those are hooded crows, so that would be my aunt. But you're right, I know. They're off doing whatever."

Boudka chuckled. "You know, you whine a lot."

"Do I?" I grumped as we made our way around a tangle of brown thorny brambles. I eyed the light above me as the forest shadows deepened slightly. "You know, it's going to get dark soon. How much farther to wherever we're going?"

44

"Not far now. And yes, you do."

Not long after, we stepped lightly into a tiny clearing. The thick veil of the canopy gave way here to just a smattering of leaves. The rays of the late afternoon sun peeked through the trees at a broad angle, casting deep shadows across the ground. The babbling rivulet that flowed within, probably from one of the nearby ridges, gave the area the feel of someplace enchanted and secret. It reminded me of the paintings and drawings I'd seen of Bethadi, right down to the wide circle of death caps poised in the center. I grinned in silent appreciation of the surreal mimicry of Fae art she'd found.

"Planning on poisoning me, are you?" I asked, gesturing to the ring of death caps.

Boudka looked back and waggled her eyebrows, but she didn't touch the mushrooms, instead stepping gingerly over them and opening her pack to lay out a blanket in a clear flat spot next to the brook. Then she sat and patted the blanket. "Come, sit with me."

I smiled. "A ring of mushrooms, you know the legend."

Boudka giggled. "Not every myth has a grain of truth, you know."

I chuckled. "True. Still, this seems like a lot of work if you just want to spend time with me. You know I'd go anywhere with you."

Boudka grinned back. "I know, but I wanted us to do something a little more special than usual."

She set the gleaning bag next to her and pulled out a bottle of honeyed mead from her pack, along with two small wooden cups. Then I understood, and a naughty grin spread across my face.

Servants weren't allowed wine, and my mother had made sure that absolutely no one in the camp would give me anything resembling alcohol. She worried constantly that I might lose control and blow something up if I stumbled around the camp in a stupor.

On the other hand, I wasn't exactly big on following the rules. I took after my Aunt Badb in that respect. I often wondered if that was the reason she spent so much time away. Of course, there was also the rumor that she had a lover and daughter of her own somewhere south.

"Hey, where are you?" Boudka asked, holding out a cup.

"Sorry, I was just thinking about Aunt Badb."

"You miss her." It wasn't a question.

I nodded. "Everyone leaves me. First, there was my sister. She left with a traveling merchant, but at least she's still alive —I think. Then Da died, not that he was around much, drinking all the time.

"When I first got here, not long before you showed up, Badb took care of me while Mother was wrapping up with the Kaushkar over on the continent. She didn't have me fetching water all the time and doing grunt work. She gave me reasonable chores—and this." I pulled out the small knife I carried with me. "And she taught me some basics of how to use it. Now she never comes around, as if my mother chased her off."

Boudka put a hand to my cheek, turning my face to hers. "Hey, I'm not leaving."

I looked at her skeptically. "You say that now."

She frowned. "Okay, stop. This was supposed to be a fun time for us. Now drink your mead."

I nodded. "Sorry. So, what herbs do you need to collect?"

Boudka laughed. "None. I made that up so that I could get away from the fort and spend time with you. All of my other duties are done, and it made a reasonable excuse."

I grinned wickedly at that and drained the mead from my cup. "Really? So, what exactly are we going to do out here rather than— "

I never got to finish the sentence as she placed a finger on my lips and shushed me.

"You talk too much, Weyna," she said, and then she pressed her lips gently to mine. "Lay down."

I laid back on the blanket, noting that the ground, while hard, didn't have any protrusions like roots or rocks. She'd clearly scoped this place out ahead of time. Boudka leaned down and kissed me once again, then she moved down and slowly slid my robes upward over my bare legs. I closed my eyes and leaned into the moment, feeling each delicate pass of her fingers as she trailed them across my knees and the inside of my thighs. Unconsciously, I spread my legs as she pushed apart my folds and ran her tongue over them and across my clit, forcing a tight gasp from my throat. "Oh, Goddess," I sighed, then she stopped, sliding up toward me, and I groaned with frustration.

Boudka drew me into a passionate kiss, straddling my hips. I slid my hand downward, finding purchase on her skirt, and drew it up. Adjusting her position slightly, she tugged her skirt from under her knees as I ran my hands over her ass, and she sighed into my mouth, filling my lungs with her breath. I moaned with abject need as she put a hand to my chin and pushed my head back, nibbling and sucking at my throat.

"You know," Boudka said as she licked at my throat. "There's this rumor of this woman," she licked again, "some girl back east," another lick, "that your mother raised from the dead. They say she drinks blood from the neck of her victims."

The rumor was true, I knew, and Boudka had hit a bit of a nerve, but I didn't want to ruin the moments, so I kept silent. Instead, I slipped the folds of her shirt open and pulled at her legs, letting her slide forward, licking and sucking at her nipples and running my tongue on the undersides of her breasts. Arousal filled me, finally, and I wanted nothing more than to drag this moment out as long as I could, to forget the rath and its chores and people, just for a moment.

Sweat beaded on my skin but evaporated quickly, sending a shiver down my spine.

"Do you love me?" Boudka whispered, but I didn't answer. I needed her. I wanted to taste her. It had been a few days since we'd last made love, but I couldn't get enough of her. Love, though, was another topic I didn't want to engage with. Her jabbering was starting to spoil this, so I slid down and buried my head between her legs.

I dug into her with gusto, running a teasing tongue at her entrance.

Boudka's breathing became labored as she bunched the

blanket next to me in her fists and moaned loudly. "Oh, Mother of Waters, more."

I moved my mouth to her clit and began to suck at it, rubbing it gently with the flat of my tongue.

Boudka arched her back and dug her fingers into my hair. "Yes," she moaned. "Right there."

I licked and sucked until her legs went rigid.

"Yes," she moaned loudly with a harsh gasp and jerked forward, dropping a hand into the blanket and bunching it up in her fingers. I lay my head back on the blanket to ease the forming ache in my neck.

Boudka kissed me, and the scent of our mingled bodies lit in my mouth as I greedily sucked at her tongue. She lowered herself down and resumed what she'd begun, first guiding her tongue around my folds slowly. Then she softened her strokes, tonguing my clit in wide, wet, languid movements.

"Oh, Boudka," I whispered, filled with the pleasure of it, the feeling of her mouth on me, and the way she gripped at my hips, pressing me to her. It wasn't long before I felt it, the building of pleasure, diffuse and sweet, taking me upward toward a delicious orgasm. Then I threw my head back and slapped a hand to her shoulder, digging in with my fingers as I crested the wave of blissful pleasure. "Oh, yes," I cried, the words coming out in a harsh whisper of ecstasy.

My legs jerked as she continued to bite and lick at me until I had to beg her to stop. "Enough," I breathed. "Enough. Please."

She lifted her head from between my legs and grinned at me. "Now," she demanded. "Tell me that you love me."

"Of course, I love you," I replied with a crooked smile, breath still a little short. "But my mother once told me never to believe anything someone says when you're between their legs."

Boudka laughed and slapped my exposed thigh. "Very funny, Weyna. I'm serious."

"Yes," I confirmed quietly. "I love you." Then I sat up and pulled her back to straddle my legs, and we sat there for a long time, simply kissing each other and enjoying the feel of each other's skin under our hands, so much so that time slipped away from us.

It wasn't until a chill wind blew through the forest that I realized the sun was dipping below the horizon.

"Oh, shit," I exclaimed.

CHAPTER SIX

Weyna

As darkness began to fall, we scrambled to pack up the blanket and the cups. Boudka just tossed the bottle of mead aside, unable to find the cork, and we rushed through the brambles. Boudka tripped on an errant root and spilled the contents of her pack.

"Leave it," I said, hoisting her up and keeping one eye on the setting sun. "It'll only slow us down."

Her expression was shot through with terror as the sun dipped below the horizon and birds across the entire copse of woods took off, startled. We were in real trouble—almost a quarter mile from the fort. We were bound to be spotted by one of Mother Darkness' minions. The wevkravna burrowed underground during the day, but at night, they rose and scurried about, looking for anyone they could find. If we were lucky, one of the patrols would come by before one of the creatures spotted us. But luck is rarely a friend to the foolhardy.

Just as the path drew within sight, I heard the crumble of earth and the scurrying of bladed legs to our rear. I pushed Boudka into a group of briars, landing on top of her. My weight pushing her into the painful thorns, Boudka called out briefly, but I put a hand over her mouth and pointed back.

Maybe thirty or forty feet behind us, the wevkrana scraped at the ground as it turned about. In this thicket, Boudka might be able to hide, but my soul would be a beacon, all spun with

Shaddani magic.

I breathed in quietly and pulled my knife slowly from my belt. Then I placed a finger to my lips, shushing Boudka, "On three, we make a run for the fort."

She shook her head vigorously, paralyzed with fear, eyes wide and terrified.

"We don't have a choice." I counted down silently with my fingers. "It will come for me first. Whatever you do, don't stop, and don't look back."

Three.

We adjusted ourselves to run, pulling loose from the pricking vines.

Two.

Boudka's terrified eyes watched me, glancing back to the wevkrana, which had begun to move in our direction.

One.

We took off. "Don't look back," I cried. "Go. Go. Go."

Boudka immediately outpaced me with her long legs, which was good. She didn't have a weapon of any kind. At least I had my knife. If I timed it right, I might be able to kill the spider-thing before it killed me.

"Weyna! Look!" Boudka said as she turned briefly, then picked up her pace.

I glanced back, and my heart sunk into the pit of my stomach. There, in the distance, maybe two hundred yards back beyond the wevkrana, loped an emisai, its muscular apelike form charging toward us on all fours, even as the spider-like beast grew closer. I was going to die out here.

I stopped and turned to face the charging wevkrana, taking only a second to glance back and see Boudka was closing on the fence line. She would make it.

When I looked back, the spider was almost on me. I crouched, waiting for it, keeping myself steady and coiled to spring at just the right time.

The scream of a massive crow echoed in the darkness, boosting my courage and driving away any fear as the creature leaped, its legs wide to impale me when it bore me to the earth.

I sprang forward as it left the ground, leading with my knife, and we collided in the air. My arm plunged right between the creatures grinding teeth, just barely missing both sets.

I turned my hand instinctively, driving the knife into what it kept in its forebody for a brain, simultaneously cutting a deep gash in my forearm on a jagged gnashing tooth.

When we hit the ground, it was under me and quite dead, not even having time to spit acid from its glands. But in its death throws, its legs closed around me like bindings, digging painfully into my back and legs, and I found myself stuck.

The emisai loped up, its headless, slick, black humanoid frame rippling with strength. It leaped forward with its foreclaws extended to tear apart my backside. There was nothing I could do, so I waited for it to land. At least Boudka was safe.

The blow never came. A massive boot stomped into the thing and drove it to the dirt. Moments later, a long sword of black steel pierced it through the body, and it ceased to move. Badb had arrived.

She quickly peeled the wevkrana legs off my back. "Weyna, are you alright?"

I felt the legs peel aside, leaving painful cuts in my flesh as Badb dug me from its death grip.

Finally loose, I ran to my aunt, throwing my arms around her massive legs. Sobs of relief wracked my shoulders as I held on for dear life. "No. Boudka and I were out. And we lost track of time. We made a run for it, but— "

She grabbed my shoulders in her massive clawed hands, drew me back gently, and chuckled. "Look," she said, pointing at the wevkrana. "You killed it all by yourself. Not bad with just a knife."

Slowly, I turned my head toward the spider-like creature. It was almost as big around as I was tall. But she was right. It was dead. My lip trembled at the sight of the dead creatures. We had come that close— no, I had come that close to dying.

I looked up at her. Her raven hair blew wild in the wind, and her massive wings spread out behind her perfectly toned and structured body. Black leather armor hugged her form, and her dark eyes bored into mine as she gave me a wide grin. "You may be your mother's daughter, but you take after me, child. That's a warrior's heart."

I sniffed and pawed at my eyes. "That was just your scream."

"No, child. I saw you. You were poised to strike long before I screamed. Readiness to die in the face of impossible odds shows courage beyond your reckoning. Now, come."

I wasn't convinced, but I kept my own counsel on that. It wasn't wise to argue with the battle crow on such matters.

Badb scooped me up into the air. "It is a good thing that my crows kept watch over you."

"I had a hunch," I said. Then I realized the implications. "Eww. Were you watching us the whole time?"

Badb just chuckled. "Let's just say I didn't pay attention to that."

I flushed, mortified. *Oh, Goddess.*

Below, Boudka had just reached the gate and was banging on it for help. We landed next to her, and Aunt Badb returned to near-human proportions, calling for the guard to open up.

Moments later, the massive, iron-bound wood swung open just enough to allow us inside. Saya stood inside, her gaze eyeing me intently. Then she shared a cryptic look with my aunt as Boudka and I made our way back into the encampment.

Looking back at the pair, I found them both talking and staring right at me. Saya had a dark look on her face, but Badb was all smiles. Something about the whole thing felt a little disconcerting, as if they were planning something.

I caught just a snippet of something Saya was saying. " — have to be pushed harder, I think." The rest was lost in the evening noises of the fort, and I sincerely hoped they weren't talking about me.

Boudka and I were both shaking as we arrived back at my tent, and Boudka was extremely quiet, eyes downcast, clearly lost in thought.

Closing the tent flap, I set about cleaning my wounded arm.

Blood flowed freely from the deep cut, and black rotted ichor covered the wound. "Shit."

Boudka grabbed a small rag, dipping it into the bathwater and wiping away the ichor. "There's no infection," she said as she examined it. "You're lucky."

She paused for a second. "I'm so sorry, Weyna. I should have been paying more attention."

I put my other hand on her cheek. "No, we both should have done. It's not any more your fault than mine."

Boudka drew in a shuddering breath to calm herself. "Are there stitching supplies here?"

"In there." I pointed to my footlocker.

Boudka pulled out the supplies, first cleaning the wound with water and then placing a medical salve on it to prevent infection. Finally, she looked me in the eyes after threading the curved needle. Tears still hovered at the edges of her lashes, making her ice-blue eyes glimmer in the faelight lamps, and she sniffed. "Are you ready?"

I put a hand on her cheek again and nodded. "It's okay. Take a deep breath and try to steady your fingers. Then just do it. I'll be fine. I can take it. I've had worse."

She gave me a confused look. "When?"

"I— " I glanced at my left arm, not sure what I expected to see. "I— " I paused again, then shook my head. "Nevermind. Let's just get this done, so we can get some rest and put this behind us."

Boudka took a deep cleansing breath, then slid the needle through the skin. I winced but kept my mouth shut, grimacing slightly at the sharp intrusions of the metal. The pain was about as I anticipated. And though I couldn't remember a single time I'd ever had a single stitch, somehow, this seemed familiar.

Despite the shaking in her hands, she drew fourteen tidy stitches that were as clean and neat as any I'd ever seen. Then she tied them off and cut the string. Looking back up at me, she said seriously, "If you feel feverish, make sure you let someone know. No toughing it out, okay?"

I grinned and nodded. "You'd make a good medhen. You

know that? You have deft fingers. You really should assist them rather than stitching clothing."

She shook her head. "No. I like the work that I do. Besides—" She paused as if she were about to say something she shouldn't.

I looked at her askance, curious. "Besides what?"

"Nothing. Just take care of it. I need to get some rest," Boudka snapped, her irritation evident in her voice.

"Aren't you going to stay here? There's a wonderful bath right there." I strode to the bath and took a moment to heat the water.

Boudka made a little squeak, and I looked back at her, puzzled. "What was that for?"

"I don't know. I just felt something. It made my insides feel weirdly warm."

I pursed my lips in thought, then yanked my hand from the water as it suddenly grew ice cold. I'd lost control of the magic again. "Shit."

I tried again, this time concentrating on the water and ignoring Boudka, directing it to heat up to a soothing temperature, and steam began to rise from the small pool. At least I could do this right. I sat down then and began to strip.

Boudka let out an exasperated sigh. "You know the rules, Weyna. We can't."

"My mother has given me permission to use her bath, so why can't you join me? It's really my decision, isn't it?" I pushed.

Boudka placed the stitching materials in my lap and stood up. "It doesn't matter what your mother said. I can't use it. Those are the rules, and they're in place for a reason. Why are you always trying to get me into trouble?"

I frowned, furrowing my brow. "I'm not. I just thought, after all that—"

"What, that I might want to get caught by your aunt or Saya bathing in your mother's tub?" Boudka interrupted, her voice rising. "Besides, your mother could return at any moment, and she already doesn't like me. You should have heard her scolding me the other day. She threatened to send me out of the camp," she added with a raw and loud tone. I held up my hands in surrender, knowing there was no winning here.

"Okay, okay. Sorry, I asked. Go bathe with the other maids if that's what turns you on," I retorted, immediately regretting my words. I knew it was a horrible thing to say.

Boudka's eyes went wide at the statement, hurt playing in her expression. Without saying a word, she stormed out of the tent, leaving the tent flap swinging angrily.

"Fuck," I muttered to myself. "Could this day get any worse?"

CHAPTER SEVEN

Aoife

Morgan hadn't been joking. Her flat was fucking tiny, just a little one-room bedsit in an ugly brick building that would have been more at home in Soviet Russia than Roxbury. The interior was alright, if a bit ascetic and dark. A tiny window at one end provided the only light into the entire room.

She did have a king-sized bed that she'd crammed under the window. That had probably been an epic struggle. But given her six-two frame, a queen wouldn't have been big enough. A small loveseat sat against the tiny nightstand.

The entire place looked like something out of a noir novel. Sparsely furnished and miserable. Even the bathroom was claustrophobic, with a coffin-like circular shower with a weird sliding door. It looked kind of like one of those capsule hotel beds in Tokyo. There was also a little sink covered in makeup remains. About the only saving grace was the little cupboard with the stacked washer and dryer and a tiny bookshelf full of lesbian romance novels. The place was also a mess.

Morgan was a slob. Clothes lay strewn on the bed, old receipts covered the small breakfast table, and the rubbish bin, though largely devoid of organic matter, was overflowing with paper products and a few old blood storage bags with remnants of blood in them, most surely rotted. At least it didn't stink.

I shook my head as we walked in, wondering what Liz and Marcella had been thinking.

"I guess I'll take the floor, then," I said as I set down my suitcase next to the couch.

Morgan looked over at me. "Why? I'm an army vet and used to cramped quarters. It's a king-sized bed, Aoife. There's plenty of room." Then she grinned. "And it's not like you'll be pressing a boner into my back at night."

I laughed at what seemed like an uncharacteristic show of humor. It was good to know that she could joke and that she had a bawdy streak. "Erect penis. No. Erect nipples, maybe." I said with a wink, and she snorted a laugh.

"That wouldn't bother me," she flirted back.

Okay, so maybe this wouldn't be so bad. I made a show of inspecting the place like an NCO. Running my hand across the surfaces and rubbing my fingers together with imaginary and, in many places, not-so-imaginary dust. "Besides, it looks like you need someone to look after you."

She frowned with embarrassment. "It's been a rough couple of months. I've been pretty depressed, honestly, and haven't been up to cleaning."

I smiled at her as kindly as I could. "It's okay. I'll straighten it up and make it better for you. It's the least I can do for having to host me."

"No, don't bother. I'll take care of it."

I nodded, not at all convinced that she would and certain that it wouldn't matter because I'd do it anyway. But I could see her stubborn streak, and I wasn't going to fight with it.

I wandered over to the nightstand and found another romance novel laying there. "Ooh, I haven't read this one." I immediately snatched it up.

"Hey, I'm reading that," Morgan protested.

I flipped through it. "From the dog-eared pages and worn cover, I'd say you'd read it plenty already. Wait, why do you stop reading right before the saucy bits?" Then I thought about it. "Oh! Oh, my!" I made a mocking gasp and clutched imaginary pearls giving her a cheeky grin. "Morgan Kennedy!"

Morgan blushed and snatched the book from my hands. "Give me that." She threw the book on the nightstand and took off her coat, throwing it on the sofa. "I'm going to sleep. It's almost midday, and I can't stay up anymore. I'm exhausted. There's nothing in the refrigerator, but the grocery guy Marcella ordered should be here soon."

I laughed, and Morgan turned, a puzzled look on her face.

"She ordered groceries or just the guy?"

Her eyebrows rose as she got it, and started to giggle. "You know, this might be alright."

I stood there and gaped as she stripped naked and climbed into the bed. I couldn't help admiring her rippling muscles. Gods, she really was gorgeous, and for a moment, I was rooted, unable to move, a creeping warmth sliding up my neck.

She rolled over, her back to me, and I could almost hear her grin at my discomfort.

Having nothing else to do until Carlos arrived, I waited until I was certain she was asleep and started cleaning. I thought maybe Morgan might wake up and protest, but she didn't move a muscle. I even shook her gently, but she refused to stir, which was perfect. I wasn't going to live in some pigsty for the next few months. Ever since my first day of basic training, my world had been neat and tidy. I wasn't going to change that now.

It didn't take long; the place was so small. So, by the time the grocery guy, and Carlos as it turned out, knocked at the door, the place was almost worthy of inspection. The dirty clothes were in the hamper. The clean clothes were put away in her small dresser, and the counters had been cleaned. The stove was scrubbed within an inch of its life. The surfaces were dusted and wiped down. The rubbish had been emptied into the chute, and I'd cleaned the bathroom sink. I didn't have time to mop or vacuum, but I'd get that later. I couldn't find a mop or a vacuum anyway. Morgan was such an animal, honestly.

"She sleepin'?" Carlos asked as he stepped in.

"Like the proverbial dead," I quipped and handed the grocery guy the ten-dollar tip that Morgan had left on the counter before shooing him off and closing the door. I waved my hand and wrinkled my nose at the sour smell of weed that lingered behind him.

Carlos gave an amused grin and set a stack of binders on the small breakfast table, sitting down in one of the chairs as I put away the groceries.

"I'm Aoife," I called as I stuffed some iceberg lettuce into one of the vegetable drawers, noting a few bags of blood on one shelf.

"Carlos Ramirez. I'm Cait's lead detective."

"Good to meet you. Hang on just a second."

Finally, I finished putting away the groceries, folded up the used bags, stowed them between the refrigerator and counter, and sat down. "So, is this everything?"

"Yup. It'll keep you busy for a few days. But I reckon most of it will be familiar." He flipped through the binders. "Evidence procedures, personnel procedures, investigative, and a manual on the case management system. That's all you'll need for the job. The hard part will be getting familiar with her life at the department. This is Maki Imai." He handed me a photo of a pretty East Asian woman. "She's in the know. She's a kitsune."

I raised an eyebrow at that. "Okay, so those are real?"

He nodded. "Yeah. And she's handy in a fight, too."

"Detective Freyer, Detective Doyle, and Detective Washington are also aware of the situation. I don't have photos of Doyle, but here are pictures of Freyer and Washington." He pulled out two more eight by tens and slid them over, one of a handsome older man with a graying beard and tree-trunk arms, the other of a cute, short black woman with a natural afro in current style. "Carol, um, Detective Washington, is on leave right now. None of us know where she is, and we want to keep it that way."

I glanced up, puzzled at that. "Why?"

"Mother Darkness is after her."

"Who's Mother Darkness? A local kingpin or something?"

Carlos snorted. "No, she's a two-hundred-foot-tall crystalline monster that lives on the other side of the black gate."

I raised my eyebrows at him. "Okay, so there's something I never imagined."

He proceeded to give me a brief rundown of the gate and the things on the other side, being very detailed about a creepy bunch of spider things called ogumo.

After he was done, he got back to the issue at hand. "No one else knows a damn thing about what's happened other than Cait got shot, was wearing a vest, and is recuperating. The responding officers were glamoured by Nastasia to forget the incident. She did the coroner, too, after Cait popped a gasket in the morgue. I round-filed the report."

"Popped a gasket?" I asked, feeling somewhere between amused and disturbed by the description.

"She opened her eyes, said something in a weird language, and almost choked out the coroner. Liz was there, fortunately. After Cait went down, Liz absolutely refused to believe Cait was dead and insisted on staying with the body. She sat at the Medical Examiner's office for two days, not sleeping, not, um, drinking. I swear that woman is fucking dedicated. Anyway, she called Nastasia and Marcella, and they cleaned up the mess."

I pictured Liz sitting in a morgue with all of the dead bodies around, just guarding Cait. *Vampire love,* I thought. *Obsessive and crazy.*

"So, as far as anyone else knows, you're Cait Reagan, the same lady they've worked next to for years." Carlos must have seen the look on my face, so he added. "Cait's been pretty private for the last few years, from what I understand, so most of the department knows little about her. Liz and Marcella probably know more than anyone, so I wouldn't get too uptight about the entire thing. And if it gets dicey and you get caught, I've got you covered." He held up a piece of paper. "I have authorization from the DA's office."

I nodded, letting that nice knuckle of gristle settle in my stomach. "I've never done undercover work before."

"Can you do an American accent? If not, we'll have to work on that."

I switched to an American accent, though there might have

been a hint of my brogue under it. I wasn't sure. "I was born here, Carlos. Of course, I can be American."

Carlos laughed. "Damn. You sound just like her. Just remember to say fuck every other word, and you'll be okay."

"Fuck," I swore. "I knew I forgot something. Fucking Da and his potty mouth."

"Oh, she doesn't call Mike Da anymore, just Mike."

I stared at him, puzzled. "Why not?"

Carlos' eyes went wide. "She didn't tell you?"

"Tell me what?" I gave him my best 'what the fuck are you talking about' face.

"Mike wasn't your father. You were sired by a goddess." He raised a hand to stop me before I asked about a million questions. "Don't ask me how that works. And don't ask me how it happened. You need to ask your mother. I don't know the details. Something about the back of a Volkswagen, I think."

My mouth dropped open. "But—"

"As I said, darlin'. You need to take up that particular bomb with your mother."

I sat back heavily in the chair. "Great way to start this."

Carlos' radio chirped. "Operations Victor 8-7-7."

"Victor 8-7-7, go ahead," he replied.

"We've got a call out for full PIU support. Carson beach. Time off is canceled. If Reagan is in contact, she needs to be on-site as well. Freyer and Kennedy "

My eyes shot wide. *Already? No way I was ready to do this.*

"Victor 8-7-7 acknowledged," Carlos said into his radio, then turned back to me. "Cait is Victor 8-9-4, by the way. Anyway, I guess you'll have to study these tonight. We have a job to do, so let's get to it. I've got Cait's fatigues and gear in the car."

"Let me get dressed," Morgan grumped from the bed. "Turn around, Carlos. This show isn't for you." Then she smiled at me, making me blush.

On a whim, I went to the refrigerator and looked inside. Finding what I was looking for, I pulled it out and took it to Morgan, who was still starkers. I tried not to flush and failed.

She didn't say anything, but she grinned broadly, obviously flattered, then took the bag of blood gratefully, draining it like a kid on the playground, adorably sucking out about every last drop. "Pitch that, will you?"

Damnit, she was supposed to be the fucking enemy. And fuck if I wasn't getting all twisted over her already. I turned around, studiously grabbing Cait's badge and weapon from my bag.

"You do know how to use that, I hope."

I slid open the chamber and checked it, finding a round inside. I re-holstered it, then grinned at Carlos. "We do carry them in Ireland. We just don't let any idiot buy one, not that most people want to. Now let's go. I'll figure things out on the fly."

"Can I get my boots on? Please." Morgan bitched from the bed. At least she was dressed now, but she winked at me and struck a pose when I looked over, and I rolled my eyes. Good Gods, if she was this much of a flirt, how was I going to survive the next couple of months with my neck intact?

A few minutes later, Morgan and I crammed into the back of the cruiser so Carlos didn't have to take the time to move a bunch of papers from the front seat. She was uncomfortably close, and when she splayed her long legs to get comfortable, I moved mine over to avoid them touching. I felt suddenly self-conscious, and my heart sped up.

"I'm sorry if I made you feel uncomfortable," Morgan said. "I'm not really body conscious, but after your display in the bathroom—" She let the statement die and grinned, making me laugh.

"Morgan, now," Carlos called from the front. "Leave the poor girl alone. She just got here."

"I didn't do anything. She's the one who flashed me in the shower."

"Good God, you move fast. You've already showered together?"

"Hey," we both protested in unison.

"I was in the shower. Morgan was bringing in towels."

"Yeah, but it's not like you hid yourself, like, at all," Morgan giggled, watching Carlos' head shake in disbelief.

"Morgan," Carlos interjected, "that's Cait's sister, you know?"

"And?" Morgan asked, crossing her arms and looking at me with a mischievous grin. Then she leaned over and whispered. "He's afraid I'll convince you to become one of us."

"I heard that," Carlos said from the front seat. "And, no, that's not it. You know what? Aoife, you're a big girl. I'm sure you can take care of yourself."

I just sat back and watched the playful exchange, feeling a combination of amusement, joy at a feeling of belonging, and a bit of jealousy that Cait had had this kind of camaraderie. I'd never gotten on like this with my peers back home.

"Yes, Carlos," I said finally. "I can take care of myself." Truthfully, though, I wasn't at all sure of that.

"Are you sure you're alright?" Morgan asked quietly, then leaned in very close to whisper almost inaudibly, "Your heart is racing."

Yes, I thought. *Yes, it is.* I wasn't sure if it was because of the callout or because of her proximity. Eventually, I decided it was the callout, but the scent of her was heady. She smelled of wild blackberries and something else I couldn't place, almost intoxicating. I had a slight shiver down my neck, but I nodded anyway. "I'm fine. Just nerves. You just mind yourself."

She nodded back, but her expression was skeptical, to say the least. Then she leaned in briefly and said, "Your sister calls me Red."

I nodded, getting the message.

We made our way through shitty traffic. The Massholes were certainly out in force, and from the swearing up front, it was clear that Carlos was none too pleased about it. As it was, it took us a full thirty minutes to go all of about six miles.

We pulled up into the parking lot at Carson Beach, a flat, fingernail sliver of sandy shore south of downtown that, during the day, was home to beachgoers and a favorite spot for local beach volleyball players. Several of the nets were still up, even this late in the evening. A line of cops, firefighters, and a contingent from the coast guard surrounded the bow of a massive cargo ship sitting high up on the beach. She was Chinese by the markings.

I glanced around as Press crews and gawkers crowded the police cordon.

"You ready, Cait?" Morgan asked as we got out, sliding me a sly wink.

"Ready as I'll ever be." I planted an excited smile on my face and followed them to the boot. Suiting up, I felt a little weird changing in semi-public. Being super flirty with Morgan was one thing, but this was something else entirely. Then again, Morgan was getting into her fatigues, so I figured that's how things were around this place. Detective Imai walked over with Detective Freyer, who looked much gruffer and a little meatier in person.

"Coast guard went on board, immediately came off and called for us," Maki said as she stripped out of her suit and started sliding on her gear. Something about her made me all gooey on the inside, and I couldn't keep my eyes off her, constantly glancing in her direction. She was beautiful with long black hair, almost fox-like features, and a cute rear. Freyer just kept his eyes on the ship and watched for peeping toms.

"Maki, give us a break, huh?" He chided as he stood between our cruiser and another one, blocking the civilians from seeing us.

"Oh, sorry." The woman looked a little chagrined as the sudden urge to get closer to her disappeared. "So, Cait, you ready?"

"Everyone keeps asking me that. I'm back and fit as I'll ever be." *Yeah, right.*

My hands shook as I took the MP5 SD from the back and checked the magazine. "That's a Qiongsha class cargo vessel. Bow reads Nan-Kang 834. She's got a massive hold, and she's a commissioned ship of the People's Liberation Army. She's eighty-six meters long, thirteen and a half meters in the beam, and has about a four-meter draft. The crew complement varies, but she can carry over two-hundred passengers." I peeked around the car at the wreck as I re-holstered my sidearm. "She had to be going at least eighteen knots to get up this far onto the beach."

Everyone stopped cold and stared at me.

Then Morgan gave me an appraising look. "Damn! That was sexy, girl. Do it again!"

"What?" I muttered, suddenly bashful, and looked away, checking my sidearm to hide my flush. "So, I have a thing for boats."

They all laughed at my discomfort.

All dressed and geared up, we meandered over to the guy who looked like he was in charge. He was a stocky fellow with what looked like a permanent frown beneath his graying beard. He also had commander's stripes on his shoulders, so he'd been around a while.

Carlos stepped in front of me. "So, Commander, what do we have?"

"Oh, good, the Zombie Squad is here. You must be Detective Ramirez. And this woman needs no introduction. Good to meet you, Reagan. No sword this time, I see." He stuck out his hand. "I'm Commander Wade."

I took it briefly and nodded. "No, sir, no swords." I had no idea what he was talking about, but I played along.

"I need you guys to clear this thing," he continued gesturing to the ship.

"How did a PLAN ship get into the harbor anyway?" I asked Wade. "I mean, shouldn't someone have intercepted it?"

"She was here on a scientific research mission, delivering cargo to Zhu Pharma's lab at MIT. They had authorization."

I snorted. "Great. This ought to be fun. So, what did you find that brought us out here?"

"A lot of blood, a bunch of dead bodies, and if you look there. Shit, hang on." Wade whistled to a crewman and ordered him to turn the light on 'the hole.' The light wobbled a bit left and right, finally settling on a two-meter hole in the side of the ship, about thirty feet above the waterline. From the looks of it, something had torn her open from the inside, though there wasn't any scorching or melting I'd expect from a blast. The metal looked ripped open like an aluminum can.

"It's not from an explosive," Wade confirmed. "Something

tore through the side of the ship from the inside. Our guys peeked in the forward cargo hold and decided to high-tail it out there. A few of them barfed along the way."

Carlos sighed, and Morgan chuckled. Then Carlos said, "Alright, sounds like our gig. We'll check it out."

"I don't know how much more of this my men can take," Wade commented as he walked us to a launch. "You know they closed the Strait of Messina."

We all nodded.

"Yes. Well, less well known, we've had twelve ships, and small craft found floating off the coast, all in perfectly good working order, with crews missing, every single one as empty as Mary Celeste herself. We've kept it out of the news for now, but it's fucking creepy. No blood, no bodies. Just nothing." He paused and pulled a cigar from his jacket. "Honestly, though, I think I prefer that to this." He waved a hand at the massive, stranded hulk. "Whatever happened here, it was quick enough that they didn't abandon ship, but they didn't get away either."

We stopped at the edge of the water in front of a small motorized dinghy. Now that we were a bit closer, I could see the rope boarding ladder attached to the huge ship's side. The wind was blowing out of the northwest, so at least we didn't have much chance of it listing over on top of us. But, unless there was a massive hole below the waterline we couldn't see, that was unlikely.

"Call down when you figure it out," Wade called as we boarded the dinghy.

I gave him a thumbs-up, and we pushed out into the harbor.

CHAPTER EIGHT

Weyna

I spent the next few days doing my chores and feeling sorry for myself. Since the encounter with the Fomori, I'd found myself sleeping alone. Boudka hadn't even so much as talked to me. I caught her eye a few times, but she immediately turned away.

"What are you doing, child?" Badb asked when she found me waiting for Boudka outside the servant's mess.

I glanced up at her. "What does it look like I'm doing? I'm waiting for Boudka."

She chuckled in that deep, mellifluous voice of hers, her tone haughty and superior. "Trouble in the palace?"

I snorted in derision. "You could say that. She hasn't spoken to me since the day you rescued us."

"You." Badb corrected.

"What?"

"You rescued her. I rescued you. The emisai was just bad luck; otherwise, you wouldn't have needed me at all."

I pulled up my right sleeve. "My arm begs to differ."

She frowned at me. "Leave the girl be. She's obviously got something on her mind, and she'll tell you when she's ready. Come away from there and get back to work."

I didn't mind the menial nature of my tasks, feeding the livestock or taking mine and my mother's laundry down to the lake to wash it. It was just work. Though, I hated actually doing the laundry. It wasn't the washing that bothered me. It was the long journey to the lake below the camp and, more importantly, the long climb back up the steep hillside.

My mother, by her own peculiar insistence, assigned me the task of our laundry, opting against the communal facilities of the camp. 'They misplace things,' she had reasoned, her voice curt. Yet, I suspected that this was merely a ploy to keep me occupied, a safeguard to keep out of trouble.

As I wrung out the damp garments, settling them neatly in the laundry basket, the Óşeni women descended the hill, their agile forms gliding over the rugged terrain like liquid down the hillside. Their speed was mesmerizing, their beauty captivating.

I was entranced by their elegant movements, their bare feet nimbly dodging past root and stone. Sunlight glimmered off their silver locks, braided tightly into neat buns, and kissed their glistening, grey skin. I stood transfixed, a silent witness to their moving perfection as they dove into the water, cutting swiftly through the liquid expanse towards the distant shore, half a mile away, and then back again. They were just—lovely, for lack of a better word.

Daydreams drifted through my head, leaving me wondering what it might be like to be one of them, with their strength, their poise, and their warrior prowess. Of course, it was a notion better born of Bethadi Euphoris flowers than reality, I knew, but still, it was something to spark my imagination amid the drudgery, and it gave me pause as I watched their nude forms retreat back up the hillside toward the top of the curving ridge and the stockade walls of the fort.

With the laundry completed, I shouldered the heavy burden of wet clothes and set off on the uphill journey, treading in the footsteps of the warrior women. The sun had slipped a couple of hours past midday when I finally reached the camp, and almost another hour and a half slipped by while I hung the laundry, tended to my mother's bathing pool, and fulfilled my water-bearing duties for the Óşeni. Like most days, I'd had to skip the midday meal. No wonder I was so thin.

As I maneuvered among the Óşeni women, offering each water in turn, they treated me with indifference, making me feel small as I scurried about their tree-trunk legs and towering frames, like some little pack animal.

Fighters to the last, they viewed anyone without skills in blade or bow as unimportant, below respect, the sole exception being the medhen, whom they happily revered as healers of their wounds.

Each day, about halfway through water-bearing, I would stop at the training circle. It was then that a distinct group typically practiced using dual blades rather than the traditional bow or sword and shield. Each carried an unmistakable blackened spiral brand etched onto their skin, just above their left breast, perhaps a symbol of honor or rank. Even among the Óṣeni, they were highly respected and, it seemed, feared.

They fought in pairs, back to back, and their movements were as one. As they turned and jostled against sometimes three or four opponents, their defenses seemed impenetrable and their attacks swift and deadly. They were artists who painted in death and often made the other Swasari seem inept.

As I watched, I noticed Saya on the far side of the training circle giving a harsh lesson to one of the soldiers. She knocked the woman's shin with a wooden practice sword coaxing her feet back into proper form. In sword work, it seemed, as in any skill, bad habits could form from lack of practice. When she'd finished with the warrior, she brushed past me gruffly, nearly knocking me down with her greater bulk and spilling a bit of the water.

"Watch where you're going," Saya barked.

Huffing out a breath, I looked up to find her staring down at me, one eyebrow raised, daring me to say something.

A reckless part of me longed to punch her in that perfect Óṣeni nose and see if I couldn't knock her on her perfect Óṣeni butt. I even had a vision of myself hooking her weight-bearing leg and giving her a shove, but I knew better. Besides, I didn't know where the thought had come from. It seemed foreign and weird. It would probably work, but still.

"Sorry, Captain Saya," I said instead, though I'm sure she could read my rage. It was painted all over my face with a red brush.

She smirked weirdly but said nothing and continued on.

A young Óşeni woman, maybe a year or two older than me, walked over after Saya was out of earshot. She looked different from the others, not just because she wore one of the spiral brands or because she was slightly shorter and fuller figured than the others, but because she wore a warm, friendly expression. She must have finished her training for the day, as her hair was down, framing her pretty face with soft curling locks like silver flames. It was beautiful, and I said so.

She tugged at it, curling a lock playfully about one finger with a shy smile that made my heart skip a little. "You think so?"

I nodded but kept my lips tightly shut lest I stutter.

A mischievous look turned her full lips impish as she took a sip from the carafe and then whispered, "Don't mind the Captain. She's just a sour bitch who needs to get laid."

I blurted a laugh, drawing dour gazes from the woman's compatriots. I ignored them as best I could, staying focused on the young Óşeni before me.

She continued. "She thinks people around here don't matter if they can't handle a blade. And don't mind the others. Most of us *do* know better. While slaves do things like this at home, so do the newosi. We've all done it, so we appreciate the help." She took another drink from the Carafe, gave me a kind smile, and bounced away, calling, "Thanks for the water."

I was honestly a little starstruck, but I smothered the burgeoning grin on my face and dutifully resumed my rounds. My path etched a familiar circuit until my task was complete, then I emptied the remnants of the carafe into the massive water barrel perched adjacent to the warrior's mess, one of the scant permanent structures dotting the circular fort. I'd never eaten there; I wasn't allowed. Yet, I found myself frequently lingering on the periphery, observing the camaraderie of the Óşeni, their laughter, and friendly exchanges. Each echo of laughter was a reminder of an experience beyond my reach, a longing that stirred within me.

Afterward, I found Boudka next to the laundry, mending a

pair of pants. They were Bethadi cloth, if I wasn't mistaken. The cloth held an odd duality—supple as lambskin and yet strong enough to take a few shots from a steel-pointed blade. Boudka's fingers deftly guided the black-steel needle, their movements swift and precise as she threaded it through the fabric effortlessly.

The Bethadi incorporated enchantments into the weave of their cloth, but the tools needed to mend it were kept secret. They seemed to prefer the spectacle of the poor humans' struggling to mend the cloth, much to the servants' dismay and the Bethadi's twisted amusement. But Boudka had always been a step ahead. Before she'd ever had the mend the first bit of Bethadi cloth, she'd gone to one of the Óșeni weaponsmiths and had her coax together a needle of the razor-sharp metal which could cut through steel like melted fats.

I sat down next to her and watched her work for a bit. When she didn't give me any kind of greeting, I finally said, "Sorry about the other day."

She scoffed and replied with feigned indifference. At least, I thought it was feigned. "I'm sure."

I grinned at her. "So that's how it's going to be?"

"Mmhmm." She continued pushing the needle through the trousers.

I took a deep breath. She wasn't going to make this easy. "Okay, so what do I need to do?"

She set the trousers carefully in her lap, gently sticking the needle into them in such a way as not to catch her fingers or push the insanely sharp thing through her leg. Then she looked at me, her eyes holding a melancholy sorrow and a grim determination. The depth of the expression gave me pause. This was going to be an unpleasant conversation, and I could tell she thought it a long time in coming.

"Weyna, your mother is the fucking Morrigan. Everyone is terrified of her and her sisters, even the Kaushkari, if the stories are to be believed. Some say she could wipe out most of this army with a stroke of her arm."

I shrugged. "Yeah, okay. So. What does that have to do with me?"

With pursed lips and hard eyes, she studied my expression, finally giving a frustrated sigh before continuing. "Weyna, look. I like being with you, but I like being up here in the camp more. This place is wonderful. You take it for granted. There are healers. There's running water. We have things like this." She indicated the small needle. "This little piece of metal doesn't even exist in my village below."

I rolled my eyes. "I know that. Don't forget that I was living in a shitty little village just like that up until four years ago."

"Yes, but no one is going to kick you out of here if you slack off or fuck up."

"Hang on. That's not necessarily true."

"Yes, it is, and you know it. You blew up a fucking lamb, and no one batted an eyelash."

"Ugh. Don't remind me, please." The poor creature had had a mildly fractured leg, and I'd tried to heal the lamb like I'd seen the medhen do to human limbs. It should have been simple, a brief stitching of the tarzhi, but my magic had slipped away from me like a wriggling trout pulled from a stream. The results had been, well, catastrophic.

"It's not about the damn sheep!" She threw her hands up in aggravation, nearly dropping the pants to the ground. "I want to stay here. I want to live with these people. Up here, I don't have to worry about being raped. Life down there," she pointed toward the gates, "is horrid and miserably short. My mother died in childbirth because I was turned the wrong way. They cut me out of her. Did you know that?"

I hadn't, but she continued before I could answer. "Up here, I can love who I want, be with who I want, and it's okay. It's not only ignored. It's accepted. Down there, I would have to marry a man selected by my overbearing father, probably some greasy bloke who chases sheep all day and wants me to give him a bevy of sons, like some breeding cow. Like you, I don't like men, never have. And unlike you, I have to earn my keep every day in this place. So, when you lay there in bed and do nothing, you remind me that you're not long-term material. You're just someone I'm sleeping with. I don't like how that feels."

The impact of her words struck me viscerally, landing in my gut like an invisible fist. "That's how you see me? A layabout?"

She nodded. "The worst part is that I like you. I want to be with you. I like the way you make me feel when you look at me and how sweet you are, at least most of the time. But you're completely irresponsible, and for whatever reason, I just follow along with it and end up stumbling into disaster with you. And that's not something I can abide. I intend to make myself useful here and find a way to move on with whichever group will have me."

I just stared at her, mouth agape. She sounded just like my mother, and I wasn't thrilled with the emotions it stirred. The cold whisper of doubt curled itself around my heart, suggesting perhaps she was right, and my mother as well. Maybe I was nothing more than a waste, marred and spoiled and worthless.

"So," she said with an air of finality, picking up the pants once more to resume her task, speaking in a hushed but firm tone, not looking at me. "You asked what you need to do. I'll tell you. What you need to do is grow up and take some responsibility for yourself. Act like someone I would want to be with and not a bratty child. Please, Weyna."

Though she had lowered her voice, every word drove right through me like a knife buried to the hilt.

I wasn't sure what to say, so I blurted out the first thing that came to mind. "I like your company, Boudka. I like you. It's not just sex to me. I want to be with you, too."

She paused mid-stitch and stared at her hands, refusing to meet my gaze. "Then act like it. Take your studies seriously, and take care of your chores with the kind of concern I'd expect from a daughter of The Morrigan and not some little palace terror. Until then, though, I'm going to stay in the maids' quarters."

"Wait. You're staying away for good?"

"Yes, Weyna, I am. I've been bitching about this for months, and you've done nothing. Maybe some time on your own will get your attention."

I wanted to say something. I wanted to wail and rage. I

wanted to throw a tantrum. But in the back of my mind, some part of me knew that nothing I said would matter, and throwing a fit would only make things worse. So, I kissed her gently on the cheek, begged my leave, and went back to my tent with only a stone in my belly for sustenance.

"Fuck," I swore when I sat down on my cot. Scalding tears threatened, pressing painfully behind my eyes.

Boudka was right, of course. I was a fuck up, a constant annoyance to my mother and everyone else. For a moment, I wished my mother had just left me to die when the Fomori had come.

I hadn't been happy with Da. He was a useless drunk and a shitty father, always leaving me to manage the shitty chores and our shitty little turf and stone cottage in that shitty little village. One night, while he'd been passed out drunk since midday, he'd left me to tend the entire fucking farm. Two men, turf men by the look of them and their wagon, had stopped by to hock their bricks. Finding me alone out of doors, they'd tried to have their way with me instead.

I'd fended them off, mostly by luck and a broken broom handle. But in the morning, Da hadn't even asked how I'd gotten two black eyes and a split lip. And where had my mother been then? She'd been off with this very army halfway around the world battling the Kaushkar, a people I hadn't even known existed. Of course, I hadn't even known she was alive back then. Da had said she was dead. But, as it turned out, she'd left me at home with Da right after I was born. She'd had responsibilities. Apparently, I hadn't been one of them.

Of course, as anyone would, when she'd flown in and saved me from the rampaging Fomori, I'd been grateful. She scooped me up, like the goddess that she was, and brought me to this place. Back then, it hadn't been much more than a smattering of tents on a hillside gingerly set up around the ancient stone tombs that already sat here, but I'd been thrilled to go, given that the alternative would have been almost certain death, but now, shit, I was tired. Tired of lessons in magic I couldn't follow. Tired of being told how important I was and yet treated like a child. Tired of being told that I had some stupid destiny.

Mostly though, I was tired of living. Everyone here hated me. I didn't belong.

And with those cheerful thoughts, I cried myself to an early sleep, praying not to wake up in the morning. And though Mother Danu certainly heard those prayers, being about a hundred yards away, she would be unlikely to answer them. And, let's be honest, my mother was also a Goddess of Death. She could snatch a soul out of the air as someone perished if need be. So, even if I died, she'd probably just send me to bed without supper and then send me back to lessons and chores the next morning.

Fuck, this sucked.

CHAPTER NINE

Aoife

"Sweet Jesus," Carlos said as he topped the ladder.

It didn't take but a second to understand what he meant when I reached the deck myself. Blood, primarily arterial spray, covered almost every surface. At least four people, or parts of them, were dead across the deck. It might have been more; I couldn't be sure, and I immediately hurried to the stern to hurl my guts out. "Sorry, sis," I mumbled, wiping my chin on my sleeve.

Morgan tapped me on the shoulder. "You okay?"

"Yeah," I whispered hoarsely as I spat over the railing, trying to clear my mouth. "I've just never seen anything like this."

She offered a small pouch of red liquid from her pocket.

"No thanks." I turned away in disgust.

Morgan chuckled. "It's just pedialite. Take it. It'll wash out the taste."

I grabbed the pouch and took a swig. It tasted like shit but was far better than the puke flavor on my tongue. I rinsed my mouth and spat over the railing again. "Why do you carry pedialite? You don't drink it."

"I can when I need to convince someone I'm human. But mostly, it's for the others. We got stuck overnight in a hostile dimension a couple of weeks ago, before I was turned, and I kept wishing I had something like this to wash the taste of sulfur out of my mouth. We were also low on water. So, now I carry it when we go out."

"We?"

"Cait and I," she said, then added quickly, "Freyer, too," and turned away.

I tilted my head at how she'd felt the need to amend the statement and, more importantly, how she'd turned away so quickly. There had been something on her face, regret maybe? Or embarrassment? I wasn't sure. But it wasn't the time. I finished the pedialite and pushed on.

"Hey, Morgan," I called to her back. "Thanks."

She turned and smiled at me, fangs and all. This time, though, I smirked. I knew she was just fucking with me. "No problem."

"I count six," Maki said with a shiver. "Most of two of them aren't here, but there are six left legs here. I see more blood over there." She pointed toward another portion of the aft deck.

Carlos sniffed the air. "This didn't happen long ago. It's only been a few hours, I'd guess."

I looked at him. "How can you tell? It was at sea. There wouldn't be a lot of flies anyway, and it's raining."

He just tapped his nose and hoisted his weapon. We cleared the aft deck relatively quickly, then moved forward, splitting into two teams. Morgan and I took the port side. Freyer, Maki, and Carlos took the starboard. All we found along the way was more blood, a lot more. The hatches were all sealed except one just before the stairs to the bridge. We gave a cursory check of the passageway beyond, but it was empty, extending straight across to a hatch on the starboard side of the vessel. Bloody drag marks led across the floor of the dark passage and down the ladder to the right, but otherwise, it was clear, so I pulled the door closed and latched it, and we kept moving.

The forecastle was mostly empty. Carlos' group had arrived there first. They were standing in the center of the deck, staring down at something. As we approached, Freyer bent down and examined what resolved itself to be a dead Chinese sailor in a PLA Navy uniform. In the corpse's left hand was a 9mm pistol, standard PLA issue.

"Shot himself," Freyer said as he pushed the face aside with two fingers, revealing a neat hole in the side of the man's head surrounded by stippling and residue. "Something scared him enough for him to kill himself rather than—" Freyer trailed off, waving dismissively at the rest of the ship.

I looked at Morgan. "You don't think all this was—"

She shook her head. "No. Too much blood. Setting aside the fact that all vampires are accounted for and that Marcella knows right where they all are, pretty much at any time, a vampire wouldn't do this type of damage or leave this much blood. The last time I saw anything like this was the bunker at Great Blue Hill, but it's cleared out." She thought for a moment, then added, "And the gate facility downtown, but that's all sealed up."

"Naw, this started at sea," Carlos agreed. "It's fresh but over an hour old, at least. A vamp could do this, but why? I've never heard of one committing this kind of atrocity. Let's check the rest of the ship."

A metallic bang sounded aft of us from the port side, and we all spun, hoisting our weapons.

"See anything?" Carlos asked.

"No," Morgan replied. "It's clear."

We moved down the port side in two by two formation, with Maki odd-man in the center until we reached the hatch we'd checked before. It was ajar, and there were new footprints in the blood. They had no toes, perfectly smooth. They led out, forward, and then back into the hatch.

"Shit! Emisai," Freyer swore.

"No way," Morgan said. "The gate room is sealed, and those tunnels were too small for an emisai to get out anyway. Besides, the gait is too narrow. It's too small to be emisai."

"Let's not speculate," Carlos ordered. "Maki can handle a single emisai if that's what it is."

Maki looked dubious. "Let's hope. I don't want to imagine anything else that could do all this."

I shone a light on the prints. "Um, these look like women's prints, maybe a size six. See how they step, riding the outside of the foot? It's common for women who wear high heels.

How big are these emisai?"

Freyer frowned. "Okay, maybe this is something worse. We stay together. We work the ship from the bridge down. No fucking around and no going off mission. Clear?"

"Yes, sir," everyone replied, and we headed up the stairs to the bridge.

"Well, that explains a lot," I said, looking at the state of the bridge. The conning chair was torn from the floor, the bolts sheered clean, and half of the equipment was smashed, including the wheel. Blood covered everything, and there was evidence of arterial spray in several places here as well.

I glanced over at Carlos, who was picking at the broken controls on the starboard side. "We're lucky it didn't hit anything. Between the lack of control and the currents, it's a fucking miracle it found the beach." I checked over the port side controls and sighed loudly. "Shit."

Morgan walked over and looked at the wreck of twisted wires, smashed sheet metal, and plastic. "What was it?"

"The CCTV system." I pointed to a camera suspended from the deckhead. "I was hoping there'd be footage."

Carlos walked over and looked at the rig. "That's a solid-state drive unit. Doyle can pull the video after we finish, assuming we get the chance. The military will be here soon; you can guarantee that. So will the Chinese Government attaché. We need to get moving."

Seeing nothing else, we followed a dragging blood trail out of the bridge.

"There should be at least a hundred sailors here," I whispered.

"So, where the fuck are they?" Freyer replied, watching our rear as we continued to move. On the starboard side of the main superstructure, we found the hatch that lay opposite the one we'd investigated to port.

"Go," Carlos whispered as he opened the hatch. "Morgan and I filed inside, only to find more drag marks, footprints, and a dead sailor in the passageway. The hatch we'd examined was directly ahead, and a set of narrow stairs led downward. Otherwise, the passageway was empty. It was like all the rest of the ship, and the slow anxiety that had begun filtering up from the pit of my stomach was blossoming into full-blown terror.

Someone or something was in here. I wrung my hands for a moment to quell their quaking and steady myself. I wasn't really cut out for this paranormal crap. *Gods, Cait, how did you do shit like this?* "Those are called a ladder on a ship here in the states," I whispered, pointing to the stairs.

Morgan stared at me for a moment in disbelief. She was probably wondering why I'd mention something so inane, but in times like this, I talked to maintain my nerves.

"Sorry," I mouthed and started toward the narrow stairs, but Morgan stopped me.

"Me first," she whispered and took point, moving quickly and quietly. *Fuck,* I thought, *it must be nice to be damn near unkillable.*

At the bottom of the ladder, we came to a long dark passageway with the deck layered in thick pools of blood. In one or two places, I saw dragging hand prints as if someone had been trying to stop from being pulled away. "Jaysus," I said, forgetting about my accent for a moment as we moved, more slowly this time.

At each hatchway we passed—there were several—we found relatively spacious quarters, most of them in disarray and most containing corpses, all mutilated in horrid ways. One, a higher-ranking officer from what I could tell, wasn't pulled to pieces. He was sliced open, his face frozen in a silent scream. He looked as if he'd been tortured deliberately.

This didn't seem like mindless slaughter anymore. It looked like rage. Whatever had done this had gone methodically throughout the ship in a couple of hours and killed absolutely everyone, tearing them apart, except for this one guy. A name tape on his uniform identified him as a doctor.

A sign on the wall pointed toward the right, indicating the main cargo hold. In that direction, the thick slicks of blood dragged away into further darkness. Another sign indicated the mess hall directly ahead.

"Mess hall or cargo hold?" I asked, my throat dry and my

tongue thick and cottony with fear.

"Mess hall first, then cargo hold," Freyer said. "There might be someone alive still."

I almost laughed, the hysterics of pure terror nearly breaking through. There was no one left alive here, no way, but we needed to at least check. I pointed straight down the passageway and moved on.

The deck was slick and hard to walk in, so going was slow. I kept my steps short, deliberate, and careful. We passed more quarters, smaller this time, with multiple bunks. Some were empty, and some contained more mutilated bodies, but that was all, no one living.

When we finally passed through the hatch to the mess hall, our tactical lights didn't penetrate as far into the darkness as I would have liked, casting shadows everywhere. Straining to see into the gloom, I tensed and turned sharply as I thought I saw something move against the port bulkhead.

"There's nothing here," Morgan whispered. "Just more dead bodies. You can relax."

I had forgotten that she could see, even in this low light. Shit, having a vampire on your side in a situation like this was damn handy. But, relax? Hardly.

"Wait, stop," Morgan said, and we all froze.

"What?" Freyer demanded.

Morgan shushed him, then turned around. "I can hear something beyond the far wall. It's faint, but it sounded like splashing."

"That's just the water outside," Carlos interjected.

"No, I can hear that, too. This is different. What's beyond that wall?" Morgan asked me.

"Should be the cargo hold. But these ships all have different configurations depending on their role, and I'm not as familiar with the 834. It's brand new, and it's not like the Peoples Liberation Army just publishes the deck plans."

"Let's check the hold," Carlos whispered. "Then we can work the rest of the ship."

We backtracked to the junction where we'd seen the drag marks leading starboard and followed them to another junction. Another sign indicated the cargo hold to our left.

"Left," I squeaked again and cleared my throat. "That's the direction of the cargo hold and the big hole in the hull."

"Lead the way," Carlos said. I hesitated for a second but followed his order.

Right into the passageway of my darkest nightmares.

CHAPTER TEN

Weyna

The days without Boudka dragged on, each indistinguishable from the last. Diligently, I wrestled awake every dawn, submitting to the whims of my mother and the demands of the Óşeni, my footsteps heavy with resignation. I yearned to become the pillar Boudka required. I truly did. Yet misery was a constant companion, weaving itself through my thoughts and imbuing my every day. Saya still harassed me at every turn. Boudka still wasn't speaking to me, and my mother was in and out. Moments of depressing nostalgia crept up on me, an unexpected longing for the simplicity of my shitty little childhood village.

At night I often climbed the high tower on the Southside of the fort, perching at the top to avoid the sleepless misery in my tent. I couldn't see much, just shapes and shadows in the land below. Not that the Kyliri watchers needed my night-blind eyes. Day or night, they had eyes like eagles. Still, they tolerated my maudlin company.

Familiarity with them remained a distant concept, it seemed. On several occasions, I attempted introductions, yet all I would glean was a moniker—Mira, Shara, Daneen—and a perfunctory nod of acknowledgment. Any further curiosity was met with polite evasions. Yet, their captivating allure was undeniable—their lustrous, iridescent skin and silver hair that shimmered in the moonlight crafted them into beings of otherworldly beauty, like luminescent specters that belonged to the night. Their mere presence lent an ethereal quality to the moonlit hours, an entrancing presence that was hard to ignore.

Sometimes being with them helped. Most times, it didn't, and the deep depression that held me refused to retreat for long.

Sixteen days into my penance, I was taking water to the Óṣeni, and as always, Saya made it a point to hassle me. This time, she knocked me out of her way so hard that she sent me sprawling, leaving me laying in a rapidly thickening pool of black mud from the spilled carafe. It had been the last of the water, too.

I had no interest in extending my evening chores to hauling more up from the lake, especially after the disastrous dalliance with Boudka in the northern woods. Between the risk of encountering lecherous men from the village, and the spies of Mother Darkness, which could often be heard scuttling about outside the fort at night, the thought of returning to the lake so late in the evening scared the shit out of me.

Fuck that bitch! I thought, and an unfamiliar hot rage bloomed in my chest, licking at my ribs and drawing them tight around my lungs.

Wracked with fury and humiliation, I pulled myself back up and gently set the carafe to rights before whirling on Saya. She was stalking toward the archers, her back to me.

"That's it!" I muttered as I charged up behind her, tangling one of her feet with mine and giving her a good shove, knocking her face into the dirt. Gasps and whispers sounded all around from the Óṣeni warriors, but I wasn't done. Bullies that weren't confronted never stopped.

"I'm done with you!" I screamed. "What I do here is just as important as anyone else unless you want your precious soldiers carting water instead of training! Not to mention that I'm the Crown Princess of Shaddan and will be treated with respect!"

My hands trembled, and through the veil of my outrage and suddenly burning hatred, I could scarcely believe what I'd done. I wasn't a fighter. I didn't even have any powerful or controllable magic at my discretion. I should have stopped there and run, but I continued yelling, fists bunched and voice full of fury, barely under control. "I'm not your fucking slave and never will be! Do you hear me? I'll die first!"

Slowly, with an indecipherable look on her face, Saya stood amid mumbles and collective stares. Towering over me at seven feet one inch, she stared down with her piercing black-gray eyes and an arch smile.

"Oh, fuck," I heard one of the warriors mutter.

Saya nodded to the surrounding Óṣeni, and the contingent closed ranks in a circle.

The ring of warriors stomped to attention with the finality of a bolt being slammed home on a massive door. They were ensuring that I didn't try to run off and that no one interfered. I was trapped. I had to finish what I started.

I glanced around quickly, and my legs trembled beneath my tunic with a mixture of fear and rage.

The circle of women gave me hard stares; I had no friends here. Not all of the looks were disapproving, though. The young woman I'd spoken with a couple of weeks earlier, the one with the long hair and pretty face, watched me with intense curiosity as if she were wondering what the encore might be. There was even a bit of grudging respect there.

"Fuck," I murmured to myself. "Next time, keep your temper under control—" I paused mid-thought, an unfamiliar name hovering on my lips. And that same sense of deja vu I'd periodically experienced since the dream returned.

Saya didn't even bother to wipe the mud off her face before casting me a vicious grin. Weirdly, I found I didn't care. I was likely going to die or at least be beaten to a bloody pulp, but I would go down fighting. I wasn't sure where all this reckless courage had come from.

"Choose your weapons, Princess," Saya growled, throwing a bit of disdain at the word 'princess' as she brandished a wooden practice weapon, jerking me from the odd musing.

"Fists," I said flatly. *Fists? Am I mad?*

An alien calm swept over me then, as if I'd decided that I had nothing to lose, and I found it liberating. If she beat me to death, so be it. But somehow, this confrontation, this fight, felt almost comfortable to me. The fear fell away, and my shaking ceased as I slid a leg back, bending my knees and setting my stance. I had barely brought my pitiful arms up to defend myself before Saya gave me a satisfied smile, dropped the wooden blade, and charged me without warning.

This was it. She was going to plow over me and stave my head in with a single punch of her meaty fist. But that didn't happen. In a breathless, heart-pounding instant, I pivoted on my toe to the right, a latent instinct guiding my left leg.

Swift and deadly, my left foot collided with the vulnerable curve of her knee, filling the air with an audible crunch, and the distressing snap of ligaments stretched beyond their limit.

Saya shrieked, dropping to one knee. Without hesitating, tunneling in on my own survival, I turned and uncoiled my right leg, her nose blossoming into a spray of blood as the heel of my foot connected with her face.

Saya's head jerked backward, but she refused to fall, trying desperately to recover.

"Stay down," I growled, my voice shaking with months of bottled fury. I brought my right arm around in a vicious arc, slamming my fist against the joint of her jaw, snapping her head to the side, and knocking her face into the mud she'd made of my water.

As the adrenaline rush subsided, I became aware of a dull but growing pain in my right wrist. If she rose now, I'd be hard-pressed to defend myself. But to my profound shock, mingled with a frightening sense of relief, she lay unconscious in the dirt.

I dropped to my knees, heaving with exertion, within the deathly silent circle of warriors. No one was staring at me with anything other than stunned surprise now. And that was okay because the feeling was absolutely mutual.

My head spun and buzzed slightly. My breathing turned shallow. Spots crawled in around my vision. A voice in my head kept telling me to breathe, or maybe it was someone nearby. I couldn't tell.

I caught the sound of my mother fighting her way through the edge of the ring. "Let me through! I said, let me through to my daughter—damn you—before I kill the lot of you!"

I looked up slowly as she grew to her full height, roughly shoving through the circle—and abruptly stopped. I glanced back down at the unconscious Óṣeni Captain next to me, then back up to my mother. I had no idea how I looked, though certainly, there was no color in my face. In fact, I was shaking and feeling a bit cold.

Slowly, with her arms out in front of her, as if I might do something insane, my mother approached me. "Weyna? It's me. It's Mother." Her voice was calm, but I could hear the undercurrent of worry in it. This had frightened her in some way. It hadn't just frightened Nemhain, my mother. It had scared The Morrigan, whose aspect she now wore. This was bad.

I looked again at Saya. Her left leg splayed at an ungainly angle. Her nose bled profusely. From the burgeoning bruise and swelling, it looked like her jaw was broken, too. I continued to stare, rooted and confused, as tears began to flow down my face. Then I gazed at my hands, dumbfounded.

"Mama?" I whimpered, looking back up at her in confusion as her hands landed lightly on my shoulders. "What did I do?"

My mother frowned, and her brow puckered in sympathy. Then she scooped me off the ground as if I weighed nothing, carrying me away. The stunned crowd parted silently as we passed. Behind us, I saw the Óṣeni close in, lifting their unconscious commander from the dirt.

A short distance away, my mother returned to herself and set me on my feet, checking me over and whispering in amazement. "Mother's Waters, girl, there's not a scratch on you."

"A warrior," Badb said behind me, her tone sounding somewhat self-satisfied. "I told you." I hadn't even known she was there.

She threw my aunt a hot glare. "Did you do this?"

Badb barked a laugh. "Me? No. This was all her."

I ignored their conversation and held up my wrist. "I think it's broken."

My mother nodded and took me by the arm, shooting Badb

another angry, suspicion-laden glower before leading me to the infirmary.

Everyone cast silent glances or whispered to their friends and companions as we passed. A few of the other servants gave me appreciative nods. Some were gossiping, and I caught a few saying things like exile and death. I did my best to ignore them.

Once inside and seated, one of the medhen, a woman I didn't know, pulled my right arm out straight, checking it, and then she placed her hand on my forearm. The excruciating throbbing vanished, replaced briefly by an uncomfortable prickling sensation. Then there was nothing.

This was uncharted territory for me. Yes, I had suffered injuries before, but I had never been deemed deserving of a medhen's precious magic.

It was logical conservation, I knew; their healing powers were limited and reserved for combatants. Especially now, with a kóşánt having been spotted lurking nearby only a few nights before. Just one of the wretched beasts could tear apart half the fort if they caught us unprepared.

The medhen treating me wrapped my wrist in a tight cloth wrap and told me to go easy on it for a few days. As I thanked her, a figure stepped lightly into the infirmary tent. "A council is called, Mother Morrigan. Your presence is requested, Weyna's as well."

I recognized the voice as Wisteria, the Summer Queen's daughter. She stood at the entrance, her hair cascading down her shoulders in golden strands and her eyes reflecting deep blue skies. I turned my gaze to her, silently pleading for a sign of reassurance, but was met with a void, impassive and somber as chiseled stone.

My mother merely nodded and shooed her away. "Come now, Weyna. Let's see what the council has to say."

As we made to leave, a pair of Óşení warriors entered, supporting Saya's slack-jawed form, her leg dangling in a way that turned my stomach. Saya's eyes caught mine as she entered, but they were unreadable. Mine, I'm sure, reflected the abject fear and horrible regret I felt.

One of the warriors supporting Saya winked at me as we passed, and I jerked my head away, keeping my eyes on Mother's back the rest of the trip to the war tent.

The blissfully short walk ended with me standing among the leaders of the army. Each sat on a small folding stool of simple wood and stretched cloth, arranged in a semi-circle, council style, facing where I now stood in the center.

Behind them sat the table upon which Bethadi glamour depicted our pitifully tiny army, various small scouting groups, and the bulk of the Fomori forces. The makeshift, magical map also showed the landscape of all Éire, as well as the gates on the northern shore, black for Shaddan and white for Bethad. There was also a gray marker for the long-closed gate to Ósen.

The golden-haired Summer Queen of the Fae, Aine, lounged in green robes that shimmered like leaves in sunlight, idly fussing at her nails, all the while sporting that insufferable, superior half smile. She looked like someone who knew more than everyone else, though I suspected it was mostly bluster. But it was hard to say, really, as she spoke so seldomly, often opting to save her voice only for when she felt it mattered. She often abstained from the council altogether, not involving herself much except when it suited her.

Malari, leader of the Kyliri, sat quietly, observing everything dispassionately with eyes like burnished coal. Her silver hair and iridescent skin gathered a slightly sallow and jaundiced cast in the faelight lamps. Despite her relaxed posture, she clearly wasn't bored. Quite the opposite. She eyed everything with keen interest, calculating and patient in the extreme.

Mother Danu took her seat at the head of the semi-circle, her soft face and fluid sea-green eyes showing a kindness belying the will of steel that drove us all to try to save this world.

Saya entered moments later, her gait marred by a slight wobble supported by Aunt Badb. Another wave of remorse washed over me as I watched the massive woman drop heavily onto her stool, accompanied by a pained grimace. I'd given her serious injury.

"I'm sorry," I said in a tremulous voice that betrayed my

guilty heart. "I didn't want to put you in the infirmary."

Saya smiled and shook her head, then her laughter burst forth, booming and light-hearted. "I shudder to think of what you might have done had you *wanted* to put me in the infirmary. Well played, my dear. Well played."

Finally, Badb took my mother's stool, her Fae leathers creaking slightly as she did so. She didn't look at all worried, letting her mouth curve upward in a haughty smirk at the entire affair as if she thought it ridiculous. She even gave me a comforting wink, as if she knew that somehow regardless of my obvious bout of insanity, everything would be fine.

Given that I was Nemhain's child, my mother was not allowed to render judgment or even speak on the matter. By law, she was only permitted to stand with me, though she kept a supportive and comforting hand on my shoulder. My whole body began to sag as I looked at the assembled group. I was well and truly fucked. At best, I'd be tossed out on my arse. At worst, I'd be made Saya's handmaiden or, potentially, given to her as a slave. It wasn't something Mother Danu supported, but she wasn't the only vote, and her voice carried no more weight in council than any other.

"Well, now, this is a bit of a conundrum," Mother Danu began, scrutinizing me with interest. "Weyna, you are a human servant, are you not?"

"Half-human, your majesty. My mother is Shaddani." My eyes flickered back to my mother then to the rugs that covered the tent floor. The assembled power in the room was beyond terrifying. Any one of them could snuff me out like a candle with a word, and I did my best to be as respectful as possible.

"First, I am Danu, or, if you like, Mother Danu, that is all. You do not call me majesty or highness or any other such formal titles." She threw a raised eyebrow over my shoulder, and I cringed inwardly at her thinly veiled rebuke. "I do not consider myself your better. Second, you will keep your eyes up in this chamber. There may be such customs beyond these walls, but in this tent, we treat everyone with the same respect regardless of station, Princess." Unlike Saya, Mother Danu spoke the title with respect, which made me feel at least a little better.

"Yes, ma'am, I mean, Mother Danu." Regardless of what she said, I still felt some honorific was better than none.

"It is my understanding that you had an altercation with Saya. Is that correct?"

"If I may," Saya interrupted before I could utter a word.

"One moment, Saya, you will have your say. I wish to hear the girl's side."

I was in so much shit. "Yes, Mother Danu. It was entirely my fault. I—"

"Danu, let me speak, please," Saya said, laying a gentle hand on her arm, much to everyone's shock. Mother Danu looked down at the offending appendage, and Saya removed it before continuing. "This is not *entirely* her fault. I have let my own prejudice and my strained relationship with the child's mother influence my better judgment. I have not treated her in a manner befitting her station."

My mouth dropped open in absolute shock. I had expected Saya to have me pilloried, not admit fault and jump to my defense.

Danu turned to Saya, her expression inscrutable. "How, then, do you suggest we reconcile the situation?"

"Give her a practice blade and train her. She downed me in three swift strikes. If she can fight hand-to-hand like that, she can learn the sword. Her reflexes are fast, and her mind is far more calculating than I first believed. She may make a good addition to the Swasari." Every head snapped around at that pronouncement, and my mouth fell open again. I should have been thankful that there were no flies in the tent, or I would have swallowed one. Only Aunt Badb continued to look at me, an enigmatic smile on her face.

My mother's hand gripped my shoulder tightly as I drew in a breath to speak. "Out of the question," she said. "She has magical aptitude that needs attending."

"All I see her attending to is your bath time, Nemhain," Saya joked, and there were chuckles all around. "Well, that and exploding perfectly good pigs." Everyone laughed even harder, sending heat up my neck and into my cheeks.

"It was a sheep," I muttered.

Everyone grew quiet as Mother Danu addressed me. "What did you say, child?"

"A sheep, ma'am—I mean Mother Danu. It was a sheep, not a pig."

The room erupted in fresh gales of humiliating laughter.

My mother's lips were pursed in annoyance. "Enough!" She barked. "Saya, look at her. She's barely the strength to lift a sword, let alone—"

Badb held up a hand. "Sister, your voice is to be silent in these proceedings. Saya has offered an interesting prospect and one that I think would be better than the alternatives."

I couldn't see it, but I knew my mother would be shooting her sister a baleful stare, and the hairs on the back of my neck stood up.

Badb continued, her words resonating in the room, each syllable thick with intent. "An offer sits in our midst, and it begs for my cherished niece to impart her voice before we cast our collective decree." Then, almost imperceptibly, she nodded to me.

On impulse, I shook free from my mother's grasp, and my declaration tumbled from my lips, my voice loud and echoing in my own ears amidst the silence. "I consent. I'll do it."

My mother's brow furrowed. "Are you certain? My protection shall be stripped away with this choice. Falter, and the repercussions will be yours alone to bear." A ripple of apprehension marred her voice, and a veiled flash of worry danced across her features.

I acknowledged her with a quick nod.

A familiar storm of anger swirled in Mother's eyes, but that was replaced quickly by another emotion that, too, flickered swiftly across her face, drawing up the corners of her mouth in an oddly resigned smile. My first instinct was to assume she was relieved to be rid of me, but when she took both of my shoulders and pulled me into a quick hug, I realized that as angry as she was, this was something else, more like—pride. But as quickly as it emerged, it receded. Then she rearranged her features into her usual impassive mask and fell back, her touch leaving my shoulders, before she joined Badb, standing resolutely behind her.

"Well, that's it then," Mother Danu said. "First thing tomorrow, you'll report to the Óṣeni for training. You will work at Saya's command performing whatever *reasonable* duties she assigns." She paused, fixing Saya with a warning stare. "For your part, Commander, you will treat her as you would any newosi, and you will ensure that she is ready for battle at the earliest, and I mean, the earliest possible moment. No delays. Is that clear?"

"Yes, Mother Danu," Saya said and nodded solemnly, but then she turned a sly smile in my direction.

Mother of Waters, I swore silently. *What did I just do to myself?*

Mother Danu turned her face to me, raising the corners of her mouth in a knowing smile. Her voice echoed gently in my head. *We shall see, child. We shall see.*

CHAPTER ELEVEN

Aoife

The corridor was dark as hell and chilly. I shivered slightly as cold air and rain blasted in from outside through the star-shaped hole in the bulkhead.

Something had definitely torn through both layers of the hull in its desperation to escape. I looked at the others, in turn, the unspoken question hanging between us. *What could do that?* Another followed behind it, though. *Was it the only thing in here? Or was it fleeing from something worse?*

My hands shook, and my body recoiled, steps stuttering to a halt as the smell of brine and blood and awful sickly-sweet death filled my nose and clogged my mouth. A long shallow puddle of brackish water, blown in through the hole, pooled darkly on the slightly canted floor, damp and foreboding. My brain refused to process the scene properly, unable to square the rectangular passageway with the crooked pool of water. The insane part of me, the part that sensible Aoife never listened to except at unhelpful moments like this, worried that something horrid might be waiting in those few inches of water, lurking just below the dark surface to reach forward and snatch at my ankle, like some horror movie.

"Dear God, Cáitlín," I muttered, out loud this time, "how the fuck do you do this?"

For a moment, I couldn't move, but a firm, cool hand touched the nape of my neck as if to say, 'I'm here. I have your back.' It was Morgan urging me to press on with the gentlest, kindest of pressure, and, buoyed by the comforting presence of her tactical vest pressed to my back, I stepped forward, once again slightly ahead of them.

A dripping, viscous goo covered some of the lights along the wall, rendering them a sickly brown color. That, coupled with a few of them flickering in irregular patterns, made it hard for my eyes to adjust. The entire atmosphere was eerie, and my legs trembled slightly as we crept toward the half-open hatch midway down on the port side.

I jumped as a flash of lightning and the crack of thunder rumbled through the superstructure of the cargo vessel. The ship rocked and creaked from the howling gusts outside. It sounded like a great beast in its death throes or perhaps gurgling for its next meal. The worsening weather only amped up my anxiety, and I stopped again.

"I don't know if—"

Morgan's hand landed on my shoulder once more, and she spoke in a reassuring and calm voice. "You can. Remember your military training. The first time is always the hardest. I nearly flipped out my first time doing this. Breathe and focus on the task. There may be innocents still alive inside."

The others said nothing, but Maki's steps seemed a little unsteady. The leadenness left my limbs as I realized I wasn't the only one here struggling with my own fear, and seeing her discomfort strangely alleviated some of my own. I took a deep breath.

Clear and move, clear and move, my mind rattled in rapid succession. *Trust your teammates.*

I signaled forward, and we strode toward the door much more quickly, weapons at the ready. I stopped for a moment, though, as Freyer's light flashed across something greasy and black on the floor. It looked, for all the world, like spilled ink or maybe wet melted vinyl, which made no sense. I knelt down and put a finger into it.

"Wait!" Morgan hissed in alarm, but it was too late. I jerked my hand back, and a bit of the stuff glopped onto my face, sticking to my skin.

I rubbed it between my thumb and forefinger, then sniffed. I sniffed again. "It's ink. Just ink." I looked around for a source, such as a spilled bottle or broken pen, but there was none. "I think it's squid ink, like you might use with an old quill. Weird."

Carlos and Freyer breathed a sigh of relief.

"You need to be more careful, Cait," Freyer admonished in a harsh whisper. "There's this black stuff from the gate that will eat your flesh and take control of you. You can't just go around sticking your fingers in shit."

I looked at him askance. He just nodded and jerked his head toward the hatch.

Something akin to an electric charge sang in my skin, making me squeak as a blue light flickered to life next to me. Maki was holding a ball of liquid fire, twirling it like I might a sliotar on the camogie pitch or a pitcher might nervously finger a baseball.

Freyer, Kennedy, and I took up positions in front of the hatch. Maki stood to the left, nine vibrant white tails fanned out behind her, standing damn near straight up, looking like a raft of yellow and blue, giant, furry fishhooks in the sickly light of the lamps and the glow of her little fireball. Her face appeared calm, but I could see the tremble in her lips and a nervous twitch in her knees.

Carlos stood slightly to the right and placed his right hand on the hatch. I took a deep breath, my hands shaking slightly until Morgan put a supportive hand on my shoulder one more time.

"Remember, monsters don't shoot back," she whispered almost too low for me to hear. "And I'm here for anything else."

I nodded, and Carlos raised three fingers, counting down.

Three—

I tucked my weapon into my shoulder.

Two—

I put my finger across the trigger guard, ready and waiting to fire with a viable target.

One—

He pulled, yanking open the hatch, which swung outward

dramatically and slammed against the bulkhead of the passageway, making me flinch.

I moved first, stepping in and right, sweeping both sides of the catwalk, which was dangerously canted forward and practically dangling twenty feet above the deck of the cargo hold. It was clear.

Morgan and Freyer filed in behind as we viewed the entire area. I took a second step to give the big vampire more clearance and slipped slightly on a wet section, sliding precariously down the tilted catwalk before Morgan snatched my tac vest in one hand.

"Thanks," I mouthed, and she winked, giving me that cocky, crooked smile that she wore so well.

The forward end of the catwalk was completely twisted and mangled, the welds and bolts torn from the starboard bulkhead as if a great hand had come down and crushed it in its grasp. Fortunately, it didn't squeal under our weight, at least not too much.

The scent of blood, decay, brine, and Gods knew what else assaulted us further. I gagged and coughed as we took up positions. Looking down, it became clear that the catwalk wasn't even near the worst of it, and it was highly unlikely there was anyone alive on the ship at all. The deck below was a horror show.

"Bloody hell!" I gasped.

Bodies, easily fifty or more, lay dismembered and in pieces, discarded all over the hold but mostly in a pile near the center. Blood slicked most of the deck, easily a quarter inch deep in places, and I blinked slowly, trying unsuccessfully to quell my revulsion.

"That must be the rest of the crew," I said, swallowing back my rising gorge at the sight of so much unbridled carnage.

In truth, it was hard to tell if it really was the crew, but who else could it be? Much of the remains had clearly been gnawed on by something. Streaks of arterial spray covered some of the walls, dribbling down in deep red streaks. Much of it still looked wet. This couldn't have happened long before the ship ran aground.

Most of the body parts were centered around a large rectangular container sitting flush against the forward bulkhead, about ten feet long by six or seven feet wide and maybe ten feet tall. From our vantage point, we could see the walls of the container were probably eight-inch-thick, solid steel, and there were shallow, bulging dents protruding outward from inside. Whatever had been inside had certainly wanted out, and judging from the twisted wreck of a door that had capped this end of the container, it had gotten its wish. The door, just as thick as the walls, had been peeled back off its thick hinges like a sardine tin and tossed aside.

The aft half of the cargo bay, to the left of the upper hatch where we stood, had been converted into an enormous aquarium-like tank constructed of thick acrylic, completely enclosed, and filled with red liquid. It was aerated by a sickly-sounding pump against the far bulkhead that looked like it had seen better days. Looking at the red liquid, the filter was likely broken.

"It's blood," Morgan commented, glancing at the tank. "See how it clouds and swirls in the water?"

I just nodded. *She would know,* I thought.

Periodically, currents shifted and moved along the water. Something was swimming around in there, several somethings it seemed, and a small man-sized hatch sat open on top in one corner, allowing access to the interior of the tank.

The rest of the hold was largely empty, but one corner held the remains of a small computer rack, twisted and laying on its side. Several large monitors sat next to it on a table with a workstation that appeared oddly untouched. One of the monitors showed us standing on the catwalk, and I glanced around, spotting the camera mounted to the far bulkhead. There had been a separate CCTV system in here.

"Fuck me sideways, Red," I whispered to Morgan, looking at the gore below.

"Yeah, glad I fed earlier. This would put me off my dinner."

I looked at her. "Jesus, Morgan, have some respect."

She had the good sense to look chastised, then said, "Cover me," and leaped over the railing to the hold floor. There didn't seem to be any threats, except maybe what was in the fish tank, but Freyer and I kept watching anyway.

Morgan landed solidly with a bang and stuck the landing like a professional gymnast, even with the slightly tilted floor. She might as well have been hopping off her bed at the apartment, and her weapon rose back to her shoulder almost faster than I could see.

"Red!" I snapped as I slid down the ladder. "Give us a bloody warning next time you want to go all Black Widow."

"I said, cover me," she responded as if that was supposed to make it better.

Freyer and Carlos kept watch from above, with Maki still holding that glowing ball of fire-jelly stuff.

From the cargo hold floor, the scene was far more terrifying. The tank, which appeared large from above, looked enormous at eye level, at least eight feet high and running probably half the width and length of the hold. The destroyed cargo container had held something massive. I shouldered my weapon and covered Morgan as she peered inside.

"It's clear," she shouted, and then we moved to the tank.

I crept closer, trying to get a good look inside. Blood swirled around in the water in whirlpool-like motions as whatever was inside moved about. A few feet away along the side, I caught a glimpse of something, but it was gone before I could figure out what it was. It looked like a shark's tail.

I moved right up to the glass and peered inside, only to rocket back with a muffled screech when a hand and a terrifying face appeared. "Holy shit!"

"Mermaids," Morgan commented and turned to the others. "Clear!"

The other three moved down with us, and Morgan headed to the workstation. Several files lay scattered behind the computer rack, and she started picking them up and thumbing through them.

"Trafficking in preternatural people? That's a new one." Freyer said. "Never seen a mermaid up close."

"Be careful with them," Maki said. "They're probably feral."

"And sick," Morgan added with a heavy sigh. "Cancer.

Every last one of them. Most of this is in Chinese, but there's a bit here in English from a Doctor Caine out of Hong Kong."

I winced in sympathy.

Carlos and I looked inside the massive reinforced container. The door had huge dents, the hinges were torn away, and one corner was bent backward like tin foil. Something enormous and powerful had forced its way out.

Morgan whistled at the twisted container door. "A vampire couldn't have done that. Shit. Even a kóşánt would have been hard-pressed to do that kind of damage."

"What's a kóşánt?" I asked, but Morgan was going through the contents of the desk.

Leaking from inside the cargo container was a runny, black liquid. Carlos pulled on a latex glove and fingered it.

"Is that?" Freyer asked, eyeballing the nasty stuff as if it might jump out and grab Carlos at any moment.

"No, it looks like more ink. Squid ink, maybe, same as outside."

"Great," Freyer said sarcastically, "now we've got a fuckin' sea monster running around Boston."

A splash sounded from the tank, and we all spun around, weapons up. A woman, clearly East Asian, climbed out of the mermaid tank. She wore a wetsuit and had a scuba tank on her back, and as she climbed down a ladder at the far end of the fish tank, we could see the terror in her eyes, eyes that darted around, not at us, but watching the cargo hold hatches. She definitely wasn't afraid of us. On the contrary, she seemed somewhat relieved we were there. Slowly and tentatively, she stepped toward us, her hands raised.

"Identify yourself!" Maki shouted in Chinese, dousing her little fireball and pulling her sidearm.

The woman halted her steps and spoke in flawless English. "I'm Doctor Victoria Zhi. I'm a marine biologist for the Chinese government, and I request political asylum."

Maki stepped forward, holstering her pistol. "What did this?"

"I don't know. I didn't see it very well," Zhi replied, but her fidgeting and furtive glances gave her away.

"You're lying," Maki continued in Chinese, raising her voice. "What was in the container?"

"I said I don't know." Zhi became more agitated, and soon they were arguing in Chinese at a speed I couldn't really follow. But Maki got the better of it when she pointed at the container and demanded to know what was inside a final time and placed her hand back on her holstered sidearm. It was a well-planned bluff, and it worked.

Zhi's eyes went wide. "Atkor Kamuy."

I frowned, bemused. Freyer was right. It turned out. Apparently, it had been a fucking sea monster.

"Akkorokamui? Nante kottai!" Maki whispered. "This is bad."

CHAPTER TWELVE

Weyna

On the morning next, I woke well before dawn, somehow sensing a presence in my tent. Saya stood over me, waiting patiently.

I dragged myself from my bed and rubbed my sleep-filled eyes, reaching for my tunic, but she put a hand on my arm.

"No. All Newosi learn to fight the Óṣeni way, regardless of station or title. Clothing is earned."

"I have to train naked?" I asked, my voice small. "But what if I get hit?"

"I guarantee you will get hit quite a bit. But that is the way we learn. Now come. Do not forget that you agreed to this."

She paused for a very long time, considering me, then added, "We will not mistreat you in any way. You will be trained in the same fashion as every other warrior. We will adapt your training to suit your frame, but you should know that we will neither go easier nor harder on you than we do any Óṣeni female."

Suppressing the pent-up sigh that threatened to escape, I dared not release the breath filling my lungs as I followed Saya out of the tent.

She led me through the gloom and quiet of the slumbering camp, skirting the tents and bedrolls of the occupants. We worked our way past one of the old stone cairns that had sat her long before we'd arrived. The camp was quiet but for the guards on watch, so for some time at least, no one other than the Óṣeni would likely see me nude. Still, my discomfort was palpable, and I wondered for a moment if this was really how the Óṣeni were trained. I had my doubts.

When we reached the practice area, bleary-eyed Óṣeni were getting ready for their near-constant training. Saya led me over to one of the warriors. "This is Óbin. She has agreed to take on the task of training you. You will do everything she asks. Questions about how things are done are encouraged. Questions about why you do them are not. The way we train and its reasoning will become clear over time. Trust is implicit. Do you understand?"

I didn't, not exactly, but I nodded anyway. My self-consciousness rose as I recognized the woman who had winked at me in the infirmary tent.

"The proper response is 'Yes, Kóhen,'" Saya said firmly. "Kóhen is how we refer to trainers in Óṣen. Do you understand?"

"Yes, Kóhen," I said.

"Louder."

"Yes, Kóhen!" I shouted.

"Excellent." Saya turned to Óbin. "She is all yours."

After Saya had left, I raised a tentative hand, and Óbin nodded. "Is this how you were trained? Nude, I mean?" I asked as Óbin turned and collected a series of heavy-looking weights, which she began piling into a bag.

"Yes," she replied perfunctorily without looking at me.

I tried not to fidget, but I was definitely nervous and felt extremely vulnerable. Óṣen was a cold and almost desolate world by comparison with the current summer months, and I didn't fancy the idea of having to train in the nude there. But then, the Óṣeni warriors were our hardest troops, capable of handling, so I was told, even the harshest conditions. In combat, they had no peers and no fear.

Óbin looked back, seeing me eyeball the weights with worry. "Don't worry. These aren't for you—at least, not yet. Come and sit." She then dropped onto a small bench.

I did as she asked, taking a second to remember a 'Yes, Kóhen,' just beforehand.

She snatched up a comb and a jar full of a peculiar, viscous oil. With deliberate strokes, she tenderly coated my hair with the oil, carefully untangling the strands without inflicting undue strain. Skillfully, she wove my hair into a single, lengthy braid, then bound it into a neat bun and secured it in place with two elongated black metal pins. "This is to ensure your vision is unobstructed and your hair unsoiled." She gave me a wink then. "The pins can be used as weapons in a pinch, too."

She replaced the lid on the jar and bound it with twine, stuffing the comb underneath the tied string to secure the jar and comb together before setting them aside. "I have assigned you a cot in the barracks. You will live with, train with, bathe with, and sleep with us. Every night you will bathe. Every morning you will do the same. Then, each morning before you dress, you will do as I have done here, oiling and braiding your hair. It will be in a tight bun before you leave the barracks. Is that clear?"

"Yes, Kóhen."

"If you require assistance with the bun, one of your sisters will help you."

The word rang in my ears. Sisters. And in that single word, I felt a sudden, if nascent, sense of belonging.

"Now," she continued, "down at the lake is a pole attached to two water pots. You will run the footpath to the lake, fill the jugs, cover them, and haul them up to fill the cistern. If you spill so much as a single drop, you will return to the lake and refill them. Go!"

I stared at her for a second, but at her glare, I took off, trotting down the path with a brief, "Yes, Kóhen."

I wasn't even halfway to the lake before I had to slow down. I'd seen the Óșeni women make this run two dozen times without stopping and without getting winded. I frowned at the ponderous seeming distance.

It took me almost ten minutes to get to the bottom of the hill. By the time I reached the water, I was out of breath, and my feet were bruised and bleeding from every stray root, pebble, and sharp stone along the way. The two clay jugs for the water sat on the bank strapped to a metal dowel. Undoing the netting holding the jugs, I took the lids off and carried them into the lake. "Mother Danu! This water is freezing!" I swore.

"That it is, wee-un."

I looked up at the speaker, a barrel-chested, bald man, slightly shorter than me in stature, wearing a grimy, brown tunic and a tightly bound wool belt that had seen better days. Bulging muscles rippled on his thick corded arms and legs as he dragged a formidable shillelagh, a kind of wooden cudgel common to the region.

Trailing in his wake were three smaller fellows, all of them gaunt and malnourished. Rotten teeth marred their mouths, and dirty clothes hung loosely on their skeletal frames, which were topped with matted, greasy hair. It was clear who was getting the lion's share of the food in this bunch.

I pursed my lips and sighed. I didn't bother calling for help, there was no one out here this time of the morning except the Óṣeni, and they were all up at the camp for morning warmup. I was on my own without a weapon. *No,* a thought intruded just as I was trying to figure out where to run. *I am not without a weapon. I have several.*

The men lazed toward me rather casually, clearly confident that I'd be easy prey and giving me precious moments to pull the slipknots binding the jugs to the dowel and shake it loose. Light as it was, it probably wouldn't stand a single hit from the man's club, but if I timed it right, I might be able to disable him with a shot to the groin, knee, or jaw. The pins in my hair were a last resort. I wanted to avoid close quarters if at all possible. How I knew that, I had no idea.

I hefted the dowel and stepped out, circling my way out of the water and back onto the shore. I wanted the room to run when this went south.

"Get on with yourselves," I called as my foot struck the shoreline. "The rest of the Óṣeni are on their way down."

The big man blurted a laugh as they started to fan out, looking to encircle me.

Fat chance, I thought and continued weaving across the

shore and toward the trees. There was no point in running. They were between me and the footpath; besides, I was starkers. They'd likely catch me as soon as I stepped on something sharp or hard or tripped over a root in my bare feet. I just needed to keep them from getting to either side of me or, worse, behind me.

"Where are they, then?" This big man leered as he continued to close, walking right toward me. He got closer than I'd have liked, and I took a few half-hearted jabs with the dowel. He jumped back.

"She's got spirit, that's for sure!" He bellowed, and they all laughed.

Somewhere in my chest, that same rage that I'd felt when fighting Saya roiled up, only more intense. It was a deep loathing of these men that coiled about my thoughts, constricting away all fear and doubt. They were going to die today if it was the last thing I did.

Baldy stood poised while one of his companions, with tangled red hair, darted forward from my right.

I proved the quicker, jamming the tip of the rod into his forehead. He teetered backward like a felled tree onto his back, blood pouring all over his face, either unconscious or dead. I neither knew nor cared as long as he was out of the fight.

The end of the dowel was coated black with his blood in the false dawn light, but I noticed something else. Thick flakes of hastily applied brown pigment had chipped away from the dowel around my grip, exposing the night-black metal underneath. Black-steel, I surmised. *That's why the thing is so light.*

Shilleleigh-man's remaining minions were much more cautious now, seeing their companion dropped so neatly. I didn't think I could take them all, but they didn't know that. The fourth man had been stupid, and my shot pure luck, but my main concern, baldy, still loomed, deftly tossing his club about with an air of seasoned familiarity.

Holding the dowel like a quarter-staff, I launched a sweeping blow from my left toward club-guy's right arm. He blocked the blow expertly, and I barely dodged the return swing, which would have easily shattered my skull.

Exploiting my distraction, the others sought to dart in. I quickstepped backward and shifted my grip to one end, swinging the staff in a wide arc. The second skinny man tried to dodge backward, but I had more reach this time, and I hit my mark, delivering a devastating shot to his right thigh, the force snapping bone with a sickening crack. He crumpled to the ground, writhing in agony, his anguished screams rending the air.

That's two down, I thought. And I began to think that maybe I might survive this, unspoiled even.

Unfortunately, baldy's compatriot charged in and shoved me while the big man, much faster than I expected, hooked the shillelagh on my ankle, dropping me to the pebble-strewn and muddy shore, the dowel skittering away.

"Just kill her," the skinny man I'd whacked in the leg shouted through gritted teeth. "I want to get paid."

Paid? Paid for what?

The big man sneered at me then looked back to his fallen companions. "No, I have a better idea." He grabbed at my ankles, and I kicked out, but I couldn't catch him any place vital. I started to panic as his mate grabbed one of my arms. "No!" I growled, struggling and kicking for all I was worth.

"I'm going to take this poor—" the big man began, but his voice died as I jammed one of my hair pins into his neck and tore it straight out, leaving a wide gushing wound. Baldy stumbled back away from me, clutching his throat, and the man holding my left arm let go.

He jumped up, but I grabbed his foot, tripping him. He kicked me in the face bloodying my nose, but he was down now.

I scrambled over and pounced on him, snatching a fat rock from the mud and banging on his face with it over and over until his cries turned to weak struggles, his weak struggles turned to convulsions, and he finally died.

I dropped the stone, my entire body shaking from the exertion, fear, and excitement of combat.

"Well then," Óbin said, holding one hand toward me, a bow

in the other. "Maybe you didn't need me after all."

I looked up, realization dawning. "You set this up. You paid these men to attack me. That's why the simple dowel turned out to be a black-steel staff. What was this?" I shouted. "Some kind of test"

"Yes," Óbin said simply. "And you surpassed all expectations, though I had a feeling you would." As I sucked in a breath to release my pent-up ire, she held up a hand for silence. "Weyna, there's no point in training someone whose first instinct is to run. You'd be a detriment to the unit and the army. I wasn't going to let them hurt you. If you'd chosen to run, I'd have sent them on their way with the gold I'd promised. But you downed them all. Impressive for a waif like you."

"But you paid them to die." I was appalled, and a stiletto of guilt began to dig into my gut.

"No. I paid them to take the dowel. But they did what came naturally to such men. They earned their fate." As if to drive the point home, she plucked an arrow from her quiver, knocked it effortlessly, and buried it in the remaining man's heart without even looking. "Now, are you injured?"

"Not seriously, just a bloody nose," I said flatly as several Óşeni emerged from the trees surrounding the lake and began piling up the bodies of the four men. None of them said anything, but two who walked past me patted me on the shoulder.

"You can quit now if you like," Óbin said as she held out the black-steel rod.

I didn't answer. Instead, I took the rod and stomped my way down the shoreline back to where I had left the water vessels, returning to the task at hand. I wasn't going to back down, and I wasn't going to give her the satisfaction of seeing me cry.

And cry, I did. I sniffled and bawled almost the entire way back to the camp with the full jugs. I had never killed anyone before, and it was a shock. Not that they'd been anything but deserving for what they'd intended, but still. After a bit, though, I thrust my self-pity aside. *This is what I've chosen,* I thought. And I'd be damned if I let it turn me inside out.

It took me almost a half hour to trudge back up the hill. I dumped the jugs in the cistern as the blood on my face and hands dried to a sticky mass. I didn't bother to wash it off. Fuck these women and fuck Óbin. No matter what they did, I was resolved. I picked up the empty water jugs and the bloody dowel and marched back down to the lake.

I made that trip seven more times until, drained and dehydrated, I collapsed from exhaustion, unable to take another step.

Óbin told me to stop. "Rest for a minute and rehydrate," she instructed. Then she had me stretch and do calisthenics until my arms refused to function.

Relentlessly, she counted the same number over and over again as I struggled desperately to lift my body from the dirt for just one last push-up. It occurred to me that she might be simply pushing me to a breaking point to see if I'd falter. I didn't. I wanted to, though.

After a few minutes of further futile efforts, she stopped counting and knelt down. "Take one last bath in your mother's tent, then report to the barracks. Your cot has been arranged. Good work today."

After that, Óbin simply watched me as I rose and staggered away to my mother's bathing tent to set about getting clean. I didn't even have the strength to heat it.

An hour later, as the sun fell and night closed in, I found the one empty cot in the barracks. Lying, neatly folded at one end, lay four Óşeni linen tunics stitched to my size, a belt, and a footlocker on the floor. I placed the tunics in the footlocker with all due care and dropped to the bed, asleep almost as soon as my head hit the pillow.

CHAPTER THIRTEEN

Aoife

We all congregated down on the beach just as the Chinese attaché arrived. I stayed near, listening to the conversation between Wade and the Chinese representative, a bloke named Yi. Maki translated between the two of them. I kept my mouth shut, though. Cait didn't speak Chinese as far as I knew, and if she didn't, then neither did I.

"Look, she's requested asylum, so regardless of what you say, Mr. Yi, you can't take her with you. Her request will be adjudicated properly, and then, if denied, she will be transported as we see fit."

Yi had a hell of a poker face. If Wade's proclamation phased him at all, he didn't show it. Instead, he just smiled benignly.

"You are quite correct," Maki translated for Yi. "However, we still need to address the fact that your team entered the ship without permission. That ship is Chinese property."

Wade's ensuing laughter was measured and nuanced— diplomatic. His words, however, were not. "Your ship is in US waters, which means we can do whatever we like with it to ensure the safety of US citizens. And since it seems your government was illegally transporting a dangerous creature on board, I have, for the time being, impounded and quarantined this vessel. Neither you nor any persons not delegated by the US Coast Guard will be permitted on board."

Maki translated this, and Yi scowled and squinted at Wade, losing his poise. Of course, he didn't doubt he spoke flawless

English. It was a stalling tactic. He was probably waiting for a call from a superior.

This had turned into a full-blown international incident, and I didn't envy either of them. They were both just doing their jobs. Hell, I doubted Yi even knew about the boat before this happened. He certainly looked genuinely shocked when Wade mentioned that there was something dangerous on board.

Yi's phone rang, and he answered it. The call was short, and he agreed readily to whatever was being said, but he didn't look happy. His face screwed up in disgust as he hung up, then he pointed to Dr. Zhi and motioned to her for a private conversation. So convinced that only Maki could speak Chinese, they didn't even bother to move away from me as they spoke.

"You do realize what they will do to your family if you do this?" Yi said.

Zhi just laughed, though there was an edge to it, not of fear but hostility. "Go ahead. That old man isn't any family of mine."

I turned my back to hide my smile. I suddenly decided I liked Dr. Zhi. She had huge bollocks. In a single sentence, she snapped any delusions of control Yi might have had.

I turned back, now having my face under control, but I still pretended to be focused on the ship, where they were bringing the mermaids down to the waiting launch we'd used earlier. Despite Maki's worry that they might be feral, they all settled into the launch, docile and quiet. So emaciated were they that several had to be carried down the ladder. As the launch motored toward land, I could see their sunken eyes, and their skin seemed to hand loosely on their bones. It was awful, and pressure built at the backs of my eyes as I watched them being lifted from the launch one by one.

Yi turned bright red and started to shout, in English now. "Those are Chinese citizens! You have no right to take them."

Wade stepped in front of him and placed his hand on Yi's chest. "You can stop right there," Wade said, his voice full of menace. "At this moment, the People's Liberation Army and your consulate are suspected of human trafficking." He gestured to the cameras. "Do you really want to escalate this further?"

I took Zhi by the arm gently. "Come with me," I whispered in my shitty Chinese and moved her to Carlos' cruiser, opening the door. "You won't be mistreated in any way, I promise, but I need to get you away from here."

Zhi nodded and sat in the back seat.

I closed the door and went back to the madness that was unfolding. Yi was positively apoplectic, shouting at everyone about our government hearing about this and whatever else came to his mind as a possible threat. Wade just stood there like the proverbial mountain, immovable and perfectly calm.

I walked over to him and spoke quietly. "So, they threatened her family. And apparently, she doesn't like whatever family she has back in China very much, so that didn't work."

Despite his calm exterior, Wade's eyes burned with sympathy and rage. "Yeah, well, Yi's having a complete meltdown, but looking at those women, I'd say he's got a serious PR problem. I mean, look at them. Didn't they feed them?"

I glanced over at the unhealthy and malnourished women. I didn't know much about mermaids. I'd never seen one. But I didn't think that was normal. What was worse, all of them had thick scars across their throats, as if they'd been tortured, and a sudden thought occurred to me, but before I could voice it, a cool crisp English voice spoke from behind me.

"Commander Wade, how are you, dear? How is your wife? Did your daughter make it into the academy?"

Marcella Carson had arrived. *Shit.* She gave me a glance and a nod, and I was more than happy to move away from her, a slight shiver of fear running down my back.

"Ms. Carson, good to see you," Wade said and took her hand. "Good God, Marcella, you're positively frozen. Don't you need a coat out here?"

"Oh, I'm fine. I didn't have time to dress properly, but I'll live. This seemed more important."

"Marie is fine, and yes, little Sara, not so little anymore, is going to the Naval Academy. She wants to be an operator. Can you believe that?"

Marcella raised an eyebrow. "Well, I know some badass women who could probably give her some advice, Jack, or at least tell her what to expect in the military." She gave me an arch smile and a surreptitious wink, then turned back to Wade.

"I'm sure she'd love to see you again," Wade said. "Between you and me, I think she was a little taken with you the last time you came by the house."

Marcella laughed a pleasant, gentle laugh that gave me goosebumps. I could see why Cait had been so taken in by her. She was extremely charming when she wanted to be.

"So," Marcella asked, "is there something I can do?"

Wade motioned to Yi with a 'have at it' gesture and backed up a step. Marcella walked over to the still fuming, though less vocal, Yi and spoke to him. I didn't catch the words, but her voice was lilting and soft, and Yi calmed immediately.

I turned away as my breath came in shallow gasps, and I put my hands on my knees. It had been bad enough when Nastasia had tried to glamour me, but this was way worse. Watching Marcella snap Yi's will like a twig brought back half a dozen nightmares I'd had over the years in full glowing color. It was always my worst fear, being forced to do something and trapped in my own head, unable to defend myself or resist. Reading about it or watching it on some cheesy vampire show doesn't do justice at all to actually being glamoured yourself or seeing it used on someone you love.

Morgan tapped me on the shoulder. "Hey, let's get you out of here," she said softly, and I felt bad for slipping out of character.

"Sorry, Red."

"What for? Cait's always doubling over in misery about one thing or another. Or so I've been told. Come on."

Carlos, Morgan, and I piled into the cruiser with Zhi and left, not waiting for Marcela to finish what she was doing or for the state department to turn up. They could have Zhi after we'd had a chance to ask her some questions.

"Shame, really," Carlos said. "I would have liked to have gotten a better look at the files and the video surveillance.

Now the State Department is going to have a chat with the Chinese Government and hush it all up."

Morgan, who was sitting in the front next to Carlos, glanced at him, then back at Zhi. "Yeah, shame." Then she looked at me and winked.

I just shrugged and turned to Zhi.

"So what was in the container? What is the Atkor Kumuy? I've never heard of that."

Zhi sighed heavily. "You should ask Detective Imai. I can only tell you that it was on board. I never got a good look at it. And all of the images of it were redacted from the research files I had. I was just trying to protect the mermaids."

"How many did you lose on the trip?" I placed a gentle hand on her arm and switched to Chinese. "They were feeding to the beast, weren't they?"

Zhi turned extremely quiet and looked out the window. Then she sniffed and tried to blink back tears as she began to cry. I squeezed her arm a little more firmly, then pulled a handkerchief from my pocket. As we'd left her apartment, Morgan had stuffed three into my hand, saying that Cait seemed to carry dozens with her at all times. It was weird, but I had to keep up appearances. After a few moments, Zhi dried her eyes and said, in English, "Thirty-five."

I covered my mouth. "Oh, Gods."

"What did she say? They lost thirty-five mermaids?" Morgan asked. I looked at her and nodded gently.

"Yes," Zhi replied. "We were at sea for almost five weeks. They only fed the thing once each day, and its appetite is voracious."

"But that tank," Morgan said. "It didn't seem big enough for that many."

Zhi just nodded, and we understood. They'd literally been packed in like sardines.

"What will happen to the others?" She asked.

Carlos spoke up from the driver's seat. "I expect Marcella will handle it. Under the current ordinance, they have to be confined to camp two with the other mermaids. But Marcella will bend that a bit and make sure they get medical care first.

Neither the mayor nor the city council bothered to set this up properly. There's no real process for bringing them in. I guess they didn't expect more to show up."

"That'll show 'em," I muttered. "They have no idea."

Zhi gave a tight smile at that, but it didn't reach her eyes. "Thank you for rescuing us."

Us. I noted the turn of phrase but simply nodded and continued my questioning. "Why did the Atkor Kumuy drag the bodies down there?"

Zhi looked away uncomfortably, then wiped her nose and changed the subject. "Will you have any clothing for me when we get to the station? I don't want to wear this wetsuit everywhere."

I didn't press my original question, giving her the space she needed. "Hey, Carlos, Is there a place to stop? I want to get her some jeans and a sweater, so she can be more comfortable."

Carlos frowned in the rearview but pulled off into a Target parking lot. Things were so different here. For a witness in this situation, I would have happily stopped to get them some clothing without thinking about it. Here, apparently, they just got those awful paper suits. Frankly, given the ordeal this woman had been through, I didn't want to put her through any more trauma. Besides guessing her sizes, it took less than ten minutes. Morgan and Carlos were in the car, and she was a little slip of a thing. Where could she possibly go in ten minutes with them watching her?

And sure enough, when I returned to the car, she was still sitting there quietly. There was something odd about the way she sat, with her legs splayed out as if she were perfectly confident rather than someone who'd just survived a major trauma, but I dismissed it. She was from a different culture, and I had no idea what to expect in terms of body language. I just didn't have experience with China.

I gave her the bag of clothing and pocketed the receipt as we drove off and headed to the station.

CHAPTER FOURTEEN

Aoife

Once we had Doctor Zhi settled into the interview room with her change of clothes and some coffee, Sesi called us into her office.

"Cait, how are you feeling?" Sesi asked as soon as I walked into her office, and it took me a moment to realize that she was talking to me. "Yoohoo, Cait?"

I shook my head. "Oh! Sorry, I was lost in thought. I'm fine. Right as rain. Disappointed that I couldn't rest more, but otherwise, all good. How about yourself?"

Morgan smirked and looked at me, 'nice recovery,' she mouthed while Sesi looked away to dig in her drawer for something.

I blew out a relieved breath, but my pulse ramped, and my blood pressure spiked. I rubbed my sweaty palms on my fatigues as it dawned on me that I was really here, pretending to be my sister. On the beach, there was no one around to confront me. Everyone knew what was going on, and I could have slipped away afterward and probably gotten away with it. But now, I was in front of the acting Chief of Police. There was no going back.

What was worse, though, was that even terrified of being caught and prosecuted, I was kind of getting a kick out of it. Unlike most twins, Cait and I had never impersonated each other, even as kids, probably because we'd had such different styles. She had long hair. I kept my hair butch short all the time. She was quiet and shy with strangers, and I was gregarious. It would never have worked. But now we were adults, and it was a bit more fun than I wanted to admit, especially with the added risk. I had never realized doing crime could be this much fun.

I sat down next to Carlos as Sesi pulled a red badge from her desk and threw it at Morgan. "I'm re-assigning you and Freyer to PIU as armed support."

Morgan just raised an eyebrow as she caught the badge and swapped it out. "Fine. It's not like we've been doing anything but supporting them anyway. Besides," she grinned wickedly, "that's where the action is these days."

I made a show of rolling my eyes, but the way Morgan had said that was kind of hot, and it was turning me on.

Morgan turned, looked me in the eye, and gave me a salacious wink as my heart rate sped up, and a flush of warmth crawled through my body, starting in a rather private place. I couldn't deny she was so my type, and the way she'd had my back on the ship, how confident and action-oriented she had been, made me wonder what she was like in the sack. I bet she'd pin me down, and—I halted that train of thought immediately. *No, no, no. Vampire, Aoife. Vampire. Stop. No snuggling with the monsters.* Morgan had an eyebrow raised and an obnoxious leering smirk on her face as I dismissed the inappropriate musings.

"Okay, what's going on with you two?" Sesi demanded.

"Nothing," I said but almost laughed. "Nothing at all. I'm fine. You good, Red?"

She shrugged nonchalantly. "Oh, yeah. I'm good. You good, Carlos?"

Carlos just rolled his eyes, and Sesi pulled a gold badge out of her desk, throwing it to Carlos. "Congratulations, Ramirez."

Carlos caught the badge and swapped it out. He opted to stand, place his old one on the desk, and sit back down.

Morgan stared at him. "Congratulations? For what?"

I raised an eyebrow and stared at Carlos, playing along with Morgan's confusion.

"We'll be making the announcement tomorrow. Ramirez is

taking the Homicide Lieutenant Superintendent position, including supervision of your team, Reagan."

"I—I'm sorry? My team?" I was baffled.

"Unless you don't want the lead job." She pulled out a third badge and tossed it to me.

I caught it. "Oh! Yeah. Of course. Of course, I do." *Did I? I mean, did she? Did Cait?* I assumed she did. Of course, Cait would want to lead her own squad, wouldn't she? Well, she was now. Again, I got another little thrill of amusement at the situation. This was craic mental, and I loved it.

"But Carlos has only been here for a couple of months, Chief," Morgan interjected.

Sesi picked up her briefcase and packed her things. "The Mayor and I have decided that this is best for the department, having someone with outside experience to run Homicide. Now, if there are more questions, ask Carlos. I'm out of here. I have to get to the temple for a kid's volleyball tournament. I'm refereeing. I'll see you all tomorrow. The office is yours, Carlos."

And with that, she blew out of the office, though she did stop momentarily and eyeball me in a way that gave me the willies before heading off to the lifts.

Morgan sat there in stunned silence. I just sat there and waited. I had no idea what the big deal was other than the promotion itself, of course.

Carlos got up and leaned against the desk. Seeing Morgan about to say something, he held up his hand and closed the door Sesi had left wide open. Then he said, "Let's chat about this later."

Morgan shook her head. "What's to talk about? I'm thrilled. It's our other friend whom we just spoke for that's going to have to deal with this. Does the rest of the team know? And Freyer's basically being demoted. How does he feel about it?"

Carlos shrugged. "He wanted it. He's sick of running a team, tired of dealing with everyone else's issues: vacation, sick days, my dog died, all that crap. I've already discussed it with him. He's an old combat vet, and honestly, like you, he'd rather be in the thick of it. Apparently, he decided that your trip through the gate a few weeks ago was, how'd he put it? Wicked Pissah?"

I laughed at Carlos' bad imitation of a Boston accent. Coming out of his Texas drawl, it was adorable.

"Alright, interview Zhi, and let's get this case rolling."

"Um, boss," Morgan said, lifting the hem of her fatigue top. "Since you're the guy in charge now, I need to tell you something." She pulled a folder from behind her back that had been tucked halfway into her trousers and set it on the desk, then she reached into a vest pocket and pulled out two small two-inch solid-state disks in an evidence bag. Finally, she pulled a thumb drive from her pocket, also in an evidence bag.

Our mouths fell open. It was all stuff from the ship.

"You sneaky bitch," I commented, impressed.

Morgan waggled her eyebrows at me and continued. "I figured that State would show up and give the whole damn thing back to the Chinese, and that just seemed like a problem for our investigation, so I collected the evidence at the scene."

Carlos shook his head. "Cait, go give that stuff to Doyle and give her the good news. Then I want you and Maki to go take the interview with Doctor Zhi. Morgan, you stay. We need to talk for a minute about not starting international incidents."

I exited quietly and closed the door. Morgan didn't look very worried, and I lingered for just a second to stare at her.

"Cait! Close the door," Carlos barked.

I laughed and did as he asked. Looking around, I found a young red-haired woman with a very intent look on her face in one of the cubicles across from the interview room.

That had to be Doyle from Cait's description of her. There weren't any other redheads around except Morgan and me, and she had her hair pulled back into a tight ponytail that bounced a little when she moved her head, though there were dark circles under her eyes, and she looked a little drawn. The placard on her desk read, "Det. Jessica Doyle."

She looked up. "Cait?"

I gave a surreptitious shake of my head, and she nodded.

"How is she?"

"Still down but alive, or so they tell me," I whispered.

She nodded again and then looked at my hands. "Ooh, what's that?"

"Goodies from the team. It's all from the cargo ship we just searched. The SSDs are from a video surveillance system. I don't know what's on the thumb drive. Morgan will provide the chain of custody forms a little later for us to sign."

She nodded and noted the time on her pad. "Okie doke. Sorry, you have to do this, but thanks." She put a hand on my arm.

"Yeah, sure," I said dismissively. "She's my sister, you know?" I stopped before walking away, though. Even in my own ears, the sentiment sounded shitty. The truth was, now that I'd started, I had developed a deep conviction that this was what I needed to do. I added a second later, "We're going to find this bastard and take care of it."

Doyle gave me a sympathetic smile. "Yes. Yes, we will. And I'll get started on these right away."

"Thanks."

"Sure thing, Cait," she said with a smile and a flirty wink, then started unsealing the drives.

Well, then, I thought. *It's like that. Good grief. Cait's had them falling all over her. I bet she's fucking clueless, too.*

CHAPTER FIFTEEN

Aoife

Maki finally arrived at HQ about a half hour after we did. Doctor Zhi was still in the interview room, but I pulled Maki aside for a few minutes to get a better understanding of whatever this Atkor Kumuy thing was. I knew there was a sea monster myth, but not much more.

"The Akkorokamui," Maki explained, "or Atkor Kumuy, as some cultures call it, is basically a sea monster of legend. Think the Sea Witch of Hans Christian Anderson, not Disney, the Kraken of Nordic belief, and a demigod of the sea all wrapped up in one."

I raised an eyebrow. So we really did have a fucking sea monster on the loose.

"It was believed to live in a bay off the coast of Hokkaido. Some folklore has it as a good spirit that grants boons and provides healing if offerings are made to it."

"Huh," I grunted. "That doesn't sound so bad."

"No, it sounds super nice, right? But—"

"There's always a but," I chuckled humorlessly.

She nodded. "There is another legend. And it's that one which should concern us most. In one ancient folk tale, the Akkorokamui flooded a low-lying village after being disrespected."

"Uh oh." I was starting to understand, and it was not good at all.

"Yup. A shape-shifting demigod of the sea may be walking

around Boston right now or hiding in the harbor, and we don't have any idea where. I don't know about you, but I wouldn't consider the everyday Bostonian to be terribly polite."

"It could be worse," I said, grinning.

Maki cocked her hip and raised an eyebrow. "Oh yeah, how's that?"

"Could be New York."

Maki just rolled her eyes, obviously not amused. "Anyway, moving on. I have no idea whether what they brought here was the actual Akkorokamui, but whatever it was, you saw the damage it did."

I pursed my lips in thought. I had indeed seen. I pushed that aside for the moment. "Do you think it might actually have the kind of magic that could flood a city?"

Maki shrugged. "There are stranger things out there. Let's go see what Doctor Zhi has to say."

I let Maki lead us into the interview room. Doctor Zhi was out of her wetsuit, which was piled in the corner on top of the blanket, dripping a mix of water, squid ink, and blood.

I spoke first, opting for Chinese. While I wasn't fluent, Maki was, and I felt Zhi might be more forthcoming if we made every effort to make her comfortable. "So, let's go over how you got here and what happened on the ship. Carlos is going to call the State Department and get you situated until your asylum request can be evaluated."

Zhi nodded. "Where are the mermaids?"

Maki answered her, placing her legal pad down on the table. "Ms. Carson has taken them to be evaluated by someone who may be able to help them. As you probably know, there's a colony of mermaids here in Boston. Once they've been checked and we've determined it's safe to move them there, they'll be housed comfortably with the others."

"That's good," Zhi murmured with a wan smile. "When can I see them?"

"One thing at a time," Maki said. "Let's get through this first. Please state your name and occupation, then start at the beginning. How did you end up on that ship?"

Zhi did as Maki asked and explained that she had been

conscripted to accompany the mermaids on the trip. They did not, however, tell her what they would be using the mermaids for until they were underway.

"And why did you move the bodies to the cargo hold?" I asked without inflection, watching Zhi closely.

She shifted uncomfortably, then replied in a tiny voice. "They were starving."

"The mermaids," I acknowledged, and she nodded.

"They weren't feeding them, just using them for food for the Akkorokamui."

"You mentioned that earlier," I said, carefully noting what she'd said about the dead sailors. "What exactly is the Akkorokamui?"

Zhi hesitated for a moment as if formulating what she'd say, then spoke with a bit more authority. "It's a cephalopod-like creature. I never got a very good look at it. I wasn't allowed. But from what I could see of some of the photographs they carried, its body was somewhat amorphous, almost humanoid and spotted. Its lower half consisted of eight powerful tentacles." She paused.

"Continue, please," Maki said. Her tone was a touch demanding, and I wondered what was going on with these two. Maki seemed to be taking some kind of dominant role with Zhi, and Zhi was responding almost deferentially. I didn't spend any time worrying about it because it was working, but it was weird.

"The entire trip was exhausting, but they treated me well. Then, about two hours out of port, the Atkor Kumuy broke out of captivity and ran rampant over the ship. The screams were —" She paused, looking a little shaken, took a sip of water, and recovered. "It was horrible. As soon as it started, I made my way down to the cargo hold and put on dive gear. I'd been nice to the mermaids as much as I could be, and I hoped they recognized that as I went into the pool. After everything happened, I tried to do something about the ship, but the steering had been smashed, and so had the radio. I didn't know how to stop the engines. There was nothing I could do, so I dragged the bodies down to the cargo hold and used them to feed the mermaids."

I raised an eyebrow at the incongruity of her statement. "Are we supposed to believe that you were so horrified by the screams that you hid in the mermaid tank, then ran around the ship and collected a bunch of dismembered body parts without a second thought?"

Her face turned angry then. "You can believe what you want, but it wasn't without a second thought. I had plenty of time to think about it before I decided that was the best thing to do. I couldn't leave the rest to die. I just hoped someone would see us before we ran into something."

I shook my head. The ship was two hours out of the harbor, and rather than try to launch a lifeboat, she thought the logical thing to do was to feed dead Chinese sailors to a bunch of mermaids. It made no sense, and I said so.

Zhi turned defensive, her voice rising once more. "I was distraught. But I'd taken care of those mermaids for the entire trip the best I could." She paused and collected herself again, then said in a soft voice, "They're dying. Did you know that?"

"We know," Maki said gently and reached out a comforting hand, but Zhi pulled away abruptly.

I wasn't feeling so charitable. Zhi had admitted to feeding dead people to a bunch of mermaids, seemingly for no reason. She'd been the only human survivor on a ship full of dead Chinese sailors. The Atkor-whatever had been cooped up for two weeks or more by these guys and yet just happened to break out just as it was reaching our city. I chose to ignore the fact that I'd thought of Boston as *our* city even though it wasn't, in fact, *my* city. It was Cait's. Most importantly, when said monster had broken loose, Zhi had apparently decided to hide with what appeared to be its preferred food source. That didn't sound scared or protective. It just sounded stupid. Something wasn't adding up for me. But I couldn't pursue it further as a knock sounded at the door.

"Fuck," I muttered and went to answer it.

Outside, Morgan and Carlos stood with grim expressions, so I said, "Just a second," to Maki and stepped out, closing the door. "What is it? We're in an interview."

"That asshole, Yi, is here," Carlos whispered. "He wants to interview Zhi."

I frowned. "So, tell him to fuck off. He has no authority here."

Carlos frowned momentarily, then cracked a mild smile. "You sound just like—"

I raised an eyebrow and stared daggers at him in a way that suggested finishing that sentence might be hazardous to his health.

He did not finish the sentence. Instead, he said, "There's a guy with State here as well and two guys from DIA."

I screwed up my face, puzzled. "That's the Defense Intelligence Agency, right? What are they doing here?" I pushed. "Nevermind, she needs representation at the very least. Can Marcella call someone?"

Both of them looked like they'd just sucked on a lemon before Carlos said, "I'd rather not ask—"

I shook my head, then withdrew Cait's phone and punched in Ma's birthday for the code. It unlocked on the first try. Cait was so predictable. Of course, it was my code, too, so I had no room to talk. I dialed Marcella.

"Hey! What are you doing?" Carlos demanded, but Marcella answered before I could respond.

"What can I do for you, Aoife?" Marcella said coolly.

I waved my badge at Carlos, mouthing the words 'Lead Detective,' and waggled my eyebrows. "Do you have an attorney available that can come to the station? We have an issue. We need someone with a background in international asylum claims."

"Phillip is here. He's not the person to handle it, but he can stall until we find someone. We'll be right there."

"Wait, you—" But I was talking to dead air. She had hung up.

Seeing me drawing in breath to speak, Carlos held up a hand. "I heard. I'll put them in the conference room."

I schooled my face and stepped back into the interview room as they walked away, Morgan practically giggling over the exchange.

Maki turned and looked at me, but I gave her a dismissive nod and sat down. She turned back toward Zhi. "So, Dr. Zhi," she said in that high-pitched voice of hers. "Where did the Akkorokamui scamper off to? The hole in the hull suggested it tore its way out. Did you see where it went?"

"No," Zhi replied. "I already said I was hiding."

I frowned. "Right. With the preferred food. Care to explain why the Akkorkamui tore its way out of its prison at just the right time to escape into Boston Harbor, and you decided that was the moment to throw yourself into the tank with the mermaids who were starving? Why didn't they eat you first?"

"Because I was nice to them."

"Keeping them alive as food for a beast," I countered, starting to press on her story.

"Yes—I mean, no. I mean—"

She was getting flustered, so I pushed a little harder. "Then, instead of getting on a perfectly good lifeboat and running away, you slunk around a ship with a monster on the loose and scooped up dead body parts to feed the mermaids. Do I have that right?"

Zhi became so upset that she started to cry.

I shoved a box of Kleenex at her that had been sitting on the table. "Well?"

She blew her nose. "I just wanted to help them. They didn't deserve that. Besides, what do you care? You didn't see what they were doing to them. It was awful." The tears were free-flowing now, and I frowned. Either she was earnestly upset, or I needed to make a call to William Morris Endeavor. Regardless, we didn't have a ton of time.

I said, "Is there anything else you can tell us about the creature?"

Zhi shook her head, turning silent and a little sullen. The shock must have been wearing off, so I decided to end the interview. We needed to deal with her legal status situation first.

"Okay, I have an attorney coming to see you about your immigration request. Stay here until they get you situated. I'm also going to ask for a security detail to be assigned to you."

Maki turned to look at me and opened her mouth to say something, but I shook my head and nodded toward the door.

"I have a visa," Zhi said softly. "But I left the paperwork on the ship."

I smiled as gently as I could. "I'm sure there will be a record. The attorney should be here in a few minutes, so hang tight, okay?"

She nodded, and Maki and I left the room. I locked the interview door from the outside to make sure that no one else got in and Zhi didn't run off.

CHAPTER SIXTEEN

Weyna

I was awakened from a restless sleep by the raucous sound of a loud bell. Bizarre imagery of a vivid and perplexing dream consumed my thoughts, in which I found myself lost in the depths of an unfamiliar building. The air lay thick with the deafening sound of pulsating music, while the frenzied movements of countless strangers gyrating in some kind of orgiastic fertility rite, or whatever it was, added to the overwhelming chaos. Amidst the throngs of people, I noticed a striking woman gazing at me intently, with one leg casually resting against the wall. Though I strained to recollect the events that followed, the details of the dream were already slipping away like sand through my fingers. Only the words, "Looks like you're alone now," still lingered as all else was lost.

Shaking my head to clear it, I groaned to my battered feet, grabbing my comb and hair oil before following my new sisters to the bathing area behind the barracks. My arms were still so sore that the simple act of lifting them seemed a monumental effort.

The Óṣeni warriors were all either sitting in or wading into the large stone and mortar bath behind the barracks, protected by an open-air canopy and a high fence. None of the laughing and joking women noticed my presence as I drifted into the bathwater. So I sat quietly in the corner and smelled the harsh scent of exotic salts as they entered my lungs and nose, opening them and slowly relaxing my stiff muscles. Between that and the warm water, my arms and legs began to feel a little better.

I brooded in silence as I bathed, then combed the oil through my hair, struggling repeatedly for a few minutes to tie my hair in the braid they all wore. My fatigued arms refused to cooperate.

Two long, lustrous, and powerfully built legs appeared on either side of me as deft fingers twisted my hair into a proper braid and bun.

"You have several bruises and wounds on your back. Did you know that?" The voice carried a woman's soft and rich tenor as she rubbed some kind of foul-smelling paste onto my back.

I flinched and shook my head but didn't look up or speak. Instead, I leaned slightly forward, giving in to the ministrations. The bruises and scrapes hurt, but she didn't stop there, working the unguent into my shoulders and neck. Goddess, it felt good. When her fingers eventually found my spine, I giggled and then pulled away, flushing in embarrassment.

"Thank you," I mumbled.

"We take care of each other," she said and patted me on the shoulder. I turned around and had to stifle a gasp. She was glorious, maybe a foot taller than me, and built to finely honed muscular perfection. Her lustrous gray skin seemed to shimmer in the artificial faelight, and her full lips were a dark ruby, almost black. It was like looking at a goddess of war. Unlike the rest of the Óşeni, there was barely a mark on her other than a spiral-shaped black brand over her left breast. It took me a moment to realize that it was the same woman who'd made jokes about Saya needing to be laid that day on the training ground.

Taking my hand, she pulled me out of the pool with little effort and absolutely goddess-like grace. "My name is Zilyana, but everyone just calls me Zilly. You're Weyna, right?"

I nodded and followed her back into the barracks, where Zilly showed me the proper way to wear my tunic and belt, whispering to me conspiratorially, "You know, we've all got bets on how long you'll last. Just so you know, I put my rations on you not quitting at all." As she wrapped her arms around me, showing me how to adjust my belt, I caught the scent of something utterly foreign but somehow familiar and comforting.

"What is that fragrance?"

"It's the oil I add to my hair. The Romans call it dracaena. You know who the Romans are, right? Do you like it?"

I nodded. I knew who the Romans were, though I'd never met one. "It's nice. So, what are the odds?"

"Forty-eight to two against you completing. The odds improve from there depending on how long you last. As for me, well, I'm going to feast like a queen in the coming month." She gave me a sly wink. "Don't worry, I'll share." Then she vanished into the early morning fog.

As I watched her departing backside, my confidence felt just a little bolstered by her unwavering belief. And by the time I had finished dressing, my doubts evaporated. If even one person had faith in me, I knew I could accomplish this.

I didn't bother with my boots, though they'd been left as if I might use them. If the Óșeni didn't train in them, I wouldn't either. No luxuries, no special treatment. Whatever they did, I would do, even if it seemed impossible. I wouldn't let Zilly down.

Tired as I was, I trudged back out to the training ground. Then my step stuttered for just a second. *Wait, Forty-eight to two?* I spent the rest of the walk trying to figure out who the other one was.

The morning was abnormally cold and dew-frosted, lending the early light a pearlescent shimmer. Spectra cast across the tents and grasses, and sparkling rainbows floated through the fog. My breath blew hot, glinting in the cold light as well, as I sprung up into a jog to the practice yard, arriving just behind Zilly.

Óbin paced around in the cold, and the other Óșeni were all deep in calisthenics, where I did my best to drop in with them. Every push-up, knee-bend, and weird drop-and-pop thing I performed was a struggle, my muscles burning within minutes, and I was suddenly a lot less confident than when I left the barracks, but I kept going, trusting that my body would toughen up before giving out.

Óbin didn't bother sending me down for water this time. Instead, she had me work with a practice blade. When my left arm finally tired, and my hand bled from banging on the wooden practice dummy, she had me use my right until that, too, was useless. Then it was lifting a bag of heavy weights, carrying them in endless circles around the training yard. After that, it was running with the rest of the platoon to the lake, where we swam across and back five times, finally returning up to the fort. I was last, of course, but I made it the entire way without stopping, though for most of it, I wasn't certain it could rightly be called running. It was more of a limping shamble on my bruised and angry feet, suffering from several cuts on the soles.

I was already exhausted, and the sun had barely moved, but at least breakfast was ready.

The portions set aside for the Swasari were insanely large, which was good because I was positively ravenous. Our plates were filled with eggs, blood sausages, fried pork belly, and other delicacies. I had third helpings of the blood sausages, deciding they were my favorite. Something about the way they crisped when fried. I had never eaten so well.

I glanced around, my eyes traveling with the bustling servants beginning their daily chores, and sighed, thinking of my empty bed. My chest squeezed a bit in memory of Boudka's arms around me and the warmth of her body before she dumped me over my bad attitude. I wondered what she might think now.

With some effort, I pushed it aside and returned to my training with Óbin, who, seeing my miserable expression as I approached from breakfast, said simply, "She came by. I sent her away. No distractions. So forget her for now."

I frowned but let it go. I had made my bed exactly as I now lay in it. There was no sense in getting uptight about it now.

She picked up a black-bladed sword from a nearby rack.

"This is a bóllom. It is made of what you call black-steel, though the more correct translation is shadowsteel. It is an alloy of iron and karanite ore. This is a nisís." She held up a long dagger. "It is also made of shadowsteel. We all carry them, but only the Valtárí wield both bóllom and nisís together in combat." She hefted one of their breastplates. "Finally, this is a karkaríné of the same metal. By the time we are done, you will know not only how to use these but how they are built, down to the last syllable of the rituals required to make them."

I frowned at that. "What good is it for an Óṣeni warrior to know how to make one if they have no magical talent to call on to forge it?"

"You do," she said simply. "You are Dark-Fae, Weyna, Shaddani. Unlike all of the rest of the Swasari here, with one exception, you can forge and mold karanite steel."

"Are you the exception?"

Óbin smiled knowingly. "Why do you think Saya asked me to train you? They tried to induct me into the priesthood, but their methods—" She grinned mischievously. "Let's just say that they met with mixed results. About the only saving grace is that, on Óṣen, there are no sheep."

I laughed, suddenly feeling the sense of camaraderie I'd felt earlier deepen.

Then she lowered her voice and leaned in. With a furtive look, she whispered, "I think that Saya just wants to prove we can teach you magic better than your mother can. Now, no more talk. Back to work!"

And work I did—like my life depended on it. I trained longer and harder than the others. Now that I'd tasted purpose, I consumed it with relish. Every day brought new trials, triumphs, and heavier demands. Something had changed in me. Failures became opportunities to work harder. Successes became that much more gratifying.

Just over a month later, I engaged in sparring sessions with my fellow sisters, honing my skills both armed and unarmed. A few weeks more and I achieved my first victory, toppling one of the formidable women in combat.

Horsemanship followed, so different from the old nag on

Da's farm. Over time, my skills improved, easily matching the prowess of the Bethadi cavalry. I was even permitted time out on two mounted patrols, riding with the likes of Lugh and Nuada, the best of the Bethadi knights. We encountered nothing of significance both times, but it was thrilling nonetheless.

In between various structured exercises and practices, I filled my time with weightlifting, endurance training, and calisthenics. I was like a woman possessed. By the time the archers began my bow training, my muscles were corded and strong, able to draw the powerful weapons with ease. Within a few weeks, I adeptly sank bullseyes from both solid ground and galloping mount. It was during that time, as she instructed me in the proper construction of arrows and bows, that I truly came to understand what a phenomenal trainer I was graced with.

Óbin was strict but fair. When I succeeded, she commended my progress and growth. If I failed, she encouraged me to continue to hone my skills until that changed. Never once did she encourage me to quit, though she did confide in me around week four that she had already lost her rations, kicking her off my short list of who, other than Zilly, had believed I'd make it all the way.

By midsummer, I scarcely recognized myself. The lanky child of a wretched village had been supplanted by a fit, extremely muscled woman devoid of excess fat.

Agile, capable, and clad in the same attire, all that made me stand out as I trained and sparred was my stature and the color of my skin and hair. Even on training runs, I excelled, despite my shorter legs, often making up time during the swimming, where I proved faster, generally finishing at least middle of the pack. In stamina, though, I outstripped them all; the longer the runs, the better I placed.

The solstice also brought my eighteenth birthday, almost unnoticed. The only indication was a modest gift, a ribbon of purple Fae-cloth, delicately placed upon my bunk, which I stowed diligently and promptly forgot, and Óbin's decision to train me in something other than Swasari grunt fighting.

I was too small to be a shield sister, so Óbin decided that my shorter stature and more limited reach were more suited to a two-handed fighting style that favored a swift and mobile art called the Valtár-Skolmeh, favored by the elite soldiers, the Valtárí.

I swelled with pride when Óbin suggested that I could be inducted into the Valtárí unit, but it gave me pause moments later as Zilly described how Valtárí soldiers fought. "So," Zilly said breezily as we selected practice weapons. "Our job is to launch ourselves over the forward line off the shields of the third phalanx unit. Then we land and slaughter the enemy back-to-back."

I froze momentarily, my hands hovering over the wooden weapons, and I turned to stare at her. "We what?"

She grinned. "I said, we slaughter the enemy, back-to-back. You really should see the chaos that ensues in the enemy front line when we suddenly land and start ripping into them from behind. It's all good fun."

I scowled at her in absolute disbelief at her rather blasé response, waiting for the punchline. None came.

"Good fun?" I scoffed. "We'll be totally exposed. I'll get cut to ribbons, assuming I don't land on the end of a spear or an emisai claw."

She took my shoulders and looked me dead in the eye, her tone soft but serious. "Weyna. I have been through four Kaushkari campaigns. I was your age when I joined the Valtárí. I've never lost a Valtárí-sister. I will train you well, and by the time we're done, you will be able to fight as one with any of us—and as well. Trust me."

I nodded, mollified slightly by her words, yet at that moment, my situation dawned on me for the first time. This was training for war, and should I succeed, I would become part of an elite Swasari unit, where the toll of attrition ran high and life expectancy woefully brief. Gnawing at my insides further was the reason I was assigned, not for training excellence but because I fit in nowhere else.

I mashed that thought violently under my foot. I'd achieved a lot in less than six months. I was a part of this unit. No one questioned that. I'd yet to be formally inducted, but I'd get there if it killed me. And I would be one of the best. I wasn't going to let doubt loose in my head now.

Valtárí training began with light work, mostly learning forms. That was followed by sparring sessions, which quickly grew swifter and more intense, Zilly pushing me back on my heels constantly. By the fourth, though, I was holding my own better—until Boudka appeared at the edge of the training ring, distracting me and earning me a hard whack on the side of the head from Zilly, along with a kick that put me on my backside. I felt the flow of warm blood down the side of my face. "Ow," I groaned with a chuckle.

"Weyna! Focus!" Óbin shouted from across the yard, then she followed my gaze, and the corners of her mouth turned up. "Five minutes, then back to work."

Zilly helped me up with a wink, and I grabbed a loose towel to stem the flow of blood from the cut on my head. Boudka stood, suppressing a bout of mirth, no doubt from the way I'd gotten whacked for my troubles.

I grinned stupidly at her as I strode over. "Good to see you, too," I said awkwardly and wiped at the blood and sweat on my face.

"I'm so sorry," Boudka giggled. "I just wanted to see you. I didn't mean to get you in trouble."

I glanced back at Óbin, who pointed toward the sun, indicating the passing of time. "Yeah, I'm not in trouble. The shot to the head was punishment enough."

Boudka reached up and touched the wound gingerly. "Does it hurt?"

I brushed her hand away. "Not really, but Zilly's practice sword might not survive. Besides, I've had plenty. I'm just happy to see you."

Boudka blushed. "Well, your mother was going to come and ask you to have dinner in her tent, but I asked her to let me deliver the invite. Um, I'll be there if that's okay."

"Of course it's okay," I replied, my lips split in the same idiot smile.

"Did you get my gift? I wasn't sure when I didn't hear from

you."

I froze. *Gift? Oh, shit.* "Yeah, I'm sorry. I've been neck-deep in training, you know?"

A tinge of disappointment colored her expression for a moment but vanished almost as quickly. Then she reached up to touch my arm. I flexed a little as she felt the muscle and followed it up to my shoulder. Then she leaned in and kissed me on the cheek. "Good. Your mother said to be there after training, but make sure you take a bath and put on fresh clothes. You stink."

I laughed then, loudly and without reservation. "Okay. I will. Thank you for coming by. I'll see you this evening."

"By the way, the muscular look suits you." She said as she backed away shyly, adjusting her clothes. Her servant's kit had been replaced by the robes of a trainee of Celestria, the old Shaddani Magic Academy. They were even made of Shaddani woven cloth, and I wondered briefly why, when my mother had been training me, she hadn't bothered to make me a set.

She turned on her toes and sauntered back into the main camp, leaving me standing there staring stupidly after her, completely flustered. I was still lost in thought when the flat of a practice blade whacked me on the behind.

"Enough gawking, lovebird," Zilly said. "Back to work."

CHAPTER SEVENTEEN

Aoife

The next few minutes were chaotic, but at least I didn't have to get too involved.

Carlos held off Yi and the State Department wonks long enough for Marcella and Phillip, her attorney, to arrive. That had been a hoot.

Yi had demanded to see Zhi and claimed he had jurisdiction to return her to the consulate and back to Beijing. Phillip then stopped and wrote down something on a piece of paper, handing it to Yi when he was done.

"Those are the relevant statutes of US law that relate to kidnapping and aggravated assault. Doctor Zhi is on US soil, so she cannot just be whisked away by you. Her claim has to be adjudicated. Now, Ms. Zhi has expressed that she does not wish to speak to you at this time."

The State guys hadn't been so easily deterred, demanding to speak to Zhi. Carlos had fought that, reminding them that she wasn't under arrest and finally convincing them that she was in no condition to talk to anyone further about the incident. I finally gave up watching and returned to my—Cait's—desk and sat down, feeling dizzy and tired.

"Hey, you okay?"

I looked up. It was Marcella.

I wiped some tears from my eyes that I hadn't known were there and sat back. "Yeah, just tired."

Marcella frowned. "No, it's more than that. What's going

on?"

I waved her off. "No, Marcella, I'm fine. Please. I just need rest."

She turned to Morgan. "Take Cait home, please." She slightly emphasized the name Cait, as if my, or Cait's rather, entire team, didn't know who I was. Morgan's head popped up over the cube wall, and she gave Marcella a hard stare but faltered under Marcella's eyes. The queen had spoken.

"Now," Marcella demanded in a low tone, and my eyebrows shot up.

I didn't like the way she talked to her. *Who the fuck did she think she was, just ordering people around anyway?* But Morgan nodded and walked around to my desk.

I wanted to argue, but Morgan said, "Let it go. It's fine. She's right. You look exhausted," and she started helping me out of my chair.

As it turned out, I needed the help. My knees buckled, and the world spun around me. I sat back down. "But what about Zhi?"

Marcella spoke up. "I'll make sure she has a place to stay, and we'll figure out what's going on. With the mermaid involvement, that's my area of expertise anyway. Now go."

I frowned and made an annoyed face at Marcella's tone and squinted at her. "You really are a pushy bitch. You know that?"

Marcella closed her eyes for a moment, her face a mask, but I'd definitely hit the right button because she reached out and touched Morgan on the shoulder and spoke gently, in an almost coaxing tone. "Morgan, I'm sorry, I have to keep up appearances. I've got this, and Aoife needs to rest."

Morgan nodded firmly, then said, "It's okay. I shouldn't have let it get to me. This is the way it has to be," and then helped me back up. Quietly we took the long way around to the lift and slipped out, Morgan keeping me upright by one arm most of the way.

Once we got to the car, as I reached for the passenger door, the dizziness got worse, and I bent over to catch my breath. And that's when the pavement decided to introduce itself to my face.

"Jesus! Reagan." Morgan shot around the car and knelt down. She did a quick check of my neck, but other than a scrape on my cheek, I was okay, except for the dizziness and now black spots in my vision.

"I'm taking you to the hospital," Morgan said as she rolled me over and scooped me up like I weighed nothing.

"No, just take me—"

"No!" She said firmly and loudly. "You're going to the hospital right fucking now."

"Jesus, okay, Red," I croaked. "No need to shout."

Morgan got me buckled in, hopped into the other side, and then shot out of the parking lot, sirens blaring. I had a weird sense of deja vu as I looked at her as if I'd seen her like this before. It was something about the angle, but instead of her black swat uniform, she had been in combat fatigues. I shook my head to clear it, but that only conjured a vice-like pain at my temples.

"No," I muttered under my breath. "Not yet. I'm not done."

"Not done what?" Morgan said, weaving in and out of traffic.

I didn't answer. My vision was closing in, and I felt hot. I finally just gave up speaking and closed my eyes, waiting until we got to the hospital.

My memory was hazy, but I must have blacked out at some point during the chaos. When I finally came to, the harsh glare of the emergency room's fluorescent lights assaulted my eyes. I tried to sit up, but a sharp tug on my arm brought my attention to the IV that had been inserted into my vein.

"Ouch," I groaned, feeling disoriented and weak. That's when I saw Morgan standing rigidly by my side like a marble statue brought to life by panic. She wore a worried expression, and I could practically feel the waves of concern and fear radiating from her.

"Hey," I croaked.

Morgan moved next to me, pushing a strand of hair out of my face in an almost too-intimate gesture. Then, as if just realizing what she'd done, she jerked her hand back a few inches and squeezed it shut. "Sorry. You okay?"

I gave her a pained smile. "It's okay. What happened?"

"You passed out in the car. Do you remember what happened before that?"

"Yeah, I was dizzy, and my vision went blurry, but I feel fine now." That was a lie. My head was still pounding, and my face hurt. But my vision was good, at least. "Did they say what was wrong?"

Morgan shook her head. "They won't tell me anything other than that you were dehydrated." She gestured to the IV.

I sighed. One of my medications had diuretic side effects, and I hadn't been drinking much water, not counting the swallow or two of pedialite hours ago. *Shit. Was that all this was?*

"I'm sorry about the hair thing. I— Boundaries are a problem for me right now."

I gave her a puzzled look. It hadn't bothered me. Actually, it had been nice, which made me scrunch up my face a little bit more with a confused expression as I mulled that over.

Morgan clearly took that to mean something else because she said, "Shit, I'm sorry. I didn't mean to upset you. This whole thing is hard to deal with."

I shook my head, then said, "I'm not upset. I'm struggling with my own issues right now."

"Shit. Yeah. I probably shouldn't be so self-absorbed. I'm sorry."

I chuckled mirthlessly. "Well then, aren't we a pair? But what do you mean this thing is hard to deal with." I figured she'd meant me living with her all of a sudden, but I wanted to be sure.

She looked around and leaned down to whisper, "Being a vampire. It's only been a few days."

My eyebrows shot up. "A few days? What's that even like?"

She sat down on the rolling stool next to the bed, and, oddly, I was reminded of my visits to the pediatrician as a kid.

"Um, isn't that the doctor's chair?"

Morgan snorted and chuckled, "I don't think they're assigned. Anyway, thanks for asking about, well, you know. No one has, really. Mostly, Liz and Marcella have been spending their time with me ordering me around or," she made air quotes, "'showing me the ropes.' They haven't really bothered to give me a chance to talk about it. And I do really need to talk about it, you know?"

"Sure," I shrugged. I didn't know, but I was happy to listen. Morgan had engendered a lot of trust in just the last few hours. I found that, in addition to the obvious physical attraction, I kind of liked her. She was no-nonsense, direct, and to the point. And she had a wry sense of humor, which I appreciated.

"I *feel* differently," she continued. "It's like all of the things— you know, my past?—they don't matter as much." She touched the scar on her face in an unconscious way. "Most of the baggage that I carried with me for so long just doesn't seem to matter as much."

I nodded. "I think I can relate to that some, but keep going." I really was genuinely interested in this. It was kind of fascinating.

"Marcella told me that we don't have empathy for people we don't already love, and that love, real love, comes hard for us sometimes. And that when we love, we get possessive. She warned me that I had to be careful who I let into my world as friends because I could hurt them badly, doing awful things in the name of protecting them."

I raised an eyebrow at that, thinking about what Marcella had done to Cait and me. Also, it confused me. "But you've been really nice to me."

She gave a snort of amusement. "Yeah, but you see, Aoife, that's not what you think. It's probably because of your relationship to Cait—" She held up a hand, I guess to forestall a protest from me that wasn't coming. "I know, I know, you're not Cait."

I smiled. "I wasn't going to say anything. Continue, please. I really want to know." She rested a hand on the bedrail, and on instinct, and probably against my better judgment, I placed mine on hers. "Seriously," I prodded.

She looked down, then back up. "Well, you're Cait's sister. And I still love her. Not romantically. We're not a good match. But I still care about her and, by extension, you. So, when you were on the ship and frightened, it was easy for me to feel, " she paused, struggling for words, "caring, I think. The idea that you might be hurting bothered me."

"It probably doesn't hurt that I look just like her," I said honestly.

"But you don't. Not to me. You're very different."

Now I raised an incredulous eyebrow. "We're twins, Morgan."

She laughed. "Well, duh. And, at a distance, you guys look alike, but up close, you're very different. You have this tiny scar that runs through your right eyebrow. Here," she reached out and traced a line next to my right eye.

I grinned, thinking of the drunken brawl I had been breaking up when one of my fellow officers punched me by accident, knocking me into the bar.

"And you have this worry line that crinkles when you squint. And when you scrunch up your nose, it wrinkles differently. Also, your smile is very different, a little crooked, both silly and attractive. It's—" She stopped and looked down. "Sorry."

I gave a dry smirk. "Yeah, well, I guess my flaws aren't hard to see." I was joking, but it occurred to me that she really had been studying me, watching my expressions and my face. When had she noticed all of this? And, more importantly, why?

She looked up at me, and there was a depth in her expression now that caught me off guard and made me flush. She said softly, "They're not flaws." Then she placed her other hand, soft and cool, on top of mine.

"Uh, Morgan, I—" *I what?* I didn't know. I had no idea what I was about to say, so I looked away, a little embarrassed, and she pulled her hands back in a gentle, fluid movement. I wondered if she was trying to put the moves on me because, if she was, she was damn good at it. And it was working.

"Anyway—" she said but stopped when the curtain pulled back, and a doctor who looked about twelve to me walked in. He was a handsome Indian fellow, clean-shaven, with dark hair and brown eyes.

"Miss Reagan, how are you feeling?" He asked, flipping through my chart and looking at the monitor next to me, which showed just my pulse rate, blood pressure, and blood oxygen. I didn't have any EKG leads, so the heart monitor was flat.

"Fine, just a little bit of a headache. Any idea what's wrong?"

He looked up at me and gave me a grave expression.

Uh oh. I turned to Morgan. "Can you, uh, give us a minute?"

She stood. "Sure." And walked away.

The doctor spoke up. "I talked to your doctor back in Galway, and I don't want to—"

I held up a hand. "Forget it. Was this related or just dehydration from the meds?"

He sighed. "I'm going to pull some blood work, but I think it was just dehydration. If it had been anything else, I would have expected other symptoms. Are you having any memory loss, disorientation, heart palpitations, or sudden loss of feeling anywhere?"

"No," I answered truthfully. "I'm not there yet."

"Um, does your girlfriend know?" He asked, indicating where Morgan had walked out with a nod of his head.

I laughed. "She's not my girlfriend. We're just friends." I flushed anyway, though.

He looked at me skeptically, like he was about to give me the 'it's okay to be gay speech,' but seemed to think better of it. "I want you to get some rest, okay?"

Like hell, I thought. *I have a killer to catch.* But I said, "Sure," instead.

"And, for what it's worth, Aoife, I'm sorry."

I snorted. "Sure, doc, aren't we all? Thanks, though."

"The nurse will come in and take some blood. Then we'll get you out of here."

"Sounds great."

He walked out, and Morgan came back in. She had a grim look on her face. "So what don't I know?"

"Were you eavesdropping?" I asked, but there was nothing in it. I didn't care, not really.

"Not intentionally, but you know I can hear a mouse fart at a thousand paces, and it was better than listening to all of the other people around here bitching about staffing, travel nurse pay, and their personal ailments. One guy down the hall just told a nurse that he was eating a carrot in the shower and fell on it. You don't want to know where it is now."

I laughed out loud. "I'll tell you when we get back to your apartment. It's probably best we talk about it somewhere quiet."

She smiled. "Okay. I'm just glad you're okay."

I gave her a forced smile.

CHAPTER EIGHTEEN

Aoife

Morgan flipped through my medical file, reading the relevant portions, then she set it down slowly on the table and leaned back in the chair as I lay on the bed, safely ensconced in jammies and under the blankets.

She looked crushed, sighed, and then hung her head for a moment before she looked up and said, "Good God, Aoife, I'm so sorry. I had no idea."

I shrugged. "No one knows."

"Do you want me to help you? Or maybe Marcella—"

I shook my head. "No. I want to go out the way I came in. I really am okay with it." I wasn't. It was a lie. But I didn't want to be a vampire. That was the last thing I wanted. I most certainly didn't want to live forever, though I didn't want to die, either.

She looked at me incredulously. And I looked away, staring out the window into the false dawn. Gods, it had gotten late. And I was so tired. I rolled over and curled up into a ball. I didn't need her judgment, not about this.

The lights went out, and I listened to Morgan move around, stripping out of her clothes. I heard the soft click of the switch as she activated the heating blanket, the tick-tick of the thermostat as she raised the heat, and the soft sound of her skin on the sheets as she slid gracefully into the bed and up against my back. Her body was cool but not unwelcome. I wasn't really cold anyway.

"You're so warm," she whispered as she draped an arm over me, and pulled me closer, then moved it to stroke my hair, her other arm sliding underneath my pillow. "For what it's worth, I'm sorry. And I won't judge your decisions. I chose to become this in a moment of panic. I won't say I regret it because I don't honestly know if I should yet, but I won't begrudge you your choices or question them."

I sniffed and pawed at my wet eyes. "Thanks. Don't tell the others. Marcella will pull me off of this, and I need to do it. I need to finish this before—"

Morgan reached her hand awkwardly around my head and placed a finger across my lips in the darkness. "I won't tell a soul, I promise."

Desperate to turn the topic away from myself and the malignancy gnawing at my brain, I asked, "Did you get that scar in Iraq?"

"I was wondering when you'd ask," Morgan said with a chuckle. "I thought you might when you saw me naked earlier."

"I wasn't going to ask at all," I admitted, glad I had my back to her so she couldn't see my smirk. "I had figured you'd mention it if you wanted to. But when you touched it earlier, it seemed like there was more there, and now I'm curious."

There was an extended silence before Morgan spoke again. The heating blanket was doing its job, and she wasn't as cold. I rolled over and could see her silhouette. She had rolled over and thrown one arm over her forehead.

"The last time I told anyone about this," she whispered. "I broke down."

I didn't respond, just waiting patiently.

She rushed forward, clearly afraid of coming apart in the telling and probably trying to avoid reliving it. "When I was living in Chicago, my ex and I had a fight. She grabbed a sword off the wall and cut me from forehead to belly. It was really bad. Somehow I got to my piece and shot her before she could finish the job." Her voice hadn't trembled or broken, not at all, and yet, I could still hear the pain in it.

Still, though, I said nothing. There was nothing to say, really.

I could have said, I'm sorry as a show of sympathy, but what for? She'd probably heard that a thousand times. So instead, I reached out, gave her a soft hug of support, and then rolled back over.

She moved back behind me and draped her arm across my belly once more. I put my arm over hers.

"Thank you," Morgan said.

"You're welcome," I replied and patted her hand. The sun finally broke the horizon outside, giving what sky I could see through the window above a golden color, and Morgan went perfectly still, tumbling away into the death-like sleep of a vampire.

I lay there for a while with my eyes closed, unable to sleep, wondering for a while what it must be like for Morgan, how lonely. Katie had said she was looking for her sister, whom she believed dead.

It must be hard, I thought. *Waiting around for confirmation that your loved one is dead while trying to cope with all of this on top of it.*

I wondered, too, if maybe that's why Marcella had put the two of us together. Morgan was alone. She had no one, really. I didn't know what her relationship with her parents was like, but if they did, indeed, live in Bumblefuck, Montana, as Katie had put it, then it was likely, not great or at least strained. Some country families here in the States didn't like their gay children for some reason I could never fathom, as if they were the greatest disappointment anyone could imagine. I suspected none of those parents had ever lost a child to drugs or alcohol or suicide. If they understood that horror, if they had even an inkling of the pain that could befall them otherwise, maybe they might appreciate their gay or trans kids and love them regardless, thrilled that they were as safe and happy as they could be—but maybe not. Bigotry knew no logic or friends.

Morgan needed someone. She needed a friend.

I turned over and looked at her. She lay partially on her stomach, one arm behind her and dangling over the edge of the bed, the other lying limply across my belly. Quietly, quickly, I leaned in and kissed her on the forehead. The skin was cool and soft. I pushed her hair aside and gazed at her face. She really was very pretty, and I decided that I really liked her. That I was interested in her romantically.

Let's be honest; she'd cracked my own prejudice the moment I'd seen her. That seemed wrong somehow, that a hot body had been what had done it, but there it was, and I wasn't going to lie to myself about it. The anger and resentment I'd felt because of Marcella must not have run nearly so deep as I'd wanted to believe. And for the first time, I began to wonder why that anger was directed at all vampires. Liz had been a good stepmother of sorts for the two years before I went to University. Yeah, she'd kind of fucked off after, but she was never completely out of touch. I rubbed my forehead, deciding to think about it later.

I rolled back over and scooted backward until I was once again body-to-body with the red-headed vampire and drifted off to sleep. What did it matter? Holding on to past injuries had no point anyway. I knew it was wrong, that I shouldn't get close to her. She'd just end up getting hurt. But still, it was nice, and I couldn't bring myself to pull away.

I woke up well into the evening to Morgan's voice. A light was on behind me, the one in the little kitchenette. I didn't move. My face was to the wall, so I just lay there.

"No, Carlos, I'm not bringing her in," she said and paused. I heard her pacing back and forth, and I smiled. She paced around like I did when I talked on the phone for long periods.

"I understand what's going on, but this is a special circumstance, and she needs the time to get squared away. We got lucky yesterday. She didn't run into Cardozo, and Sesi was only around for a few minutes. She needs prep."

There was another long pause as she listened, then gave an exasperated sigh of resignation. "Yeah, fine. Two days. Yes. Okay. We'll see you then."

It got quiet, and I heard her set the phone down on the

table. Then she sat in one of the breakfast chairs, the one closest to me by the sound of it, and I heard her flip papers. Going through my file again, I suspected.

I didn't know why I hadn't turned over or made any noise. There was something comforting in just listening. It was just the knowledge that she was in the room. A warm feeling crept into my chest over it, and this time I didn't shove it aside or stomp on it. I knew what it was. And I didn't mind. Again, I was dying. I should just enjoy the ride.

For a moment, it turned very quiet, then Morgan said, "I know you're awake."

"Only barely," I replied in a sleepy voice. "Are you really ready to get up?"

She chuckled at that. "Yeah, that's the problem with being a vampire. When you wake up, there's no idle time being sleepy. One second you're dead, and the next, bam, you're wide awake."

I scowled. "Where's the fun in that?"

She didn't answer, and I turned over to find her still reading my file, a cup in front of her, full of blood, I assumed. I watched her for a while, a creeping smile slowly pushing up the corners of my mouth as I admired her figure. She was in undies and a sports bra. Her long legs were muscled like some CrossFit goddess, as were her abs and arms. Still, though, I didn't move.

Morgan paused and peeked at me over the file then went back to reading it, raising it up slightly and shielding the lower half of her face, but a soft crinkle of a smile formed around the edges of her eyes, and the barest hint of a blush bloomed under them. There was a sense of accomplishment in that. I'd made a vampire blush. Points for me.

"What?" Morgan asked from behind the file, trying to sound stern.

"What?" I repeated, feigning innocence.

"Why are you staring at me?"

I did my best to turn on the charm, hard to do with bleary eyes and wild, auburn bedhead. I said, "You really are stunning, you know that?"

She lowered the file then and turned up a crooked smile, her scar curving around it and giving her a slightly rakish cast. *Jaysus,* I thought. *Yeah, for sure, you're fucked, Aoife.*

Morgan set down the file and stood, stretching her arms upward and giving me a full view of her gorgeous physique. I laughed out loud, knowing full well that vampires don't need to stretch their muscles. Liz had taught me that much.

"So," she said, her voice low and sultry enough to give me goosebumps. Then she crossed her arms, and her expression changed from mild amusement to something else entirely. "Are we doing this?"

I stared up at her, transfixed and unable to speak, as she started walking toward me.

She sat down on the bed and lowered her head, dipping her face so close I could feel her breath on me when she spoke. "What? Cat got your tongue?"

The scent of mint toothpaste, coupled with the coppery tang of blood, wafted into my nose. There was also something else, something uniquely her, blackberry and a scent that I couldn't identify but brought back long-buried memories of home. I closed my eyes and shivered. She leaned in further and kissed me lightly on the cheek, then pulled away.

"You are so easy, Reagan."

"You're shitting me, right?" I protested as she started digging into a bag on the floor and threw some clothes at me.

"No, I'm not shitting you. We can't, at least not right now. Get dressed. We have things to do."

I picked up the clothes and looked. Panties, a bra with a weird pocket sown on to the left strap, a Boston PIU women's polo, and a pair of loose cargo pants.

"Don't dawdle, Aoife. It's late. Now go get a shower."

"Aye, ya' bloody slave driver," I said, letting my accent slip out. "For sure, you're a right ginger bitch."

"Back atcha," Morgan replied with a smirk as she started pulling on some jeans and a t-shirt.

Twenty minutes later, showered and dressed, I piled into her cruiser, and we headed out toward Cambridge, stopping at Dunks so I could get some coffee.

"You know," Morgan said with a grin. "I'm glad they ditched that whole Double-D Perks ad campaign they had."

I snorted my coffee and had to wipe it off my upper lip. "The what?"

"Oh, yeah. A couple years ago, someone in Dunkin' Donuts marketing decided to call their rewards program the Double-D perks."

Fortunately, I'd waited until she was done talking to take another sip because I burst out in peels of laughter. "You'd have thought there would have been one woman on the team."

"Oh," Morgan said with a chuckle, "There were, but they were shouted down by the men."

I laughed again. "So, where are we going?"

"To see your mother."

I almost choked on the coffee again, this time having to snatch up my napkin quickly before it dripped on my new shirt. "Thanks for the warning. Just pull over here and let me out."

"Now, now, Aoife. Time to see the penguin," she said in a fair imitation of Dan Ackroyd's Elwood Blues.

"But I don't wanna see the penguin."

"We gotta see the penguin," she said again.

"You do that really well," I said with a chuckle.

"Ten years in Chicago. I better," she said, then added, "asshole," and swerved around a cyclist who'd decided to take his half out of the middle of the Mass Avenue Bridge, which was four lanes.

"Do we really have to go see my mother?"

"No, Aoife," Morgan replied with a touch of irritation. "But I need to take you to see Bian and have your tumor looked at, and she'll be there. I don't understand why you don't want to see her. If I could just go see my parents and have them love and accept me, I would."

I paused at that. "They rejected you? Because you're gay?"

She nodded.

My hand moved reflexively, but I stopped. I wanted to touch her, show that I cared and, maybe, to show some sympathy, but I figured she'd probably had plenty of that in her life, so I just said, "I'm sorry. That sucks."

"It's okay. Things were getting better until Caileigh disappeared. They blame that on me."

"What happened? Who took her?"

Morgan sighed. "I—I guess you'll find out eventually, anyhow. Please don't judge me too harshly. An FBI agent named Carter Reese, a vampire hunter. His crew kidnapped my sister and forced me to feed them information on your sister—and Liz. It didn't help that Nastasia told them how to get to Marcella. Reese said they killed her."

"Do you believe him?" I asked, batting aside the obvious worry she had for the moment.

"Yes, and even if they didn't, she's probably dead by now. We looked into how to find her, but we had no leads. Reese covered his tracks pretty well, at least financially, and we never figured out who was bankrolling them."

Morgan turned very quiet, and I studied her face for a moment, then said, "It's okay, Red. I don't have any room to judge you. A man shot my sister, and I'm here to kill him. You did what you had to do." Now I did place my hand on her leg and gave it a gentle squeeze.

She sniffed and wiped her eyes. I dug one of Cait's handkerchiefs out of my pocket and used it to dab at her cheeks. She chuckled a little.

"So, anyway, about your mother," she said mysteriously. "She's a little, um, different now, so you should prepare yourself."

"Different how? Has she finally lost her last marble?" I asked with no small amount of cheek.

"No, she's fine, better than, really. But it's not for me to give away the surprise." She glanced at me with that crooked smile again, and I had to stifle a literal sigh. "And I think I like it better."

"What's that?"

"When you call me Red." And the way she looked at me then made my insides go all melty and my heart flutter.

Yeah, Aoife, for sure, yer fucked, all the way around. But then again, I thought, *so is she.*

CHAPTER NINETEEN

Weyna

I stood in front of my mother's door, fidgeting with the folds of my tunic for about the tenth time to control my trembling hands. After going barefoot for months, the gray leather boots I now wore felt stiff and uncomfortable. I'd walked barely fifty yards here from the barracks, but I was sure I'd raised a blister or two on my heels.

I raised my hand to knock but paused, taking in another breath as a sudden overwhelming feeling hit me that I'd done this before, and it hadn't gone well, which was ridiculous. Never once had my mother invited me to share a meal with any of her guests unless I counted the meal that I'd been made to cater for her and Lugh, Aine's champion, which I certainly didn't.

Just as I was about to knock, something funny brushed my nose, the scent of something burning, not unpleasant, but still. I looked around. There was nothing, nor should there have been. This was the heart of the camp. Just a dozen or so feet away sat Aine's massive tent, taking up a ridiculous space and enchanted to be even larger and more luxurious on the inside. Around it, at the center of the camp's protections, lay the tents of her magi.

I frowned and turned around, briefly considering just returning to the barracks abutting the fence only fifty yards away. But then I'd have to hear about it later and not just from Boudka. After all, the barracks was, ironically, only a dozen feet from my mother's bathing tent, owing to drainage needs.

I checked my tunic and belt, even my boots, one last time, knocked, then entered, hoping that my mother, for once, would keep that tongue of hers in check. On her best day, her biting comments could pierce armor. I had never lived here, but it had a homey feel, and the only complaint I ever had about the place was the perpetually faulty door that never quite closed right, getting stuck or bouncing weirdly back half the time. Once, I even thought I'd heard it squeak in protest. Tonight though, it gave me no trouble.

Though it likely didn't compare to the Vermillion Palace as anything more than a hovel, Mother's residence was almost opulent. The interior of the wood and stone structure was decorated in a pseudo-Shaddani style. Dark rugs covered the floors replete with the spiral patterns so common in Shaddani art, some identical to the Valtárí tattoos, which I thought an interesting coincidence.

Woven tapestries depicting Shaddani history hung tightly bound to the ceiling and floor, hiding the stacked logs of the outer wall. But to be honest, I neither recognized nor held any genuine interest in the intricacies of the mythic narratives. They had always bored me.

The artwork in the one that hung behind the wide Bethadi couch, however, always drew my eye, portraying the tragic downfall of Shaddani, the relentless battle with the Kaushkar, and the cataclysmic devastation that followed.

On every visit, I gazed at the weaving. And on every visit, I found some detail I'd missed before. Tonight, upon closer examination, my eyes caught sight of a minuscule crystal, radiating hues of blue and purple, delicately embroidered into the cloth. Its size, if brought to actual scale, might have been the length of my forearm. I frowned at it, somehow expecting it to be much larger, gigantic even, but unsure as to why.

I meandered around the room, stalling for a minute more and taking time to glance at the portal tablets, intricately carved of Óșeni karanite-infused stone. Each bore engravings of the sixty verses of power. There should have been ten, but there were twelve. She had made two more. I shifted my perception and skimmed the inscription. This one bore only markings for an odd ritual and included one of my mother's prophecies, a dark one about a woman bonded by two birthrights. As usual, it was cryptic and weird.

"Are these two new?" I asked, hearing my mother shuffle into the common room from the kitchen.

"Yes," she replied. "I created those last night after a particularly distressing vision, but don't touch them, please."

I raised an eyebrow at that, still staring at the inscription. "Why?"

"Because," she said, entering the room behind me, "They're keyed to you."

I turned to ask about that and was shocked to find her standing in the kitchen doorway with an apron over her thin black dress.

"Have you been cooking?" I asked, gobsmacked by her attire and the subtle hints of spiced meats in the air. The tablets were instantly forgotten.

She said nothing for a long moment, pausing even in wiping her hands on her apron as if I'd caught her at something naughty. Then she said, "Yes. I thought you might like a home-cooked meal." Then she gave me an appraising look, glancing up and down with a frown before turning on her heel and leaving the room.

I shook my head. *Couldn't she just let it be and be proud that I chose something for myself? Gods, she's such a bitch.*

"I heard that," she called from the kitchen.

Then hear this, I thought coldly. *Stay out of my fucking head.*

My mother poked her head around the corner. "I'm sorry, Weyna. It's a habit. I'll try not to do so in the future."

I rolled my eyes. "That's what you said last time."

She came out of the kitchen a few minutes later and closed the front door. "Come sit with me, please, so we can talk."

Uh oh. "Okay." I sat down at the table, and she took a seat across from me.

She didn't waste any time. "Weyna, why?"

I considered playing dumb and dragging out the conversation, but Boudka would likely be here any moment, and I didn't want us arguing in front of her again. "Because it's what I want. I'm eighteen years old, mother. I'm well old enough to make my own decisions."

"But your magic training—"

"Was going terrible, and we both know it," I interrupted. "I trained for two years and five months, and I can barely heat water. I know you tell me that I have all this great potential, and it may be that I do, but I can't wrap my head around the lessons. The equations alone bake my brain. I'm not being intentionally obtuse here." My voice turned pleading, almost begging her to understand. "I struggled for so long and got almost nowhere. The threads of magic that you taught me to see fight me. Even the ones in my own body. And for the first time in my life, I'm finding I have some talent in something, and now you want to stand in my way. I'd like to have a success, you know? Can't you give me that without a fight?"

She scowled at me. "But if you don't master your magic, you can lose control. You're a bomb, Weyna. Like me, you've got the power to destroy this camp and half the countryside around it."

I didn't know what a bomb was, but I scowled right back at her. "Oh really? Where is it when I need it, then? I try to do the simplest tasks, and it always backfires. Never truly spectacularly, but always a problem. I tried to heal a sheep and ended up blowing it to hell." I paused and muttered, "Okay, that *was* a spectacular failure, but it's a far cry from flattening the fort. And when I try to use my magic, it always resists me, like it's fighting me or something. Can't you just accept that I don't have what it takes to master it? I have."

My mother sighed and placed her hand on mine in a truly condescending gesture that she probably thought was motherly. "Weyna," she said in that voice she always used when she thought she was right and that I refused to see it. "The Óşeni are battle troops. They die, sometimes by the dozen, in combat. I don't want you to be doing that. You're better than that."

"Mother, I am no better than anyone else here. I keep trying to tell you that. You should have kicked me out of the camp long ago." I stood and placed both hands on the table, raising my voice in fury and disbelief. "Boudka was right! I can't be kicked out of here, no matter how bad I fuck up. You won't let it happen."

"You are my only living child, Weyna. I just want to keep you safe."

"But that's just it. Boudka has to work her ass off just to stay here. And she certainly doesn't want to go back to living down there," I pointed sharply at the door. "It's wrong."

"Boudka's human, you are not. You are my child," she shot back harshly. "Of course, I'm protecting you."

"But she needs protection!" I shouted. "She needs to know that her place here is safe. I don't. I have a path of my own! Sometimes you forget that I'm not you! And I really wish you wouldn't ignore that Boudka means something to me. What is the human girl not good enough for me? If not her, then who? One of those Bethadi idiots? Or are you hoping to find one of our lost Shaddani brethren who's just as arrogant and self-important as you are? It's sad the way you and your sisters cling to each—" I stopped abruptly, realizing I'd gone too far, and tried to look away.

The fingers of an enormous hand grasped my chin and pulled my face savagely around, forcing me to look up. Grown to her full height, she stooped beneath the rafters, her wings unfurling in a threatening gesture, and a fearsome rage burned in her glowing green eyes as her aura darkened the room almost to pitch. "Watch your mouth," she growled.

I swallowed hard. For the first time in my life, I was afraid of her. She now truly embodied The Morrigan, a divine creature with an unpredictable nature, and there was a real possibility she would kill me. She wouldn't mean to, and she would be devastated, but it could happen.

She stared hard at me with a gaze that could have turned me to cinders. Then she squinted. Something flashed across her face, some expression, some realization, but it was gone too quickly for me to catch.

"Now, you listen to me, girl." Her voice had dropped and taken on that unearthly quality. This was the aspect that inspired terror in enemies and turned their hearts to ice as it did mine now. I tried to keep her gaze, but my courage failed. I could barely stand, but she suspended me almost off the floor by my chin and neck. "You will treat my sisters and me with respect. Is that clear?" With each word she spoke, my body quaked in fear.

I continued to stare at her, unable to speak or move.

She repeated herself, enunciating each word with absolute clarity. "Is that clear?"

"Y-yes, Mother." My voice was small, and tears had begun to slip from my eyes. I was about ready to piss myself; I was so scared.

She shrank down and released my face. Her wings slowly shrank away behind her, and then she sighed and ran her thumbs under my eyes, wiping away my tears.

I didn't wait for her to say anything further, instead turning with what little dignity I could muster and walking out the door, brushing past Boudka, her fist still hovering to knock.

Even as I stormed out, my anger twisted, tumbling over with a sinking feeling of guilt. I had transgressed our relationship in a way that probably would have left most people dead by her hand, and it was a testament to how much she loved me that she had kept her more chaotic nature in check.

Boudka's soft call barely registered as I walked away, lost in my own thoughts.

CHAPTER TWENTY

Aoife

My watch ticked over to eight-thirty as Morgan tapped on a large metal door. We were in an old disused side tunnel of one of the Harvard T stops. I hadn't realized it was even a door, it blended so well with the side of the tunnel. Not until she knocked. And I didn't think she'd knocked hard enough as the wait seemed exceptionally long, but she held up a hand when I said something, and moments later, there was the clang of a lock or crossbar, and the door slid to the side on well-oiled casters.

My eyes went wide, and I gasped audibly. Behind the door was a thing of beauty from my most twisted and, certainly, prurient nightmares. From the waist up, she had beautiful black skin and Nigerian features, but from the waist down, she was all snake with black pearlescent scales.

She smiled. "Hi, Dr. Reagan. We've been expecting you for some time now. I'm Alitash. It's good to meet you finally, Morgan. I've heard so much about you from Liz."

"Any of it good?" Morgan asked wryly.

"Mixed reviews," Alitash replied with an enigmatic smile, then she twisted around gracefully and began sliding down the hallway with a noise like a heavy sack dragged over sand. The torch she carried undulated with every move.

"People live down here?" I hissed to Morgan.

She smiled mysteriously but didn't answer.

"This is just the entrance tunnel, Dr. Reagan," Alitash

answered. "The rest of the facility is very different."

I rolled my eyes. "No one calls me doctor. That's my mother. Aoife's fine."

If Alitash heard me, she didn't acknowledge it.

The word facility brought up a host of imaginings from my youth of watching Sci-Fi shows, dark plots, cages, and secret government labs. Already this was giving me creepy Stephen King vibes.

Maybe two or three minutes later, Alitash came to a stop and faced the left-hand wall. With a wave of her hand, it vanished, revealing a watertight hatch.

"Holy shit," I whispered, and Alitash smiled.

She said, "We've had to make some improvements to our security of late, what with the Mayor and her nonsense."

"Oh really?" Morgan asked. "Like what?"

"Well, the illusory wall, for example. If someone is feeling around, they'll find the hatch, but otherwise, they'll just walk right by it. We've also added guards at the entrance." She gestured through the hatch.

Inside stood—I supposed stood was the right word—six lamia in black bullet-resistant vests with 9mm sidearms in cross-draw chest holsters, spears in their hands, and short swords and daggers at their hips. I half expected shotguns or assault rifles on their backs. As Alitash closed the hatch behind us, they banged their spears in unison. They were all gloriously female, or at least looked that way.

"They look so young," I commented as we passed, and one cracked an arch grin.

"Yes, we live a very long time. All of them are far older than you are, Aoife. It is okay if I call you Aoife, isn't it?"

"Yeah, sure," I murmured, still in awe of the world beyond the hatch. The walls were polished stone, tightly fitted together with master craftsmanship. They flanked a set of stairs that descended to a landing far below.

What looked like wireless cameras sat mounted high up the walls. They rotated to follow us as we passed, and I raised an eyebrow at the weird mix of ancient architecture and modern technology.

"The cameras are new as well," Alitash continued as we descended. "With Ms. Carson's return, we've managed to at least update our security somewhat, with more changes to come.

"Previously, we relied solely on secrecy, keeping out all others. But we won't close our eyes to the needs of the other people around Boston, especially those who are now being penned up by the current government. Your mother was quite persuasive about that particular point. We have contracted Ms. Déra to provide training for our troops. She's shown herself extremely adept at adjusting her Óṣeni fighting style to our specific body type."

"Speaking of my mother, is she here? Can I see her?" I asked, feeling a mixture of trepidation and hope.

Alitash turned back to me. "No, I'm sorry. She's attending a deposition with lawyers downtown. She'll be some time. She is attempting to convince the courts that she is still the same person she was, and that she's fully capable of returning to work. She's fighting the city ordinances as unconstitutional. She has a good case. But she did send her regards."

I looked at Alitash. "I don't understand. She got the sack? Why?"

"She's one of us now. Did no one tell you?"

My head swiveled slowly toward Morgan, who cringed slightly and then shrugged. "It wasn't my story to tell."

"No," I said, turning back to Alitash. "No one told me."

"I'm sorry if it comes as a shock, but she had suffered catastrophic neurological damage. Human science couldn't help her. This really was the only way."

I had a sudden pang of guilt. She'd been sick and then changed in a way I could scarcely understand. Cait had begged me to come to see her, and I'd just ignored it because of my own situation. In my own defense, it had been the same day I'd received my prognosis, but still, I felt like an awful daughter. And that was why, now, tears started to overflow my lashes. I wiped them away, but my steps came to a halting stop on the stairs.

Morgan touched my neck and shoulder with a cool hand

and said, "It'll be okay, I promise." Then she added, "She loves you."

I looked up at her. Gods, she was perceptive.

Morgan gave me a gentle squeeze around the shoulders and then took my hand in hers.

I looked down, startled, but I didn't pull away. It felt good. No, it felt really good, like 'butterflies in the stomach' good, like 'infatuated teenager' good. Which was bad. Not because she was a vampire but because I was sick.

We continued on.

At the bottom of the stairs, the floor leveled out into a short hallway before a pair of gigantic doors. The symbol of the ouroboros was carved above them, which I found fascinating. It was carved in an early-kingdom Egyptian style that predated it by almost a thousand years. Alitash made an offering gesture, and I pressed on the doors. They opened with surprisingly little effort. I looked back at Morgan, grinning wildly.

She said, "Okay, so that's kind of cool."

I kept grinning.

She looked me in the eyes and gave me one of those crooked, flirty smiles.

My insides went mushy, and I blushed and looked away, making her laugh. I had forgotten how much fun it was to just flirt.

Past the doors, the floor sloped for a bit before we entered another chamber. The ceiling was supported by black and grey marble columns made to appear wrapped by marble serpents. Along the walls were sculptures set within deep alcoves presenting lamia doing everyday work.

"Those are to remind us of where we come from," Alitash said.

I nodded, and Morgan shrugged in an 'okay, I guess we're getting the nickel tour' kind of way, then we pressed on, finally reaching a large temple lined with columns. Several lamia slithered around stacking boxes of various supplies, mostly medical.

The room itself was amazing. At one end was a raised dais

beyond which was a dark passage. In its entirety, it was lit by, of all things, moonlight that gleamed off the walls and columns, giving the entire place a magical glow.

"Okay," I said with a gleeful laugh as I stared at the ceiling. "That's not just kinda cool. That's awesome."

"Yeah," Morgan agreed, watching clouds pass in front of the crescent moon above, then asked of Alitash, "It's magical, isn't it?"

"Yes, just a simple spell, but we like it, so we keep it. We've started updating the lighting to more modern options everywhere else, though, in preparation."

Morgan and I looked at each other and then said at once, "Preparation for what?"

"The battles to come," Alitash said smoothly, without even a hint of angst or concern. "All is not well in the world, you know."

I snorted. *No shit, that was an understatement.*

"Well, this is interesting," Morgan said as a Lamia carrying a heavy-looking crate nearly slithered over her and disappeared down a side hallway with a passing, "Sorry!" over her shoulder.

"I guess we caught them unloading the truck," I joked, one eyebrow arched in amusement.

Morgan chuckled. "What do you think is in those crates?"

"Snacks," I retorted with a mischievous glint in my eye. "Never have an underground compound without snacks."

"Or invade a bird sanctuary," Morgan joked.

I kept the joke running. "That's only if your Ya'll Qaeda."

Alitash turned an annoyed glance at us. "They're medical supplies and food."

"So, snacks," Morgan confirmed wryly, and I laughed even harder, wanting just to kiss this woman and get it over with, if for no other reason than her sense of humor. Gods, it was grand.

Alitash just rolled her eyes. "Do come along, *children.*"

I looked at Morgan as we followed. "Ooh, we're in trouble now."

Morgan stifled a chuckle, but her shoulders shook.

Alitash stopped, then, and turned back to us. "Mother Lamia would like to talk to you, Aoife, when you have some time."

"Honestly," I said, swallowing hard. "I really just want to talk to Bian first."

She frowned at that but nodded. "It is, of course, your prerogative."

I looked at Morgan, suddenly feeling a little nervous.

"It's okay," she said, placing a hand on my shoulder. "Bian's a friend, and I'm here. Whatever you want to do."

I suddenly felt a little off balance, emotionally, that is. I wasn't the domineering alpha type, but Morgan's constant prodding and gentle support were starting to make me feel small. Or maybe it was just my insecurity making me feel that way, and Morgan was reacting to that. But regardless, I felt out of my depth, a little lost and alone.

I took Morgan's hand in a tight grip. "Can Morgan come with me?"

"Of course," Alitash replied and slithered on past the dais and down the back passageway, the two of us in tow.

I turned to Morgan as we followed, "Who's Bian again?"

Morgan smiled. "A ninety-foot-long Naga. Liz says you'll like her. Which reminds me, how long have you two known each other?"

"Liz and me? Sixteen years. She took me to Ireland when Marcella split up Cait and me. I wouldn't call her a friend, more like an aunt. We were never mates or anything, but she was nice and kind of raised me until I was eighteen, whereupon she promptly took me to my first lesbian bar.

"She left a few months later, fucking off to London and, I think, Turkey at one point. But she did stop in from time to time. If Uncle Donny was on a bender, she would help me manage him."

I must have frowned or something because Morgan said, "Manage your Uncle Donny?"

I sighed. "He was a drunk. Sometimes he got so pissed that I had to take him in for alcohol poisoning."

"And he?" She prodded.

"Died last year," I finished sadly. "Liver failure. It was awful to watch. I don't want to talk about it. Despite his foibles, I still loved him."

Morgan nodded.

I gave her a questioning look. "I gather that you and Liz don't get along?"

Morgan shook her head. "No, not really. It's not that I don't like her or that I'm jealous or anything. Cait and I resolved our feelings for each other and let them go." She paused for a minute, then added. "That Liz doesn't like *me* is probably fairer to say."

"She's a vampire, Morgan," I said, as if it explained it all, then remembered who I was talking to. "Sorry."

Morgan chuckled. "It's okay, but I don't really know what you mean by that."

I stopped, still holding Morgan's hand, and she turned to me. I looked her in the eye. "She trusts you way more than you think to have me live with you, especially for protection. Vampires are extremely protective and possessive of the people they love. I call it the Dracula syndrome."

Morgan snorted a laugh.

"No, seriously," I continued, "it's how I know that Bram Stoker really did know a real vampire. Love, real love, for a vampire, is an almost obsessive thing. I don't know why. Like Marcella told you, they—you just love differently. And while Liz is usually more relaxed than most, I've borne the brunt of it before. She had a habit of scaring off my girlfriends." I could see the wheels turning in her head. "So, if she thought it was a good idea for you to do this, she has a much higher opinion of you than you can imagine."

Morgan seemed to consider all that. "Then why is she always a bitch to me?"

I shook my head. "I don't know. It probably has something to do with my sister."

"Your sister?"

"Everything is about Cait, Morgan, or haven't you noticed? She's an attention whore. She always has been, even before we were separated. It's just how she's wired." It was harsh, but I didn't care, and it was good to finally say it, despite the scowl Morgan gave me.

I thought maybe that would put her off, but she didn't let go of my hand, so I continued.

"When we were kids, she was always calling attention to things that drew my parents away from my accomplishments. One year, I drilled three tries to seal our high-school rugby championship, but *no*, Cait went on and on about taking first place in her fucking harp competition, and my killer sportsmanship took second place, as always. It drove me mad."

Morgan raised an eyebrow. "Cait plays the harp? I'd like to hear that."

I scowled at her, and she laughed. "I'm fucking with you, Aoife. That kind of competition among siblings is normal. Try being ten years older than your sister. Now that's maddening."

I scowled again, but she just pulled me in, chuckling and putting an arm around my shoulder.

"Oh, get off," I said half-heartedly, but I couldn't help but laugh.

I spent the next few minutes of the walk explaining the finer points of rugby football to Morgan as we traversed the halls. To her credit, she seemed to catch on quickly. Then she asked if I still played.

"On occasion. Maybe we can find a group around here sometime."

She nodded and smiled, but it didn't reach her eyes, and it was all I could do not to break down and bawl right on the spot. *Fuck, this sucks.*

The facility, as Alitash had put it, was positively sprawling, and the further from the temple we got, the newer the walls looked and the wider the corridors. We rounded a final bend and were met with a bright blast of light emanating from a room with an open door.

Alitash stopped on the far side, pulling her considerable bulk around and motioning us into a large infirmary and laboratory space, brightly lit by harsh white LED lights. In one corner sat a large containment cell of thick bullet-resistant glass, which I thought was odd. But it was the chief occupant of the infirmary that struck me. Bian, I assumed.

She was breathtaking, at least ninety or a hundred feet long, her green scales glimmering beautifully in the light. Her snake body partially coiled under her as she gazed into a microscope. On the lab bench next to her sat five vials of blue liquid like something out of a sci-fi movie. Five women lay on gurneys, all in soft linen gowns, the mermaids from the ship. They all appeared to be of Chinese descent and were extremely quiet, none of them speaking at all, just watching us as we walked in. They all looked so sad.

"Bian, your appointment is here," Alitash called and slithered off.

Bian held up a finger. "Grab a seat on the open gurney, Aoife. I'll be right with you."

I started toward that direction, but I was drawn away when I looked into the eyes of the oldest of the women on the gurneys. She looked so haunted and terrified. I walked over to her and spoke in Chinese.

"Can you understand me?"

Some of the terror left her eyes as she nodded, and I saw a touch of relief there, as if maybe, just maybe, there might be some way she could understand what was happening.

"You speak Chinese?" Bian asked, turning abruptly from her microscope and jostling it, almost knocking it over.

"Yeah. Some. What's wrong with them?"

Bian's face and chest were covered with tiny scales giving it an almost skin-like appearance. She frowned briefly. "In an effort to curtail their charming song, someone cut out their vocal cords. All they had to do was wear baffles. They didn't have to mutilate them."

I was aghast. "Oh, Gods, that's horrific."

"Yes, and I'm glad you're here. They've been pretty compliant, but I don't speak Chinese, and they don't speak Vietnamese, Thai, or HMong. I've tried to pantomime some ideas, but I'm not sure I'm getting through to them. I even tried Google translate, but they just stare at me when I show them the translations."

I laughed, and Bian glowered at me.

"Sorry," I apologized. "Google translate is great for going from any language to English but not so much the other way. And it's worse going from most Asian languages to just about every other Asian language."

I glanced over, Morgan was leaning against the wall, preternaturally still, but her eyes were on me. I shrugged my shoulders in a silent 'what' gesture, and she just smirked, but she kept watching me, her emerald eyes burning my back as I turned away.

"So, I take it you're Bian. This is Morgan Kennedy, and I'm Aoife Reagan."

"Oh, sorry, where are my manners?" Bian said with a touch of sibilant irritation in her voice. "I've been so busy." Bian introduced herself to Morgan.

I stepped back to the bed of the oldest mermaid. "Can you read and write?" I asked.

The mermaid shook her head.

I said as gently as I could, given my limited command of the language, "That is Bian. She is going to help you."

Through me, Bian told them, "We're going to make you well and then take you to stay with other mermaids." At least, I hoped that was what I was saying, and I didn't know the word for mermaid, so I just pointed at her and pantomimed a fish swimming. She seemed to get it, though, because she threw her arms around me, and, through a whisper, I heard her thank me, over and over in Mandarin.

"What are you going to do to them?" I asked the naga.

Bian sighed. "For years, Marcella and I have worked on a serum to help them." She gestured to the vials. "We almost had it perfected when Carter Reese raided my lab in Hockamock. Fortunately, your sister recovered some of it."

"With help," Morgan commented from her spot against the wall, waving her hand.

"You don't get points for that, Detective Kennedy. You almost got them all—" Bian started, but I interrupted.

"No. We're not going to talk about that," I said a little more forcefully than I meant to. "Her sister was in danger. I'd kill a brick for Cait. So let that go."

Bian snapped her jaws shut, and Morgan looked at me strangely in a way I couldn't read.

"Yes, with help," Bian admitted, finally. "Morgan did put her life in danger, and it made a difference as I understand it."

"Thank you," I said flatly.

"Anyway, at this point, with Mother Lamia's help, it's probably as much magic potion as formula now, but we think it will work."

I hopped up on the gurney she had directed me to and did the mental math. "Wait, they have cancer. Is that what this is? A cure for cancer?"

"No. We tried to do that, and the results were less than ideal. Instead, we've created something specific to the mermaid physiology, specifically an enhancement to their immune systems, allowing it to kill the cancerous cells more readily. It's worked on samples, but we don't know if it will work on them."

"Is it dangerous?" I asked, starting to understand something that I didn't like the sound of.

"I hope not, but I can't be sure. The tumors in some of these women have spread across their systems. I'm afraid that the strain on their bodies will kill them."

"And if they don't get it?" I asked quietly, knowing the answer.

"Then they die," Bian said flatly and without inflection, almost coldly. "Slowly, painfully, and horribly. And I need your help to explain that. If you don't mind, that is."

I nodded solemnly, suddenly feeling a tremendous weight, and I wished Cait were here. I also felt the fast-falling hammer of misery landing on me.

Morgan stepped over to the gurney with an expression that told me she understood exactly what had just happened. I'd found my magic bullet, but it wouldn't work on me. It was both heartening for the women around me and infinitely depressing.

I nodded to her, wiping my eyes. The least I could do was help these women. So, before having Bian examine me, I walked around to each of the mermaids and explained as best I could what was about to happen. To the last one, they agreed to take the risk. I translated for Bian.

"It'll be a bit before I'm ready to administer the serum, so tell me, what brings you to me? Morgan wasn't clear on the phone."

I looked her dead in the eye. "I'm dying of cancer."

CHAPTER TWENTY-ONE
Weyna

After the fight with my mother, sleep was slow in coming. The argument still turned over in my racing thoughts until, succumbing to fatigue around midnight, I finally drifted off. By morning, I was back in comfortable form on the training ground, drilling with Zilly and working to learn and hone my skills in the Valtárí forms.

I had expected learning to fight back-to-back with a much larger fighter like Zilly to be a challenge for both of us, but, truthfully, it was pitifully easy, and by the middle of the sixth day, we were sparring with the other Valtárí, and we were holding our own. Better than, really. Finally, after two more weeks of practice and sparring, we had our first victory.

Zilly and I developed a smooth rhythm, easily anticipating each other's moves. When she went high, I went low. And when she went low, I used my smaller form and swifter movements to cover her in a non-traditional fashion. Against the other Valtárí, I was at a significant reach disadvantage, but I was able to adjust the combat forms to compensate. Moving out of the back-to-back fight to push back assailants, and yet always being back in proper form to turn and move at the right moments. In the end, I was just much quicker than the larger women, and it threw off the other Valtárí with whom we sparred. I left several of them bruised and bloodied from sharp whacks of my practice blades.

There was something intimate about the way we fought

together that sometimes made my pulse quicken, not just from the adrenaline but the feel of Zilly's back against mine and the way I came to know every inch of it, responding to the slightest twitch of her muscles, and her to mine. During training, it was never an issue, but afterward, when we broke up, I often came away feeling flustered and frustrated.

We had to train with different Valtárí partners from time to time, getting to know how they fought and moved and separating the nuances of the individual from the overall combat style. I often watched Zilly when it was her turn with someone else. She wasn't as stately or statuesque as Saya. On the contrary, Zilly was a little curvier than the others, and it accentuated the lines of her body as she dodged, moved, and struck. I tried not to stare all the time, but it was difficult not to. And every day we trained together, it became harder for me to deny that I was growing really fond of her in a way that had nothing to do with her combat skills or professionalism.

We were the last two in the bathing area late one night, lounging around and enjoying the late summer breeze. She sat in the water, and I lay on the stones around the edge, staring past the canopy into the starry sky. As we talked about nothing in particular, I bitched about a kink in the side of my neck I'd had for days. Zilly abruptly sloshed over and drew out of the water, straddling me at the waist, effectively pinning me to the rocks.

"Here, let me," she said and began rubbing my neck and shoulder.

I looked into her eyes. Her black irises, threaded with stria in beautiful silver and gray, glinted in the faelight. We were so close I could feel her breath on my face, and I licked my lips, almost certain that she was about to kiss me. But then she cleared her throat, asked how my neck was, and dragged herself away and back to the barracks, leaving my heart racing and my breath coming in almost heaving gasps of foiled anticipation.

I lay awake in bed that night for quite a while, feeling butterflies dancing in my stomach and trying not to think of kissing Zilly or the burgeoning guilt in my chest over Boudka because of it.

During the following afternoon sparring practice, I'd just swept the legs of one of my sisters, Megana, and was about to deliver the killing blow when I was called out.

"Weyna!" Óbin shouted, halting our sparring practice.

"Aww, Óbin," I grumped good-naturedly. "I had Megana down. For the first time, even."

Megana threw a hand to her forehead melodramatically and gave an exaggerated swoon. "Saved by my hero, the mighty Óbin."

"Yes, well, you'll have to kill her later, Weyna. I need you to come with me."

I leaned heavily against Zilly and pantomimed a sigh of misery. "Save me, Zilly," I joked before reaching down a hand to haul Megana up off the ground with a light grunt. "You've been eating too much, Meg."

The joke elicited a laugh from everyone, and she rolled her eyes. "More like it's your tiny physique."

I stuck out my tongue at her amid more laughter from our group. When I turned back, Zilly was looking down at me with her beautiful, gentle smile, and my heart skipped a beat as a hot flush ran up my chest, neck, and face like a wave of fire. She blushed, too, and we both looked away.

A shiver ran down my spine, and I felt Zilly's eyes on my backside as I stowed my practice blades in the rack and trotted over to Óbin.

"Yes, Kóhen? What can I do for you?"

Óbin gave me a sly look and waggled her eyebrows. "Magic training. Grab a set of proper weapons, and come on."

"Real weapons?"

"Mmhmm."

I did as she asked, wondering what we needed real blades for if it was to be magic training, but then I found out as I jogged to catch up to her longer strides. We were leaving the fort.

"So," She asked as we picked our way through the woods on the western side of the valley until we reached a large clearing. "How long are you going to pine for your Valtárí partner?"

"What?" I sputtered. "What are you talking about?"

"You two really should just fuck and get it over with, honestly, Weyna."

"Óbin!" I protested. "Really?"

Óbin laughed and gave me an arch smile. "What? Everyone sees how you two look at each other. It's obvious. And it's not *that* uncommon. That kind of combat is intimate. You have each other's lives in your hands. And Zilly's gorgeous. So don't deny it."

"Can we talk about something else?" I griped. Not that she was wrong. Obviously, she was dead on. I had it for Zilly pretty badly, and I knew it. But I loved Boudka, and I wouldn't ruin what we had. Assuming we had anything, of course, because it wasn't like she was visiting often, or at all for that matter, and I wondered what I'd done this time to deserve the silent treatment.

"Yes, we can. Come, sit."

Óbin led us to a clearing with a small circular wooden deck covered by a plain ruddy-brown rug of woven grass. She sat down on one side of the deck and tapped the other side like she was asking a dog to sit.

I shook my head but sat. "Now what?"

"So, your mother told me about your challenges mastering your talent."

I sighed. "What, did she seek you out and tattle on me?"

"No. I sought her out and asked. I wanted to get an understanding to see if I could help you." She studied me for a moment. "Answer me this, are you good at mathematics?"

I snorted. "No. I'm terrible."

Óbin held out her hand. I felt the tug of magic and watched as she easily summoned a small ball of blue flame that danced and circled around her fingers. Óbin smiled at me. "So am I. I don't use maths to control my magic. I can't even count right half the time. It's not that I don't understand the concept of what numbers are. I just struggle to put them together."

My mood brightened as she spoke, and I realized she was describing exactly what I'd been struggling with. My mother's approach to Shaddani magic involved cold calculation and specific ratios of force applied in a lattice of magical threads. It took a strong, calculating mind to manage. I couldn't do the simplest word problems, let alone understand the relativistic forces as she did. Bethadi magic was similar, which was why their efforts to teach me, too, had come to no avail, of course.

"It's a mental divergence, Weyna. We're just wired differently. So, I'm going to show you how I did what I just did, okay?"

The very idea that I might be able to handle my own magic with some facility made me almost giddy, but then I looked around and sobered. "We're all the way out here in case I blow us up, aren't we?"

Óbin laughed and nodded. "Yes. I'm not worried. But your mother has the insane idea that this is a terrible way to teach you. She thinks that you'll split an atom or something."

"What's an atom?" I asked, my expression puzzled.

"Nevermind, magic doesn't work that way, anyhow. Now, this will be the easiest magic lesson you've ever had."

I raised a skeptical eyebrow. "Okay."

"I want you to create a little ball of fire like I just did, right between us."

I closed my eyes and began to concentrate, but Óbin's hand shot out and grabbed my own.

"Not like that. Don't focus. Just relax and observe the tarzhi. See how they move."

I did as she asked, relaxing and shifting my perception. Out here, away from the camp and the myriad magics used by its occupants, the threads of light and Dark-Fae magic flowed freely from the open portals to the northeast, undisturbed by the chaotic churning and turbulence of static magical effects—Aine's tent specifically. From the ground, thick blankets of green and turquoise threads flowed upward, Earth magic that ultimately broke into tiny little spinning spirals, just like the ones on my mother's rugs, wrapping around and warping the paths of purples, blues, golds, and whites. The effect was breathtaking and instantly calming.

"Don't try to influence them. Just watch for a minute." She still had a hold of my hand, and she adjusted her grip, sliding her fingers to my wrist. "Now spread your fingers. I want you to feel the magic. There's a buzz, a movement, a frequency that sings. Do you hear it?"

Hear it? All I heard was the birds, and I tried to concentrate.

"Stop, Weyna. Relax and let it come to you."

I took a deep, steadying breath, allowing all my muscles to drift. My thoughts became unfocused, and a high-pitched, tinkling sound like the colliding of glass shards sang in my head. The music, if I could call it that, drew me into an almost dreamy state, and my voice sounded far away. "It sounds like wind through chimes almost."

"Yes," Óbin responded. "Feel their essence. Find a thread, any thread, but make certain it is a Shaddani thread, and bring it to your fingers."

"How?"

"Feel it. It wants to obey; you just need to let it." She still had a hold of my hand, and she'd raised it, fingers pointed loosely to the sky. "Don't force it or concentrate. Feel it. Let your talent call to it."

I allowed my thoughts to flow, not stopping on any particular one. Something—something I could only describe as feeling like a presence in my chest grew, expanding throughout the core of my body from my abdomen to my throat. It seemed to be waiting. As I relaxed even further, being aware but focusing on nothing, the tarzhi drew around me unbidden, swirling ever-tightening circles. I panicked for a second, and the threads flew apart, returning to the flow of magic.

"What is that?" I asked, opening my eyes.

Óbin laughed with excitement. "That's your magic—*your* magic. Call it your power if you like. But it's not Shaddani, Bethadi, or Earth. It's pure, unspilt, untainted, and alive. It is also uniquely you. Everyone has it in some amount. It's part of our souls. Now, relax and try again. This time, feel it and hold it. Concentrate on your magic, not on the tarzhi. Don't look for it. Feel it."

I took a deep, slow, cleansing breath. Sweat beaded on my head, chest and dripping down my arms, but I ignored it. Now that I knew what it felt like, returning to that state was almost simple. I let my feelings flow, quickly tuning back into that magical music. I allowed that part of me, indescribable and yet undeniably me, my core or my soul, perhaps, to reach out, and I found that with just the feeling of intention, not even actual thought, I could control it.

I allowed my attention to drift to a blue thread, midnight and glimmering like spider silk on top of the water. The thread stopped moving, then it arced toward my fingers, rolling into a tiny shimmering ball of blue light. More threads gathered as I gently let the pull increase slowly.

Somehow, instinctively I knew that I could have pulled in tremendous power right then. I could have gathered everything around me and bent it to my will with ease, not by forcing it but by feeling my way through it.

"Open your eyes," Óbin said softly.

My lids lifted and were met with a small ball of blue fire that hovered perfectly still between my fingers, hot and burning but controlled. I looked at her in surprise, and even as I did so, some instinctive part of me held the little ball of fire perfectly still. A single ecstatic tear flowed down my cheek.

Óbin grinned widely at my success. "Isn't that so much easier than fucking mathematics?"

CHAPTER TWENTY-TWO

Aoife

"Please come with me," Alitash said as we returned to the temple area, my mood much changed-- ruined, really.

It wasn't that Bian hadn't actually had options. When they'd created the original serum, they'd thought they'd had success, so much so that they started a trial run with two terminal patients at Margaret Chastity. But they'd been wrong in the end. All they'd succeeded in doing was turning a young girl into a werewolf, whom they'd subsequently had to kill because of some stupid werewolf rule, and an adult male into a vampire, Marcella's friend, whom she'd had to kill because he'd gone off his rocker. We didn't need a serum for that. If I wanted either of those options, I could just ask someone—or maybe start a fistfight with Carlos.

"Where are we going?" I asked.

Alitash held out a hand. "Come along. Mother Lamia would like to speak with you, and—given your circumstances, I think you should talk to her."

I pursed my lips and looked at Morgan.

"Just you, I'm afraid," Alitash said in answer to the latent question in my eyes.

Morgan nodded to me. "It'll be okay. I'll just wait here."

I pressed my lips together, suddenly feeling even worse than when we'd arrived, not just small, but afraid. The shock and, well, the awe of the place and the people in it had worn off, and I'd come to realize that I was the only human here. It was isolating. But, I hunkered my shoulders and took Alitash's hand, finding it surprisingly warm.

"Do you feel that?" She asked as we moved further down the hallway.

"Yes," I said. There was something in the air, something cool and refreshing. The further we went, the more prevalent it became. It took me a few minutes to realize that what I was feeling wasn't a breeze on my skin, but something inside me, something powerful and disorienting.

"What is that?" I asked as a shiver of gooseflesh ran up my arms.

Alitash gave me an arch grin. "Look at your arms."

I did as she asked and gasped. "What the hell?"

"It's not permanent. It's magic. Your body is responding to it."

What I'd thought were goosebumps popping out on my skin were fucking scales, midnight-blue scales. Abruptly, my back jerked in a painless spasm and popped strangely. "Oh, Gods, what's happening?" I shrieked. "Am I becoming one of you?"

Alitash squeezed my hand, and her other arm shot out, grabbing mine. "No. Not really. You're a shifter by nature, Dark-Fae, like your sister. During the ritual that saved Róisín, she transformed both herself and Elizabeth Medlyn fully. It was quite a surprise, to be sure. How much has anyone told you about your mother? Your *other* mother?"

I shook my head. "Nothing. Carlos said something about a goddess but nothing else."

"Relax and feel the flow of the magic. It will not hurt you, nor will it change you permanently, I promise." Alitash's words were calm and soothing, and her demeanor helped steady my nerves. She didn't push or pull, simply holding my hand and waiting. "Let it wash through you. Focus on yourself."

My first urge was to run, and I pulled my hand away. Alitash didn't resist. Then I took a step back. She didn't follow, either.

"There's no need to run. Just focus on yourself," Alitash said again, her voice still quiet and gentle, coaxing. "Simply think about who you actually are, remind yourself of what you look like, in the mirror perhaps."

I did as she suggested, closing my eyes and reminding myself of how I looked while brushing my teeth that afternoon. The weird gooseflesh feeling settled away. I looked down, and my arms and hands looked normal. I shiver ran down my back, and the smell of grass and loamy earth filled my nose and mouth.

"Come inside, child," a raspy voice like sand over glass called from down the hall. "No one will harm you here."

The voice was resonant, filling my head, devouring my thoughts, and making me feel the need to see from where it originated. It wasn't like vampire glamour. I felt completely different. It wasn't an actual compulsion, more of a relaxation of my fears and a distracting pull, but not a draining or smothering of my will. So, I chose to follow it. It wasn't just the curiosity. There was something implicit in the promise of safety, something real that I couldn't put my finger on. It spoke to my very soul, like some kind of pact. And I *knew* at that moment that I would be unharmed.

"Your mother and I have an arrangement," the voice said as I followed it and rounded into a chamber decorated in fabulous frescoes, showing scenes from all of history.

I felt something else, a sameness, a familiar presence. "Cait's been here," I whispered to the ancient-looking lamia reclining in a huge bowl of a chair.

She smiled genteelly at me and offered me the large papasan-like bowl across from her, replete with massive pillows.

I sat, Alitash and the temple and even Morgan totally forgotten.

"Mother Lamia?"

The old lamia sat up a bit then performed an odd bowing gesture, her hands out. "In the flesh, as they say. Though not likely for long."

I tilted my head. "You're dying." It wasn't a question. Just something I knew somehow, not just from her words either. I could feel it, like a ragged wetness dragging at her insides.

"Even lamia do not live forever. And my time is almost here. A few days away. I go to join my children."

I knew the story as well as any scholar of the classics, and I understood what she meant. "Ας ξεκουραστείς καλά," I said. 'May you rest well.'

"και σε ευχαριστώ," she replied and adjusted slightly with a pained expression. "Arthritis is a bitch," she laughed and gave me an agonized smirk. "We're not here to talk about me. Tell me about you. How are you feeling?"

"Are you putting me on the couch?"

"I am," she replied with a soft smile that reached her watery eyes. "So, tell me."

"I'm angry. I'm trying not to be, but I am. I don't want to die. But I don't want to be a vampire or a werewolf or anything but human."

She gave a hoarse cackle. "Aoife, you're not human now. You're Sidhe, Dark-Fae, a faerie, barely human at all."

I blinked. "What do you mean?"

"Your DNA is mostly Fae, probably just human enough to look okay in a DNA analysis, but you are far from human. You are the daughter of The Morrigan. More than that, you are tied to her soul. When she fades, you will become her successor. There's nothing you can do to stop that."

"So you're saying I should become a vampire. That doesn't sound like the life I want. I've watched—"

"Oh, no, of course not. But your future is far from over. Death is never the end, especially for one such as you, or your sister. But you are different from her in almost every way that counts. Three there must be, Aoife. One who reigns, one who battles, and one who secures the crown. That is your legacy. And, as much as you may feel it is not your place, you must reign. And I do not envy you that."

"How am I supposed to reign from the grave? And what am I to reign?" I demanded, my voice rising, irritated at her proclamations, which completely ignored my impending demise.

"Young one," Mother Lamia snapped sharply, then her

voice softened. "This I know. You must reign. How you make that happen will be up to you. But you will find that the pragmatic often forces us to make hard choices."

She coughed once more, a wracking, hacking thing that made my chest hurt to listen to. I realized that she was missing a few scales, and most of her tale section was covered in flakes of dead skin.

"For what it's worth," I said solemnly, "I'm sorry that you are sick."

"Whatever for? Death is the ultimate end of life. Even for Morgan or Marcella, or Elizabeth, one day, their time will come. Even vampires have an end. No one escapes the call of death, not even gods and goddesses. But, if we are lucky, for a time, we will be remembered and leave behind a legacy."

I paused for a moment, pondering the fate of the Chinese sailors on the ship, wondering what legacy they might have left, which set my mind on a different track. "What do you know about the Akkorokamui?"

Mother Lamia's face turned dark then, and her eyes grew narrow and penetrating. "She is a broken thing of a long bygone era, much as I am. Unlike me, she has no children to carry on traditions and build upon what she has wrought. She is bitter. Take care with that one, for she is old and powerful and not to be trifled with. But she will never be as powerful as you can be."

I didn't feel particularly powerful at the moment, so I filed that away for another time. "Do you know what she looks like? Or how I might find her?"

"You already know what she looks like. Read the stories. They will tell you. But to find her, you must remember, she is a creature of the deep, moving beneath things. She is also highly intelligent, so expect anything from her."

I nodded. "I understand."

"Now, I wish I could show you more of what you must know, but I simply haven't the stamina anymore. But I will leave you with one last tidbit you might find useful."

I raised an eyebrow. "And what's that?"

"That feeling you have. The magic you feel even now

blowing through your soul, it is a part of the very heart of you. It is also the source of your illness." Mother Lamia let out another horrid cough and slumped down quietly in her chair.

I stared at her, utterly confused. "Wait, how is this connected to my cancer?"

"The first time Cait touched the tablets, she connected to you. Do you not remember?"

My eyes flew wide. I *did* remember. It was a late night around Halloween last year. I had thought I heard Cait calling my name, and I'd had a horrible headache. I'd blown it off at the time as stress and the imaginings of an overtired and overworked mind.

"Mother Darkness," she wheezed, "used that opportunity to try to corrupt Cait. She failed, but she also used Cait's link to you to try and extinguish your flame. Did you think it a coincidence that you were only recently diagnosed with cancer —right after the gate opened?"

I sat there in silence, stunned as she worked to recover her breath. Then she said, "I have a question. Are you quite resigned to your own death?"

I shrugged. "So far, no one has offered me an acceptable alternative, so yeah, I guess so. I'm pretty much okay with it."

Mother Lamia frowned. "I suspected that might be the case. In that event, there is an alternative that, at least, will help someone else. Would that interest you?"

I looked at her askance. "I suppose so. I mean, I'm not much use to anyone in the ground." I really wasn't liking this morbid conversation. I had been avoiding thinking about the final disposition of my remains. But I didn't want to leave that to Cait or, worse yet, Morgan in the event that Cait didn't wake up in time, or at all. So, I sat and listened to Mother Lamia's proposal.

Mother Lamia sipped at her tea. "There is one here, Déra. She is in pain. The love of her life, Umbrá, has died. However, her soul, and all that she was, is encased in a small creature. If that creature is introduced into a human body, a dead one, it will use that body as material to bring her back to life. Déra will not ask you. Her people believe that the dead are

184

sacrosanct and should be left to rot in the earth to provide life for the next generation, but she is torn—"

"That's fine," I whispered, quickly writing the last line on this conversation.

"Déra will be very happy to hear it." She said, then slumped down once more. "I'm sorry. I must rest now."

"Thank you for your time," I responded.

She gave a wan smile laden with deep pain. "You're much more polite than your sister. That is good. She is meant for battle. You are meant for more. Now, go. Perhaps we will see each other in another life."

"Yes, Mother Lamia," I said. Then, on impulse, after wiggling from the awkward seat, I approached her and bent down as close as I could get, and opened my arms. She pulled me into a gentle, brief hug, then released me and waved me away.

"Go, child," she choked out. "Go."

I left the room, feeling both deeply disturbed and a weird sense of wonder. As I walked down the hall, I thought I heard the whisper of her voice. "I do not envy your coming choices, Aoife Aisling Reagan."

I paused at that, listening for more, but I only caught the soft sounds of my breathing, and another of Mother Lamia's coughing fits.

CHAPTER TWENTY-THREE

Weyna

"Your mother is distraught," Badb said a few days later while we both sat on a bench at the edge of the sparring circle. "She thinks you hate her."

A sigh welled from my chest. "Of course, I don't hate her. I love her, Aunt Badb, but why can't she accept that I've chosen a different path? For four years, she's treated me like a servant and a student, but I've never been her daughter." I bent over and sunk my fingers into the ground, gathering a handful of dust, gritty and real under my clammy palms. My turn in the circle was coming up.

Badb waved her hand reflexively, engaged in battle with a small fly that for some time now had refused to leave her be. Finally, in exasperation, she eradicated the thing with a spark of magic, watching it drop to the ground. "You bear her blood, her legacy. You're her only child, and yet, you are as much a mirror to me as you are to her, and that grates on her. But mostly, it's fear. Fear of losing you. And the guilt she carries— she was the last queen of Shaddan. When our world fell, she was on the throne. It's a weighty burden. So, try to remember, Weyna, everyone you encounter is facing a battle of their own, hidden and secret, some more than one. Even your mother. Especially your mother."

I looked up at her then, curiosity edging my voice along with a bit of playfulness. "So, what's your secret battle?"

I hadn't expected her to answer, but a cryptic and wan ghost of a smile haunted her lips, and then to my surprise, she spoke, sounding almost sad. "Jealousy."

I puzzled that over in my head, trying to make sense of it. "What could you possibly be jealous of? Even among the rest of us, you're peerless in battle. Your sisters love you. Certainly more than they do me."

Badb put a finger to my lips. "Hold your tongue unless you've tasted the truth, child. Your mother loves you more than anything, even me. You'd do well not to forget that."

I nodded and changed the subject, not liking the feeling that the current line of discussion was giving me. "There's a rumor that you have a family here, somewhere to the south. Did you know that?"

A laugh, full of genuine amusement, erupted from Badb. "A lover, yes. A family? Not quite." Her laughter turned into roars of mirth but was cut short as Óbin signaled me. "It's our turn now."

As Aunt Badb sauntered past me on the way to the sparring circle, a realization hit me, leaving me suddenly filled with anxiety and not a little excitement. She was my opponent. "A challenge?" I asked, the chill of fear seeping into my voice.

The question pulled a playful smile onto her lips. "Would you like it to be?"

I shrugged off my fears. This was the chance of a lifetime. "Sure."

A predatory grin, sprinkled with a bit of amusement, spread across Badb's face. "Choose your stakes, challenger."

"If I win, I get a set of leathers like yours." I had always been enamored by her Shaddani armor, the intricate design, the flexibility, and the protective coverage it provided. But it was the boots, rising just over her knees and beautifully wrapped, that I coveted the most. They were simply spectacular, and I thought they might look rather fetching on me.

She chuckled. "In your dreams, girl. And if I win?"

I bowed. "If you win," which she surely would, "I will mend things with Mother."

She hefted a pair of bóllom, glanced at me with a wicked

grin, and for a moment, my heart skipped a beat, believing she'd actually select live weapons for this, but she set them back on the rack and picked up a pair of African Blackwood practice swords. "I accept the stakes. As the challenged, I choose practice blades. You may select any style of practice weapon as suits you. I will take these."

"The limits?" I called, following the proper Shaddani dueling form.

She cocked her hip in a show of confidence and, if I was honest, arrogance. "Three strikes to the torso or head wins, or of course, unconsciousness. Let's not make this to the death if that's alright with you, Weyna."

"Thanks for that," I said wryly and chuckled.

Óbin was standing in the circle, looking bored. "Are you done?"

"Indeed," my aunt said and bowed to me.

I returned it. "Ready."

Óbin raised her arm and dropped it. "Begin."

The quick shushing of dust, bare feet, and shoe leather sounded as Badb and I circled each other, both of us grinning with excitement. I wasn't confused about my odds here, and no one was taking bets, but quite the assembly of women had surrounded the ring to watch. My aunt's motions were smooth, fluid, and graceful, rivaling even those of us in the Valtárí. Of course, the upside of this pairing was that no one expected me to win, so I had nothing to lose. It was just a spot of fun.

Badb darted forward, launching a series of high and low swings, all in a pattern I recognized, and I blocked them all deftly. At the end of the series, she swapped her attack. Instead of swinging high from the right, she brought her left blade in toward my head, followed by a lightning-fast jab at my torso. I shoved both blades out to my left and spun, snapping a leg toward her ribs, but she was the swifter of us and parried the blow with one arm. I dropped and ducked on the recover, narrowly avoiding a nasty shot that might have whacked me in the head.

"Alright now," I said as we moved apart, the thrill of the

fight sparking between us. "Let's try not to brain each other."

She laughed. "Not to worry, sister's daughter, I won't hurt you too badly."

I chuckled in return, my confidence starting to build. "Oh, really?"

I darted in, executing a high-low combination that should have left her right side open for a strike, but in the midst of it, she stepped into a blow to block me at the forearm and spun.

Only a swift backward dodge of my upper body kept her from elbowing me in the nose. As it was, I almost fell. Almost. I bent backward, nearly all the way over, like a willow, and turned the off-balance scramble into a swift recovery by dropping one blade, flipping, and pivoting onto my now empty left hand.

From there, I coiled, inverted, and popped both feet backward directly into Badb's chest, sending her into the air and onto her backside. The momentum carried me a short distance away in roll, where I sprung back to my feet. Several whistles of approval sounded from the ring. Point for me.

I scooped up my nisís and rushed forward, executing a swift one-two strike at Badb's head and body as she rolled up. But she was too fast. She deftly blocked both shots at a weird angle and then slid her blades together, drawing my weapons into the center of the V of hers. Seemingly from nowhere, a snap of her right foot struck me in the ribs and sent me flying across the ring.

"Ugh," I groaned, pulling myself up and struggling to catch my breath. She'd cracked a rib for sure.

Badb charged. As she approached, I scissored my legs and caught the side of her knee, much as I had Déra's in our first fight months ago. Badb was ready for it, though, and turned her knee to avoid injury. I kicked out with my other leg and caught her in the face, bloodying her nose and sending her staggering backward.

Two to one in my favor amid more noises, my sisters giving shouts of encouragement now. I drew myself up, struggling to keep my breath. She'd taken a ton out of me so far, and she looked none the worse for wear as she licked a drop of blood from her upper lip and grinned. "You fight well, Weyna. I suppose I'll have to put some effort into this."

She darted forward, her hands a blur, and I barely kept up with her swift strikes. Each hit came quicker than the last. For a moment, I seemed to be holding my own, but she grew faster still, and my blocks began arriving later and later. I desperately sought a way to escape the chaotic fray.

Scrambling backward, I dodged low and then came up inside her guard, striking at her chin with my right elbow, but it passed through empty air.

Badb had spun completely around my back and to my left, where she whacked me across the head with the flat of her practice blade and then kicked my legs out from under me, sending me almost horizontal before she landed her final strike right into my fractured rib cage once more.

I grunted as I slammed to the ground, losing my weapons and sucking for breath. Slowly, the world turned black on my last conscious thought. *I did pretty well.*

I awoke a little later in the infirmary to the sounds of Saya and Badb arguing while a medhen treated my ribs. I kept my eyes closed and listened, curious.

"This is unacceptable." Saya's voice, hot and angry, lashed out.

"Captain," my aunt replied, her voice nonchalant and calm in the face of Saya's irritation. "She's fine. And she's very well trained. Be proud."

"I am proud, damn proud. What I am not thrilled with is you inserting yourself into her training and giving her enough of a beating to end up in the infirmary. That kick to the ribs could have felled a bear."

I cracked an eye at that, watching. Neither of them paid me much attention.

"Clearly not," Badb said, gesturing toward me.

"Captain," I tried to protest, but Saya snapped at me.

"Quiet, Weyna!" Then she turned back to Badb. "You are the Goddess of Battle, any ten of us couldn't match you, but you're not invulnerable, Badb."

Whoa, I thought. *Was that a threat?*

Badb crossed her arms and pursed her lips. Then she turned to me. "Are you quite alright?" She asked the question in an almost perfunctory fashion, not like her at all. At least she'd never spoken to me with such indifference. And her coal black raven's eyes were unreadable.

"I'm fine, Aunt Badb," I answered quietly, thoroughly confused by her gruff demeanor.

Without another word, she stalked from the infirmary.

Saya turned to me, speaking quietly but firmly. "You should not have taken that challenge, Weyna."

I furrowed my brow in confusion.

Saya shushed me. "Listen to me very carefully. I have known your Aunt for years. She and her sisters were once inseparable, but something has happened recently. I don't know exactly what, but she and your mother seem," she paused, "at odds lately. Badb knows how to pull her punches. I've seen her do it. That strike to your ribs was meant to injure."

I winced as I adjusted myself and looked back up at my commander. Her eyes were hard, but her ire wasn't directed at me. I just nodded my agreement and lay back, allowing the medhen to finish her work while my thoughts roiled, thoroughly unsettled.

CHAPTER TWENTY-FOUR
Aoife

The following week brought me to a better mood. I was getting on well with the team and finding myself settling into an easy rhythm of life: work, home, nights sitting around watching TV or reading with Morgan, when she wasn't out feeding, that is.

The 26th of January started especially pleasant when I woke to find Morgan curled up into my back. It was a little unexpected, but I didn't really mind it. I still couldn't bring myself to move away from her in the bed. I didn't want to. I wanted to stay right where I was, and abruptly tears started flowing again from nowhere.

"Hey. Hey. Come here," Morgan whispered. "It's okay."

I closed my eyes and sighed. "I'm sorry. I didn't mean to wake you."

"Sun's not up yet, so you didn't. You don't have to go through this alone, Aoife."

"But I don't want you to be hurt when— " I couldn't get the words out. They got stuck in my throat with the fat lump that lay there.

"That's my choice to make, now come here."

I sighed once more, fresh tears tumbling over my lashes, but I let her wrap me up and draw me in close. And she was so warm with the stolen heat of whomever she'd fed on the night before, and it felt so good not to be alone. It was easy to fall back to sleep in her arms.

We both woke again at around one when her ridiculously loud alarm clock blared the world's most annoying tone. It was the kind of clock that some sadist had designed for CIA black sites, for sure, bleating its noise at us until I finally found the snooze button, whereby I curled back up into Morgan's back and closed my eyes.

"Comfortable?" Morgan asked as my arm draped across her chest.

"Very. You know, the mix of this heating blanket and your cool skin is definitely a cure for insomnia. We should bottle that and market it."

Morgan chuckled quietly. "That's easy. We just buy some corpses from a medical school and sell them with a warming pad."

I slapped her on the shoulder lightheartedly and gave a wry smile. "Ha ha. Dead bodies smell way worse than you do."

"Are you saying I smell bad?" She asked and rolled over.

I could feel her eyes on me even though mine were still closed. "No, you don't," I whispered, feeling extremely turned on all of a sudden. "You smell like blackberries and home."

"Are you trying to get into my pants?" Morgan asked, her voice low and a little husky.

The corners of my mouth quirked up. "You're not wearing any pants, love."

"Love, is it?"

"It's an expression, Morgan, like dear or—"

"Sweetie pie?" She finished saucily, then slid out of the bed.

I groaned. "Five more minutes, Ma."

"Nope! Time to get up, recruit. We have work to do."

"I left the army as a Captain, so I outrank you, Specialist. I'm also the lead detective."

"No, your sister is lead detective, so you're not the boss of me. Now come on." She jerked the covers off, and I squealed in protest.

"Fine. I'm up. But you suck."

Morgan snorted a laugh. "Yes. Yes I do. Now go get a shower."

"Why me first?" I grumbled, still laying in the bed, but now turned toward her as she began fishing out clothing.

"Because you're more sleepy than I am, clearly, and you were sweating." She pinched her nose at me and waved her hand like she was shooing away some foul miasma.

I drew in a mock gasp of indignation. "You cunt! I do *not* smell bad."

She laughed. "No, you don't. But we have to go, so let's get moving."

<hr />

At HQ, I poked my head over the cube and looked down at Doyle. "So, anything?"

It had been almost a week, and Doyle had been struggling with the drives we'd brought her. They'd been encrypted. She had borrowed some horsepower from a local contracting company to work the decryption, but finding the key was turning out to be harder than we'd hoped. The Akkorokamui was nowhere to be found, so I hoped we'd dodged that bullet, and the BOLO on Reynolds, if he really was Cait's shooter, had turned up nothing. All in all, it was deadly dull.

Doyle looked up and shook her head. "No," she muttered tiredly. If anything, she looked even worse than before. There was no more bounce in her personality. Her eyes were sunken, and her entire complexion had taken on a waxy, almost ghoulish pallor. If I didn't know better, I'd have said she'd succumbed to some manner of drug addiction.

"Jess," I probed quietly. "Is there something you need to tell me or one of the other team? You know we'd understand."

"No, Cait," she spat, shaking her head with a little more vigor. "I'm fine. So quit fucking asking!"

I raised my eyebrows in shock and sank back down to my desk. "Okay," I muttered.

Morgan leaned around the cube where Carlos once sat and wordlessly pantomimed drinking coffee, then she jerked her head toward the break room. I got up, almost grabbed Cait's 'Big Busts' coffee mug but opted for the plain white one, and followed Morgan to the breakroom.

"What's up?" I asked as we walked in.

"So you noticed it, too?" She said. I didn't have to ask what she meant.

I sighed. "Hard not to, Doyle's looking really rough."

"Think I should talk to Nastasia about it?"

I frowned. "Nastasia? Why?"

"They're a couple, didn't you know that?"

"Well then, she should know about it anyway, shouldn't she? She must be bleeding her dry, and—" I stopped myself and let out an exasperated breath. "Sorry."

"No," Morgan said seriously. "It's okay. It's a valid point. Nastasia should be aware of what's going on with Doyle, so why hasn't she said or done anything? It's possible she's the cause, but that wouldn't be like her. She's eight hundred years old. She doesn't have to feed that often."

I pursed my lips. "I don't know. But you should say something to Nas, anyway."

Morgan nodded and changed the subject. "Did you find anything in the files?"

I shook my head. "Not really. There's a description of the creature, which they have termed the Enteroctopus Maculosa Mimicus. Imaginative, huh? The description doesn't add much to Zhi's statement, though. It's a giant octopus shapeshifter, basically."

"What did Zhi's notes say about the mermaids? Anything relevant?"

"Zhi's notes aren't in the files. We must have missed something. Either that or it's on that thumb drive."

"Which is also encrypted," Morgan confirmed. "So, we're still waiting there. Well, I'm sick of sitting around, so I took the liberty of getting us a chat with the head of the Zhu Pharmaceutical lab over in Cambridge."

I chuckled. "You sneaky bitch. Give me the shitty paperwork to translate while you go do the easy job?"

Morgan laughed at that. "Yup. So, We'll have to rise and shine at the ass crack of 2 PM, but tomorrow we might be able to get some answers."

CHAPTER TWENTY-FIVE

Weyna

Once more, I approached the cabin, decked out in my dress tunic, boots, and formal belt, per my agreement with my aunt. A young girl exited, glancing at me over her left shoulder as she closed the door. Her strawberry blonde hair caught the smoldering twilight, each lock falling in a perfectly chaotic bundle across her shoulders and obscuring most of her face, though I saw a swift gleam of her eyes, captivating and gray. A rebellious gust of wind unveiled her impish smile as it sent her tresses flying, and just like that, she was gone like vapor, vanishing into thin air as if she'd never been there. I frowned and blinked. *Fae perhaps?* I wondered, but I brushed it off. Such things were commonplace among Aine's weird git.

I stepped up to the wooden door, gave a soft sigh of lament, and knocked.

A voice chimed from within, not of my mother's but a familiar lilting alto I knew all too well. "Coming!"

The door swung open to reveal Boudka's face, and a fresh furrow creased my brow, "Boudka? What brings you here?"

"I live here now. I'm your mother's apprentice." She pulled me inside and smoothed her academic robes just as the bitter notes of jealousy and irritation began to salt my tongue. I held it in check, fixed on one simple idea. The stakes had been reconciliation, and that's what I would do.

"Be out in a minute, Weyna," my mother called from her bedroom. "Grab a seat anywhere."

I looked around for a moment, then took a seat on the sofa.

Boudka seemed different, more settled, and more confident as she glided over into a seat next to the dining table. Several books, mostly Shaddani magic tomes, covered one end of the tabletop.

"Where did you get those?" I asked, knowing full well the answer. I tried desperately to control my heartbeat, now banging under the twisting knife of betrayal.

"Your mother gathered them a few weeks ago. She snuck her way to the Vermillion Palace and the old library."

A flush of mad rage shot up my face and crushed my chest, but I still said nothing, and in the ensuing awkward silence, my eyes began shedding silent tears of frustration and hurt.

I felt small, like a child, as I had one cold winter morning in a half-burned home, when a woman I didn't know, dressed in fine robes with her raven-black hair braided and clean, hoisted the dead corpse of my father off of me. 'Come with me,' she had said. 'I am your mother.' And as she touched my hand, a spark of something grew between us, and I knew without question that she told the truth.

To be laid bare like that, unable to control the emotions in my chest in front of Boudka, embarrassed and humiliated me, and I thought to leave. But before I could rise, Boudka joined me, took my hand, and put her other to my cheek.

"You look so beautiful," she said softly. "I know that it is you, but you are so different, so directed. I would be proud to be with you."

I looked down, momentarily flummoxed by the sudden mix of emotions conjured by the compliment. I pawed at my face and eyes, wiping away the tears. "I envy you," I whispered and finally looked back to her face. "She really cares about you."

Boudka gave me a look full of sympathy and heartbreak. "It's not what you think. She didn't do all of this for me. She did it for you."

I sniffed. "I don't understand."

"She helped me unlock my magic so that I could have a purpose here beyond laundry and sewing. She wanted to ensure that I had a place here so that we could be together."

Almost on cue, my mother drifted into the room, her black robes moving with a soft sound that reminded me vaguely of the falling of water or perhaps the tide. Slowly, gingerly, she set herself next to me on my other side and pulled me to her.

"I love you more than I ever thought possible, Weyna. For all of my life, almost fifteen thousand years, I have held out a fruitless hope that one day I'd be more than just the queen of a dead world. It never occurred to me until I took you that day to the infirmary that there might be a greater cause. I'm so sorry."

I said nothing. I couldn't. Humiliation and comfort still mixed in my heart in equal measure as I sat there until finally, my turmoil resolved, after long thought, into the realization that I was among family who loved me and that it was okay not to be alone. "I'm sorry, too."

And then the strangest thing happened, something I had never seen, felt, or heard. My mother, the mighty Morrigan, shook with soft sobs. A wet tear fell and landed on my cheek, burning its way down, hot and heavy, to land on my chest. I sniffed once more and drew back, looking up at my mother as more tears fell.

I wondered briefly what stories the locals might tell, if they could see this moment. When Nemhain, The Morrigan, the Goddess of Magic and Battle and Death, wept for her love of her child. Would they make up stories of rivers that then ran from them?

A sudden storm of emotions made me throw my arms around her once more and squeeze her tightly. "I love you, mother. And I am thankful that you brought me here. I am thankful that you are my mother."

Boudka wrapped her arms around us both, and there we sat for long minutes, all of us in tears, and it turned out that the pact I'd made to Badb wasn't nearly so onerous to fulfill as I'd thought.

After a bit, we all pulled ourselves together and sat at the table. Boudka stepped away for a bit to make us a light dinner of mixed greens, local vegetables, and seasoned lamb slices.

We drank wine, ate, and whiled away the time with my mother regaling us with descriptions of the Vermillion Palace.

"It's still there," she said. "Literally untouched, the library is still full of books, tomes of magic, flights of fancy, and histories. Tens of thousands of years worth.

"It was bittersweet to see, though, with the devastation all about it. That and the throne room where I once sat and dare not place my royal arse again lest the palace spring to life and become a beacon to Mother Darkness."

She paused, taking a sip of her wine. "The trip was taxing and treacherous. The gate sits so close to her on that side, resting almost in easy sight of her. And it's the weird contradiction of magic that it takes tremendous effort to hide it. The more magical power you possess, the more it takes to obscure it."

I stood and walked over to the tapestry and looked at the depiction I'd been eyeing earlier with some interest. "Where did they go? The people in this depiction? They're shown leaving by a gate, but there's no indication as to where."

My mother shook her head. "We don't really know." She stood and joined me, Boudka following suit.

"Is that her," Boudka asked, pointing to the small crystal embroidered in the fabric.

My mother nodded. "Yes, at the beginning. We left her for the Kaushkari in the Heroes' Field, trapped in a soulstone, and there she remains today. Though, with the power she has gathered to herself, the stone has twisted and grown into a mockery of the magic it once held. She has shaped almost a body from it."

"Can it be destroyed?" I asked.

"Perhaps, if I could get close enough, or— " She placed a hand to her mouth.

"Or if you collapse the gate." I finished and looked over at the tablets.

My mother turned to me. "You've been speaking to one of the council."

"Captain Saya said you collapsed the gate at Dwarka."

My mother looked a bit stricken as she ran a finger over the figure of Mother Darkness within the tapestry. "It was a last resort, and only the council know that I and your aunts were the cause. It sank the city with most of our army still battling inside. Badb still hasn't forgiven me for that. She lost many friends that day, including someone special."

Jealousy, I thought. *Was that why she was jealous?*

I changed the subject, trying to steer away from the suddenly dour mood of the conversation.

"I think I've got my magic under control," I said flatly with a grin. "Finally."

"So I hear?" My mother replied with a raised eyebrow and a playful smile. "Show me."

I felt a little silly, like a child reciting with some instrument, but I did as she asked, showing her what Óbin had taught me, conjuring small lights, faerie glamours, and small balls of fire, nothing too fancy, but everything was cleanly summoned and dismissed.

I wouldn't say she was impressed, but she did applaud my efforts, which was all I cared for, honestly. Magic wasn't my thing, and I was okay with that.

"Still, though," my mother warned after I'd done my little demonstration. "Those little tricks may serve you well if you put enough power into them, but please be careful. Summoning enough tarzhi in that way can have unimaginably powerful effects, unforeseen and uncontrolled effects." She continued her short lecture after taking a sip of wine. "Your human blood gives you access to use magic that I cannot. In a way, Weyna, you carry more potential power than I ever will. Like Boudka, the paths of Earth and Bethadi magic are not closed to you as they are to me. So, please, be thoughtful."

I shrugged. "I never use it except to assist the weapons smiths."

She chuckled. "Yes, crafting with their stolen metal."

I frowned, my face a mask of confusion. "Stolen?"

"Has it never been a wonder to you why the Óșeni haven't tried to close their own gate to Shaddan? Especially with the threat of Hel but thirty miles away?"

"Oh," I said, then I understood. "Oh!"

She nodded, noting that I understood her meaning. "Quite so. Better them than others, though. At least they put it to good use. One day, when we've recovered our home, things will be put in order."

Finally, as the evening drew late, my mother announced her intentions to retire for the night. But she'd barely spoken when there was a rather insistent knock at the door.

I rose from my seat. "I'll get it."

Outside, a Bethadi soldier in a scout's camouflage stood, looking haggard and winded.

"Yes?" I queried, having a fairly solid suspicion as to his purpose.

The man peeked past me toward my mother. "Mother Morrigan, you are summoned to the council. There is a force of Fomori approaching."

My mother frowned at him and acknowledged the warning, sending the man on his way, then she turned to me. "You'll need to report to the barracks. It seems you're about to find out if this truly is your calling."

I nodded and stepped out the door.

"Weyna?" Boudka called and rushed to the door. "Here, take this with you."

I looked down, but she carried nothing, then threw her arms around my neck and pressed her lips to mine in a long and passionate kiss. "I missed you," she said. "Be careful."

"I missed you, too," I replied and started back toward the barracks, a slight flutter in my chest.

CHAPTER TWENTY-SIX

Aoife

The next day, around four PM, we found ourselves in the lobby of a modern brick building fronted by gleaming glass that showered the entire entrance in sunlight. A large round reception desk sat in front of us, manned by a young Asian man in professional attire.

"May I help you?" The young man asked with a frown and narrowed eyes. Let's be honest. We both looked like cops. It was a pretty common reaction when we arrived anywhere.

"I'm Detective Kennedy," Morgan stated, her face beaming that dazzling smile. "This is Detective Reagan. We have an appointment with Doctors Williams and Jing."

"Ah, here it is. Just one second. Ms. Willis will be down momentarily."

Morgan's gaze fixed on the kid. "Who's Ms. Willis?"

"She is our US General Council. Just a moment." He dialed a number and spoke in Chinese into the receiver.

"What did he say?" Morgan whispered as we turned our backs to him.

"Just that we're here. Now he's telling her that he had specific instructions to call Ms. Willis when we arrived. Apparently, at the request of Dr. Jing."

"You're dead handy. You know that?"

"Why thank you, Red. That's a compliment coming from you. You're dead handy, too."

Morgan rolled her eyes at the obvious pun.

A few minutes later, a tall black woman walked in. Her red heels, red blouse, and black skirt all looked expensive. Morgan wrinkled her nose a bit at her top-brand perfume. "I'm Nancy Willis. Right this way, Detectives."

She led us up a set of switchback stairs that ascended directly over the lobby. Rising against the massive glass fronting as they did gave the entire entryway a sort of Frank Lloyd-Wright kind of feel. Near the top, they gave a striking view of the skyline across the Charles, and I had to yank on Morgan's arm to keep us going as she stopped to admire it.

"Come on," I hissed, and she smirked at me. "Arsehole."

"Bitch," she whispered back, and I had to suppress a grin.

"What was that?" Ms. Willis called back.

"Um, nothing," I responded, glaring at Morgan. "Just admiring the view."

"Oh, yes, the building is brand new," Willis commented absently.

A few moments later, we found ourselves in a minimally decorated conference room with two men in lab coats, one Caucasian, the other Asian, and two other Asian men in black suits. I recognized one of the black-suited gentlemen from Attaché Yi's retinue at the harbor. The two doctors looked extremely nervous. And the two Asian men standing behind them looked hostile.

"So, what can we do for you?" Ms. Willis asked. Her voice was perfunctory and held zero warmth.

"Well," I started, but Morgan cut in.

"Ms. Willis. We can have this conversation here or at the station, it's really your choice, but those two gentlemen can leave. Now, please. The Chinese government is not invited to this party."

Nancy Willis stared at us for a moment as if debating whether she should argue, then turned and asked them to leave in nearly flawless Chinese. The two men looked perturbed but eventually stalked out and disappeared down the hall.

"Fine," Ms. Willis said, and there was a bit of irritation in her voice. "Now, what can we do for you?"

I looked at Morgan, waiting to see if she wanted to lead, but she stayed quiet, so I continued. "Ms. Willis, what do you do for Zhu Pharmaceuticals?"

"I am our Senior General Council for the America's, Detective, uh—"

"Oh, my apologies, I'm Detective Reagan. This is Detective Kennedy." I said and slid one of Cait's business cards across the table to her. Kennedy followed suit. "Now, maybe you and the good scientists here can help us out. We're currently trying to locate a large predator that was stored aboard the ship that recently grounded at Carson Beach. Perhaps you can tell us a bit about it, and more importantly, why it was being brought here. After reviewing the permits sent to the US Government, the State of Massachusetts, and the City, it seems I can't find the required paperwork for importing a dangerous species."

One of the men spoke up. "I'm Dr. Jing. We had no idea that the creature might be dangerous. But, it is a one-of-a-kind specimen, and our facilities here are best suited to examine it."

"I see," I said, plastering on an obviously fake smile. "So, the eight-inch thick steel container it was placed in was for what—in case someone wanted to hurt it?"

"Well, no," Jing started. "But—"

Willis cut him off. "I think Dr. Jing has answered your question, Detective. Can we move on?"

Morgan looked at her with narrowed eyes. "Yes, Ms. Willis, he has. We're just trying to understand the nature of the precautions. Also, we're trying to understand why you took perfectly innocent-looking women who are suffering from cancer and stuffed them into its pie-hole."

Jesus, Red, I thought. *Real sensitive.* I had to press my lips together to keep from laughing.

Willis looked like she might be ill, and the two gentlemen looked extremely uncomfortable and a little aghast.

I tilted my head at that. "You didn't know." It wasn't a question.

Willis shifted uncomfortably. "No."

"Well, then, let me help paint the picture with clarity," I said, putting just a bit of menace in my voice. "The Chinese

Navy placed a large creature into a big steel container and then fed living women to it."

Willis found her voice. "It's my understanding that these were mermaids and not human—"

"Let me stop you right there," I interjected. "I have met these women. They speak and understand fluent Chinese, and at least one of them reads and writes. Setting aside their interesting proclivities when they enter saltwater, they walk on two legs and look and act perfectly human. So, despite the fact that the courts have not ruled on their status as 'people,'" I air quoted the word, "I can assure you that they are as sentient and have the same emotional capacity and the ability to feel terror and pain as you or I. So, as far as I'm concerned, at this time, this is a murder investigation."

"We didn't know," Jing said again. Williams was pale as a ghost but still said nothing.

"And what was the purpose of having Dr. Zhi on board the ship?" Morgan asked.

"Who?" Williams said, finally speaking for the first time.

"Dr. Zhi? The Marine Biologist on the ship?"

They all shook their heads, and Willis said, "Detectives, we weren't aware that the Chinese government had a Marine Biologist on board."

"Well, they did, and she was pretty distraught the night the ship ran aground. She said they fed almost three dozen mermaids to the Akorokamui."

Williams blanched again. He really looked ill. Jing started looking a little peaked, too.

"Dr. Williams, are you alright?" Morgan asked, mild alarm rising in her features.

Williams began to cough, and a bit of spit and foam peeked from the corners of his mouth. Then he erupted in a fit of choking and fell to the floor. I started to stand, but Morgan grabbed my arm. "Poisoning. I'll deal with him. Call an ambulance."

Willis pushed away from the table, staring at Williams. Then she looked down at her glass of water, untouched. Then looked at the two men. Glasses of water sat in front of both of them.

"Shit," I said as Jing began to choke as well. I called 9-1-1, gave them Cait's badge number, and requested an ambulance for a possible poisoning with imminent death.

Morgan looked up from Williams, whose eyes were bulging now, and shook her head gently.

Both men were dead by the time the ambulance arrived, and we took Willis into custody.

"She doesn't know anything," Morgan said as she came out of the interview room with Maki after a marathon interview. "She stonewalled me for a while, then I glamoured her within an inch of losing her mind, and she stuck to her story. She got a call from Beijing. She was instructed to meet with us and the Doctors. The two men were instructed to be there. The water was the same water they left in the conference room all day."

"Well," I said. "The hospital confirmed it was an ingested neurotoxin, probably cyanide. We'll know more when the lab results come back. So—"

Before I could ask even a single question about the interview, our phones buzzed, and Morgan rolled her eyes. "Now what?"

I answered first, "Reagan, PIU."

"Detective Reagan, PIU presence requested by Cambridge Police at Zhu Pharmaceuticals."

I looked at Morgan. She was getting the same message from another dispatcher. And we hung up. I left Willis in the care of Freyer and Doyle as we hustled back over to Cambridge.

When we arrived at the building, we were escorted around back by two officers, their faces etched with unease. Then the pungent stench of decay wafted through the air, assaulting our nostrils as we approached the grim scene. The alleyway was dimly lit, casting elongated shadows on the surrounding walls. As soon as we hit the alley behind the building, I smelled it.

"Ugh," I said and put my hand to my nose.

Morgan didn't even flinch. "Yup, that's bad."

Two other officers stood next to what Morgan referred to as a dumpster. I wanted to inform her it was properly called a 'skip,' but she would just argue about it. Beneath said skip, though, a massive blood pool had formed. As we approached, the sound of buzzing flies grew louder, and the putrid odor intensified, mingling with the metallic tang of blood. The sight that greeted us was a haunting one: the mangled body of the receptionist sprawled amidst the refuse. He had died violently, very violently.

The body bore the unmistakable signs of decomposition, its flesh discolored and bloated. A sickly sweet odor hung in the air, intermingling with the acrid scent of trash and decay. Deep lacerations marred the once-familiar features. Some of the wounds mirrored the grotesque injuries suffered by the sailors on the Nan-Kang, an unnerving connection that sent a shiver down my spine. He wasn't in rigor mortis, so it had likely been less than twenty-four hours.

"Didn't we just see this guy?" Morgan asked as we stared down at the body.

I nodded. "Yeah, just like two hours ago."

"Shapeshifting octopus monster?" Morgan asked, looking at me.

I looked at the four officers around us. "Did anyone see anything? Who found the body?"

"That lady over there." One of the Officers, Caldwell, by his nametape, pointed toward a young Latina in black pants and a yellow blouse sporting a cleaning service logo. She was pale and looked extremely tired, about as tired as I felt.

I switched to Spanish. "I understand you found the body?"

She replied in Spanish. "Yes, I found him in the dumpster a little while ago."

I nodded and went through the usual questions. Her name was Maria Vasquez. She didn't have much to add. She hadn't touched the body. She notified management. They called the Cambridge police. Who, in turn, called us because of the state of the body. Pretty much the expected answers.

"We have a problem," Morgan said as we gave Maria a card and asked her to call if she thought of anything else.

"No shit. If this guy was dead back here for the last twelve hours or so, who did we see up front?" I asked, watching as the Coroner and her assistant lifted the guy from the dumpster.

One of the Cambridge detectives walked over, an Asian woman about five feet tall and, as my mother would say, her expression looked like a bulldog licking the piss off a nettle, not happy.

"Lisa Nguyễn, CIU," she introduced, sticking out a hand. In her other hand, of all things, was an apple turnover.

"This is Morgan Kennedy, and I'm Cait Reagan."

Lisa laughed. "You don't remember me, do you? We worked a double together two years ago."

Shit, I thought. "Oh! Yeah. Gods, I forgot."

"That's alright. I'm sure you've taken a lot more cases than I have." She took a bite of her turnover and spoke around a mouthful. "Anyway, what do we think? Same thing that killed all those sailors on the boat?"

I watched for a moment in awe at the woman's stomach. That she could eat with the smell blew my mind. "Yeah, looks like that."

"Wow!" Lisa said and grabbed my left arm, sliding up my sleeve.

"I'm sorry?" I asked and pulled my arm gently from her grasp.

"Your arm. Last I saw it. It was covered in scars." She started scrutinizing me closely.

I looked at Morgan, who shrugged, clearly unable to come up with anything.

"Oh, that? I had some special work done. Killer skin grafts."

"I bet," Lisa said, but her expression held something I didn't like.

"What?" I asked. My anxiety was rising, and it was starting to irritate me. This wasn't what I needed right now.

"Nothing," she replied. "So, what are we looking at?"

"Honestly," Morgan replied. "We have no idea. We have no pictures. Only a vague description of some vaguely octopus-looking thing like Ursula from Disney's The Little Mermaid.

Whatever it is, it's amazingly strong and pretty much a total terror. I wish we had more. But it's intelligent, and it seems focused on this place."

"Great," Lisa said wryly. "Well, fortunately, it's not my problem. Looks like there's something to investigate, but not solvable by our department, so best of luck." She handed me her card. "Call if you need our support. I'll have the analysis unit send over the reports and details as soon as they're done."

We said our goodbyes, and she walked off, giving me a disconcerting backward glance.

"Well, that sucks," Morgan said flatly.

"Yeah, for sure." I tried to ignore the sinking feeling in my chest. She was going to call the department, no doubt. "I'm fucked."

"Maybe not," Morgan replied, but she didn't sound convincing, and I gave her a skeptical stare.

"Well, let's see how things go."

We stopped off for lunch at Boston Burger Company off Boylston, a place I'd been wanting to try. Specifically, I wanted to see if the 'Pigferno' was everything people said it was.

We were escorted to a booth in the back where a waitress, a cute girl covered in tattoos, took our order. "What can I—Oh, hey!"

I looked up at her. She had a bright smile splitting her lips, and her eyes twinkled a little. "Um, hi?" I said, feeling a little taken aback at being confronted by two people who knew Cait twice in a few hours.

"It's me, Nohemi. You probably don't remember me. I waited on you and your friend, the big Latino guy with the cowboy hat. You know, over at Yankee Lobster."

"Oh, yeah!" I said, playing the part. "Sorry, I didn't recognize you. I meet a lot of people."

"I was pretty bummed when you didn't call."

Morgan raised her eyebrows and donned a cheeky smirk, then pressed her lips together to hide her shit-eating grin as I began to get the gist.

"Yeah," I said. "Sorry about that. We were working."

"Sure. I understand," she responded, looking a bit

crestfallen. "I met someone anyway. She tends bar at Leslie's."

"Oh, which one?" Morgan piped up, picking up the conversation. "It isn't Carrie, is it?"

Nohemi laughed. "No. She'd break me in half. It's the new girl, Sandy."

Morgan's eyes shot wide. "Really? I always figured her going for the mousy librarian type."

"Yeah, I could see that," Nohemi chuckled. "Sorry. I don't think we've met."

Morgan stuck out her hand. "I'm Morgan. And this is Cait. We've started dating."

Nohemi just nodded. "Ah. You're a cop, too, then?"

I thought it an odd question, given we were both wearing our badges on our hips, but then I realized she probably couldn't see them because of the table.

"Yup. Well, I'm not really hungry, but my girlfriend wants the, what did you call it?" Morgan turned to me.

"I'll have the pigferno," I stated flatly. "And a coke. Oh, and a side of fries."

"You sure you don't want something?" Nohemi asked Morgan, cocking a hip as she wrote on her pad.

"No, I'm good. I'll just snack on her fries."

"Well, it was nice to meet you, Morgan." Morgan gave the waitress a half wave as she trotted off.

"See," I said. "I told you. Cait's had them falling all over her. Probably forever."

Morgan nodded. "Yeah, not shocked. She's gorgeous. Who wouldn't want a jacked girl with auburn hair, pretty green eyes, and a beautiful smile?"

I blushed and stared at the drink menu, then changed the subject. "So, you going out again tonight?"

"Yeah, I have to. Girl's gotta eat, you know."

I looked down and pawed at the table, then fiddled with my napkin. "What's it like?"

Morgan gave me a puzzled look and stepped closer. "What's what like?" Her tone wasn't confrontational, which I'd expected. She sometimes bristled when I asked about being a vampire, but this time it was just a curious response.

"Um, you know, feeding, I guess." I looked up, wincing slightly in preparation for her to lose her cool about it, but she just smirked at me.

"I won't lie to you. It's hot. There's an almost sexual component to it that makes it enjoyable for both me and the person I feed on. Is that what you wanted to know?"

I looked away. *Was it?* I wasn't sure. "I just wondered what it was like for you. You go out to these bars, find women who are interested in you, and then, what? Ask them to donate a pint?"

Morgan laughed. "You're really funny. You know that? No. It's not like that. Usually, they come on to me. Something happens when the hunger spikes. It's like we become this embodiment of attractiveness that jerks everyone's gaze around, at least for a moment. After that, it's a spot of glamour, a nibble, and another spot of glamour. It's not really intimate, though, you know? I don't know them and don't really want to."

I thought about that. "What would make it better? Knowing the person?"

She shrugged. "Liz told me that being in love with someone makes it very different. You don't have to glamour them, for starters."

I nodded, not really sure how I was feeling. No, that wasn't right. I felt jealous, and it felt weird. I didn't have any right to feel jealous, but it was there, and I didn't like the feeling. "I'm sorry," I said. "I shouldn't have pried." I looked back to the glass of water in front of me and swallowed the lump in my throat before I reached for it.

Morgan touched my arm, taking it gently. "Aoife, what's wrong?"

"That," I said, running a hand through my hair. "That waitress, Lisa. I'm scared. I know it's probably nothing. I just. And all of this, it's overwhelming sometimes. And I don't know—" I sighed. "I guess I'm just being ridiculous." I looked back up at her, those beautiful green eyes watching me with such intensity. My heart sped up a bit under her gaze. I'd been blasé before about my feelings. Now the depth of them constricted my throat. "Mostly, though, it's not that. I feel a little—" I couldn't get the word out.

Morgan watched me for a moment longer, then said, "I like you too, Aoife."

Fuck, why did she have to be so perceptive?

"Come on," she said with a genuine smile that spoke volumes and squeezed my hand for just a moment before letting go. "Let's get you fed and get back to work."

CHAPTER TWENTY-SEVEN

Weyna

In the haunting light of Aine's conjured moon, the valley stretched before us like a tapestry woven from shadows and silver. Cresting the hill, as if bursting from darkness itself, crawled a small group of Fomori—each movement a sinister, glistening dance beneath the ethereal glow.

"There's not a lot of them," Semi, one of our fellow Valtárí, murmured.

"No," I answered with my brow furrowed. "A hundred, maybe?"

Semi seemed unconcerned, but it was far more than the number that had overrun my village shortly after the gate yawned open in the northeast. Since their first forays five years ago, where the living and the dead they'd collected had become raw material to make more of the beasts, they'd simply lingered, spilling like ink from the gate only to mass some fifty miles away, halfway between our position and the gate. We hadn't the strength of arms to go on the offensive, so we simply kept an eye on them and waited.

This sudden emergence from the quiet shadows marked the first stirring of a massive tide that had been ominously silent. A hundred of the spindly horrors we called wevkrana scurried about, the terminating blades of their six legs catching the spectral moonlight and casting eerie glints. And yet, every time I looked at the things, another word, born from my odd dreams of late, intruded on my thoughts, 'Ogumo.'

Behind them, emisai bounded forward, twisted visages blending both strength and aberration, muscled and headless, their dragging arms ending in sharp claws like a bear. Their forms were akin to the apes of my mother's stories, if apes had been shaped by the shadowed hands of some forgotten malevolence, which, I supposed, these had.

Soaring above the macabre parade flew the pteraket, the 'flying blades,' so named by the Óṣeni. Their chitinous wings could be heard buzzing on the wind, even from this distance, and their tri-folded arms, mantis-like and bladed, paid homage to the twisted mind that created them. Their legs dangled beneath them, clawed instruments of snatching despair, poised to pluck the living from the earth and cast them from the skies above.

But it was the kóṣánt at the rear of the legion that concerned us most. Armored behemoths, their triangular heads housed deep sensory pits that seemed to taste the fear and screams of the night air. With claws that could easily rend steal, they moved as if the rugged terrain were flat carpet beneath their three-toed feet. Among all of these beasts, they were ours to fight. They were the whole reason the Valtárí had been formed from what I'd learned in my training.

To the last, of course, they all bore the hallmark of Mother Darkness' creation, shining with a slick, inky sheen, as if they were covered in black oils plied from the depths of the earth that oozed and moved almost on their own.

Fortunately, our bóllom were perfectly formed for slicing through all of their chitinous hides, and shadowsteel had a dampening effect on both Shaddani and Bethadi magic, so for most of the creatures, one or two deep strikes in the torso would take them down.

Watching the three kóṣánt closely, I realized that they were directing the others, like generals or captains or something. It had never occurred to me that there might be a true hierarchy among Mother Darkness' forces.

"Probably just a probe of our defenses," Saya commented as Zilly helped her buckle on her breastplate. "But it's not a good sign. They're gearing up for a real assault later, for sure." She turned to me. "Well, Weyna, it'll be your first real battle as Valtárí. How do you feel?"

I gave her a nervous smile. "Bloody terrified. But I won't let you down."

"Oh, I know you won't. But it's not me you have to worry about. Right, Zilly?"

Zilly grinned at me and winked. "She'll be fine. Besides, this is just a bit of fun."

I felt my lips mirror the curl of her grin, and her confidence stitched the fraying edges of my nerves somewhat, reminding me that, over the last six months, I'd been well-trained. I could do this.

We watched as the creatures swarmed in neatly formed lines across the dirt, moving almost in unison around the lake. The kóşánt lingered at the rear of the force, looming like the titans of gloom and chitin they were, as if watching with eyes they did not possess. The flyers weren't much of a worry. I looked back as the archers prepared, stringing bows and loading quivers, perfectly capable of dropping them in droves.

As soon as the Fomori reached the halfway point of the lake's southern flank, the widest point, we descended to meet them in the open maw of the valley below. By now, the fort was more fortress, melded to the land by earthworks and protected by a high stockade wall of solid timbers constructed by a mixture of local muscle, Bethadi magic, and even Óşeni efforts, myself included, for I felt much more Óşeni than human or Shaddani now. The ridge upon which had started our small encampment now wore a crown of timber and defiance.

Walls, once thin and weak, now stood as sentinels—their timbers embraced deeply by the earth before the trench that carved its way around, designed to guide the monsters straight to the most defensible points. While they'd likely be little use against the pteraket or wevkrana, the other beasts, more formidable and immune to steel, would be funneled into a hail of shadowsteel-tipped arrows. It was a good design.

Down in the field, we assumed the defensive lines we'd trained so diligently to construct with absolute perfection. The front and second Swasari shield lines held spears. Their bóllom kept sheathed for close combat that should never take place.

Stoney faced, the third line faced us with their backs to the enemy and their shields angled to the dirt. A thrill ran up my spine as I thought of my training, all funneling down to this moment. I found that my nerves had steadied, the fear fled, and a giddy sense of exhilaration filled me for what was to come, well worth the sprained ankles and fractured toe I'd suffered learning how to do it.

We were well set in position when the shadowy tide hove around the final bend in the lake and surged forward, chittering and screaming. The alienness and proximity of the monsters gave me a brief shudder, but I reminded myself once more that this was precisely what I'd trained for. And this was just a scout force. We could handle them.

The front line of wevkrana plowed forth into the Óşeni shield wall, scrabbling and tearing. Several of the things impaled themselves on spear tips. But the real danger of the charge was the emisai, who sprung forth behind them in an attempt to overtop the Óşeni shield structure. But we had a surprise for them.

"Valtárí!" Saya called as the emisai charged, and we all lunged forward, the third-line shields becoming the bucking earth beneath our feet as we were catapulted over.

I tucked and flipped, drawing my legs up to ensure they cleared the front-line spears. Then I unfurled like a flower, arms flying outward to cut down two passing emisai and steady my descent. We decimated the initial line of emisai, slicing into the lot of them and painting the air with their black ichor like a lance of forgotten goddesses.

Zilly and I, our movements bound by countless hours and days of work, landed a little further than the rest and began sundering the remaining forces. We spun and moved in a dance of death that was both effortless and graceful. The wevkrana practically threw themselves onto our blades.

We flowed, we embraced; she soared above as I kissed the earth beneath. The wevkrana were but ripples upon a pond, casting themselves in waves across our blades, and I embraced their charges with perfect focus. As one threw itself at my chest, I bent and passed under it, trusting implicitly in Zilly to dispatch it as I spun around, pivoting along her hip to end one of the wretched things leaping toward her back. Four more charged us from almost all sides, but in a ballet kissed by the phantom moonlight, we whirled around one another, cutting them down.

A triad of emisai, likely the last, charged directly at us. Zilly coiled low, her leg a cascade of moonlight, taking one of the emisai to the ground. I twisted and spun in the opposite direction, soaring over her sweep and slicing the creature neatly in two.

In a fluid motion, landing behind my partner, I buried my nisís into the heart of the second emisai. It still barreled into me, though, and the sheer momentum forced me back at an odd angle, my boots sketching whispered lines in the dirt.

With a scream, I stabbed it with my bóllom, and, for a moment, I lost track of my position and had to turn back toward Zilly as I silently cursed my lack of battle experience. She was facing me, the third emisai added to the growing pile of dead in our wake. I was about to dart forward and return to my space behind her, but her eyes shot wide.

"Behind!" Zilly's voice pierced the air as she anchored her weapons into the earth now soaked with the black ichor of dead Fomori. I launched forward into her cupped hands and was hurled backward into the night, only to plunge blades first into the charging kosant's chitinous hide, driving it to the packed earth.

I rolled smoothly back to my position at Zilly's side, my blades wrenching through the thing and spraying us both with black foulness. Covered in grime and doused in ichor, we stood ready for more. But the sounds of battle had hushed, leaving only the night breeze and our own breath.

About Zilly and I piled the bodies of the enemy, a dozen at least, cut down, inert. I turned, desperate for an enemy, but all I found was Zilly looking at me with the same intensity of feeling that burned within my own breast, and the shield line looking rather bored. Several of them had found the ground with their asses as if they'd simply been watching us dispatch the enemy the entire time. Many were staring at me specifically, smirking or grinning.

"Oye Konbom!" Saya shouted.

"Oye Konbom!" We returned, raising our blades high.

Zilly and I weren't even that winded, and I glanced around, taking in the carnage. The entire enemy force had been decimated, and not a single serious casualty lay among us, just a few cuts and scrapes. Saya was standing four feet away from us, her sword buried in the chest of another kóşánt.

"See! I told you," Zilly said as she bent down and cut a clawed finger from the kóşánt I'd downed. "Just a spot of fun."

I felt like I could take on the entire world right at that moment, and a slow, beaming smile spread across my face. I was a fucking hero of song. We all were.

"Come on, woman. Let's get drunk!" Zilly said and threw an arm around my shoulder, practically dragging me away from the battlefield while the Bethadi Magi, assisted by Boudka, burned away the mass of Fomori corpses.

CHAPTER TWENTY-EIGHT

Aoife

An insistent banging at the door dragged me out of bed. Looking around, I found one of Morgan's massive t-shirts and pulled it on, and looked at the alarm clock. It was eleven-thirty. *Fuck!*

"Okay, whoever you are, you better have a damn good reason—" Liz stood behind the door as I opened it, stopping me in my tracks. "Oh, it's you? What are you even doing up?"

"I'm here to take you to Marcella's so we can go over Cait's files. You've been avoiding this for almost two weeks, and I don't know why, but you are coming with me to go through this."

"Why? I'm doing fine. No one is the wiser."

"No, not yet, but Sesi knows Cait's history pretty well, and you don't. Carlos has made it clear that you've slipped up or glossed over important things several times, and he doesn't want that happening again."

I raised my eyebrows in surprise. *I had?* Well, that was a little distressing, and my face began to heat, so I sighed, still a little fatigued. "Sure, let me get dressed." I pulled on some work clothes, took my meds, grabbed Cait's sidearm and badge, and left, leaving Morgan a short note.

When we arrived at Marcella's, we found her standing in the doorway between the foyer and the kitchen. She was dressed in her usual pencil skirt and blouse with her Greek column legs stuffed into a pair of black patent leather heels.

Her hair had grown out faster than I'd expected and was looking a little more suave. Evil as she was, she was fucking hot, no doubt. I could understand why Cait liked her. She gave me a flutter or two myself, but still.

I scowled at her, and I thought I saw a twitch of annoyance break her impassive expression, but only for a moment. *Good, you evil cow.*

"We need to talk to you about Cait," she said, turning and walking with her seductive hip sway. "You need to catch up on all that's happened since—" She trailed off, probably not wanting to piss me off even more.

"Since what?" I said impassively. "Since you wrecked our lives?"

She stopped and looked back over her shoulder, face indifferent. "Sure, if you insist on putting it that way," she said quietly. "Now, let's get started."

I shot a nasty look at her backside and followed. "Fine."

We all sat down at the table, and Liz placed one hand on a set of files in front of her. Her face was solemn. Marcella sat beside her, giving me a shitty, ice-cold stare.

I glanced at the top file. It was Cait's service record.

"So, we're going over Cait's military service?"

"We're going over Cait's life," Marcella intoned from her seat on Liz's left. "It's been quite extraordinary. At least from the time you two were separated. But, yes, we'll start by showing you her service record, which, I think, is the best exemplar of the shoes you're filling."

I raised an eyebrow. "So this is before you lured her into your bed?"

Marcella stood and slammed a fist on the table, startling me and sending a crack into the thick wood. "Aoife!" She shouted. "Your sister is one of the most selfless people I've ever met. She deserves better from you."

"From me? That's rich, coming from you." I retorted hotly, shooting to my feet and jabbing a finger at her, toppling my chair in the process. "You—"

Marcella swept forward faster than I could see and grabbed me around the throat, growling a low warning. "We're not talking about me. I know what I've done. And frankly, I'd do it all over again if I thought it would keep you two safe. Now, enough!"

I bashed at her arm, even though she wasn't actually squeezing terribly hard. It might as well have been made of steel for all the good it did me.

Liz stood and placed a hand on Marcella's arm. "M, this isn't helping." Then she turned to me. "Please, both of you, sit down. We really need to go over this."

I picked up the chair, sat back down, and glowered at them both, then made a 'let's get on with it' gesture.

"I understand that the military is viewed differently in Ireland. It's the same in the UK, as you know." Liz said gently. "But your sister saw some extraordinary circumstances." She pulled out an official-looking piece of paper and slid it across the table to me. "This is her nomination for the Congressional Medal of Honor."

My jaw fell open in shock. "Cait was awarded the CMH?"

"No," Marcella said flatly. "She wasn't. She was nominated, but the Pentagon declined to give it to her. After some digging, I found out that her rape at the hands of Sgt. John Holley had something to do with it."

"She was what?" I stared at them both in horror. Hot tears burned behind my eyes. *Cait had been raped? Oh, Gods.*

Marcella made a pained face and nodded. Liz looked stricken. This had hit something raw for both of them.

"She reported it," Marcella continued softly, "but it was determined there wasn't enough evidence to prosecute Sgt. Holley. He also had connections at the Pentagon, which complicated matters further. Cait doesn't know that part. I didn't think it was wise to tell her. I was afraid of what she might do."

"With the abilities of a vampire? She would have hunted him down and torn him to shreds," I said flatly. "And, honestly, I wouldn't blame her. As it is, he's a dead man if I get to him first. Keep going."

Marcella paused and looked at me for a long moment before finally nodding. "In the end, when she was nominated for the

CMH, someone decided that she might make waves when she returned home. And it wouldn't do politically at the time to have a CMH awardee running around saying she'd been raped by another soldier, especially when it was swept under the rug by the brass, so they knocked it down to a Distinguished Service Cross instead. They had to give her something, you see. She had jumped on top of a grenade, and it almost killed her, an act that saved the lives of two other soldiers."

I sucked in a breath through my nose and ran my hands through my hair. "So, let me get this straight. Some guy raped Cait, and because she reported it, she was denied the highest award for valor given to any soldier in the US military? After jumping on a grenade? That's beyond fucked."

Liz nodded. "Yes, it is. But that's not the worst of it. One of the people she saved from that grenade was the man who raped her. Beyond that, though, just before that happened, she saved the lives of an entire patrol by picking off a kid in a suicide vest at five hundred yards with a sniper rifle."

I blinked. "She had to shoot a kid?"

Marcella nodded. "Yes, and it pretty much destroyed her. She struggled for ten years until she and I met, most recently, that is. We worked through some of it, but it still haunts her from time to time."

"Worked through it how?" I squinted at her suspiciously.

Marcella's scowl returned. "That's not important. She can tell you about it if she wants when she wakes up."

"Let's move on, please," Liz said, and I nodded. She slid a photo across the table.

Morgan, Cait, Carlos, and Freyer were standing outside of some kind of hatch. They were all disheveled and covered in blood and some kind of black goo. Cait looked awful, miserable, and deathly pale. "They look like they've been through hell."

Liz explained this time. "They had, quite literally. Cait led those four down into a tunnel full of monsters under Boston. It led to a chamber that had been carved from the rock beneath Elliot Norton Park, which houses something we have named 'the black gate.' It's a portal to another world."

She slid another picture over. This one was terrifying. The photo showed a gaping black hole in a dark underground cavern. Worse, monstrous spider things curled up in thick black webs surrounded it. The thing looked like an entrance to the pits of hell from some horror movie, and I said so.

"No," Liz said. "It's real. That," Liz continued, "is the black gate. And those creatures you see are what the Japanese call Ogumo. Cait, Morgan, and Freyer went through it to rescue a federal employee who had survived an attack on the facility where that gate is housed. Cait nearly died again, saving Morgan and Freyer from a group of creatures called emisai, which she faced down with nothing but her Bowey knife. Had Déra, not been there, she would likely have died."

"Jesus. When does she have time to bloody eat, for all the heroic shit she does? And who is Déra? Mother Lamia mentioned her, but I know nothing about her."

"It's not important. You'll meet her eventually. Anyway, that's your sister, thoroughly selfless," Marcella replied. "She saved me from certain death. She kept Detective Doyle alive after they'd been in a bomb blast. She rescued Nastasia from a car bomb in her bare feet, suffering third-degree burns in the process."

She slid two more photographs across the table. The first was a mangled, nearly unrecognizable wreck of a vehicle, burnt out and destroyed. The second showed the devastated remains of a house that had collapsed in on itself. Marcella pointed at the photo of the house. "She saved five people that day with her intuition and quick thinking."

I sat back in the chair, stunned and unable to speak, as the sheer immensity of the person that was my sister landed on me. She was a fucking hero. I was shite.

"So, you see," Marcella finished. "That's who your sister is. Quick thinking, compassionate, and selfless."

Liz slid the files across to me. "Study these. You need to know every detail."

They got up and exited the room, leaving me to go through the files, but on her way out, Marcella stopped and placed a hand on my shoulder.

"I know you don't like me, but your sister has had a very hard time of it. Blame me if you must, but don't blame her. She's made the best decisions she could under extreme circumstances."

Marcella left, and I scooped up the files, calling Morgan to let her know I'd be taking the day off. She said she'd come by when she got off work. Then I retired to Cait's room to read with a horrible feeling welling in my stomach, the kind of sadness and self-pity that spiraled inward.

I spent the entire rest of the day reading through the files until my eyes burned. Every page was like something out of a spy novel or an action film. There were the details provided in her CMH nomination. She had saved a platoon of soldiers by shooting a kid in a suicide vest, then when a grenade had landed on her position, she'd pushed it under some blast blankets and laid on it to protect Morgan and Sgt. Holley. There was a picture of Holley in her files. I studied it carefully, memorizing every detail. On the back of the photo was an address in Decatur, Georgia, his last known. I took a snapshot of both sides with my phone.

Her medical records—I didn't know how Liz had gotten them—detailed seven complicated, long, and horrendous surgeries used to cobble her arm back together. There was also a fairly recent note that she had some kind of hemolytic anemia. *I chuckled at that. So that's what doctors call it*, I thought.

Marcella had provided a handwritten statement to supplement an official police report about how Cait had taken on a vampire all by herself just one floor below me and survived, killing two assailants practically with her bare hands and sinking an arrow into the fleeing vamp. *Where the fuck had she had time to study archery?* I wondered.

She just didn't seem to be afraid of anything. It wasn't like she had a death wish, either. She was just a badass. I'd seen SAS blokes with less bollocks.

Schaeffer had offered up details on her interactions with Cait, how they had gotten along, and a long report on their rescue of Liz, Katie, and Marcella. It practically glowed with admiration, in at least as much as the reserved Agent ever glowed about anything.

There was even a letter from Katie, hand-written in flowing script, about how wonderful "mama" was and the things she'd done to protect her from the Finchers and Carter Reese.

According to all this, she was a fucking saint. Not that I couldn't read between the lines in places. Cait was brash, almost reckless in her dedication to others. She had ruthlessly tortured a man for information about Katie's and Liz's whereabouts. Nastasia had written that in glowing terms as well, which was a bit creepy, and told me all I needed to know about Nastasia.

I snorted when I began to realize that Cait had slept with almost all of them, except Katie, of course. "Making up for lost time, I bet," I muttered when it hit me. The only person who hadn't offered a perspective on Cait was Morgan, other than the official report from the "hellscape," as she called it.

It was hard to imagine. When we'd been kids, Cait had always been the shy and quiet one. Yeah, she had been goofy and silly at home, but in public, she was almost bloody demure. The only time she'd ever been in a fight had been to protect me. She'd always been at my side. But I'd secretly hated that. I'd hated that she was the good kid, always doing the safe thing, always with the straight A report card, Dad's favorite. I'd always felt like I had to measure up to her. Now, I realized I never could.

I sighed heavily, dropped the papers on the floor, and went back down to the sub-basement. And sitting there next to Cait's inert form, I spilled the truth.

"You know, I always knew you were out there. It wasn't like what they did to you. Marcella didn't even bother. She and Liz told me to leave you be so that you'd be safe, and like a dullard, I'd just done what they'd said. But I always knew what I'd lost. In truth, though, Sis, I didn't want you to know that feeling." Deep pressure pushed at my eyes as tears came unbidden. "I'd like to say that I wanted you to be safe, and that's why I never looked for you or tried to contact you, but that would be a lie. I wanted to be alone. To have a chance to prove myself without you around. I wanted to shine with my own light. Instead, I did fuck all. I know that you always looked up to me when we were kids, but if you could see me now, you'd be ashamed and disappointed. Especially knowing that I didn't want you around.

"I could do whatever I wanted without you in my ear about bad decisions. Now I wish I could take it all back. But I can't, and now look at us. I'm so sorry, Cait. I should have been there." I leaned over and kissed her on the forehead, stroking her hair and finding her body warmer than I expected. "Please come back," I whispered. "You're my other half. I need you."

As if in answer, as I watched, Cait screamed aloud and arched upward in tremendous pain. A smoking spiral brand appeared on her chest, just over her left breast.

"Cait?"

I returned upstairs and brought down Liz and Marcella, showing them the brand.

"It just appeared," I said in explanation. "She screamed, then it was just there. What does it mean?"

Marcella and Liz both shook their heads.

"I don't know," Marcella said. She checked over Cait's body but could find nothing untoward. "I'll look into it and call Bian. I'll let you know. You look exhausted, Aoife. You should get some rest."

I nodded. Still, I waited for almost an hour, sitting next to Liz, maybe hoping that Cait might just suddenly open her eyes, but she didn't.

I sighed, bid Liz goodnight, and left, heading back to Cait's room, where I curled up and cried. I didn't know who I cried for, Cait or me, maybe both, but the tears were furious and had clearly been a long time in coming because I sobbed until I fell asleep.

"Aoife? I'm here. Do you want to sleep here tonight? I can stay with you if you like."

I opened my eyes and then closed them against the glare of

the hallway light. Exhaustion gnawed at my thoughts, and depression weighed heavy on me. The last thing I wanted was to stay at Marcella's. "No, Morgan, I want to go home."

I tried to pull together Cait's files from the bed. More had slid onto the floor while I slept, so Morgan gathered them up while I found my shoes and put them on.

"You two were together, weren't you?" I asked once my shoes were tied.

"Only for a night," Morgan replied, still cleaning up the files and not looking at them.

"Do you—"

"Stop. Let it go, Aoife. It's not worth the time. I'm not in love with your sister. I was infatuated with her when we were kids, that's all."

I nodded. I shouldn't have asked. It wasn't my business anyway. But I felt like shit, and I just wanted confirmation that I was second fiddle like I'd been all my life. Everything had always been about Cait. Cait's grades. Cait was the good one. Now, Cait is the heroic one. Cait the vampire. And me, Aoife, the dim echo, the shadow, the reflection that would always be less than the original. Second born, second loved, second rate. But that's how it was. And now I was the sister who had cancer. A disappointing end to a disappointing life. It was a bitter pill to swallow.

With the files straightened, Morgan looked down at me, sitting on the bed still, staring at my now idle hands.

"Come on, Aoife," she said tenderly, taking my hand. "You still look exhausted. Let's get you home."

This had been a shit day, and she was right. I was still tired. But I was tired all the time these days.

Before we left, I stopped at Katie and Leah's room and waved goodbye. Leah was asleep, looking like the little angel she was. Katie was looking at her phone intently with her earbuds in and waved at me half-heartedly. I gave her a wan smile and waved back, but she was back in her TikTok or Insta feed or whatever.

"They didn't ask you to write your own take on Cait?" I asked once we were on the road back toward the apartment.

"They did," Morgan replied. Her voice was quiet and reserved. "I just didn't see the point. Cait's a hero, sure, and there wasn't anything else I could add on that count."

I could tell there was something else. "And?"

"And she's an emotional wreck, Aoife. She doesn't take care of herself well. And she was all over the place. She slept with me, Nastasia, and Liz. I didn't think that was something any of them would want me to write. I certainly didn't think they'd show that to you."

"What do you mean?"

"Cait wants to be loved," Morgan explained. "But she's too broken to take it. Well, until recently. She and Liz seem to be getting on well."

"Eww, don't remind me. My sister and the four-hundred-year-old vampire that I used to call Auntie Liz."

Morgan laughed. It didn't have the silk in it like Marcella's or the tinkling beauty of Liz's. It was an honest laugh, born from her tenor voice and large frame.

"Aoife, Cait doesn't have your history with her, nor does Liz have that history with Cait. What else can I say? They fell in love. And boy, are they in love. It's pretty sappy."

I ran a hand over my face. I was still trying to digest that. In addition to staying with me from the time I was sixteen until I went to University for my undergraduate and helping me manage Uncle Donny, Liz had been there with my mother when I'd graduated, and when I'd shipped off to Afghanistan for a six-month stretch. She even attended my graduate baccalaureates at Oxford for both my Master's and Doctorate. She really was like my aunt, though now, she treated me like she probably did any other woman my age, less the biting, of course. Still, it was weird and a little isolating in some ways. I felt like Cait had kind of stolen her in a way. *And that's it, isn't it?* I told myself. *I feel alone and isolated.* But that wasn't the worst of it.

"I know she doesn't take care of herself," I said softly. "This may sound a bit weird, but sometimes I feel what she feels. At least, I think that's what it is."

Morgan glanced over at me. "What do you mean?"

"I didn't understand it then, but after reading what happened to her when she was Schmidt's captive, it kind of became clear. On Halloween last year, one of my first armed responses, after we'd grabbed a fugitive suspect, I had this searing pain in my arm, like someone was stabbing me. Later that night, my arm felt like someone was ripping it off. And Mother Lamia said that the first time Cait touched the tablets, Mother Darkness used our connection to, well, give me cancer."

Morgan scoffed. "Well, I'd say that's weird, but, well, vampire, you know?"

I snorted a laugh. "But that's not all. Then, when she got shot, I woke up early in the morning, unable to breathe, like I was suffocating."

"Shit. That's like out of The Corsican Brothers or something."

I nodded. "I know. And saying it, even though I lived it, it sounds crazy."

"No, it doesn't sound crazy. It sounds about as fucked up as anything else in this town. Aoife, you have no idea. All that, the gate, vampires, werewolves. It's all just the tip of the iceberg."

"Wait, werewolves are real?"

She pulled off the side of the road and stared at me. "Were you not paying attention when we told you Carlos was a werewolf?"

I smiled. "I was. I'm just fucking with you."

She chuckled and smirked, then got out of the car. "Okay, we're home."

"Home," I repeated to myself. It was a weird word for me to use. I hadn't had a real home in sixteen years, but this little dingy apartment felt more like a home than I could remember. Especially when Morgan was there.

CHAPTER TWENTY-NINE

Weyna

After the battle, we retired to the barracks. I was the last one in, and as soon as I'd stripped off my karkaríné and boots, the platoon seized me, carrying me bodily and throwing me into the bathing pool out back with the sound of hoots, hollers, and grand laughter. Then they all jumped in with me, except Saya, who stripped in a dignified fashion as befit her station and waded into the bath.

"Okay, ladies! Bring it out!" Saya called once we were all in and naked.

One of the women, a Valtárí named Sadai, retrieved a jar of what looked like black goo while the others surrounded me in the pool.

"What's going on?" I asked Zilly, but she only stood at the edge of the circle and gave me a crooked smile that beamed with pride.

Reni, one of the medhen, entered the tent, carrying the claw of the kóṣánt I'd killed. She stripped as well and entered the pool.

My nervousness heightened as I waited, only made worse when Zilly and Semi grabbed me, one on each arm to hold me. They were all still laughing though as the medhen entered the circle.

Saya delivered an ear-splitting whistle and held up a hand, and everyone turned serious. "We welcome one of our sisters into the ranks of the blooded fighters today!"

"Hurrah!" They all shouted in unison.

Saya continued. "Indeed, when I saw this scrap of a thing, I expected little. She was so small any one of us could have snapped her in two with one hand. But now look at her. How many of us have been downed in training by this little waif, myself included?"

There were some uncomfortable looks around the group, and I blushed furiously, uncomfortable at all the attention. The answer was eight, not including my first fluke of a fight with Saya. I had kept count, but I wisely kept my counsel on that point.

"On her first time out, she and her Valtárí sister took a kóṣánt in a single move! So, now we honor her with the brand." My nervousness became a burning anxiety in my breast as understanding dawned.

The medhen took the claw, and using a shadowsteel knife, she sliced it in half, exposing the spiral structure within. Everything began to make sense as she dipped the cross-section in the black liquid that Sadai held.

"Hold her!" Saya said, and the two women on either side tightened their grip. I gritted my teeth. I knew whatever was to come would be painful. I just hadn't a clue how painful.

Sadai pressed the sliced end of the claw, dripping with the black unguent, just over my left breast, and my heart skipped a beat as agony burst from my skin. My whole body felt like it was on fire, with the burning brand at its core. I shook and grunted with the pain, biting my lip painfully and tasting the liquid copper in my mouth, but I didn't cry out. I wouldn't cry out. I wouldn't—

I opened my mouth and let out a scream. My entire body seemed to seize up, and it felt as if every muscle contracted at once in a sharp convulsion. Darkness swam at the edge of my vision as the poisoned ink ran through my body. Black lines traveled through my veins, leaving a burning trail of pain in their wake. Stars burst in my eyes as the ichor reached my head, and my heart stuttered once more, fighting to beat in the wake of it.

The sisters held me steady for long moments before the

burning lessened, and the medhen removed the claw. She placed a hand over it and vanquished the poison, leaving behind only the blackened tattoo and a lingering sting spidering through me.

Grabbing my shoulders, the sisters dunked me under the water. I rose, spluttering slightly, as the medhen spoke again. "Rise from the water. Rise into your new life as a blooded Swasari and Valtárí. You are Weyna no more. You are now Skaja. Rise, Skaja, and embrace your sisters."

They all shouted, "Oye Konbom!" as pats and hugs rained down. And then it was over.

As we set to cleaning ourselves and enjoying the evening, Saya pulled me to her roughly and squeezed me so hard I groaned. "I am so very proud of you!"

"I couldn't have done it without you. You and Zilly and Óbin."

She leaned down, whispering in my ear. "No. You earned this. Never let anyone tell you otherwise, little shadow." Her eyes glistened with tears as she spoke, and I realized I'd never seen an Óşeni cry before. She wiped her eyes and turned away.

Later, as we celebrated by the campfire, Boudka appeared, dressed in black Shaddani robes, her hair braided and her face striped with three lines of woad across one eye. She didn't even look at me as she fixed herself a plate and then sat primly on the bench at my right side. Her plate was covered in food, making me laugh.

"Are you going to eat all of that?"

"Of course I am. I never waste food. Besides, I'm hungry. I'll need my energy for later," she said, giving me a salacious and appraising glance. "You know, you look really sexy in your kit."

I was dressed in the Valtárí casual uniform, plain grey boots, a black skirt of tough but supple hide, and a grey and black patterned bandeau across my chest, leaving the tattoo just above my left breast proudly bare.

"Did it hurt?" Boudka asked, reaching up a hand to touch the raised flesh, tracing the spiral pattern gently.

I snorted. "Yes, like nothing I've ever felt." I couldn't stop grinning. I was sure I looked like a smitten child.

Boudka watched me, her eyes twinkling in the light of the fire as I ate my roast pork and wild greens. She ate in a much more dignified fashion, and I suddenly felt like a clod, my hands covered in grease. Blushing furiously with embarrassment, I tried desperately to wipe my hands on a cloth napkin that, till then, sat unused next to my plate, and flushed furiously in embarrassment.

"I'm so sorry. Living with the Óşeni, I forget my manners."

"Hey!" Zilly protested from across the table.

Boudka chuckled at my discomfort and watched me, periodically picking food off her mountain of wild greens and fruit. Gingerly, she plucked up a slice of fruit and held it toward my lips. "Try it."

I looked at the strange red fruit, finally opting to bite into it. I tried to be sultry about it, but juice spilled down my chin, and I had to wipe it away quickly before it got on my uniform. Boudka laughed again. This time her eyes crinkled mischievously, and then she took my chin and leaned forward, pressing her lips to mine.

Semi gestured to Boudka's plate as she dropped down next to Zilly on the bench. "You going to eat that?"

Boudka shook her head, then took my hand and drew me from my seat.

Zilly snatched my plate and moved the food to hers, then called, "Hey! See that you bring her back in one piece, Boudka!"

Boudka threw a three-fingered gesture over her shoulder that basically meant 'get fucked' in Óşenic parlance. Zilly and Semi just laughed and continued to eat and drink.

Boudka was very quiet as we walked through the camp. I asked several times where we were going, but she said nothing until we arrived at my mother's bathing tent.

She pushed me down on the cot. "Sit."

I sat.

She stripped out of her robes, revealing her beautiful, lithe body. Boudka was captivating in a way that was so different from others in the camp. It wasn't just her form, though, with small, firm breasts, wide hips, and gentle, curving legs. It was her movements. Despite growing up in the shabby village nearby and spending her days toiling in the camp, she moved with a grace that belied her upbringing.

I watched, unable to move or even to breathe, as she moved to the bath, set a hand over it, and spoke a single word. "Tednia."

Soft steam rose from the bath as she stood wordlessly and drew me off the cot, reaching around and undoing the clasp on my bandeau, which fell to the ground.

She kissed my lips, wet and soft and sweet, pressing my arms back to my side when I tried to raise them and touch her. Then she undid my skirt, letting it fall to the floor. Finally, she lowered slowly to her knees, kneeling on the rug and unlacing my boots, lifting each leg gently as she removed them.

She looked up at me with her beautiful blue-grey eyes. Her expression was impassive and hard to read as she ran teasing fingers down my right thigh. I almost squirmed at the sensation of the light tips just brushing my skin, and I shivered.

She laughed a light lilting giggle. "Cold?"

I shook my head and closed my eyes, suddenly feeling very shy and vulnerable. I had slain one of the most feared beasts of mother darkness in a single strike, and here I was, trembling in front of a woman barely a year my elder. She was kneeling before me, but I was in her power, unable to do but what she bid.

I heard her stand, and I opened my eyes once more. She walked away toward the bath, casting a beckoning glance over one shoulder.

The bath water was hot and comforting, and once we were both fully immersed, she pulled me closer.

"I missed you," she said, taking a fistful of my hair in her hand and drawing me into an intense kiss that melted me in her arms.

"I missed you, too. So much." I pressed my lips back to hers, and she parted her lips, bringing heat to the already passionate moment as my tongue probed gently across hers.

A soft hand stroked the inside of my thigh, and I jerked involuntarily. "Sorry," I giggled, then gasped as her hand found the line between my thigh and a more intimate place.

I leaned against the ledge of the bath for balance as her fingers began to massage me. One leg rose and wrapped around her, pulling her closer. I leaned my head back and felt her gentle, wet, silky tongue slide across my throat and up my chin as her thumb made slow circles around my clit.

"Oh, mother of waters," I whispered between heaving breaths.

She didn't change her pace at all. She still moved around me in slow, languid circles, drawing out my pleasure almost to the point of begging for release from the excruciatingly slow rise and fall of my need.

I squeezed her closer, and she slowed her pace. "Oh, no, not yet."

My legs quaked, but she didn't stop, keeping me on the edge, bringing me toward orgasm only to slow her strokes and pull me blissfully, needfully away. I grabbed the walls of the bath, sloshing water over the edge as she pressed me against the side.

"Please," I whispered, pleading for her to make me cum.

"Oh, is the big bad warrior woman begging? That's so cute." Then she pressed, massaging my clit harder. "Like this?"

"Oh, Goddess, yes!" I cried as the building wave of orgasm pelted toward a crescendo.

She stopped again with a vicious laugh, and I groaned in agony and frustration.

"Oh, dearest," she cooed. "I'm going to have so much fun with you tonight."

"Oh, really?" I said, a wicked smile cracking my face. I hoisted her out of the water and set her down on the side of the tub, pushing her legs apart and burying my face between them before she could react. Immediately, I went to work on her, running my tongue through her folds and across her clit in wide wet strokes. She gasped and dug her hands into my hair, her fingernails digging under my braid.

She moaned loudly as she came, arching her back and

raking her fingernails across my neck, and her legs tightened around my head in orgasmic spasm after spasm. But I kept at it, drawing another climax shortly after the first.

Boudka jerked my hair, pulling me back as she dropped into the water and pressed her lips painfully to my mouth.

"Tell me that you love me," she whispered as she nibbled at my ear and throat. Her hand slid down between my legs, massaging me toward climax. She grabbed the back of my neck and bit painfully into it. "Tell me," she growled.

"I love you," I panted, lifting my head up. Unbidden thoughts came to my mind then, memories of my dreams, a stream of them, rode in on the waves of pleasure from Boudka's hand: a beautiful woman with black hair laying in the moonlight, a red-headed woman kissing me in the wastes of Shaddan, a blonde woman with ice blue eyes, tall and imposing, grinning at me with lust, blood on her chin.

"Oh, Goddess," I gasped as I crested the waves of pleasure between my shaking legs and squeezed Boudka closer until the orgasm finally passed, leaving me in the soft bliss of afterglow.

Boudka wrapped her arms and legs around me then, squeezing tightly, holding me as we kissed, my breath now coming in shallow gasps.

"I love you," I said again, more fervently, before we finally separated, breathing heavily.

It was hours later before the night truly ended. We lay on the floor, spent and exhausted. Boudka snored peacefully in my arms, but my thoughts were elsewhere, lost in the strange visions from my dreams, settling finally on a nagging image that wouldn't leave my mind, Zilly, her eyes flashing with lust on the battlefield. My stomach fluttered slightly as I thought of her pressing against my back on the practice field and straddling me that night next to the bath. And that was how I fell into slumber, not with thoughts of Boudka at my side, but with visions of Zilly, naked and beautiful under the stars.

CHAPTER THIRTY

Aoife

I would never forget the morning of January 30th.

"Let's do Valentine's."

I lifted my head from my book, one of the many lesbian romances that Morgan had laying around the house. It wasn't bad, and it was short, one of those 'girl meets girl, girl flits with girl, girl is clueless, girl gets it, sex ensues, complications arise, more sex, and, surprise, happy ending' books. And if anyone asked me, I'd lie and say I'd read it only once, but the condition of the cover suggested it was a household go-to, and this was my second go-round.

"What do you mean, precisely?"

Morgan looked a picture of innocence as she suggested it. "Let's get dressed up. Maybe even a little fancy. We can go out on a friend date and gawk at people. That way, neither of us has to feel bad about not having someone on Valentine's."

I shrugged, sounding non-plussed. "Okay. That sounds fun."

And that was all it had taken to pull me right out of my funk. I had been nonchalant in my answer, but as soon as she'd asked, my heart picked up a little and warmth crawled up my cheeks. I lifted my book a little higher.

"Good book, is it?" Morgan asked, obviously noting the physiological changes and maybe the bit of curl at the corners of my mouth.

"Mmhmm," I answered quickly. "I'm at the good part

where Lilly and Jesse brush hands over the cupcakes.

"Huh?" Morgan said with a smile of her own. "I could have sworn that was later in the book."

I ignored the comment. "You ever try these?" I asked, eyeballing some of the recipes that filled the last few pages. The book was about two chefs, and the author had added some recipes for the dishes mentioned in the story.

"No, but they're not earth-shattering, Aoife. Who's never had good cornbread or biscuits and gravy?"

I stayed silent. I'd never had either. I looked up. Morgan was watching me.

"What?"

"You mean to tell me you have never had a good country breakfast?"

I frowned at that. "Of course I have. Fried egg, tomatoes, mushrooms, white and black pudding, and bacon. It's delicious. Except for the black pudding, it's disgusting."

Morgan tilted her head. "One, black pudding *is* disgusting. I have no idea how Cait can eat it. Two, I'm talking about eggs, grits, sausage, American bacon, not that weird rasher stuff, and biscuits smothered in sausage gravy."

"What's a grit?" I asked flatly.

"Oh, honey. We need to fix that right now." She began throwing on clothes and grabbing her keys. "Just stay put."

I lay back on the bed. If she was going to get breakfast food, then who was I to argue? I was hungry anyway.

When she got back, Morgan grabbed a flannel shirt out of her closet and threw it at me. "Put this on and join me in the kitchen."

"Yes, Ma'am!" I replied, snapping a solid British salute.

"Here, follow this." She pulled a small index card out of a file and handed it to me.

"Cornbread? Can't *you* make it?"

Morgan continued removing a few items from the bag. "I could, but I want you to learn how to."

I scowled at that and crossed my arms. "Morgan, I'm dying. I don't see—"

She stepped right into my space and put a finger on my lips.

"Now, you listen to me. There's nothing for that, so we're going to go on as if it's not happening until it matters."

I opened my mouth to say something, then shut it abruptly. Then I said out of nowhere, "You know you have the prettiest green eyes." It wasn't a lie. She did have some of the most startling eyes I'd ever seen.

She narrowed those eyes at me. "Don't think flattery will get you anywhere with me, Missy. Now, can you manage that recipe?"

I looked down at the card. It was beyond simple. "Do you have a cast iron skillet?"

She pulled out a well-seasoned skillet. "Here you go." Then she gave me a smirk. "And, um, thanks."

My mouth curved up into a slight smile, and I got to work.

An hour later, we were sitting at the table. In front of us, we had cornbread, biscuits and sausage gravy, scrambled eggs, and sausage patties. A total cholesterol bomb and it was delicious.

Morgan even ate, saying, "I know I'll pay for this in about an hour, but I don't care. I haven't tasted a good breakfast in weeks. I so miss this. Also, the cornbread is fantastic. What did you do?"

I grinned. "Substituted butter for the oil."

We sat there for a moment as I downed my orange juice. "You know, when—" She stopped and then looked away. "I like having you as a roommate. I thought it'd be hard, but Aoife, you make it easy."

I just shrugged. "Yeah, sure, but what can I do? It's tough being perfect."

We both laughed and finished up. Then we laid down back in bed after putting away the dishes and the food. Morgan, almost on the hour, darted to the bathroom and heaved up the breakfast, brushed her teeth, and came back. I felt bad for her, and it reminded me why I'd turned her down. I didn't want that. I wanted to grow old, eat eggs, die of a heart attack or something, even the cancer growing in my brain. But I never wanted blood to be my favored diet. It seemed monotonous and a little miserable.

Morgan didn't seem to mind, though. When I said something, she just shrugged and got back in bed.

"You get used to it. Now go back to sleep before we get called in."

We passed out for a little bit longer, and it was nice until both our phones buzzed around noon.

"Please get that," Morgan muttered, and I slapped at my phone.

"Reagan, PIU."

It was Carlos. "We've got a lead on your assassin, and it's odd. Meet me there. And bring Kennedy." He gave me an address in West Roxbury.

I leaned over and tapped her shoulder. "I heard," she said tiredly.

There was a chuckle on the phone. "You know I can hear everything, including the bedsheets rustle."

"Fuck you, Carlos," Kennedy snapped, though half-heartedly. "We're not having sex. Not that it's any of your business."

I rolled my eyes. "We'll be there," I answered, annoyed at both of them, and hung up.

"Come on, Red. Get up," I mumbled as I dragged myself to the bathroom for a shower and to brush my teeth.

An hour later, we were pulling up to a relatively nondescript blue two-story house in West Roxbury.

"Oh, my God!" Morgan said as we pulled up.

"What?" I asked, but she didn't answer immediately. Instead, she threw the cruiser into park and launched herself out, stalking toward Carlos, who was standing by the door with a few uniforms.

The house and lawn both looked unkempt. Of the two mismatched front doors, one had clearly been recently replaced. From the half-finished repair work, it looked like someone had kicked it open from the inside.

"What happened here?" I asked as I walked up to Carlos and Morgan.

Carlos immediately grabbed me by the arm and pulled me away from the other officers. "I should have said something.

This is the place where Gabe used to live," he hissed.

I shook my head, befuddled. "Gabe? Gabe who?"

"Parkman. Cait's ex. He's locked up in Bridgewater. Marcella sent him off the deep end. Or at least we think Marcella did it. I was never clear on that part. He murdered his own mother."

My eyes went wide, but I kept my voice low. "Wait, Cait was dating a guy who murdered his own mother?"

"Long story. If you want more details talk to Marcella. But, someone's been living in here. Come on."

We followed Carlos into the building, and immediately, every hair on the back of my neck stood up as if I was being watched. Everything about the place felt off. If I didn't know better, I'd have sworn the place was haunted. Of course, when I thought about it, I realized that I didn't know better. Vampires were real, so why not ghosts?

The house was split with the ground floor providing one apartment. Looking around, it was clear that no one had cleaned in the place in months. Dust covered everything, and the kitchen was full of opened canned goods, partially eaten, straight from the cans.

"Is it Gabe?" I asked, genuinely concerned. Maybe he was Cait's assailant, and we'd just missed it. "Could he have gotten out?"

Carlos shook his head. "Nope. I checked on that the day Cait got shot. He's still locked up tight."

The bed in the back bedroom was a mess. It was dirty, and the bedclothes were matted with grease as if someone who hadn't bathed in months had been sleeping here. The smell was awful, and I turned away until I got used to it.

Carlos pointed to the floor next to the bed. Lying there were a shotgun and an open FBI badge wallet belonging to Matt Reynolds. Next to those lay some black goop. It looked a little like the ink we'd seen on the Chinese ship, but this stuff was definitely different.

When Carlos shone his flashlight on it, it moved.

"Jaysus, Mary, and Joseph," I shouted and jumped back about three feet. "What the fuck?"

"That's the stuff we were talking about," Morgan said, bending closer to get a better look.

"Careful," I squeaked as it seemed to pull toward her.

"Fascinating." Morgan sounded like Mr. Spock.

"Hey, get away from there. That's mine," Doyle said from the doorway as she came bouncing in. She looked about a thousand percent better than the last time I saw her.

"Nice necklace," I commented, noticing the gold collar around her neck etched with strange markings even I couldn't identify. I hadn't pegged her for a sub, but if she wanted to wear it to work, who was I to stop her?

"You like it? Marcella gave it to me," she said nonchalantly as she rummaged in her kit.

I frowned, puzzled. *Marcella? Not Nastasia? Good Gods, but this girl got around.*

Doyle pulled out a Petri dish and scooped up the little bit of ooze with a pair of forceps, placing it in the dish before sealing it with a couple of rubber bands. Then she held it up to her light, looking at it. For all the world, it looked like a wiggly piece of black silly-putty.

"Wow," she said, then jumped as it scooted closer to the side facing Morgan, pressing against the side of the dish. Doyle turned the dish, and it kept moving over as close to Morgan as it could get. "Neat."

"Yeah, for sure, fair play to you, Doyle, but neat isn't the word I'd use. Creepy as all fuck, maybe."

Doyle stuck her tongue out at me, and for a moment, I wondered how it might taste, then stomped on that idea. She wasn't my type.

Carlos sighed. "Well, great. It's a vampire seeking ooze."

"What are you doing here, anyway, boss?" Doyle asked.

"I wanted to see for myself what they'd found. I have a vested interest in finding this son of a bitch, same as all of you."

I tilted my head. It sounded reasonable, but I could see by the twitch in his face that he was holding something back, so I prodded.

"And?"

Carlos turned on me, his face hard and about eating the head off me. "And nothing. Cait's my friend."

I raised my hands in a placating gesture. "Sorry, I just thought you were going to say something else."

Carlos frowned and then stalked out, calling over his shoulder, "Just find this bastard and bring him in."

Morgan and Doyle both looked shocked.

"I take it that's not normal?" I asked. It did seem a little out of character from what I'd learned of him over the last couple of weeks.

We did a full sweep of the house. Other than the shotgun, which I suspected a pin test would show was the murder weapon, or rather attempted murder weapon, we didn't find much else. Doyle took samples from the bed for DNA testing. Reynolds, being an agent, would be in the database.

Outside, Morgan and I talked to the officers from E-5 down the street while Doyle kept working inside. Apparently, there was a report from a neighbor that someone had been going in and out of the house. From the looks of things, he'd been doing it for some time before he got caught. We thanked the officers and reminded them to send in their reports, for which we got a pair of unkind gestures and a laugh.

"It's odd that he'd hole up here," Morgan said as we gazed up at the creepy ass house.

Having been in it and seen the goop for myself, I felt like the house had taken on a darker, more menacing appearance. As if it were looking down on us, as a snack maybe. "He knew about the place from the reports, I'm sure. I mean, Gods, it was all over Twitter, Facebook, and TikTok."

Morgan paused for a moment. "You always say Gods, instead of God. Any particular reason?"

"For sure, God's an asshole. If he's so all fucking loving, why create gay people and then lambast them in the Bible. No thanks. The whole Jaysus, Mary, and Joseph thing is just habit."

"Fair enough," Morgan said, but she didn't say more, her eyes narrowing at the house. "Come on."

With two patrol officers still outside to keep Doyle safe, I followed Morgan. Though, we didn't get two steps before a familiar voice piped up. "Is this a private venture, or can anyone join?"

We turned to find Agent Schaeffer standing there.

"Sure, come on. The more, the merrier." Morgan said, and we followed her lead.

"Hey, go easy on Marcella," Angela said. "She's not as bad as you think."

I stopped abruptly and turned to Angela, my jaw working as I thought about how to respond. "Angela, she took away—"

"I know," she interrupted and flinched as if I might go off on her.

I just waited, arms crossed.

"She knows she fucked up. You should go talk to her."

I nodded but committed to nothing. The last thing I wanted was to go talk to Marcella Carson.

"Hey! Moonlight's burning, y'all!" Morgan called, and we hustled after her.

We followed her down into the basement, weapons drawn. The stairs creaked like a rocking chair with each step, and we dismissed all pretense of stealth. The entire place was covered in the same black goo, but it didn't seem to be moving, which was both good and disconcerting all at once but, truthfully, not a bit comforting. I expected the stuff to just snap closed on us like some smothering blanket.

The entire place was more than dark; it was oppressively black. Our pitiful torches did nothing to lighten the gloom, and the wall switch was covered by the same black shit as everything else, even the washer and dryer.

"Yeah, fuck this, Morgan. Why are we down here?" I asked. I didn't bother to try to keep the shaking out of my voice.

"Over there," Morgan said, and we followed her as she strode to one corner as if we were just walking across the foyer at home. "I knew it."

We walked up, Angela groaned, and I stared in disbelief. There in the wall of the house was a hole leading into a dark vertical shaft.

"Nope," Angela said flatly. "Nope. Nope. No way. This

one's on you, Kennedy. I'm not going down there. Huh, uh."

"I'm with her," I said flatly. "It looks like a one-way tunnel to hell right there."

"Don't be ridiculous. If you can get into it, you can get out."

Morgan reached down and plucked her radio from her hip. "Victor 8-8-3."

"Go ahead, 8-8-3," dispatch replied.

"I need the full PIU team here, full gear." She gave the address, and I sighed.

"Acknowledge 8–8-3. Also, tell 8-9-4 that Yankee Charlie 2 is looking for her."

Yankee Charlie 2 was the Chief of Police unit number. Sesi's number.

"Fuck," I swore. Lisa must have called her. I knew it.

Morgan held up a finger, keying her mic. "Is it urgent?"

"Not urgent," dispatch replied, and I felt at least a little more calm about it. I was still going to jail, but it wouldn't be until tomorrow, at least.

"PIU en route," dispatch added, then signed off.

"Let's go get dressed. Sure you won't come, Angela? We've got toys to play with?"

"You know what?" Angela answered, clearly unimpressed. "Shooting guns isn't actually a pass-time of mine. So, no. I'll wait up here."

CHAPTER THIRTY-ONE

Aoife

When Maki and Freyer joined us a short time later, we took a few minutes to gear up. Freyer dug out a pair of portable spotlights and set them up in the basement with the winch. Just as we were all ready, Doyle joined us outside, taking a few minutes to get one of the patrolmen to deliver her samples to HQ.

"Can I go with you?" She asked me as we started toward the back door.

"You know how to handle an MP5-SD?" I pulled one and handed it to her.

She checked it out like a pro, sighted in, flipped and unflipped the safety, and set it back down. "That good enough?"

"You can go," I responded.

About a half hour later, we were all set. I checked my watch. It was just after midnight, and the sunrise was marked for 6:43 AM, plenty of time.

"How far are we from the gate chamber," Doyle asked.

"Six miles," I answered automatically.

Morgan looked at me. "How do you know that?"

I laughed. "I did grow up in this town. Besides, google says it's six miles." I held up my phone.

"Glad I'm not crawling six miles," Schaeffer bitched as we set up in the basement.

"Hey, at least the worm's dead," Morgan responded, and

Schaeffer shivered. So did I, for that matter. I had seen the picture Freyer had taken of it. Eww.

After our radio check, we lowered Freyer into the tunnel, which, on closer examination, was only about a fifteen feet drop. "You suck, Morgan," he said as she started the winch. "You couldn't just leave well enough alone."

"Sorry, Freyer," she called down. "It's the job."

Freyer's voice came over the comms. "No contacts. Tunnel runs straight northeast toward the chamber; this is the end of it. But I think I see a couple of side tunnels."

I closed my eyes. "Are we sure this is a good idea," I asked again. But no one was listening.

"Up next," Morgan said, clipping me in.

I secured the chin strap on my helmet and stepped over the lip of the hole. "If I get eaten down there by some oily beast, Kennedy, don't expect any more sex."

Morgan laughed and gave me the finger. Angela's eyebrows shot up. And I thought Doyle was going to have kittens.

"Already?" Doyle asked.

"She's joking," Morgan said, and she shot me the finger one more time for good measure as she started the winch. I gave her two fingers in return.

"She sure didn't sound like she was joking," Doyle said loudly.

"She's joking," Morgan assured her again. Her voice was actually full of mirth rather than irritation, and I grinned in the dark as the cable lowered me down.

When I reached the bottom, I found Freyer in a low crawl position, his weapon pointed down range. "Did I hear that right?" He asked.

"She's joking, Freyer," came Morgan's voice over the comms.

"Fucking vampire ears," He griped, although a little quieter.

"I heard that," Morgan said as the line disappeared back up above us.

"Okay, kid, ladies first. So you just move up there and take point," Freyer said, rolling to the side so I could squeak past him.

I gave him a wry look. "Yeah, sure, thanks."

Morgan was down last, behind Maki and Doyle. She clipped the remote for the winch to the end of the line, and we started forward. Going was slow, and I now had a good feel for the misery they'd endured when they'd investigated the tunnel under Councilman Waller's house. It wasn't hot, though. The tunnel was cool and relatively easy to traverse, if a bit damp in places where rainwater had obviously seeped through. It also had a relatively shallow downward slope.

"You ever do this?" Freyer asked when we'd come to the first junction.

I looked left and right before answering. "No." Both tunnels continued for some distance, off to where my torch wouldn't reach. "Which way?"

"Straight up, I'd say," Freyer said. "Anything behind us?"

"All clear," Morgan replied. She was in the zone, responding professionally and perfunctorily. Having her here watching our backs gave me significant comfort, more so even than on the ship.

"Is anyone else hot?" Doyle asked behind me.

"It's gotten a little warmer, but not much. Why?" I paused to look back at Doyle, who was pushing up the sleeves of her fatigue top.

She fanned herself with one hand. "It feels like a million degrees to me."

Morgan reached forward and handed over her pouch of pedialite. Doyle guzzled it down.

I shone a light on her face. Her pupils looked a little blown, and her face was pale. "Hey, you feeling alright? You want to go back?"

She shook her head. "No. I'll be fine. Keep going." She waved me on.

I frowned with concern but let it go as I pulled up to my feet and frog-walked forward. The slope didn't change one bit, taking us further under the city. After what I gathered was probably another six hundred feet by my steps, it opened into a chamber, a cave, really.

The walls were clearly dug out by the same clawed

creatures that had cut the tunnel, the ogumo, but it was strange. A plush carpet of strange moss spread out before us, a riot of purples ranging from soft lilac to royal, subtly pulsating with a phosphorescent glow that bathed the entire cavern giving it an unearthly and unsettling beauty.

Nestled in the moss were blooms of flowers, almost surreal, some of them swaying gently, their long stamen undulating as if dancing to an unheard melody.

Deep blood reds and vermilions covered mushrooms and fungi that filled the room among the multicolored flowers, all colored in dark hues of blue.

Perhaps most eerie of all was the silence. Everything that moved or swayed did so with absolute quiet. The only sound we could hear was our breath and the shuffles of our feet echoing off the walls.

"What the hell is this?" I gawked as I slowly slid from the tunnel into the open cave.

The floor formed a long bowl, and several tunnels moved off in other directions. There were no signs whatsoever of the ogumo or the black slime we'd encountered earlier. A few of the flowers had tendrils, stamen, that flittered about along the petals, tossing bits of pollen into the air, and the entire place smelled like—well, I didn't know what it smelled like. It was floral, but nothing I recognized. There were notes like honeysuckle and roses, but they were subdued, not quite as sweet.

I moved aside to let the others in. Doyle drew on a latex glove and reached for one of the mushrooms, but I caught her hand before she touched it. "Don't. This is alien stuff, Doyle, and all I can imagine right now is Jess and Aoife, the fungus zombies. So let's not go there."

She nodded, but her eyes were wide with fascination, not fear. I could see on her face that something about the place captivated her. And she took a slight step forward, almost stepping on another mushroom before I pulled her back. "Watch it."

"I've seen this before," Doyle said softly. "In a dream."

It wasn't until I wiped the sweat from my brow that I

realized how hot I was.

"What about you two? You ever see anything like this?" Maki asked Freyer and Morgan, who both shook their heads.

"No," Morgan said. "The other side of the gate is a wasteland. Nothing grows there, at least not anywhere we went."

I moved to the right a little further, trying to edge around the circumference of the cave, but a smattering of little midnight blue mushrooms crawled from under the red ones and moved to block my way.

"Well, that's not normal," I said, watching them.

I tried going around the other way, but the mushrooms followed me, and more surrounded me. Then a path opened to the other side of the cave.

"Um, guys," I said nervously, suddenly extremely uncomfortable with being down here at all.

"Don't move," Freyer said cautiously.

I froze. "What?"

"There is something small and furry climbing up your back."

Now that he'd said something, I could feel it, four little appendages grasping at my fatigue top and moving up my right shoulder. "Well, get it off," I said, panic starting to rise in my voice. "Please, Freyer."

Something furry tickled my ear, and I heard Freyer release the safety on his weapon, but then Morgan said, "Wait. Look."

The thing, whatever it was, started chittering in my ear. It wasn't a scary sound, like my imaginings of what the ogumo sounded like. It was almost cute, mixed with purring and cooing.

"You see, this is how it gets people," I whispered. "It looks cute, and then, all of a sudden, it gets big somehow and mean and nasty, and then it eats me." I started to whine. "So, please, get it off me."

But it didn't get big or mean or nasty. It climbed down onto my forearm and perched there, looking at me. It was the strangest little creature I had ever seen, and bloody cute. It had an almost mouse-like face and was covered in purple and blue hair. Large eyes filled most of its head. The closest thing I could compare it to was a lemur, right down to its long prehensile tail, which was wrapped around my arm.

In a moment of absolute insanity, I reached down and touched its fur. It nuzzled into my finger like a cat looking for strokes.

"Okay, that's really cute," Morgan said.

"Um, guys, I don't feel so good." Doyle's complexion turned pallid, and she dropped to the ground in a faint, sending a massive puff of bright red spores into the air. The blue and red mushrooms all skittered away across the floor, leaving her there in an empty space, like some twisted and dark Alice in Wonderland. As if Alice in Wonderland hadn't been twisted and dark enough.

"Jaysus, Doyle." I dropped down beside her. The lemur-thing, or whatever it was, squealed in an adorable little protest but didn't dislodge, so I used my left hand to check her pulse. Doyle was breathing, and her pulse was strong, but her skin was hot and feverish, really hot.

"Okay, I'm calling it," I said flatly. "We're over our heads here. Time to back out. As soon as we can, call for an ambulance."

It was fortunate that Doyle had her helmet on, because dragging her inert form was a chore. We bumped her head at least a dozen times, no matter how careful we tried to be, mostly because we felt like we were racing against the clock. Her fever kept ticking up, I could feel it every time I touched her. If we didn't get her cooled down soon, it'd kill her.

"I don't like this," Freyer said as Morgan lifted away into the shaft.

"What's to like?" I asked. "We just got pelted with alien spores, and Doyle's burning up with fever. I'm not seeing an upside here."

Freyer coughed, and then so did Maki.

"I'm not feeling well either," Maki said, then she barfed red goo all over the ground, followed immediately by Freyer, who just threw up what looked like lunch.

"Shit," I muttered. "Hurry up, Red! They're getting sick

down here."

The cable came down, and I hooked in Doyle first. She was the sickest, at least as far as I could tell. Strangely, I felt fine. The little creature on my sleeve seemed okay as well. I'd tried to shake her off a dozen times, but she just kept coming back and jumping on me. I didn't have the heart to kill it, and I didn't really have time for anything else in the rush to get Doyle out.

Maki, you're next, I said when the cable returned. She didn't argue. She was barely coherent. Whatever they were suffering from, it was some kind of fungal poisoning.

Morgan's voice came over the line. "Aoife, you okay?"

"Yeah, but these guys aren't doing so well. Maki's on her way up. She's going on about something, but I can't understand her. It's a mix of Chinese and Japanese. I can't follow it."

The cable returned a few minutes later. Freyer was a little less out of it. He just looked pale and miserable, more like a hangover.

"You okay, John?" I asked as I hooked him up.

"Yeah, I just feel like I've got a sudden stomach flu, aches and pains."

"That's inflammation response. Your body's fighting it off. Just hang in there." I felt his head. He was running a low-grade fever, not nearly as hot as Doyle.

"Take him up," I called, then sat down as far from the vomit as I could. It was only two minutes, but it was probably one of the longest two minutes of my life as I sat down there alone with my weapon aimed down the tunnel. Thankfully nothing came running down after me. Which I thought strange. If this was a nest for the ogumo, then there should be a bunch of them, and there were none.

Finally, the cable returned, and Morgan hoisted me up. This was going to be a long fucking night.

CHAPTER THIRTY-TWO

Aoife

Morgan and I sat in the hospital in paper gowns while they ran tests on us for the third time in four hours. As expected, Morgan's blood came back normal. It was someone else's blood for sure, probably whomever she had last fed on, but it was still just blood. With a little effort and some breathing, she could even make it move around fairly normally. I began to realize that Liz had actually given me a pretty good education in vampire physiology.

"Ms. Kennedy, you can step into the next room, please. You're clear," the Doctor said. "We want to keep you under observation for the next twenty-four hours, but we think you dodged a bullet."

Yeah, I thought. *She was dead and didn't breathe.*

"How are you feeling, Detective Reagan?" The doctor asked a guy named Eidelbaum, who specialized in infectious diseases.

"I feel fine," I answered. And I did. Whatever was making the other sick didn't seem to be affecting me. "And I don't think it was the fungus that made Detective Doyle sick. She passed out before it exploded around us."

"Tell me about that," he said. He seemed nice, dark-haired, short-trimmed beard, well dressed, a typical doctor in my book.

"Well, we were crawling through a tunnel, and Doyle complained of being hot. I checked her out. Her eyes looked a little glassy, and I thought maybe her pupils were a little big, but it was dark down there. Then we came across some kind of artificial cave. Inside were a variety of fungi and flowers I didn't recognize. And then there was Fiona here." I rubbed the fur of the purple lemur sitting on my shoulder. They'd tried to take her off me a dozen times, but she freaked and scratched several people and kept hopping back into my lap until I told them to pack it in and leave her be.

"We were talking," I continued. "Then Doyle fainted. She fell into a bunch of mushrooms, and poof, a cloud of red dust exploded in our faces. I got the worst of it. But, as I said, Doyle fainted before the puff of fungus."

"So you've all been infected by what looks like an odd form of cladosporium, but it's not like anything I've seen before. I've sent some off for evaluation, but it's dying off pretty quickly inside of all of you, which is typical for most fungi. Typically the human body is far too hot for it."

"Okay, so we're good."

"Yeah, probably. But I need to catalog your symptoms and work up a profile on the stuff. And you need to be decontaminated."

"Lovely," I answered wryly. "Please tell me it doesn't involve wire brushes."

He chuckled. "No, Detective, no Silkwood showers. Just some anti-fungal soap. I am very concerned about Detective Doyle though, she's very sick. We're keeping her cool with ice packs, but it's only slowed the rise in her body temperature."

"Can I see her?" I asked.

He seemed to think about that. "There's not much more that we can do at the moment, so I don't see how it would hurt."

We stepped out of the negative pressure room and over to Doyle's. She looked fine, just a little flush. But I looked at the monitors. Her temperature was one-oh-five, and she was packed in ice. As a watched, it ticked up a tenth of a degree.

"Gods," I muttered. "Please hang in there, Doyle."

"Where is she?" I heard Nastasia say outside my little room the next morning. I wasn't officially in quarantine, they were just keeping me for observation, so I got out of bed and looked through the doorway.

"Are you family?" A nurse was asking.

"I'm the only family she's got," Nastasia replied, and I felt something, like a draw, deep within my stomach. Magic. Vampire glamour.

"Second room on the left," the nurse said and moved aside.

I followed Nastasia. "Hey."

Nastasia whirled on me. "Why didn't you call me? What the fuck, Aoife? I mean Cait. Oh, you know what I mean."

I looked at her, then frowned. "I'm sorry that my quarantine was inconvenient, but I had no fucking phone!"

She threw her arms up in exasperation. I knew she wasn't mad at me. Nastasia and I walked into the room and then were hurried out by another nurse. "You can't be here."

I caught her body temperature on the monitor, though. It read one-hundred-ten. "Oh, my Gods," I whispered and covered my mouth as a man in scrubs pushing a cart of cold packs about knocked me out of the way.

Nastasia grabbed me, desperation flashing in her eyes. "I can't lose her, Aoife. I just can't."

"Send them out and turn her," I suggested, apparently unhelpfully because Nastasia looked enraged by the suggestion.

"I can't!" She then lowered her voice to a hiss. "She's wearing the Sanguineward, the collar around her neck. No vampire can feed on her while she wears it. She was double-dipping."

I didn't know what that meant, but I could guess. Instead, I peeked into the room again and saw that, yes, she still had the gold collar on her neck. "Why didn't they take it off?"

"They can't. Only she can. She has to take it off willingly, and she's unconscious. It's magic."

I went to close my eyes in burgeoning grief when something caught my attention. Her heartbeat was a steady sixty-five. Her blood pressure was one-twenty-one over sixty-eight and holding firm. Her heart should have stopped by now as high as her body temperature had climbed.

The entire entourage of nurses and doctors were just standing around now, watching anxiously as her body temperature continued to climb.

We were all transfixed, unable to do anything but watch Doyle and the monitors. Her temp topped out at one-eighteen point one. She should be completely cooked out, dead, but her heartbeat was steady. I stepped quietly into the room and stood next to the nurse. Everyone was standing with mouths open.

"Look at her eyes," I said, awestruck. I could feel the pull in my stomach again, but this time it was much more powerful, like a cold wind passing through my body. My little lemur friend's hair was standing straight up, as if he felt it too. Doyle's eyes were rocketing back and forth under the lids.

"Impossible," one of the doctors said. "She should be dead."

"Yes. But she's not," I answered.

Then, after a minute or so, sweat beaded all over her body, and her temperature began to fall, precipitously. In minutes it was back down to one hundred, ultimately settling at ninety-seven point four, probably base normal for her.

"Get an EEG on her," I suggested since everyone else was just standing around and staring. One of the doctors I didn't recognize nodded to one of the nurses, and before long, they'd wheeled in a machine and hooked her up.

The paper began rolling, and we watched. I didn't know much about EEGs, but the wild movements of the needles suggested heavy activity to me. "Is she dreaming?" I asked.

"You can't be in here, Detective," a man's voice said behind me. It was Eidelbaum.

I slowly backed out of the room, saying nothing. The cold wind that had blown through me earlier had ceased, and I was quite aware that I had just seen something magical take place, but I had no idea what.

Nastasia stayed. "I'm her only family," she repeated, this time to Edelbaum, who just nodded.

"Is she okay?" Morgan asked when I walked outside.

I was in a bit of a daze and shrugged, unsure what to make of it. "I think so."

Morgan breathed a sigh of relief. "What happened?"

I shook my head. "I— I don't know. Her body temperature shot to an inhuman level, and she just shook it off. It should have killed her. I mean outright. She should be dead, but she's blissfully dreaming right now, asleep."

I walked back into my room, and Morgan followed. We sat on the bed together, and she held my hand as I just stared at the floor. "That wasn't those spores," I said and looked up at Morgan. "I don't think Doyle's human."

CHAPTER THIRTY-THREE
Aoife

The next morning, I checked in on Doyle, who was awake but snuggled up next to a sleeping Nastasia, holding on almost desperately to her. It was about as adorable as Nastasia got, I suspected, all cute and curled up.

"So, how are you feeling?" I asked, trying to figure out what I was seeing. It wasn't that Doyle was different. She was the same Doyle if a touch paler, but not in a sick way, maybe a touch closer to Nastasia's coloring—just a touch, though. And she had a glow about her like people say pregnant women get, but more so.

"I'm okay. Why are you looking at me like that?"

"Your body temp shot to one-eighteen. By all rights, you should be dead."

She gave me an incredulous stare. "Aoife, half the people I hang out with have either died and come back to life or are literally the walking dead. But I do feel weird."

"How so?" I sat down in the chair next to the bed, between her and the window, so we could see each other.

"I feel," She replied, and her face seemed to be struggling to find an expression to rest on.

"You feel what?"

"No, you don't understand. I'm what most people call a sociopath," she replied as if it were the most normal thing in the world, and yet there was a weird sadness in her eyes. "I have never felt anything real, not love, not empathy, not even real joy, for anyone or anything. I do police work because I want to be good, but I'm not. I'm more manipulative than Marcella. Everything I do is to get what I want.

"At work, I don't feel anything for the victims. Haven't you noticed that I never get upset at crime scenes? I don't like the smell sometimes, or I find something challenging or interesting, but I don't care about the people. I was diagnosed with severe antisocial personality disorder at nineteen. But now, I hurt—a lot."

I had suspected as much, but I'd never dug into it. "But you flirt with like half the women at HQ. And you seem to care a great deal about Nastasia."

"It's the sex. I like sex. It feels good. But up until about three hours ago, I didn't really care who I had it with. Nastasia's just good at it. And I like her bite. That's why I was double-dipping with Andrea and not telling Nas. I liked the feeling that getting bitten gave me. I liked it a lot. But now, I feel a bunch of things I don't understand, and I don't like it. My stomach hurts, and I— " She started to cry.

I offered her a box of tissues from the table next to me.

"And when I look at her," she glanced at Nastasia hopelessly, "it's suddenly like she's the most important thing in the world. And I have these butterflies right here," she pointed at her stomach, "and I'm—I'm—I suddenly don't want her to be away from me. I'm scared, Aoife."

She kept reaching back and scratching at her back, so I coaxed Nastasia into the lounger chair I was in and had Jess sit up so I could get to the spot for her, but when I touched her, I felt a charge of something, like a connection. It made my pulse race and drew me closer. I tried to push the feeling aside. Fiona scrambled over to my left shoulder and stared at Doyle with those huge eyes.

"Did you feel that?" She asked, looking at me but refusing to meet my eyes.

I nodded. "Yes, but tell me more about what's going on."

She looked down at the floor as if ashamed of something. Then when she spoke, it became clear. "When I was little—like five—I killed the neighbor's cat. I just wanted to see what happened. My mama was so mad. Daddy looked at me like I was the devil himself. And I didn't understand why. I didn't feel any remorse or anything. Now I can't get it out of my head." She squeezed her eyes shut and shook her head before she continued.

"Then later, after my daddy died, I started lying all the time, doing everything I could to get others to do things for me. I was ruthless. I used sex. I threatened people. I did some bad things. And I was only twelve. It didn't turn out well in the end. I got arrested for something, and Mama was about at her wit's end, so she took me to get some help, inpatient. I lived in a special home for two years. The doctors and therapists didn't teach me how to feel; no one could do that. But they taught me that to be productive, I needed to emulate people who did things that kept society flowing smoothly and to focus on small things for myself. It worked, mostly."

I shook my head skeptically, "But I've seen you cry."

"Crocodile tears," Doyle said. "When David died, Detective Mills, I didn't feel nothin', but I summoned up some tears to try to get your sister to go home with me. I was manipulating her to get sex. It was all I cared about.

"At least until today. I don't know what's going on. I feel like I'm coming apart. I don't have any coping mechanisms for this." She started to sob. Then she turned irritated. "Don't scratch so hard. What the hell is going on back there?"

"I'm not scratching at all," I protested. "I was just rubbing your back." I pushed aside the flaps of her gown. She had two long lines running down just inside her shoulder blades. Not scratches or injuries, but humps. When she moved, it was clear there was new muscle there, and something else. "Hmm."

"What is it?" She sounded a little panicked.

I reached out and touched the marks on her back where something jutted up just under the skin. Something was growing there for sure, and quickly. "Well, you've got two muscular lines here, I've never seen anything like it."

I examined the protrusions again and touched a spot that was hard, like bone, and Jess jerked slightly. "Ouch."

I grimaced. "Sorry. It's just—" I tried to be more gentle.

Then I got a good look in the sunlight and drew in a harsh, shocked breath.

"What!?" She almost shouted.

I put my arm around her shoulder and pulled her close. "So, stay calm and tell me. Where were you born?"

"Outside Charleston, West Virginia—coal country. I grew up in a small town. It's gone now. Disappeared in a flood a few years back. Why— "

I jerked a little in surprise. "I had no idea you were from Appalachia."

"It's pronounced apple-atch-ya. And one of the first things I did was ditch my accent when I moved here. It wasn't good for dates or the job. Now why are you asking?"

"Who were your parents? What were they like?"

She shot me a glare but continued. "They were great, as far as adoptive parents go, I guess. They tried really hard. Daddy died in a mine accident in 2010. Why— "

"Wait," I interrupted again, trying desperately to keep her calm and on track until I could get to an answer. "I meant your birth parents?"

"I don't know. No one does. I was left at a hospital in the middle of the night in Beckley. Eventually, I was put in foster care with my parents. They adopted me a year later."

I raised an eyebrow. "I'm sure it's never occurred to you that you might not be human."

She pulled away and turned, staring at me. "You're kidding, right? Of course not."

I shook my head. "No, I'm not. And I don't think you are, at least not totally. Yesterday when we entered that cave under the city with the plants, you didn't get sick, per se. I think something in there started a change in you."

"What kind of change?" Jess's words were a whisper, tinged with panic.

"I don't know. Are you hungry?" I asked.

"You're asking about food? I'm probably turning into a monster."

"Are. You. Hungry?" I asked again, enunciating each word.

She crossed her arms and grumped, "Yeah. I'm starved."

"What would you like to eat?"

"Something fruity, like berries or apples or something. And maybe some hibiscus tea."

I raised an eyebrow. I didn't think the hospital had hibiscus tea, but I'd check. Moreover, the order seemed weird for Doyle, who was more of an animal protein person. "I'll see what I can do."

Fiona hopped off of me and sat in Doyle's lap as I got up, earning a puzzled stare. "So now you find another friend."

Doyle stroked her fur. "She's kinda cute. You sure she's a girl?"

"Yeah, Morgan looked up her skirt. Did you know she has a degree in Agriculture?"

Doyle just nodded and kept stroking Fiona.

I stepped out and asked the nurse to get Doyle some food per her request. When I got to the hibiscus tea, the nurse rolled her eyes, and I shrugged in a 'hey, I'm just the messenger' kind of way.

"She's working on it," I told Doyle as I sat back down. "Given your body temperature last night and that you're growing new tissue, you need to keep your strength up. I suspect you're fast-burning calories."

Doyle just stared at me. "You sound like me, all cold and sanitized. Aoife!" She groaned. "What the actual fuck?"

Startled by the sudden outburst, Fiona squeaked and jumped up onto my shoulder.

I whispered to her. "And your girlfriend is a vampire. My sister is a vampire. There are mermaids and lamia under the streets. And I'm a Dark Faerie, apparently. I feel magic whenever it's used around me like you did last night without even knowing it."

She started to snivel again. "Well, why don't you have these humps?"

I shrugged and held her close. "Maybe I do, and they just haven't come out yet. Why are you crying?"

"I don't know," she answered, throwing her hands up and then dropping them in her lap like a little kid, and I couldn't help but laugh a little at the answer.

Nastasia finally woke up, her eyes snapping open. "What's going on? What's wrong?"

"I'm a Faerie!" Jess wailed, and I was forced to press my lips together to keep from laughing out loud. It wasn't funny, but it kind of was.

Nastasia stared at Jess. "Jess? Are you alright?"

She looked up at Nastasia. "No, I'm not alright. I love you, Nastasia!" Then she dug her face back into my shoulder and bawled some more.

Nastasia looked like she was about to fall over herself. "What happened?"

"Um, I think the larval stage is over," I said in all seriousness.

"I'm not a larva," Doyle whispered, sounding like she was about eight years old.

Nastasia moved to take my place on the bed. "No, darling, you are not a larva."

I whispered to Nastasia. "She's having feelings."

"So I gathered." Nastasia's tone wasn't nasty, but it made clear her desire for me to leave them alone.

"I guess I'll just go now," I said, feeling a little lost, and I walked toward the door. As I reached for the handle, I had this strange feeling come over me, almost overwhelming, as if Doyle was something precious and rare and that I should be protecting. As I began to close the door, Doyle looked at me in a way that was just as strange, like she needed me. Her mouth opened, then she seemed to think better of it and closed it. I shook it off, mostly, but the remnants of it nagged at me as Morgan and I waited for Liz.

CHAPTER THIRTY-FOUR

Aoife

They kept Doyle for observation for quite a while, but the rest of us were all released over the next seventy-two hours. Maki was in a right strop over being held the longest, but when I picked her up to take her home, she was all smiles. The next few days were, fortunately for us all, relatively quiet.

All we had on the Akkorokamui was a boatload of dead sailors, two poisoned scientists, and a dead receptionist. There was, in fact, DNA, but it wasn't human. Big surprise there. The closest relevant species was an octopus, no shock there, either. There was a piece to this that was nagging at me horribly, I couldn't figure out how the Akkorokamui knew about the scientists. And the poisoning, that wasn't exactly on form for the creature either, at least from what I knew of it. This had gone from the rage we'd seen on the boat to something more, like vengeance. *Gods, Cait,* I thought. *I wish you were here.*

"Reagan, Homicide," I answered when my phone rang with an unknown number on Tuesday morning around three AM. I was awake because Fiona was busy looking for a comfortable spot to curl up in the pit of my knee. That wouldn't normally keep me up, but her claws kept poking me through the comforter.

"Goddess, you sound just like her," Marcella said on the other end of the phone.

"That's the idea, isn't it?" I replied, shooting Morgan two fingers when she started snickering from the other side of the bed at my irritation. She knew I didn't like Marcella and seemed to relish in the conflict a little too much.

"Well, I'd like for you to come see me. Can you meet me at Legal Seafood, Copley Place, for lunch?"

I frowned. "Why?"

"Oh, for heaven's sake, Aoife, for once, can't you just be civil and join me for lunch? I need your help with something." Her tone was less irritated and more pleading, but there was a touch of annoyance. And, if I was being honest, I was being peevish, and I knew it.

I rolled my eyes and let out a harsh breath. "Fine. I'll see you at noon."

"Mind if I borrow the cruiser?" I asked Morgan as I tossed my phone to the floor next to the bed.

"Take my Honda. The keys are on the table over there," she muttered tiredly. "I want to go back to the ship. Wade had it towed down to a shipyard in Connecticut, and I want to see if we missed anything."

"You want help?" I asked, really just looking to get out of lunch with Marcella.

Morgan laughed and rolled over, giving me a silly smirk. "No. I'm good, thanks."

I stuck out my tongue at her, and her eyes lingered on it for a minute, then she grumped back over and laid down.

"What?" I asked playfully. "Cat got your tongue?"

"Oh, shut up," she replied. "Go to sleep. You have a lunch date to attend to."

I rolled my eyes and then turned my back to her. For a long time, I lay there, feeling absolutely agonized and thoroughly sexually frustrated. But sleep did finally claim me.

Marcella was sitting at the bar with a martini in front of her when I arrived, looking the picture of business perfection in her usual attire, though her pumps were bright yellow to match her blouse, and her skirt was a little longer with an almost scandalous side slit.

"So," I said, trying to be as polite as possible. "What can I do for you?"

Marcella turned to me. "Would you like a drink?"

The place was dead, probably on account of it being eleven in the morning. "Sure, Jameson, neat," I answered, and the bartender nodded.

"Cait drinks Scotch, you know," Marcella commented as my drink arrived.

"Scotch is for heathens, and don't get me started on that juniper rubbish you Brits call liquor."

She laughed, and the resonant tenor of her frye washed over me like warm water, making the hairs on the back of my neck stand on end.

"So, how are you holding up?" She asked, taking a sip of her Martini.

I blinked and turned my head, looking at her a little sidelong. "Um, fine."

"And how is Detective Doyle?"

I sighed and hung my head a bit. "Out of commission. Nastasia says she's a wreck, and I have this icky feeling like I should be protecting her or something. It just won't quit. It feels almost—I don't know—motherly. In the meantime, Nas says she's gone fruit crazy. All she'll eat is fruit, pretty much any kind. Nas tried to give her some fruit-flavored drink, and she spit it on the floor and accused Nas of trying to poison her. Apparently, if it's not pure fruit juice, she won't drink it. It's all very weird."

"Hmm. Nas was a little vague with me about all of it. What happened to her?"

I shook my head and sighed. "I don't know. We found this weird wild garden in a cave under Gabe's old place. You know where it is?"

Marcella raised an eyebrow and made a face I couldn't really read. "I do."

"Well, something down there changed her, pollen, weird spores, who knows. So, setting aside the antisocial personality disorder that just vanished, she discovers she might not be human after all. I mean, it's a lot, isn't it?

"Nas also said she's been acting strange in other ways. Like the day she left the hospital, she was practically obsessed over their house, talking about what I would or wouldn't like if I happened to stop by. I don't even know where they live. Fiona seems to like her, though, which is odd. Other than Morgan and me, Fiona's practically a hermit. She hides when anyone knocks on the door."

"Doyle's Fae," Marcella said as if that were an explanation. "She just didn't know it. Something in that cave must have triggered her transformation. And she's not just Fae; she's a Dark-Fae, like you and your other mother, The Morrigan. And as for your sudden need to protect her, that's your heritage as well. Your mother is the queen of the Dark-Fae. You're royalty, Aoife, and Fae, at least from legend, have very tight bonds. Unlike humans, Fae relationships are almost instinctual."

I looked at her askance. "And how do you know so much about it?"

"I went to Mother Lamia and Bian. They're pretty well schooled in such things. After Nastasia told me what little she did, I decided to see if I could help. Unfortunately, there's not much for it."

I looked at her, unable to decide how to feel about that. "And did they say anything about why her emotions are suddenly switched on?"

"Not really. But Bian suggested that she might be going through some kind of long term transformation. Things like that can affect brain and body chemistry. Truthfully, it's as good a guess as any. Speaking of Fiona, how is she?"

"My purple rat-monkey? She's fine, a pain in the ass, mind you, and she won't eat anything but red meat. She must have been starving down there. But she does sleep during the day for the most part, so I left her curled up next to Morgan. I know you didn't bring me here to ask about work, Jess, or my little purple pest, so what's on your mind, really?"

"I'm going shopping, and I wanted you to join me, that is if you don't have anything pressing."

I raised an eyebrow. "I don't know the first thing about fashion, Marcella, and I'm not sure I'd be the best company for you."

"Pish. Come on. I have things I want to tell you, and I need to grab a few items."

I rolled my eyes. "Okay, but don't expect much."

She smiled and it genuinely reached her eyes. "Lovely. Come along then."

We strode out of the restaurant and into the mall proper. Copley Place is an ultra-high-end shopping mall in Boston. Coach, Gucci, Louis-Vuitton, Louboutin, they were all here. I felt a little underdressed, which was ironic considering we were clothes shopping.

The first place we stopped was Alexander McQueen. Now I really felt underdressed.

"Ms. Carson," the attendant greeted us. She was a nice young woman in her twenties with caramel-colored skin and gorgeous eyes, smartly dressed, and her smile lit up her face. "Welcome back. How can I help you?"

"That double-breasted suit jacket I looked at yesterday, is it ready?"

"Yes, ma'am. Are we here for a fitting?"

Marcella clapped her hands. "Wonderful. Yes, can you bring it out?"

I noodled around and let my eyes bug out repeatedly at the price tags. Just a shirt in this place was two weeks' salary for me if I was working for real at the department.

"Aoife?"

I turned around and found Marcella holding out a gorgeous double-breasted black women's suit. "Here, go try this on."

I raised an eyebrow. "Why?"

Marcella pursed her lips and stared at me, her eyes hardening. "Aoife Reagan, if you don't try on this suit right now—"

I held up my hands. "Alright, alright. Don't get your knickers in a twist, ma."

I went into the dressing room and put it on. Now that I was out of sight of Marcella, I about jumped up and down. The suit was fucking beautiful. It was a black double-breasted jacket with full-length pants.

"Try this top on underneath," came Marcella's voice as she laid a white blouse over the door.

"Yeah, for sure," I said, trying to sound absolutely nonplussed.

I had never tried on things like this. I just didn't see the point. But actually trying on a thirty-five-hundred-dollar suit from Alexander McQueen was getting me a little excited. Who was I kidding? This craic was ninety, and my hand shook with anticipation as I took the top, more camisole than blouse, but it fit perfectly with the suit.

After I was dressed, I turned in the mirror, left then right. "Jaysus," I whispered. I looked like a fucking movie star almost.

"Miss?" The attendant called. "May I come in? I need to check the fit."

I opened the door, and Marcella whistled. "Perfect."

The attendant checked the shoulders, waist, and pants for measurement, but they were spot on. I figured they would be. My twin was happily laying in repose in Marcella's basement for convenient measurement.

"So, what do you think?" Marcella asked.

I stuck a hand in a pocket of the pants and leaned against the door. "Yeah, sure, you know."

"Don't be an arse, Aoife. Seriously."

"It looks, good," I said with a grin. "But it's out of my league."

"Okay, go take it off and bring it out."

Once I was back in normal clothes, I stood with Marcella at the counter where the woman bagged up the shirt and suit.

"What are ya' doin'?" I asked, my eyes about to bug out.

"I'm making sure you don't look like a fucking clip on your date."

"Date?"

"With Morgan? Valentines Day?"

"Oh, shite, I forgot." I hadn't, actually, but I was trying to get her to stop. "But it's not a date. We're just two friends going out."

Marcella nodded. "Sure. I understand." But she didn't stop.

She put the clothes on her credit card, handed me the bag, and tugged me out of the store. "Come on."

"Marcella, this is four thousand dollars worth of clothes. Are you out of your mind?"

"No, I most certainly am not. Now," she stopped and turned toward me, looking me in the eye. "Tell me you're not done in over your roommate and make it sound believable."

I looked away, heat flushing my face.

"Exactly," she said. "It's a date. Now let's go. Don't you want to look good for her?"

I took a deep breath then spoke firmly. "Yes, I do. But this isn't necessary."

Marcella looked back at me. "No, it's not. But I want to do it. And not because I feel guilty, though I do. I would like to do this because I believe you deserve happiness, and Morgan seems to make you happy. You both seem to be getting along extremely well."

I took a moment then nodded and scratched an imaginary itch on my nose. "Yeah, we do, but—"

She stepped closer. "No buts, Aoife. I screwed up. Please, it doesn't make up for anything, but it will make me feel better. Just let me do this. Besides, I know where you're going for dinner."

"Where are we going?" I asked, my interest piqued.

"It's a surprise. So, is it okay if I do something nice for you?"

I nodded. "Okay." She started down the walkway toward the shoe stores, and I followed suit, right to Christiane Louboutin, where we picked out a pair of Adox booties and she dropped another twelve hundred.

"Can I ask why?" I said after we left the shoe store and stopped at the Cafe Nero. After walking around with Marcella, I was on edge and needed a cappuccino. She had been perfectly nice so far, but I still felt nerve-wracked. There was still a lot between us.

"This is for Morgan as much as it is for you. You two make a cute couple, and I thought it would be a little fun to meddle. And before you ask, yes, I thought you two would hit it off, which is why I stuffed you two together into her apartment. I'm not sorry about that."

Honestly, I wasn't either, but the fact that she'd been matchmaking rankled me a little. "I can find my own dates, you know."

She nodded. "Yes, but I find them better and faster. Now, drink your cappuccino."

"Why did you separate us?" I asked out of the blue. "I know you said it was to protect us, but why not put us both somewhere."

She stood and held out her hand. "Come with me. There's something you need to see."

Marcella and I left the mall, and I followed her back to her house. She said nothing as we walked down the seemingly interminable stairwell to the sub-basement. Inside the Ark Room, as I thought of it, Cait still lay peacefully in repose, undisturbed. I stepped over and looked at her. A few bits of dust had collected around her, so I brushed them away and ran two fingers through her hair. "Please come back, sis. I just want to see you one more time."

"Aoife?" Marcella called. Her voice held a tinge of concern. "Is everything alright?"

I nodded and looked up. "Sure, yeah. Fine. So, what did you want to show me?"

Marcella was already pulling down an immense volume from her bookshelves. It was bound in leather and looked ancient. She set it down on her desk, reached into another cabinet nearby, and pulled out two pair of white cotton gloves. "It's old and fragile. The oils on your fingers will damage it."

She opened the book to a place held by a large bookmark of ancient fabric, a little moth-eaten. "I rescued this from a library in Constantinople over a thousand years ago. Can you read this?"

The book's binding looked to be about early ninth or tenth century, but the pages were much older and carried writing in several languages. This particular page was written in nišili, the script of the Hittites. I chuckled. "It's been a while. Let me see if I can figure this out." After a few minutes of study, I was pretty sure I had the gist of it.

I looked back up at Marcella. "Wow, the Hittites sure loved their alliteration. Would you like me to maintain it in translation?"

Marcella's mouth curved into a crooked smile. "Sure. Why not."

I took a few minutes to rewrite it in English and read it aloud.

> In distant days, a decree declares,
>> Twins of tumult, one guarded, the other braves.
>> Battles and magic, their tales intertwined,
>> To save the world, they leave mankind behind.
>
>> Guardians grim shield the sorcerous sister,
>> In the dark, her powers persist and blister.

I paused. "I'm not sure about 'blister,' but it rhymes, so we'll go with it."

> The warrior, bold, battles ancient strife,
>> Ventures vast voids for her twin's life.
>
>> When chaos climbs and shadows fall,
>> Together they triumph, answering the call.
>> Their strength united, but the price undefined,
>> Salvation secured, yet the world of men resigned.

I looked back up at Marcella and laughed. "And you think this is about us? Cait and me?"

Marcella wasn't laughing. Her gaze was deadly serious. "No. We *know* this is about you and Cait. That's not a question. When I was made, I was given a task. To turn Cait and to protect you."

"You what?"

"Your mother. Your *other* mother. She is the one who turned me, made me into a vampire. Nastasia, too. And a few others. She told me that, in the future, I would find a child, her child, one of two. She said I would know her when I saw her. And I did. As soon as I laid eyes on you both, I knew. So, here I am. I know you hate me for what I did. And parts of it were unforgivable. But I was doing what I thought was right.

"It was her guidance, The Morrigan's, your mother's, that took me to Constantinople, to the library near the city center where these pages rested. I stole them in the night. A few days later, the library burned to the ground." She stepped forward, removing her gloves and placing her hands on my shoulders. "This was my destiny."

I shook my head. "No, that's not possible. It's just not."

She closed the book and placed it back on the shelf, then held out her hand to me. I took off the cotton gloves and handed them to her, watching her put them away. Then she led me out of the chamber and back up to the kitchen where we took coffee, or, at least, I did.

"Even if all this is true," I said after she'd explained a bit more of the story, mostly about the fact that she and Liz had been keeping close tabs on me but hadn't wanted to interfere with my life. "It doesn't excuse what you did to Cait. It was horrible."

Marcella looked down, and I saw something I thought I'd never see from her, genuine shame. "No, it does not. I would like to say that I was— No, I won't bother. There is no excuse. But," she held out a hand to me. I stared at it for a long moment before I took it, tentatively.

"But what?"

"But your sister and I have resolved our feelings on the matter. I wish you and I could."

My eyes started to burn, and I cleared my throat. I shook my head. "No. I—" I swallowed hard and a tear ran down my cheek. "You don't understand what it did to me. And it's not really you I'm angry at."

Marcella gave me a puzzled look of concern. "Then who?"

I broke down then. "Me," I howled. "I hate myself for not trying to find her. I hated her. When we were growing up, I loved her, but I hated her. She was little miss perfect." I stuttered and hiccuped. "Da took her fishing. She always had the best grades. She played the harp. She danced. I was a dumb jock in the family as far as my parents were concerned, and I hated her for that. So, when you and Ma sent me to Ireland, I decided I could do something else, be someone else. I didn't have to live in her shadow, so I forgot her, left her in the past. And where was I when she was raped? Where was I when she threw herself on a grenade? I checked. I looked. While she was being raped, I was at a party at Trinity getting drunk and getting laid, pretending like she didn't exist, and I was—"

I couldn't continue for the pain in my chest and the sorrow that was bubbling forth. Marcella had moved closer, pulling me to her.

"I abandoned her," I whispered. "Ma came to me two years ago. She asked me to come back to Boston. She wanted us to be a family again. She was sure that if I showed up, it would break your glamour. I told her no. We argued. Then I threw her out. I threw me own ma out of the house where she was born. What kind of person am I?"

Marcella knelt down and pushed aside my hair, taking my chin in her thumb and forefinger and turning my face to hers. "Aoife, it's okay. Your ma doesn't care about any of that, nor does Cait. When she wakes up, I'm sure she'll tell you so."

I looked at her. And for the first time, my ready rage didn't surface. I had no jibes or insults. In those ice-blue eyes, I just saw sympathy and remorse, no judgment. Marcella pulled me forward, letting me lean on her shoulder as I sobbed my guilt out in a torrent of tears.

"I'm so sorry, Aoife," Marcella uttered as she began to cry with me.

And there we sat, each of us released our own grief and remorse and found something in common in the sharing of it.

CHAPTER THIRTY-FIVE

Aoife

I lay next to Morgan early the following morning, well before sunrise, and stared out the window, the entire encounter with Marcella swirling through my head. I felt better. Marcella and I had spent the rest of the afternoon going over the things that had happened to me, to her, to Cait. We talked until I finally felt tired and decided to leave. But in that conversation, I realized something else. Despite the horrible thing she'd done to Cait, using her glamour to shroud Cait's identity from herself, she had come to love her. And she really did understand just how wrong it was. And Liz really did love Cait with all her heart. Despite the drama, that house was full of love. This group of people, my team, Marcella, Liz, Katie, and Leah, they were a fucked up bunch, but they loved each other.

And that led me to Morgan. Who, in their last few months, gets to find someone so wonderful to spend their days with or finds a team that instantly becomes like family? Despite my illness, I was extremely fortunate.

I rolled over, finding myself nose-to-nose with Morgan, who was wide awake. I started to draw away, but she placed a hand on my arm. My eyes drifted across her features in the dim light of the moon outside, and my breathing settled into something wholly unfamiliar. I'd been in bed with plenty of women, but I'd never felt like this, so suddenly shy. I pressed my lips together, not sure what to do. The attraction to Morgan was richer somehow, almost like I was looking into the eyes of a predator who wanted my soul. And I would give it to her if she asked. I didn't know why.

We lay there, staring at each other, knowing what was in our hearts and our thoughts, but we still didn't move, and the moment drew out. Finally, after what seemed like an excruciating eternity, Morgan raised a hand to my face and stroked my cheek, and spoke, her voice the gentlest, barest, tenderest whisper.

"You're a wonderful person, Aoife. You should know that. And I don't think you're second to anyone."

I swallowed hard, feeling the hint of tears welling up and an ache in my breast that felt as if it was slowly consuming me from the inside.

"And I don't care that you're sick. I love you, anyway. I *want* to love you."

I blinked rapidly, both in confusion and to stem the still-threatening tide of hot tears. I shoved down at the anguish I felt at finding such a lovely person and knowing that before long, it would all be over. It just wasn't fair. A shitty end to a mediocre life.

"And it will all be okay, I promise," she whispered into my ear, finally.

We both knew it was a lie, but it was so sweet, the way she said it, and it broke me. Tears gushed down my face. Morgan leaned in and kissed me gently on the lips. Her kiss was soft and cold and refreshing, like kissing someone who had just come in from a frosty winter night.

I caught that scent, again, of wild blackberry and something else I hadn't been able to define. It was the loamy fragrance right after a fresh spring rain back home, when water clung to the dog's-tail grasses, and fresh earth, coaxed forth from the spatter, drifted on humid winds. I breathed it in like air, unable to get enough of it. I wanted it to fill me. To take it with me, when—

The moon had drifted low behind the apartment and now shone through the tiny window, a short sliver of silver light against her fair skin giving her a soft glow like a photo through gauze, or perhaps that was just the tears. I didn't care. She was so beautiful.

She pulled me to her, cradling my head and letting me cry softly on her chest, shushing me and telling me that it was okay to cry and that she was there with me and would be until the end.

I didn't know how long I cried, but it wasn't long. I'd needed this. I'd needed someone to care. And the feel of her cool body against mine was soothing. When my tears finally faded to nothing, Morgan crooked a finger under my chin and lifted my face to meet her gaze. I felt the lightest brush of noise in my thoughts, and then I was flooded with warm affection that drew gooseflesh and sent a shiver down my back.

Then it vanished so quickly that I wasn't sure if it was real, but Morgan said, "I wanted you to know how I feel about you."

"But why?" I whispered hoarsely. "I'm a disaster."

She gave a soft snort of amusement and smiled gently. "We're all a mess around here, Aoife. You're no different."

That drew a mirthless smirk from me. And yet, I still didn't say anything. I just pulled her in a little tighter, settling in.

"Are you comfortable?" She asked. "I'm not too cold for you?"

We'd ditched the heating blanket when the weather had started to turn. I snorted a laugh. "Funny you ask now. We've been sleeping in the same bed for weeks." At her mildly scandalized expression, I added, "Obviously, you're not. You're perfect."

"There's that smile. It really lights up your whole face."

I flushed with embarrassment and turned my face away for a moment, self-conscious. I was always unsure how to react when people complimented me. When I looked back, she was still watching me, and though her mouth was impassive, the corners turned up slightly.

I couldn't take the agony anymore. I raised myself up so I could get a better position and then lowered my head into the stream of moonlight and kissed her on the lips. It was neither hurried nor forceful, but her hand came around and pressed my body to her all the same. Then Morgan opened her mouth, deepening the kiss, and I swept hers, feeling the sharpness of her fangs.

A few weeks ago, that would have bothered me, but now it was different. It was a total turn-on, and I pressed harder, my earlier maudlin feelings utterly forgotten as a light kiss turned to passion, and the spark we'd been struggling with caught flame.

My chest fluttered with the beating of moth wings, as here, at the end of my life, I finally found love. God, if such a being existed, was a cruel creature. But I wouldn't trade this feeling for the world.

Her hands roamed across my back, raising goosebumps across my arms and neck, forcing a soft moan from my lips as her fingertips trickled down my spine in a gentle stream that pushed me further away from control and into the arms of blessed surrender. The kiss of her breath stole my will as she nibbled at my throat. I could almost feel the pulsing pound of the hunger under her skin like ground glass. She wanted me, but then she drifted to my collarbone, drawing out her need and tending to mine.

Our fingers intertwined as Morgan pressed my arms to the bed, almost painfully holding me in place, giving her tongue free rein of my chest. She ran it across my left breast, bringing an unbidden intake of breath as it passed around the sensitive areola.

I wanted her to take it in her mouth, suck it, bite at it, but she was slow and teasing, and the electric need pooled between my legs, sending a shudder down my neck.

Drawing my wrists together, she bound them in with the wide grip of one hand, so tight as to draw a whimper from me, but was it of pain or pleasure? I didn't know.

"Are you alright?" Morgan asked, her voice low and husky.

I simply nodded in affirmation. The feeling of helplessness under her powerful grip was exquisite. Again, I leaned my head back, but she ignored me, bringing my hands to my belly, drawing them down until my fingers could just brush my clit.

She moved them back and forth, keeping the tips just barely

touching. It was agony, and I groaned with the scintillating frustration that grew with each motion, clouding my mind in a bright haze of lust. "Morgan, please," I begged, but she wouldn't relent, slow and intent.

Morgan pushed my hands away, releasing them as she moved downward, wrapping her arms around my hips and burying her face in the crease of one leg, her tongue still moving across my skin. Gods, she was good at this, unhurried and sensual.

One of her fangs dragged across my right thigh, just over the pulse of my femoral, and yet still, she didn't bite down. She was still drawing out her need with my own, and for a moment, I worried what it would bring when she finally relented. I knew I could tell her to stop. I'd argued against it so hard, but a part of me, naughty and needful, wanted to know.

I let out a whisper, just a breath, "Will it hurt?"

Morgan looked up and smiled at me, soft and kind, and yet there was something dark in it that wouldn't be denied, and I was suddenly afraid. And it only served to heighten my desire to the level of wanton, abandoned need.

"Only for a moment," she said, the words coming out in a lust-filled whisper, just before she descended on me and pressed her tongue into me, causing me to moan loudly in obeisance to her mouth and lovely licks, sliding deliciously over my folds and brushing the edge of being within me. She was an unbelievable lover, and, at this moment, all of her need and all of her want were mine. Even her hunger was mine to have, to draw out, to take.

The crashing waves of orgasm shuddered through me without warning, filling the space with my grunts and moans. She lapped at me with her tongue for a moment longer, then slid it up my sweat-soaked body as I shivered with the afterglow. Gliding over me, she buried her face in my neck. I felt her mouth open against my skin and whimpered at the needle-like lance of her teeth as she bit down then tore the artery wide, releasing a gush of hot blood.

I drew in a harsh gasp at her first pull when euphoria blasted away all thought, leaving me heaving and clutching.

"Oh, Gods! More!" I begged as she drew my blood into her mouth and away into the ravenous consumption of her gift. My whole body locked tight, my fingers digging into her back, nails renting open the skin in slick bloody lines. "Please," I growled from somewhere deep in my throat as she continued to drink the blood from my body. Deep within, a welling of light and strength rose and fed her from my very soul.

My heart palpitated once, then again. My vision swam at the edges, and a cold numbness suffused my skin. She was taking all that I was, and I was loving it, sliding down into a darkness that was enfolding and comforting, and euphoric. Dark purple and blue mist seemed to sing through my vision, darting about like sparkling stars, and the room faded, leaving within my perception only a strange tinkling noise, like crystalline chimes.

Then her bloody lips were on me, hot and desperate, forcing my own blood into my mouth, coupled with something syrupy and cold as she saved my life after taking me to the brink of death. And I gulped it down, desperate to have more of my own blood in my throat.

Gods, the salt taste, the euphoria, the unabashed glee that blistered through my heart at this most intimate and carnal of acts. Vermillion magic burst forth from me, and Morgan gasped aloud as it enfolded her and filled her. She arched her back with me as the magic crested, then died, leaving us in the darkened room once more.

Strength flooded through me, immediately clearing my vision. The burning that had begun in my neck abruptly vanished, and I pushed her onto her back, licking my blood from her face and neck and chin.

I lowered myself down between her legs, desperate to bring her to climax, running my tongue as deep inside her as I could, listening to the gratifying soft noises that came from her, so small and desperate, so different from what she'd come to represent for me, a rock—a tower of strength.

It didn't take long at all before her hips lifted off the ground, and she grabbed a handful of my hair, pushing me harder against her as she came under my lips and tongue. The musky headiness of her scent filled my nose and mouth, and she cried out before crashing back to the bed, truly spent.

I rolled off of her, gasping for air, needing to breathe. My arms turned leaden, and my thought sluggish.

"Oh, Gods," I breathed. Unable to think of anything to say. But there was no need.

Morgan pulled me to her, cradling and holding me against her larger frame. We cuddled like that for a long time, neither one of us speaking. We lay in the darkness with no sound but that of my breathing and the banging of my heartbeat in my ears.

Almost an hour passed before Morgan asked how I was, pulling me from my drowsy state.

"Physically or emotionally?" I asked.

"Either, both," she whispered.

"Physically, I'm exhausted, but emotionally, I feel good, settled."

She quirked an eyebrow, "Settled?"

"Would you rather I was unsettled?"

"No, but—"

I kissed her gently. "I'm fine. It wasn't at all what I expected." At her seemingly confused expression, I added, "The feeding, not the sex."

She kissed my forehead. "I understood what you meant. And just so you know, it's not normally like that. No, I take that back. It's never been like that." She paused for a moment, and I thought she might be scrambling to explain something, but then she said, "Get some rest. Tomorrow, I'll be out of it until probably two, and we have the day off."

"Love is a weird thing, don't you think?"

"Love?" She sounded puzzled. I'd rolled over, and she'd spooned up behind me. "So you think I love you?"

I grinned, though she couldn't see it. "You must. You were very, very compassionate tonight."

She barked a laugh. "Busted. Now go to sleep, Aoife. You need rest. And tomorrow, take the iron supplements in the pantry. Oh, and make sure to eat a steak or something. You need the protein and iron to replace the blood I took."

I closed my eyes and scooted further into her. "Yes, ma," I answered, and I could almost hear her eyes roll as I closed my own.

"I love you, too," I whispered as I drifted off.

CHAPTER THIRTY-SIX

Skaja

"Wake up, blossom."

I rolled over on the rug, my body all twisted up in the blanket we stole the night before from my old bed, to find no one there. "Five more minutes," I groaned.

Boudka laughed. "Nope. There are things to do. As it is, I'm going to be late, and so are you. Now get up and get bathed."

I opened my eyes, finding it still dark out. Boudka was already in her undergarments, hurting about the tent to gather up her robes and shoes. "Move it, Skaja!" She commanded with a nudge of her foot. "There's a note for you on the bed."

"A what?" I asked blearily as I dragged myself off the floor.

Boudka laughed again, hastily wrapped her robe around herself, and shot out of the tent.

I shook my head, confused. "What the hell?"

On my old bed lay a formal Óşeni dress uniform and a pair of freshly polished formal boots. Neatly folded on top was a scrap of paper.

> Full dress on the training ground at dawn. Tardiness will not be tolerated.
>
> —Captain Saya.

I looked outside. False dawn already glowed in the sky. "Shit!" I ran to the bath and jumped in. It was thankfully warm. "Bless you, Boudka," I whispered as I scrambled to wash, oil my hair, and get it braided and bunned.

"Someone could have told me last night," I bitched into the empty air as I dressed in the smart uniform. I took just a moment to check my appearance, glancing about to make sure nothing was out of place, then I left the tent at a brisk jog, just making the training ground as the sun was rising.

The entire contingent was gathered in a circle. Positioned at the heart of it were my mother, her sisters, and Boudka. Just behind them and flanked by Óbin, Saya stood and seemed to be sucking in her gut to accommodate an ill-fitting sword belt, holding two shining and new empty sheaths crafted of Óșeni leather but bereft of blades. I hastily filled the final open slot facing the center of the ring and the assembled leaders.

Boudka looked beautiful, adorned in the raven-colored ceremonial robes of our Shaddani clan, embroidered in vermillion, royal purple, and blue, the circling crows of our house symbol emblazoned on the hem. Her brilliant blond hair was woven in a traditional Shaddani thick braid, twisted with a thick cord of the same three colors symbolizing the old Dark-Fae court.

Gleaming and black upon a table before them rested a bóllom and a nisís of karanite alloy. A sash, seemingly woven from shadows and whispers of purple twilight, blood, and midnight, lay draped over my mother's arm, undulating in the soft breeze.

We all stood at attention, though a few whispers and smiles flickered like fireflies through the company. Zilyana tried to gaze stalwartly forward, but periodically, a curve of a smile tugged at her lips, and her eyes twitched in my direction. My heart thundered in my chest like a drum.

What on earth was going on? Something odd was happening. All of this most certainly wasn't for me.

"Skaja ni Nemhain! Step forward!" Saya shouted as she stepped to stand before the small table.

Or maybe it was.

I took a disciplined step into the ring, beating back the panic in my breast as two warriors behind me, Atta and Nisya, closed ranks with Zilyana.

"Front and center!" Saya called.

I marched forward until I stood at attention before her, clearly understanding now that this was a formal ceremony. My eyes furtively darted to Obín, who was clearly struggling to keep a shit-eating grin off her face.

"It is the duty of every Swasari commander to keep the compliment of her unit confined to the best available warriors. It is also the requirement of every commander to recognize when one of her soldiers is no longer fit to fulfill their role, either through age, injury, responsibility," she lowered her voice slightly, "or competency."

I curled my hands into light fists to stop a nervous shake. And even as everything and everyone assembled spoke of an honor being bestowed, my nagging self-doubt dragged at my mind.

"I have been a sister of the Valtárí for thirty-three years," Saya continued. "For all that time, I have comported myself with honor and discipline. I have fought in many campaigns against the Kaushkar. However, as Commander of this group, it is my grim duty to inform all of you that I will no longer be filling that role."

There were no surprised gasps, no whispers, no comments of any kind. The group was supremely silent. *Did everyone here know what was going on but me?* Then realization dawned, and I fought to stay composed in a fit of budding excitement.

"Though it has never been done before, as the Swasari and the Valtárí have been reserved strictly for Óșeni women, it is now, in my estimation, my honor to welcome you, Skaja, to take your place in the Valtárí as my replacement."

Now, all of my Óșeni sisters were openly smiling. By contrast, my jaw was hanging open. I snapped it shut as Saya continued. I probably should have been thankful a bug hadn't flown in.

"This decision came neither lightly nor without a measure of my own disappointment at leaving the field of battle. But, you have shown yourself to be dedicated in your training, deft with your blades, and honorable in your comportment with your fellow Swasari. It would be unjust to deny you your place any further simply to satisfy my own ego, a place which you have thoroughly earned through combat."

I shifted my eyes to my mother, who had donned a beaming smile that warmed my heart. Boudka and Macha smiled as well. But it was Badb who wore her pride blazing as she carried her trademark crooked smirk and winked at me.

"Valtárí stand!" Saya shouted.

"Valtárí attack!" The warriors replied in unison, shaking the ground with a thunderous stomp.

"Valtárí defend!" Saya shouted.

"Valtárí stand!" The warriors returned, stomping again.

"The Valtárí bring the battle to the enemy!"

A smaller group, the nineteen Valtárí among the encircled warriors, stepped forward and shouted, "We are the tip of the blade!"

"Oye Konbom!" Saya shouted.

"Oye Konbom," they returned, with me joining them automatically.

"Skaja, you are at this moment inducted into the Swasari Valtárí." She removed the sword belt and held it out to me.

I took it and glanced around a little uncertainly. Óbin made not-so-surreptitious hand motions of putting it on, and I slid it around my waist, securing it with the buckled knot, a perfect fit for my smaller frame.

"Thank you, Kóhen," I said, carefully keeping my face serious—at least the best I could. The corners of my mouth were proving undisciplined at that particular moment.

"I am your Kóhen no longer. You may call me commander or simply Saya."

"Yes, Commander," I replied. I couldn't imagine actually calling her Saya to her face.

"With the blade of the bóllom is a Swasari's fate carried." She offered me the Bóllom from the table, one-handed, hilt first, blade resting on her forearm. I took it and placed it in the sheath now at my hip with an expert turn.

"With the tip of the nisís is the enemy's fate sealed." She claimed the nisís from the table, dancing the blade across her hand in a poetic flourish. Then she held it out, the hilt delivered as both offer and contract securing fealty among my sisters.

As my hand found the waiting hilt, time turned to honey, a slow current in which past and future murmured their assent. I raised my eyes to meet Sayas, and in that gaze flickered a wink alive with the pride I felt at her approving expression. It was a breathless moment for me, the pinnacle of all I had struggled to achieve for over half a year.

I slid the dagger from her grasp, duplicating the flourish with which it had been offered, and slid it sightlessly into the sheath at my right. Then I returned to attention, still forcing some measure of decorum into my features, but not much.

My mother and her sisters then stepped forward. "In our Shaddani clan," my mother began, "when a woman comes of age and completes training, they are considered an equal." She handed the sash she carried to Badb.

Badb spoke next. "While magic is the common tradition of our clan, it is not the only one. Our clan's mandate within the Shaddani court encompasses the sovereignty of the court, the magic of Shaddan, and the defense of her borders by strength of arms. In the area of battle, your accomplishments have been ones of excellence that would make any Shaddani instructor beyond proud, and I believe you to be my worthy successor. You have earned your place among your kin in our tradition."

Badb passed the sash to Macha. "As the duty-bound arbiter of sovereignty for our people, I welcome you, the Crown Princess of Shaddan, the last of our line, to the House of the Morrigan. And when your time comes, sister's daughter, long may be your reign."

Macha placed the sash, embroidered with the circling crows of our clan, over my head and laid it carefully across my breast, making sure not to block or interfere with my blades.

I kept my poise, though I really just wanted to burst into fits of bawling, and placed my flat open hand on my sternum and nodded in Shaddani salute.

"Welcome, sister," Saya spoke, the words woven with strands of kinship, of ancient ties that murmured through the fabric of my soul. Her touch was a warrior's bond as she clapped my shoulder and then drew me into an embrace, which carried the shared breath of battles fought with and before me. Just before she released me, her voice slipped close into a whisper. "Zilly and I are going to eat very well for quite a while after today. Thanks for that."

In a roll like thunder, the collected Swasari gave a whoop before disintegrating into happy applause and general chaos. I still stood there suspended on a thread of time and stunned into silent reverence for what I had accomplished. I blinked back hot tears of joy, placing a hand to my mouth and nose as the circle closed in about us.

Badb placed a hand on my shoulder, then she leaned in and whispered almost inaudibly. "I always knew you were more warrior than witch."

I grinned wildly at her as I looked up, tapping my bóllom. "Really? Care to go a few more rounds?"

She laughed loudly at that. "Anytime, anywhere, young one."

CHAPTER THIRTY-SEVEN

Aoife

The week leading up to Valentine's Day had been the kind of absolute boredom you get from days worth of paperwork and answering useless phone calls. The 'twatline,' as I'd started to refer to the PIU hotline, rang off the hook with one thing or another, but most of it turned out to be crank calls or mistaken identity.

Morgan's trip to Bridgeport had turned up almost nil: no more information, no more missing hard drives, thumb drives, files, or anything. The government had been pretty thorough in its search of the ship. Though, she did come back with one tidbit that filled in a missing piece for me. Zhi wasn't on the crew manifest. It wasn't really conclusive since she was a biologist and not PLA Navy, but it fit an idea I was cooking up.

The hotline turned up one or two things worth investigating, mostly calls about werewolves in the surrounding countryside. Maki told me to write them off as misidentifications of local animals or dogs, which made sense, but there were just too many of them. Certainly, there were more than we'd come to expect, given the meager statistics we had. Until recently, crime analytics didn't track such things.

In the end, on a hunch, I told Marcella about it, and she put in a call to some bloke called Anton, apparently the current leader. But he didn't respond, which Marcella told me was very unlike him.

Then I took it to Carlos, who said he'd check into it, but I

289

knew a blow-off when I heard one. From what I understood, being caught out in public was a no-no that brought the ultimate penalty for werewolves. Something very fishy was definitely going on. In the meantime, there was no sign of Cait's killer, and I was starting to lose hope that the idiot would show himself. Honestly, it was possible we'd simply scared him off when we found his hideout.

And all that left me in a weird space. Despite the boredom, I was enjoying life in a way I never had before. Morgan and I were getting on so well. We'd fallen into the routine of living together as a couple. I still did most of the housework, which in that place was all of five minutes. Morgan kept me flush with groceries in return, and, well, we did other things in our spare time. New love and all that.

So far, my head hadn't exploded, and, other than Lisa, I'd managed to avoid any weird conversations that involved things I didn't know about Cait's past. Frankly, this whole charade had gone far better than I expected, and I probably should have anticipated that something would go wrong, but I was really having too good a time with it.

On the morning of the thirteenth, I found Chief Williams leaning against the wall next to the lift as I got off on our floor. "You got a minute, *Cait?*"

Uh oh. My pulse ramped with worry, not just because she'd clearly been waiting for me but because she had a suspicious glint in her eye, and there'd been something in the way she'd said, Cait, that I didn't like.

I tried to beg her off. "Can it wait? I have to sit an interview with Cardozo." I made a vomiting gesture at Cardozo's name, but Sesi didn't laugh, and my stomach fell. *She fucking knows,* I thought in a panic.

"It'll only take a second," she said. "Let's go to Carlos' office and talk there. And leave the purple lemur at your desk."

"Um, I can't," I replied a little sheepishly. "It won't stay there, and I don't want him getting into trouble."

She shook her head and just started walking.

Shit. I followed her to Carlos' office like a dead woman walking. *Yeah, for sure,* I thought. *I'm fucked.*

Carlos was working on reviews when we walked in. "Sesi, Cait, what's going on?"

Sesi turned to me. "Cait, you remember that time we talked about Vic and his wife after that whole fiasco with the Caldwell case?"

I froze for a second, then I sat down in one of the chairs in front of Carlos' desk and leaned forward, elbows on my knees, eyes closed. "No, Sesi. No, I don't."

"Yeah. I got a weird call from Detective Nguyễn over in Cambridge a few weeks ago. She said you were acting strange. I chalked it up to the fact that you'd just been shot. But I figured I'd see what was up anyway. So, you want to tell me who you really are?"

Carlos started to speak, but Sesi held up her hand, waiting for me to answer.

"I'm Cait's twin sister, Aoife. On leave from the Garda Síochána."

Carlos reached into his desk and pulled out a sheet of paper. Holding it out. Sesi waved him off and ignored it. Instead, she sat down in the chair next to me and stared at me.

I looked up. "How did you figure it out?"

She smirked. "I'd like to say it's because I'm a good fucking detective, but apparently not good enough. Though looking back, it was obvious. The first day you walked in, you didn't give me one nasty look. In the last conversation Cait had with me, she compared the PIU to the Gestapo and damn near accused me of being Göring. Also, she hates the mayor these days and typically refers to her as Madame Hitler. You didn't say a word when I said the mayor had picked Carlos to take Larson's place.

"I was suspicious, but I let it go to see if maybe you were just trying to be conciliatory. But after Lisa's call, I started reviewing your case notes, and I noticed something odd. You were suddenly more thorough, which I could easily overlook. Hell, it even made me happy. But then there were the odd spelling mistakes, weird ones, color spelled with an 'ou,' realize spelled with an s instead of a z, that sort of thing, the kind of spelling someone from England or Ireland might use.

And, of course, your tongue, which I only noticed at the elevator just a minute ago. By then, though, that was just confirmation.

"So, which of you wants to tell me what the fuck is going on in my department?"

Carlos spoke up then. "Sesi, will you fucking read this?"

She took the paper and skimmed over it. "You had the ADA set up an undercover with a foreign officer? You went around me?"

"Look, we're pretty sure someone in either the Mayor's office or in the department was involved in the attempt on Cait's life. I didn't think we could trust anyone outside of mine and Freyer's squads."

"Since you said attempt, I assume that Cait's still alive." Sesi looked beyond furious, but she kept her voice level.

"Yes, but she's indisposed. We just didn't want the bad guys to know that."

"Do you have any idea the risks you're taking? Ms. Reagan here is basically a civilian, and you're playing chicken with her life."

"I'm a cop. I know the risks," I said.

"You should be quiet," Sesi said to me. "You're lucky I haven't arrested you." She turned back to Carlos. "And why didn't you ask me? I would have at least considered it, and you ought to know I'd never have anything to do with hurting Cait." She sounded genuinely hurt that we might think so, which made me feel like a fucking twat.

Sesi continued her explanation. I would have liked to say rant, but she wasn't ranting. She was just talking, angrily and with some fervor, but still, it was talking, not ranting.

"I know you guys think I'm up the Mayor's ass, but I'm not. We're in each other's faces on an almost daily basis. I hate what she's doing, but better me in here, trying to temper it, than having some handpicked asshole that will happily start loading the mermaids and whatever else in box cars. You could—no, you *should* have told me."

"I take full responsibility for this, Sesi," Carlos said firmly. "This isn't Aoife's fault."

Sesi squinted at him coldly, then she got up and walked to the phone, dialing the switchboard. "Hi, this is Chief Williams. Can you please have Charlie McCoy come down to Homicide from Human Resources? Immediately, please. Tell him to drop everything he's doing. Also, ask him to bring a form two-ninety."

I had no idea what a form two-ninety was, but it didn't sound at all good. I looked at Carlos, but he looked as clueless as I was.

"Sesi, we were trying to—" Carlos started, eyes wide with fear.

"Can it, Ramirez. This is a clusterfuck. Shut up and sit there quietly for your own good."

I still sat in the chair, my head in my hands. "Fuck." I was going to jail, and Carlos was going to get fired or worse.

A few minutes later, a guy in his late forties with brown hair and a slightly graying beard entered carrying a file folder and a stack of forms. "I have what you need, Chief."

Sesi walked over to me and stood looking down. "Well, stand up," she said.

I stood.

"I know you're Cait's twin, so I assume you're an American citizen. Is that correct?"

"Yes." At least I wouldn't be deported. Though, that'd probably be better than a stint in prison, no matter how short.

"Hold up your right hand," she said.

I put up both my hands, expecting her to cuff me.

She rolled her eyes in agitation. "Do you not know your left from your right? Or can you just not count to one? Right hand only, please."

I raised an eyebrow but did as she asked, now thoroughly confused.

"Now, repeat after me. I, Aoife whatever-the-fuck-your-middle-name-is Reagan, do solemnly swear that I will bear true faith and allegiance to the Commonwealth of Massachusetts and will support the constitution thereof and the constitution of the United States. I will obey all department rules and regulations with integrity and to the best of my ability. I will faithfully and impartially discharge and perform all of the duties incumbent upon me as a police officer of the Commonwealth."

I repeated the words, shaking like a leaf. At least I had the presence of mind to use my middle name instead of her epithet.

"Charlie, do you have that form?"

Charlie handed her the stack of papers and the file folder. "It's on top of the personnel file."

She snatched a pen from Carlos' desk and signed it, had Charlie sign it, and then said, "Great, now get out, Charlie."

Charlie did exactly that, closing the door behind him.

I couldn't see what was on it the form, but she wrote something else on it. Then she handed it, the stack of papers, and the file folder to Carlos.

Her voice was firm and taut, full of irritation. "Get her to fill out those forms and give them to HR, and start a fresh file of your own." She turned back to me. "Do you have a US Passport? Or Birth Certificate and Driver's License?"

I nodded. "Yeah. Passport."

"Anything shitty in your background that would disqualify you from serving in the department? Besides impersonating an officer, I mean."

"No, Ma'am," I responded, now just in shock.

Sesi glanced back at Carlos. "If you ever pull a stunt like this again on my watch, I'm going to have you hauled up in front of the review board. Is that clear?"

"Crystal," Carlos replied, his expression cool and relaxed.

Sesi turned back to me. "Welcome to the BPD, Aoife." Her tone was anything but welcoming. By contrast it was harsh and clearly pissed off. She opened the door and made to leave but then closed it and turned back to Carlos. "If this blows up, the shit rolls down on you, Carlos. You're the scapegoat." Then she left, and never once the entire time did Sesi Williams raise her voice.

"What just happened?" I asked as I dropped heavily into the chair.

"She just hired you, Aoife. Welcome to the Department. Just

so you know, the paycheck sucks."

Carlos rubbed his forehead and blew out a relieved sigh. "Who the fuck spells color with an ou?"

"The rest of the English-speaking world, Carlos," I muttered.

CHAPTER THIRTY-EIGHT

Skaja

What followed my induction was what came before, ceaseless training and work. Now, however, regular patrols of the countryside with my sister Swasari broke up the monotony. Sometimes they proved fruitless. Sometimes they were filled with the vigor and wild excitement of all too brief battles. And so, two weeks passed, and though I saw little of Boudka, my thoughts drifted to her often. And for those two weeks, I lived on high, the queen of my domain as far as I was concerned, happy and fulfilled. At the end of that fortnight, though, it all came crashing down.

Semi and I were on the practice field for an evening sparring session, trading our usual barbs.

"Are you ready for another thrashing?" Semi asked, waggling her eyebrows.

I snorted. "You haven't beaten me in our last two sessions."

"Third time is golden, they say," she shot back.

I rolled my eyes. "If you say so. Your just too slow old—" I stopped as our heads turned toward the sounds of screaming from the other side of the camp.

I didn't wait for orders, scooping up my bóllom and nisís and charging off into the failing light, my legs pumping quickly as I kept pace with Semi.

"Mother of waters!" I swore as we came upon three kóṣánt cutting through the servant's tents.

I rushed forward, leaping and bringing both weapons down

in a cross pattern on the first kóşánt I encountered. It swerved aside like a whisper in the dark as I landed.

I rolled under the returning rake of its clawed fingers. There was no pause, no breath between heartbeats as my blades danced and sang in a flurry of swipes, pushing the monster backward to reel defensively as it stumbled over one of the dead servants. I followed, sliding low on the earth beneath it, and hacked off one of its legs, my blade a shadow over moonlit waters sending the monster sprawling.

It tried to rise and launch itself off on its remaining leg, foul-smelling ichor draining from its stump, but I was the quicker, leaping onto its back in a single balletic movement, driving my weapons through its sensory organs and deep into its skull. I rode its lifeless body to the ground, and my blades tore loose in a gout of black gore.

I dropped to a crouch and surveyed the unfolding battle. Semi and the other two kóşánt were nowhere to be seen, but the creatures hadn't been alone. A small group of emisai prowled quickly through the camp as if searching for someone or something. I trailed three of them out of the servant's area until they encountered their first victim, a young man of maybe thirteen or fourteen years running the wrong way in the confusion.

Charging in, I tore through two of the beasts from behind before they could strike. Then I struck out with my foot, sweeping the remaining emisai off its feet before plunging my bóllom into what passed for its foul heart.

I caught a flicker of movement from the corner of my eye, reflexively sending my nísis past the boy's shoulder. The weapon buried itself in the chest of a fourth emisai, dropping it.

I turned the young boy around. "Go take cover with the Fae," I ordered, sending him back toward their tents. *Speaking of,* I thought, *where were they?* They would have made short work of the emisai. Something wasn't right about this.

As if in answer, a massive gathering of magic stole my breath, and storm clouds gathered overhead from nowhere. Lightning sang down, accompanied by deafening blasts of thunder as the bolts seared through the Fomori infiltrators. One blast shook the camp from the direction of my mother's cottage.

"Boudka!" My voice vanished in the chaos of the fighting and cracking of thunder as I ran in that direction. On the way, I found Zilly and Semi surrounded by four kóşánt, fighting for their lives. I didn't think. I just waded back into the fray, dropping into a Valtárí triad, the three-warrior version of our typical style.

In a swift motion, dodging beneath wide arcs from both Zilly and Semi, I used my smaller size to angle around. Then I came up and cut through the neck of one of the foul creatures before it even knew I was there. Zilly dispatched one, and Semi caught another across the gut, sending it to the ground in two pieces. The fourth launched itself away high into the air before scrambling up the outer wall and out of the camp.

As quickly as it came, the storm vanished, leaving a ringing in my ears and the horrid smell of scorched Fomori, ozone, and rotted ichor in my nose.

Cries of "Oye Kombom!" erupted from various places around the camp, and we returned it.

I rushed to my mother's cottage. The door was open but undamaged. Boudka was nowhere to be found, nor was my mother. The kitchen, the bedrooms, they were all empty.

"Boudka!" I shouted again as I returned to the servant's quarters. I scoured the servant quarter frantically, running from ruined tent to ruined tent, picking through the remains. I found the bodies of four dead servants and a Fae warrior who'd apparently been caught unaware. He was wearing no armor nor carrying his weapon. He must have been sleeping. *He shouldn't have been there in the first place,* I thought. *This was the human quarter.*

"Oh, Goddess and Mother Avra! Skaja!" Semi called from behind me.

My heart sank like iron in a river as I turned to find her carrying Boudka's lifeless body. I covered my mouth as the tears erupted from my eyes, and a hiccuping sob blurted from my lips.

I couldn't breathe.

I couldn't think.

Semi knelt down in front of me with her body, and I dropped to my knees with her.

"Be careful," I whispered as Semi set Boudka onto the cold-packed earth. She had a gaping wound in her thigh and a ragged puncture in her chest, right through her heart. Someone's discarded steel dagger dangled from her fingers, dripping with black ichor.

I snapped my eyes shut in the hopes that this was all a terrible dream, but when I opened them again, she still lay there, lifeless.

"She killed one of them," Semi said softly. "It was scorched through with magic. I found her in a tent with the three laundry maids she was trying to protect."

A hand landed on my shoulder, and I looked up to find my mother gazing down, her eyes wet with tears. "Come away, Weyna."

I didn't move. "Can you do anything?"

She paused, gazing from me to Boudka's body. "Nothing that you'd want me to do. Nothing that *she* would want me to do. She wouldn't really love you any longer—or herself." Her expression showed sympathy, but there was fear in her eyes, as if I might ask her to do the horrible thing she suggested.

I didn't ask. Oh, I wanted to, but I knew better. Shaddani magic did not give. It took. It possessed. It remade. Whatever intentions I might have would be twisted and warped into a pantomime of life, shrouding the light that was her soul. I couldn't ask that of my mother or visit that on Boudka.

So I handed my weapons to Semi, and as tenderly as I could, I gathered my dead lover in my arms, cradling her as a mother might a child. Then I turned toward the medhen tent to have her prepared for her journey.

My mother's soft fingers wrapped around my arm as if to stop me, but then she gasped. Her head rocked backward in a motion I recognized immediately, her eyes turning up as she listened to the voices of destiny speak in whispered cacophonous tones.

"Wait, her skein is not yet tied." Her eyes, fully black and still swirling with an unspoken mystery, turned toward me, couched in a steely expression. Then she spoke again, her voice resonating in the air. "Stay here. Don't go anywhere."

She launched herself upward, transforming, wings unfurling, beating furiously for her cottage.

"Mother! What did you see?" I shouted, but she was gone.

Minutes later, she returned, the mantle of her ancient power resting on her shoulders. She clutched a large crystal that shimmered like a star in the heart of the night sky. A soulstone. "Set her back down and work with me."

I stood there, lost in complete shock, holding onto Boudka's body, pressing her tightly to me as if somehow the closeness might make this all go away, but the force of her command snapped me to attention, and I did as she asked, gently placing Boudka back on the ground.

"What are we doing?" There was no word for how numb I felt, how lost. Everything I did felt distant, automatic, empty.

"We are going to try to save her." She looked up and snapped her fingers in front of my eyes, raising her voice. "Weyna! Skaja! Whatever you're calling yourself. I need your help! Now focus!"

I jerked at the sound of my Óşeni name and blinked, pulling my thoughts back to order and frowning. "Okay. What do I need to do?"

She handed me the soulstone, which I accepted, heavy in my hand. Then she tore open Boudka's robes and placed my hand on her bare chest. She placed her hand on my arm, bowed her head, and closed her eyes.

The world vanished in a flash of light and a gust of magic that blew through me like a cold, bitter wind, forcing a harsh gasp from my throat and sending a screaming shudder through my body. I dropped my head and closed my eyes. They were useless anyway. My perception was sucked down into a place for which I had no name. It was a black pit of nothing and mid-winter cold. Shadowy smoke billowed around me.

My mother's voice sounded in my head and seemingly

from all around. "Love, my daughter, is one of the most powerful magics in all worlds. It binds others to us and us to them. If you truly loved her, then the tendrils of your being will be entwined with hers. Follow them."

I had no notion of what I sought. Trailing the tarzhi of the physical world, I understood, but not this, not the threads of the soul. I had no idea what I was looking—

"I see it," I whispered. A thin thread of brilliant green magic caught my notice, winding vinelike and entwining with a long stretch of silver that tethered it directly to me. It shimmered and pulsed as I thought of Boudka, her honey-gold hair and striking blue eyes. I followed it, feeling it circle and spiral and twist away from my own body. The further I trailed it, the faster my perception drew to its end, where I found a small sphere of crystalline light, exploding within with color and life and beauty. Tears sprang down my cheeks as a hollow feeling of loss melted in a warm and wondrous love. Her love.

"Now, reach for her."

Tentatively I reached out, willing it closer. Something akin to a spectral hand reached forward and touched the ball, cradling it. And as I did so, my mouth and nose filled with her scent. Somewhere distant, I still cried, but she was with me, her soul warm and alive and in need of my love.

"Gently now, feel her and move her. Guide her to the crystal."

It was beyond easy. The orb of light before me, her tiny drop of the eternal spring, pulsed with yearning, drawn to me, trusting and believing. It glided from the shadow, and my perception returned to reality, almost. I saw the world around me, Boudka's body, an empty shell, dark and quiet, Semi standing next to us with wide eyes, watching. She glowed with a shimmering mosaic of spirit, fearless and light, happy and unconcerned about the future. Greens and grays and beautiful yellows all spun about her. I didn't dare look at my mother, though the dark specter of her presence flitted on the edge of my vision, a thing of both beauty and darkness that tugged violently at my perception, almost as if it begged for me to see her in all of her glory, her soul laid bare, woven of stars and shadows.

The ethereal sphere traveled along my body, causing me to gasp with the sensation. As it flowed, the veil between my body and her spirit turned paper thin as her soul tried to burrow into me, despite my coaxing. Every place it passed, the whisper of her fingers caressed me, crossing my skin. The scent of her filled my nose and mouth once more, and the brush of her breath caressed my face and throat. Eventually, the light reached the crystal. Then it seemed to pull away, not wanting to lose contact, even as bits of it streamed away. I was losing her.

"Mother! Mother! What do I do?"

"You must bond her to the crystal, push or coax. But you must do it quickly."

"Boudka. I love you. I know I haven't been the greatest of lovers, but I love you. Please. Let me help you. Please trust me." It was all I could think to say, a pleading bound in love and loss.

It was enough.

Her light, her essence, her soul slid into the crystal, and light exploded in my eyes. My real eyes. My tear-swollen eyes.

The strange ethereal sight ended, and I looked up at my mother. "What did we just do."

My mother smiled in a kindly way that I'd seen so seldomly. "You saved her in a way I could never have done on my own. Now give me the crystal and bring her body to my home. I will meet you there."

CHAPTER THIRTY-NINE

Aoife

Valentine's morning, I went to work early so I could get out in time for my date. Morgan had just taken the day off. In addition to the running case with the Akkorokamui, we had three other human-on-human homicides on our plate. Up until the day before, Carlos had had me filing my case notes as Cait, which was all kinds of iffy if it came to court. So far, though, the one case we'd closed had resulted in a plea arrangement, and my notes hadn't been a factor. The last thing I wanted was for this whole misadventure to lead to someone getting off for murder, so I was thankful when I could finally use my own login and file my notes properly.

I spent most of the day wrapping up my notes and reports, getting them filed. At one point, I passed Doyle's desk and stopped. At least a dozen 'get well soon' cards lay strewn across it. It seemed the 'sociopath,' as she called herself, had touched a lot of hearts. She had to have tremendous strength of character to garner such goodwill without a conscience. Despite what she said, there was something there, a sense of right and wrong. I was probably projecting, but still. Well, at least now, she could appreciate the outreach. It'd probably make her blubber like a baby, poor kid.

Later that afternoon, on a hunch, I called the detail guarding Zhi and asked a few questions, the most important of which was if she'd left the building, but she hadn't. As a matter of fact, the detail had eaten breakfast with her in the condo at the

Sojourner the very morning that the two scientists at Zhu Pharma had died. I'd thought I was on to something, but it was a dead end. It was maddening.

"Did you know that Octopi can swim at twenty-five miles an hour?" Maki said. "That means the Akkorokamui could have been on shore over an hour before the ship grounded."

I looked over at her. "So, it could be anyone."

"Pretty much," Maki said. "I asked around. It probably doesn't have to shapeshift into a like-sized creature. Like many shifters, it probably expels and draws mass through magic."

"Who could possibly know that?" I asked.

Maki proceeded to explain to me that one of her ancestors lives in her head. After all that I'd seen here, beyond what I'd already known, I just took it in stride.

"Okay, is it reliable information?"

Maki just shrugged. "She's usually right. But honestly, who knows."

I suddenly realized that I had a wealth of knowledge about all things paranormal sitting right next to me. "How much do you know about the Fae?"

"Which ones? Bethadi or Shaddani?" She asked absently, now typing once more at her computer.

"I don't know the difference," I admitted. "But based on the words, I'm assuming Bethadi is the Light-Fae, from the old Celtic word. Which makes the Shaddani the Dark-Fae, which is Germanic in origin, though both have similar roots in earlier languages."

Maki turned toward me slowly, her face an unreadable mask, then she asked, "So, are you like a genius or something?"

I looked away, a flush creeping up my neck. "No, I'm a linguist by training. I mean, I'm smart, just like all the women in my family, but not what you'd call a genius."

Maki raised a skeptical eyebrow. "Uh-huh. So, let me ask you a question first. What's the Riemann hypothesis?"

I raised my eyebrows. I hadn't expected a maths exam. "The Riemann hypothesis is a hypothesis that the Riemann zeta function, a summation of one over n to the nth, has its zeros only at the negative even integers and complex numbers with real part one-half. It's never been proven, but—wait, what? Why are you looking at me like that?"

Maki stared at me with a hard-to-read expression, one corner of her mouth crooked up slightly. "So, in addition to linguistics, you have a background in number theory?"

"No, I've always been good at maths. It just didn't interest me all that much. I prefer more personal expression. Not that mathematics isn't cool. It is. I mean, it's the language of the universe, really. But I'm not big on the hard sciences—now what?"

Maki had started to laugh. "Nevermind, you nerd. I just wanted to see if you'd actually answer the question. Anyway. What do you want to know about the Fae?"

"What are they, really? I mean, I know the legends that grew from Irish myths, leprechauns, fairy rings, and so on."

Maki pursed her lips in thought and closed her eyes for a moment. "Okay, so—" She took a deep breath. "Everything I know is legend or research. The Fae used to be one people in a single world. Then something happened, no one really knows what, and they were split into two worlds, dark and light. There's no record of how or why. Shaddan was once considered a protectorate by some rather unsavory groups and revolted, so it was shattered, decimated, at least according to some ancient Sanskrit texts."

"Wait, you have ancient Sanskrit texts? What, just lying around?"

Maki laughed again, a beautiful tinkling sound that gave me goosebumps. She must be getting into the conversation because her glamour was slipping. "Well, no, not just lying around, I keep them very well preserved, and I have already digitized all of them. They belong to my family. Anyway, Shaddan was decimated long ago."

"And what about like flora, are there kinds of faerie flowers or fungi?"

"Sure, Shaddan is a world, so it probably had flowers and—oh!" Her eyes lit up. "That freaky garden."

"Yeah," I said, seeing the lightbulb go on.

"I don't know if that place is related, but the color of the flowers determines the nature of the faerie. Dark colors like deep red, dark blue, or dark purple are Shaddani. Gold, silver, lilac, and other bright colors are indicative of Light-Fae, but there's some conflicting information about all this. None of it is terribly clear in many cases."

I thought about that for a moment. "So, dark red, like blood-red or vermillion, would be Shaddani."

"If you believe the legends, yes."

I pursed my lips. "What are the chances that someone on Earth might be a pure-blooded Fae."

Maki turned and narrowed her eyes, searching my face and watching my body language. "Where are you going with this? Humans don't just become Fae, not that they can't, but that takes powerful magic, transformational magic." She lowered her voice to a whisper. "There are Bethadi living in several of the camps here in Boston, though it's another of Marcella's secrets, like the lamia. But Shaddani? Not that I've ever heard or read, except your mother and her sisters."

I began to paint a picture in my head, Shaddan, destroyed by some disaster and a massive diaspora. That meant there were likely other latent Dark-Fae here. There might even be Dark-Fae still living that had seen Shaddan at its height.

"Then it follows that the ogumo are dragging seeds and pollen here, assuming the legends are true. How much do you want to bet that there are pockets like that all over the city."

"But the land beyond the gate is a wasteland, how would that be possible?" Maki asked.

"It's the nature of plant life," I replied. "Did you know that in Israel, an archaeologist and her team grew an extinct palm tree from a two-thousand-year-old seed they found at Masada? It was called the Methuselah palm. Imagine an entire world of them just waiting for the right conditions. In the case of the Dark-Fae, a dark warm place and a little moisture. Could you imagine what would happen if there was a massive rain or a storm surge?"

Maki's eyes went wide. "An entire alien ecosystem could spring up underneath the city."

I nodded. I thought I should feel alarmed about it, but I didn't. An invasive species, or an entire invasive ecosystem, could change the world in ways we couldn't imagine, but maybe with effort, it could be transplanted. If I was really Dark-Fae like Mother Lamia said, if I was really royalty, then maybe we could save Shaddan and reclaim it by cultivating the ecosystem here and transplanting it there. Not that I'd live to see it, but maybe Umbrá. I kept that thought in my head for a while, hoping that maybe, when she took over, she'd see it through.

"So, what time is your date?" Maki asked, a sly curl forming on her lips.

I looked down at my watch. "Oh, shite. I have to go. Marcella's expecting me at her stylists."

I snatched up my stuff, waved a quick goodbye to Maki, and jetted from the building.

A couple of hours later, I sat in Marcella's sitting room, 'gussied up' as Morgan would say, and nervous as all fuck, one leg bouncing in anticipation. I even stared a few times at the fresh, brand-new, red soles of my Loubs trying to decide if my outfit actually suited me or if I was just putting on airs. I stood up and started pacing in front of the fireplace.

"Why are you so nervous?" Marcella asked from the doorway. "You've been living together for a month now."

I looked over at her. "I'm not sure. Up until now, it's been so easy, and when she asked me out, it was just a friend date, but now we're a couple. This is a real date, and shite, Marcella, I don't know." I sat back down and then stood again.

Marcella laughed and then walked over. With her in her flats and me in my booties, I didn't have to crane my neck quite so much to look at her.

She took my shoulders and said, "Take a deep breath. Morgan is completely head over heels for you. And you two are a good match. Now, have you taken your Keppra?"

I nodded. "Yes. And Gods, I feel like a teenager going to

prom."

Marcella laughed, then the doorbell rang, and my eyes went wide.

Marcella waggled her eyebrows and pointed to the end table. "Don't forget those."

I retrieved the bouquet of roses Marcella had bought for the occasion on our way home from the salon. It was ridiculous and beautiful, and about the sweetest thing I'd ever seen.

Marcella opened the door while I stood in the doorway to the sitting room. My mouth dropped open when Morgan walked in. She was in a dress. Not just a dress, a work of art. It was a spaghetti-strapped black sheath with a wide belt at the waist that perfectly flattered her every curve and muscle. In the matching black patent leather heels, she looked like a goddess and towered over me, even in my heeled boots. Her short hair was slicked back. The scar that ran down her face and over her collar displayed itself proudly, and when she saw me, she grinned. Marcella gave her a kiss on each cheek and then winked at me and left.

"Those for me?" Morgan asked with that crooked grin of hers.

I nodded. "So, was this your plan all along?"

Morgan nodded. "It was my idea, but I asked for a little help." She held out her keys. "Do you mind driving?"

"No limo?"

She shook her head. "It seemed a bit much."

"Oh, aye, and the Versace dress you're in is low-key," I said with a bit of sarcasm.

She did a turn. "Do you like it?"

I pressed my lips together to give my cheeks a rest from the permanent grin nailed to them and nodded.

"Let's go," I said as I handed her the flowers.

The restaurant at the Sojourner was nice, with wood paneling, the smells of wonderful food, and an upscale clientele. It was one of Marcella's special places, so they served appropriately for Morgan. We had a private room with a single table that held a small vase with two roses, double doors separated it from the rest of the dining area, but Morgan insisted on leaving the doors open so we could hear the crowd. Besides, we spent almost every waking moment in each other's company, so the people-watching gave us more to talk about. We made a game of it, relaxing in our chairs with a full view of the most important area, the bar.

Hotel bars are a wonderful location for people-watching, especially when they're in upscale buildings. You can get a good view of who is scoping for a date, who's looking for no-strings-attached sex, and of course, spot the occasional closeted gay person, which, for us, was a little sad to watch.

Morgan would pick out a couple at the bar, listen in on their conversations, and then ask me what I thought of their relationship, his or her chances of getting laid, that sort of thing. Then I'd look to her to see if I was right. We decided on a scoring system, too. I got a full five points for nailing it. We deducted a point for anything significant that I got wrong.

"Okay, how about those two," Morgan said when she spotted two women at the bar.

I nodded and watched them. One, a beauty with Mediterranean features with long raven hair draped over the shoulders of her gorgeous evening gown, was sipping on a vodka martini so dirty, I could almost smell the olive brine from here. She oozed class and sensuality. From the way she moved and the color of her skin, I decided she was probably Italian. It was just something in the darkness of her features coupled with the brightness of her mood. She was making the most of life tonight.

The other, a woman with modestly short light brown hair, was drinking a pretty straightforward gin and tonic. I decided she was from the US Midwest and more conservative. Nothing stood out that said that. It was just a feeling. And though she was in an evening gown, it was a simpler cut, less plunging in the chest, and her earrings were simple studs of diamond or maybe even cubic zirconia. On her left ring finger was a simple gold band, no adornment, no engagement ring. Definitely midwestern, I thought. Disciplined, pinched, and full of family secrets.

They were chatting pretty openly about something. The

Italian woman kept touching the Midwestern woman on the shoulder every time she laughed, and the Midwesterner would touch her hair nervously almost every time.

"Okay, I got it," I said with a grin as I looked back at Morgan.

She gave me her best poker face. "Okay, tell me."

I looked back at them. They were closer together now and speaking in hushed whispers about someone. "The one on the left, with the black hair, is Italian or maybe Spanish. The one on the right is American with a Midwestern accent, interested but scared. It might even be her first time. She's also cheating on her husband."

Morgan laughed loudly. "You get zero points for that."

I looked at her incredulously. "Zero?"

"Okay, I'll give you one point. The one on the right is from the Midwest. The one on the left is her half-sister, who is Boston born and bred. They are not at all talking about each other but about us, and they are wondering which one of them you are staring at."

I snapped my head back around to Morgan. "Oh, shite. Really?"

She nodded.

I looked back at the two women, and they were both looking at us, so I raised my glass. The raven-haired woman raised hers, and the Midwesterner raised hers but looked down and away in a cute, almost timid way. Then she said something to the other.

"Actually, make that two points. The one on the right is definitely trying to decide if she should approach you. So she *wants* to cheat on her husband."

"Crap," I said and turned back to the table, staring at the half-eaten slice of bread.

Fortunately, I was saved as Morgan put her hand out and took mine, bringing it to her lips and making me blush. "There, now they know we're on a date. And you didn't even have to break her heart."

"How do you know she wasn't looking to come talk to you?"

Morgan laughed again. "Apparently, I scare her. It seems I'm too butch."

I chuckled at that. "Butch? Really? I don't think so."

Morgan rolled her eyes. "You're kidding, right? Oh, wait, I forgot. You're from Ireland. The older the women get, straight or otherwise, the more butch they look."

I broke out in gales of laughter at that. She wasn't wrong, not entirely.

We did eventually order dinner for me and another glass of blood for Morgan, but I barely ate. Then Morgan had them close the doors, and we spent the entire time talking. And not once for the rest of the night did either of us mention my sister or Marcella or work. All in all, it was likely the best evening I had ever had.

Later, in front of the apartment, we sat in the car for a few minutes, neither of us talking.

"I meant it," Morgan whispered. "When I said I love you. I do." And when she looked at me with those beautiful green eyes, I just melted inside.

I leaned forward, but Morgan stopped me, placing a finger on my lips. "Come on. Let's go inside," she whispered.

I got out and walked around the car, intent on finishing out that near-missed kiss. Morgan slid out of the seat, and I took her arm. "You're not getting away that easy," I said with a grin and moved to cup her face.

Something abruptly nagged at the back of my senses, a feeling of rage and violence, and the hair stood up on the back of my neck. I pushed us both to the ground as a car squealed down the street. Automatic gunfire sounded, and the distinctive plunk-plunk-plunk of bullets hitting metal in rapid succession rang out. Agony burned through my back and chest as we fell hard to the concrete with a whoosh of air. All of the strength fled from my body in a vast and overwhelming feeling of fatigue.

"Ow, fuck," I wheezed. "Morgan?" Blood fountained from my chest in quick spurts, then stopped cold. Spots filled my vision as hypoxia immediately engulfed me. My last words came out as a whisper, just a breath, and a few tears flowed over my lashes as I looked up at Morgan. "I'm sorry."

CHAPTER FORTY

Morgan

"Aoife? Aoife? Baby, come on. Stay with me?" I almost shouted at her, but she was already pale and limp. "No, no, no, not yet! Not yet!"

I set her on the ground and reached into the still-open door of the cruiser, snatching the radio. "Victor 8-3-3. Officer Down, 2098 Holworthy. Send EMS."

I didn't wait for an acknowledgment. I felt for a pulse, there was nothing.

I laid her down and pressed on her chest, but the sudden flow of blood into my fingers told me all I needed to know.

"God!!! NO!!!" I screamed.

I pulled Aoife into my arms and held her close to my chest, begging all that was holy to bring her back. "Please, please, please." I had no other words. "I'm so sorry, Aoife. I should have protected you. I love you."

My voice dropped to a hoarse whisper, "Please come back to me, baby, please."

Time seemed to stretch on and on as I waited for the ambulance. Not that it mattered anymore. She'd been hit in the heart. There was nothing I could do.

"Ma'am?"

Someone was speaking to me. I looked up, unsure of what was happening.

"Please, ma'am, you have to let her go."

It was hard to focus through my tears. "Let her go?" I

whispered and pulled her as close as I could. "No."

I wiped away the tears on the back of my wrist, and the speaker resolved into a woman in an EMT uniform. "Please, ma'am. You need to let go. I'm so sorry, but she's gone."

I swallowed hard and sniffed, laying Aoife gently on the ground, keeping my hand under her head to make sure it didn't fall. Then I slowly pulled myself to my feet. I was in a haze of rage and burning heartache. A horrible weight seemed to collapse on me, and I walked over to the front stoop and sat down, staring at her blood.

I smeared it on my face as I lowered my head into my hands, imagining there was something special in the way it smelled like maybe it *was* her. I placed a bit of it on my lips as if somehow that would let me just hold on to her for one minute more. Just one more minute. *God, I thought we had more time. Why didn't we get more time?*

I was still sitting in the same spot, listless and unable to move, when the team showed up a few minutes later. Maki worked the scene, but the pain in her soft eyes was unfathomable. Freyer and Carlos were both broken, struggling to do their jobs. It was a shit show.

"What did you see?" Carlos asked, blinking back his own emerging tears.

"Um." I couldn't think, really. I kept looking over at Aoife's lifeless body, still laying where I'd left her.

"Late 90's Caprice. Black. It tore past in a spray of automatic gunfire. Bearded man behind the wheel. Why Carlos?"

"Why what?"

"Why did she push me down? He couldn't hurt me. She knew that."

He gave me a sympathetic look. "Because she was protecting you. It was her first instinct. She loved you, Morgan. Everyone could see it."

I lost it then, breaking down, as sadness and rage, and heartache tore through me in rapid waves all over again. I grabbed Carlos, yanking him down as I sobbed loudly and beat weakly at his back.

"I miss her already."

I stared down at Aoife, laying quietly on the gurney in Bian's lab. I had no idea how I'd gotten here or any clue what time it was. Someone had brought her here rather than the morgue, but I didn't know who, Marcella maybe? It had all been a blur.

Leaning over, I ran my hand gently against Aoife's forehead and through her hair, pushing strands away before leaning down and kissing her gently. "It's okay. I know we didn't get much time, but you can go now."

A hiccuping sob escaped my lips as I tried desperately to contain my grief, but I couldn't. There was nothing I could do but wail as the wretched heartache and sorrow burst forth in a torrent of tears and pain once more. The ache in my chest was beyond words. It was as if a deep part of me that I'd never known was there was wrenched loose, loved and caressed, and then stolen away, leaving a dark empty void that would never be filled.

I hadn't thought I could feel such pain anymore. Vampires aren't supposed to hurt like this. My chest grew even tighter, and a deep knot of misery crushed my body. I placed my head on Aoife's chest and whispered a final, choked "no," as if it might deny the truth of her passing.

Róisín placed a hand on my head and stroked her fingers through my bloodied hair, the pained utterances of her own sobbing grief mixing with mine.

I would never be whole again. My soul was beyond fractured, beyond broken. Half of it was gone. I would never again be right.

Bian's hand landed gently on my shoulder. "Morgan, we need to proceed."

I nodded and backed away, burying my face in my hands. But I had to see. I had to know, so I looked up, watching as Bian carefully extracted the tlehos from the container with a pair of forceps and placed it on Aoife's still face. The creature slid across her face quickly, burrowing effortlessly behind her eye, and we waited. I sniffed and wiped my nose. At least her death wasn't the end of all that she was. Umbrá would have her memories, or so Déra told me. Some part of her love would live on, though I didn't think I'd ever be able to look at Umbrá when this was all over. I'd just see Aoife.

Róisín sniffed and spoke a few words of Óṣeni over Aoife's body, initiating the ritual magic. There was a soft sound, almost like the rushing of air, and I felt the cool rush of something flow around and through me.

Some part of her would survive. And I could take a small bit of solace in the fact that her death would return life to Umbrá and happiness to Déra.

We all stood around and waited. My brow was furrowed so hard in grief that it hurt just to watch.

"How long will this take?" I asked. Aoife had touched my heart in a way that no one else had, peeling off the layers of pain and misery from my time in Chicago, and the rejection of my parents. Being with her had even helped me forget for a short time that my sister was missing, probably gone forever.

I looked around at my friends then. All of them sniffed and bawled as if something magical had just been snuffed from the world, even Nastasia. Aoife had wormed her way into all of them in the short time they had known her.

"Not long," Déra whispered.

As if it somehow had been waiting, Aoife's body moved, and the heart monitor wailed to life. Aoife's skin bubbled and cracked as a whirling mass of blue and silver magic shrouded her, and a sound like thunder mixed with a soft, lilting, almost musical tone filled the room. Through brief glimpses within the maelstrom, I watched the transformation. It wasn't subtle, but it wasn't nearly as drastic as I had thought. Her body did not change in structure or form. It was still her body, still her face. But her hair washed from its coppery auburn to an almost shining silver right before my eyes, and the cracked layer of skin flaked away to reveal alien white skin that shimmered iridescent in the cold fluorescent lights.

Aoife's old skin dissolved first into flakes, then powder, then disappeared altogether, vanishing as the cascade of magic that had transformed her pooled to the floor like liquid silk and disappeared. Before me, naked and whole, was someone else. Someone who looked much like Aoife but was clearly no longer her.

I watched as Déra lifted Aoife's body and took her away. Rage, jealousy, and a dreadful desire to tear Déra apart filled me to bursting, but Liz strode over and caught me in a tight embrace. "Shh. . .It won't bring her back."

Hours ticked by, and I sat in the Temple, staring at nothing. I couldn't stop crying. My face was streaked in ugly brown, the remnants of the blood that stained my tears. I should have gone, but I just couldn't bring myself to stand, let alone trudge back to my apartment. I had just begun to think of it as *our* home. How could I go back there? Just the thought made my heart wail in misery, and my chest constrict with empty claustrophobic cold. And the rage wouldn't subside. I wanted to kill someone, almost anyone. I wanted to die just so I could be with her.

Then, for just a moment, I thought I heard Aoife's brogue in the compound, swearing up a storm.

In the movies, this was where the grief-stricken hero smiled to themselves, and the healing began, but all I could think about in the echoing memory of her voice was what I was going to do to Matt Reynolds when I found him. "You're a dead man walking, Matthew Reynolds," I muttered. "Fucking dead. I am going to tear your heart from your chest and take a bite while you watch."

CHAPTER FORTY-ONE

Skaja

I lifted Boudka gently from the earth as tears of rage painted my cheeks in long pale streaks amid the dust and grime and ichor of the battle. I caught bits of mournful and angry voices as I walked, some counting the dead, some asking how the Fomori had been able to enter the camp in the first place.

I passed Aine's tent, where she and Saya were in a heated argument. It wasn't hard to hear. Saya was screaming at Aine. Mother Danu seemed to be trying to mediate.

In the end, though, the situation was clear. All of the Light-Fae scouts had abandoned their posts. When found, they were drunk and in the midst of accosting one of the local women. As a result, we lost fourteen, including two Swasari archers and our first Shaddani magi in over fifteen-thousand years, Boudka.

I entered Mother's cottage, bearing Boudka's pale form. I kicked at the door, but it merely bounced back open, so I left it, placing Boudka gently on the sofa. A bustle of Óṣeni warriors passed by, headed toward the central tent, their angry shouts telling me all I needed to know about their intent. This could tear apart the army, though I couldn't bring myself to care.

I just sat there for a long time—alone with Boudka. Her sweet face was drained of color, held in the embrace of death. I tried to re-arrange her robes, smooth them out and cover the massive wound in her thigh. There was nothing I could do about the hole in her chest.

I took a shuddering breath, and then I wailed, pleading at first and then demanding. "Please, Mother of Waters, bring her back to me! Bring her back!"

I had no idea how long I sat like that before my mother strode into her home and pulled me away. "Aine is coming, child. Come away. Let's see what she can do."

The Summer Queen arrived with one of her healers, an advisor named Veria, tall and lanky with short blonde hair and pale green eyes.

"Please, Aine—sister—I need you to heal her." My mother looked at the Summer Queen with pleading eyes. "I do not know why yet, but she cannot be allowed to expire here."

The Summer Queen looked down on Boudka for a moment, then at me with an almost disdainful expression. She turned to my mother. "Absolutely not. The thread of her life has ended. And despite your claims, it is a violation of the laws of Bethad to snatch life from the clutch of death. You know that, Nemhain."

"But, Your Majesty—" Veria began, but she silenced him with a wave of her hand.

"Our laws exist for a reason. It is the balance of things that must be maintained at all costs. The price of such meddling is as ruinous as the dereliction that led to this girl's death. I will not condone or participate in such an abomination."

My mother squinted at her. "You know, Aine, I should have expected this from you. What might you do if this were Wisteria or some consort of hers, I wonder."

Aine stood toe to toe, staring down The Morrigan, and for a very long time, it seemed as if they might come to blows, but Aine backed down, her voice turning softer. "I feel your pain, Nemhain, but I cannot, will not, do this. Unlike the Shaddani, the queens of Bethad rule by acceptance as much as ordination. If it were discovered, our participation here would fracture and shatter like so much glass on stone. I would lose my mandate to rule, and my people would likely disperse. I'm sorry."

In a flourish of her handkerchief skirts, she turned away and left, my mother's eyes following with hateful rage as she disappeared.

To his credit, Veria didn't flinch as my mother turned to him. He immediately began examining Boudka's body. "I can try," he said, glancing at me with sympathy, but a slow frown spread across his face, and his eyes bunched up in irritated defeat.

"There's nothing I can do here. Her body is suffused with a mixture of magic, even Bethadi. I've never seen anything like it, not since— " Veria paused. "She's a true mage, isn't she?" He glanced up at my mother. "You did this?"

"I only showed her the way to her own Earthen magic," my mother replied. "She unlocked the rest on her own. I certainly couldn't have managed Bethadi magic. And what do you mean there's nothing you can do? We have preserved her soul. You have her corpse!"

I flinched at the harsh description of Boudka's remains.

"Heal the body and reseat the soul," she demanded. "I've seen Bethadi do this before, several times."

"I cannot. Any magic I apply to her will simply float away like so much smoke in the wind. Look at the jewel, for water's sake."

I looked down at the soul stone, it pulsed with the white light of Boudka's human soul, but that was partially obscured by strangely swirling lights of gold and purple, blue and dark green, but most of all, blood red.

I glanced back at Veria, confused. "What does it mean?"

"It means she is beyond my power to help. Shaddani magic takes. It swallows Bethadi magic. Anything I give to this body will be drawn away immediately into the flow of energy from the Shaddani gate to keep balance. On the positive, her body will not decay, but neither can I heal it. Only Mother Aine can heal her, and, well—"

"Out," my mother said sharply.

"What are you going to do?" Veria asked, his eyebrows raised in a horror-stricken expression that painted his features.

"I said out!" Her voice cut through the air like lightning with a roll of thunder that shook the cottage and the ground beneath it. Veria swiftly scampered away, his robes trailing after him.

My mother turned to me, placing a hand on my shoulder. Her touch should have been comforting, but it wasn't. I knew what she planned.

"Give me the stone, and go, Weyna."

I handed my mother the soul stone and turned to leave.

"I will bring her back," my mother said as I made to leave. "And, for what it is worth, I am sorry."

I closed my eyes at that last, knowing that whatever came out of the cottage, and my mother's ministrations, wouldn't be the Boudka I knew. Not entirely.

It seemed like hours, though it was only a few minutes before the door opened and my mother appeared. As always, she looked the image of health, but I could see the strain in her eyes, not of fatigue, but sorrow and no small amount of rage made impotent and turned inward.

"You can come in, Weyna. She is asleep for now. I am keeping her that way to keep the camp safe. But at some point soon, I will need to wake her, and you should be prepared."

I gasped and brought a hand to my mouth. I knew what my mother had done. Her skin showed none of the injuries she sustained; it was perfectly smooth and milky pale, with blood-red lips.

"Vampir," I said, using the old Shaddani word. My mother had reseated her soul and given her the darkest of gifts. It was old magic, long forbidden by the ancient Shaddani queens a hundred thousand of my years ago. I looked up at her, still shocked at all that had happened.

She answered the unspoken question that hung between us like a veil. "The thread of her life is not closed. I do not know her destiny. I cannot fully see it. But she has purpose still."

Her hands rested on my shoulders, and she gazed at me with the millennia of wisdom she carried. And there was a kindness in her eyes that I so rarely saw, soft and compassionate, and a pang of sadness, too. My mother, possibly the most powerful being on the planet, was heartbroken. "I'm sorry," she whispered and pulled me into a hug. When she finally released me, she said, "Now, say your goodbyes."

"But," I protested quietly, "she's not dead. Why—"

She still had a hold of my shoulders. "Because for a very long time, she won't be safe for you to be around. I did this once before and was less attentive to that." She looked away and then back to me, a single solitary tear slipping from her eye. "It ended poorly."

I nodded. I wanted to protest and argue. I wanted to beat my mother to the ground. I wanted to cry and scream and rage. But it was done—it had to be done. And venting my feelings that way would serve no purpose.

My mother stepped outside the door, pausing momentarily as if waiting for something before closing it finally, and I approached Boudka. I ran a hand over her shining hair and kissed her cold blood-red lips.

"I'm sorry, Boudka. I should have been there." I paused for a moment, breathing slowly as rage and grief filled me to bursting. Scouts had abandoned their posts, and this was the result. I'd make them pay. All by myself if necessary.

Outside, I found my mother speaking with Zilly and Semi in hushed tones, and they turned quiet as I stepped through the door, the silence of mind-numbing anger sealing my lips. My mother said nothing, simply giving me a sad look before returning inside.

Neither of the other two women said a word, choosing not to lay on thick and pointless sympathies. They just waited for me to speak, but loud voices from the training ground caught our attention, and we swept off in that direction. I suspected the missing scouts had been retrieved at last.

A few minutes later, my heart a maelstrom of rage and sorrow, I stood with Zilly and Semi at my sides as the very air weighed heavy upon me. The bond that bound Boudka and me had been snapped, and the resonating echo in my head screamed for the loss of what was and what would never be.

The circle of Swasari crowded loose and unruly as we

awaited the return of our sisters sent to fetch the missing scouts. In the center stood the entire leadership council except for my mother. All were staring at Queen Aine with disturbed and questioning eyes.

Aine, for her part, looked not at all thrilled to be under such scrutiny, especially from Mother Danu, who, for the first time since I'd met her years ago, looked angry. But if Aine cared one wit for the dead rather than her own reputation, it wasn't clear, despite her words to the contrary in my mother's home.

Eventually, the missing Swasari returned, marching through the circle and pushing down a half dozen Fae scouts, all male and all stinking of spirits, their hands bound behind their backs.

"We found these six down in the village on the far side of the ridge making trouble," one of the Óşeni women said to Saya, who looked down at the men with disgust. "They had one of the village women on her back while they made her husband watch. They gave us little trouble in their state."

An unassuageable rage twisted in my gut, and as I looked around. The hateful glares among my normally reserved Óşeni sisters made it clear what they expected. The leadership stood together, whispering until my mother finally joined them, her very presence digging at the deep wound in my heart.

"What are you waiting for?" I called, unable to contain my grief and anger. "We lost two of our sisters because of their dereliction, not to mention their behavior toward the humans!"

And that was all it took to start a veritable riot. We all pressed in, grabbing at the men until Saya shouted us all down.

"Silence! All of you. Back in formation! Now!"

Automatically, we all returned to the edge of the circle and came to attention.

That insufferable smile was nowhere to be found on Aine's face now as she turned to the men. It was supplanted by a terrifying scowl. "Well? Do you have anything to say?"

The Fae warriors were quiet, all but one, who said, "The farmer disrespected us, so—"

Aine's eyebrows shot up, then she snapped her fingers, and

the Fae warrior exploded into a fine gold mist that glittered away to nothing. "I want to know why you weren't at your posts, not why you were abusing a lesser species. We can not return to the summer lands until the Fomori are pushed back. Now, would anyone else like to explain?"

The other Swasari and I had assumed that the Summer Queen was a showpiece, a figurehead, here to provide a symbol for the Fae to rally around. No one thought she had any real power except the Fae, of course, who seemed to worship her. Certainly, we'd never seen her use it before. Clearly, we were wrong. Even the leadership appeared to be taken aback, all except for Mother Danu, who watched and waited with hawkish intent.

The Summer Queen spoke again. "Who wants to explain to us why you weren't at your posts? Or do you need more incentive?"

One of the Fae soldiers opened his mouth to speak, then closed it again, thinking better of his answer. Aine raised her arm, clearly about to level the same punishment on the rest, but it was my mother who intervened, placing a hand on Aine's hovering wrist. "It doesn't matter. We can't lose any more scouts. There are too few already."

Fury moved through the Swasari like a wave. These men had not only abandoned their posts, they'd made sport of the very people we were dying to protect.

"Mother!" I exclaimed, ready to throw my weight behind a harsh judgment. But Badb and Macha returned a moment later, landing in the circle and shifting back into their humanoid forms. Both of them said in unison, "The enemy is on the move."

CHAPTER FORTY-TWO

Umbrá

"Doséyetí." I utter the arcane word as I wave my hand over the last of the candles I purchased in the marketplace, watching it flare to life.

In the darkness, the harsh light of the three candles allows me to see my own face clearly in the small mirror. It has the added benefit of banishing the myriad insects so familiar in this part of the city. I glance down, watching them scurry under the door to my oubliette-like room.

I pass a brush across my soft, silver hair, touching my cheek lightly as I examine my face. It is glimmering and iridescent in the reflection, with a silvery cast underneath, atypical for my kind, or so I am led to believe. My visage carries none of the waxy, zombie-like lividity of the Kylr as described in various texts on the subject. Neither does my face show any of the drawn, bony countenance of my kin. On the contrary, my skin is positively radiant, and my cheeks full. My liquid eyes and black irises reflect brightly rather than sitting sunken and drained of color. I look—healthy, by the standards of most.

I gaze about my sparse six-foot by nine-foot quarters, ensuring everything is in its place. Once, some hundreds of cycles ago, it served as solitary confinement and a chamber of torment for disobedient slaves. I simply cannot remove the ancient deep brown stain on the wall over my cot. It has seeped so deeply into the stone that no amount of scrubbing will remove it. Despite that, though, this is home, such as it is.

I suppose I should be thankful. As the only slave in a dilapidated

& semi-disgraced Óşení house of no importance, I have my own room. That is better than most.

In the corner, a washbasin juts from the stone. I never use it. There is only one other occupant in the house, the Ánámensí herself. Thus, I use the house bathing pool on the floor above for washing. A luxury, yes, but one the Ánámensí permits.

To the left of the basin, a stone outcropping serves as both a makeshift bookshelf and a place of constant annoyance. I rub the back of my head instinctively, recalling the last time I accidentally cracked my skull on it. Finally, the tiny cabinet that doubles as clothing storage on one side and sacred space for my altar to the right.

I glance at the three books stacked on the shelf. My favorite is a voluminous treatise on the various known worlds written by the Óşení Sage Exalt, Ophir Glaurwin. This is also my most recent acquisition, a gift from the current Ánámensí. I reach out and run a hand over the black, worm-skin cover, embossed in a platinum script that flows and moves with the harmless enchantment that identifies it as a first edition copy produced by the students of Mens-dé, the sage college.

Within the book's covers, I have learned two noteworthy things. First, I am, as far as I know, unique. I have been born naturally, if such a word can be used to describe anything Kyliri. According to the text, pregnancy is supposed to be impossible among the Kylr. Secondly, and more importantly, I come from somewhere. I have an identity beyond that of 'slave.' It provides a pleasant contradiction of thought, allowing me to fantasize about having another life. Besides, being Kylr has drawbacks, it seems, at least according to the book. The typical reproductive cycle of all Kylr is less than inviting. Involving the implantation of a wormlike creature into the corpse of a bipedal, intelligent host. Almost any will do.

The sketches and lithos within the book's pages make it clear that most Kylr aren't particularly pretty. It's not just the self-mutilation, piercings, or ritual scarifications. It is the flat, almost corpse-like look. Their hair is always white and long, thick and coarse, described as beast-like. The pictures make it clear, though, that despite the apparent differences, I am, in fact, Kylr. I might be an aberration, perhaps, but my silvery-white hair, pale skin, sharp features, and shapely pointed ears are clearly Kylr.

I wonder, assuming I ever travel there, if the icy plains would claim me as their own, likewise twisting my features into the aged pantomime of my youthful appearance, or if my beauty would hold. If I died, would my soul be snatched from this world and stuffed into a waiting husk? I have no way to know because, to my knowledge and everyone else's, I am an unknown. Frankly, I have no desire to find out. While I'm not overly fond of my appearance myself, others find it pleasing, and I'm just fine with that. And self-harm is something I simply cannot do.

Once, I heard a gripping tale in the marketplace in which one of the city guards of Ishir had hacked off his own arm. Apparently, said guard had suffered a xitíngá bite, generally lethal. Supposedly, the guard survived.

Umm—yeah, no, I thought upon hearing the tale from a market vendor. You could just kill me right there, I'd be fine with that. I shiver at the hideous thought. There's no way I could hack off my own limb or scar my own flesh. Ick.

I stop obsessing over my appearance and thoughts of my kin and kneel down to open the right-hand door of my small cabinet, my threadbare gown brushing across the cold stone floor with a whisper. Within is a small black candle, and mounted to the back of the shallow shelf is a solid midnight-blue disc surrounded by a thin purple border.

Religious practice is also forbidden to slaves lest they gain some semblance of cohesion and develop a sense of group identity. Such covert observances have apparently been the end of many an established social structure on other worlds, and the God-Empress, Avra, has no interest in allowing that.

I light the small candle within and whisper a small prayer to the Mother of Darkness, the Kyliri deity, commonly called Hel or just Mother Darkness.

I obtained a small prayer book via a black market connection. Yes, it's a little odd that one lights a candle to pray to the Mother of Darkness, but there you go. At least the candle is black. I have no tutelage in any religious observance except that of the God-Empress, so I can only hope I'm doing it right. But I have researched the belief system of my people thoroughly and am confident that, if what I have gleaned is to be believed, my approach is at least mostly correct.

"Embrace me, Holy Mother of Darkness. Cover my eyes. Hide my truth from the world, that I may be yours in your eternal grace in the end."

This is my favorite short prayer. Every time I speak it aloud, even in a whisper, I feel as if the Goddess is somehow with me and protecting me. In general, it gives me a sense of personal power that I otherwise lack, as if I have secrets within me that only I know and no other can touch.

I feel my prayers are tainted in some way, though. I would have preferred to deliver the prayers in the common language of my own people, but I know not a lick of it. I can't even ask where to find the privvy, vital if traveling to the Kylr plains for sure. Of course, the perception that the Kylrí language is somehow better or more holy than Óṣenic is simply a conceit. Indeed, I believe the Goddess hears my prayers the same as any other. I stamp down on the distracting thoughts and continue my prayers.

"Dark Mother," I whisper so softly that I can barely hear myself. *"I pray for your guidance and protection as I seek escape."* This brings no feeling at all, though I'm not surprised. I've made this promise so many times before that the personal intention has become a platitude at best, a lie at worst. I'm going nowhere.

Investigations of numerous avenues of escaping Óṣení enslavement have come to nothing. I haven't bothered to pursue the effort in over a year. When I was much younger, I felt a burning desire to see open skies, other worlds, and to have control of my own life. Lately, though, the desire to leave has lost its luster, and the realities of my life have settled upon me. A single emotion comes unbidden to me as I idle briefly on leaving all that I know, leaving her. Sadness. In truth, I no longer wish to leave. Déra, the Ánámensí, she needs me.

Besides, running away is an awful risk. Even setting aside the horrible things visited upon escaped slaves, scourging or death, there's something about this place, this house, that feels more like home now than a prison. Even as the old Ánámensí lay dying, I felt a kinship with her and a need to ease her burden and protect the Ánámensí's children from the worst miseries and ravages of the house matriarch's illness: the agonized screaming, the cleaning and bathing, the comforting. I don't know why; the woman was a shrew *and cruel.*

I quickly blow out the candle and close the cabinet quietly as the lock to my door clicks, and the door opens, revealing the anchor that holds me in place.

I woke from the vivid reminiscence in pitch blackness, feeling a little lost and disoriented. There was the soft sound of movement somewhere to my left.

"Hello?"

No answer.

My body ached as if I'd pulled every muscle. I flexed a hand. It felt normal. A strange shuffling noise came from somewhere to my left.

"Hello?"

Lights came on, practically blinding me, and I snapped my eyes shut.

"Wake up," a soft, professional voice said in Óṣeni.

I opened my eyes. A woman, enormous and well-muscled, like some kind of gray-skinned Amazon, looked down at me, a deep frown on her face. "Who are you?"

"You must be Déra. I'm Aoife, Cait's sister. How did I get here?"

A deep frown marred her angular features, and embers of rage glowed in her eyes. She stood and assessed me.

I sat up. My physique was mine, but silver hair fell long and full around my shoulders, laying across iridescent arms and breasts. My nipples had the lightest shimmer of gray. Even my pubes were silver. "Son. Of. A. Bitch! Motherfucker! That dosshouse dry-shite scaly wagon bitch. I'm gonna kill her."

"Who?" Déra asked, her arms crossed, her thoughts hidden behind a stony expression, but one didn't have to be a mind reader to read the ice in her tone.

"Mother Lamia," I said. "She told me to do this. I don't understand what happened."

Déra pointed at a beautiful blue dress in an unfamiliar style laying at the foot of her bed, then sighed dejectedly, "Get dressed. Let's go sort this out."

I grabbed her arm. "I'm sorry, Déra. I know this was supposed to be your time with her."

She turned around and stared down at me. "I knew something was wrong when your body didn't transform properly. But I had hoped it was just something new or something I didn't fully understand." She put her hands on her hips and stared at the ceiling blinking back furious tears. "Fuck. Is she even in there?"

"I don't know. I don't feel any different. I mean, I'd expect something. I can understand Óṣeni, and I think a few other languages I hadn't known. And—" I closed my eyes for a moment, just feeling everything around me. "And I think the magic around here feels different, more distinct. But I don't sense another person in here."

"Then she's lost." Déra dropped to the bed and placed her head in her hands. "All this was for nothing."

I sat down next to her and put my arm around her on instinct. "Maybe not. Maybe she's just dormant. I have skills that are obviously hers. Maybe there's more here, you know."

"No. But I don't understand. You were dead. Shot through the heart. I watched the ritual. Bian placed her tlehos at your eye. Your mother said all the words. There was the flow of magic. It all seemed right."

I shook my head. "I don't know either. But we need to find out. Where are we?"

"You are in my quarters in the lamia compound," Déra whimpered. Her tears were free-flowing, and it was breaking my heart. I put my arms around her and pulled her close, letting her cry on my shoulder while I stroked her beautiful hair.

"I'm so sorry, Déra."

"Tell me you didn't mean for this to happen!" She said, suddenly pulling back and standing, her voice rising to a shriek. "Tell me that you didn't just kill my wife for your own survival."

I gasped at her, horrified. "Dear Gods! No! I don't know what went wrong. One minute I was shot. The next I was here. That's all I know. I mean it."

She gestured to the dress at the foot of the bed again. "Get dressed."

Putting on the dress was a little difficult. Déra had to show me the proper way to wear it with several strange wrapping components. The dress had a weird high-necked, almost Edwardian appearance, except for the wide cleavage window. "Is this a Kyliri design?"

"No, this is a replica of the dress she wore when we became betrothed. It's made of embroidered cotton, the closest material you have to our kind of wool, but it is nonetheless a perfect recreation of a formal Óṣeni court dress."

"It's beautiful," I murmured but said nothing else, driving my feet into a pair of pretty slippers and following Déra out the door. She stopped as we exited the room in a part of the lamia compound I didn't recognize.

"Which way?" I asked.

Déra looked at me, and endless depths of sorrow filled her eyes. "Straight down the hallway and to the right is Bian's lab."

I nodded, starting to feel really ticked off myself. "Good, let's go find Bian and see what the actual fuck is going on around here."

Déra nodded, but she didn't move. "You should know that Mother Lamia has died."

"Yeah, okay. I'm sorry for your loss, but I know she had something to do with this, too. Come on."

I stalked down the hallway with Déra, bursting into the lab like Dan Sheehan on a try. "What the actual feck, Bian! I told you I didn't want to be changed! I told you dat I wanted to die as I was. But no, here we are. You knew I was Dark-Fae. You knew this would happen."

Bian twisted around from whatever she was working on, eyes wide and nearly dropping the beaker in her hands. "Aoife?"

"Yes, Bian, who did you expect?"

"Umbrá, of course. Though I was terribly confused when your body did not complete the transformation."

I narrowed my eyes at her. "Why did Mother Lamia recommend this? She had to know this would happen. She sees the future, doesn't she?"

"I don't know that she did," Bian replied coolly. "But if you have come into my lab to hurl accusations at me, I'd ask that you leave."

"Look," I shot back hotly. "I get that you have the bedside manner of the average pit viper, but—"

Bian shot forward, her arm out, but Déra intercepted her with a firm shot to the jaw, knocking the naga's head around and sending her torso crashing into a tray of instruments.

"There will be none of that, Bian," Déra said firmly. Then, from nowhere, she drew out a wicked-looking shadowsteel dagger. "Keep your temper, snake. I've killed bigger, more dangerous things than you."

"Whoa! Let's everyone slow down, please," I shouted before anyone could do anything else to escalate this further.

Bian twisted back up, clearly recovered, and shot a baleful gaze at Déra.

I stepped between them. "Déra, leave!" I commanded my eyes on Bian. "Go cool down."

There was a moment of frosty silence, then Déra's bare feet padded out the door, only to be replaced by Morgan.

"Aoife? Is that you?"

I pressed my lips together, and I gave her a rapid nod. I couldn't hold back the tears anymore. I launched myself into her arms and bawled like a baby. Every angry moment poured out of me in a torrent of sobs. It was all too much: Cait, my time here, Mother Lamia and her machinations, the Akkorokamui, dying. It was just more than I could manage. I almost fell to the ground, but Morgan held me in her arms. Her effortless grace and strength had to be enough for both of us because I was done.

CHAPTER FORTY-THREE

Skaja

A few nights later, the barracks door opened as I lay sleepless in my bunk. Standing in the doorway and haloed by moonlight, a figure watched me in silence like a statue of dark stone. I stared back for a few moments.

"Boudka?"

There was no reaction. The figure still hovered, motionless.

Then I heard my mother's hissing whisper from outside. "Come away from there. You can't." The door closed with a click as the figure vanished back into the night.

I lay there for long hours after that, my mind racing with anger and disappointment. I tried to understand my emotions. I loved Boudka, but even before the attack on the fort, we had been drifting in different directions. We'd made love, yes, but my heart had been steadily looking elsewhere in Boudka's rather common and long absences. I was going to miss her, but I wondered many times that night if this might be what was meant to be. At least she was still alive—after a fashion, anyway. Eventually, I gave up trying to sort out my conflicted and guilty feelings.

My dreams were filled with terrible images of a young girl with long, matted black hair and gray eyes bleeding out in a small stone room. I screamed fruitlessly for help, but none came, and I woke with a start.

As I slept again, I dreamed once more of that same young girl, now wearing Boudka's golden hair and sky-blue eyes, curled up in my lap as she drank blood from a cup.

After that night, I caught glimpses of Boudka leaving the fort every few nights. I had assumed she was feeding on the local humans, but one by one, the scouts who had failed us also disappeared. No signs of struggle and no blood. They were just gone. We all knew what had happened to them, but no one said anything. Even the Summer Queen kept her counsel on the matter.

Three weeks later, I finally tired of catching glimpses of her in the distance. So, I cut training early to get cleaned up and wait outside my mother's cottage. Almost as soon as the sun set, Boudka appeared in the doorway.

"Hey," I said as she stepped out the door and headed toward the gate, dressed in a black robe and a simple black cloak.

She halted without turning. "You should go back to the barracks."

"No. I want to speak with you."

Despite the fact that I never thought Boudka might actually hurt me, I was armed with my bóllom and nisís at my hip and wearing my boots. Casual uniform or not, I was ready for combat if needed. From what I had read in my mother's texts, such spells as created vampir were unpredictable, and the results, on occasion, could turn out badly—very badly. It's why those spells had been forbidden in the old court.

She turned around slowly and gazed at me through those beautiful blue eyes, pale and alight with keen intelligence. But there was no love or affection in them, only cold calculation. She glanced me up and down.

"Why, Skaja," she said, her voice taking on a seductive and not altogether unfrightening quality, predatory. "Are you afraid of me?"

"No," I responded firmly. "But I do know that what my mother did can have unintended consequences. Now, why have you been avoiding me?"

She paused for a moment as if to say something. A hint of hurt and misery flashed across her face. "Is that what you really want?" She moved closer to me, just a step.

My heart sped up slightly, but I kept my cool, leaning back against the cabin wall, my legs crossed at the ankle, arms across my chest.

She moved forward another step, this one bringing her within arms reach. Still, I didn't move.

"I just came by to say that I miss you," I said softly.

The wind picked up a little, blowing her blonde hair out over her right shoulder. She pushed a few strands out of her face as she stepped even closer, moving into my space. Instinctively, my hands landed on the hilts of my blades.

"That's why," she whispered, and I could smell a hint of blood on her breath. "That's why I won't come to see you. You may think you love me, but I know you love someone else. And you're afraid of me. I didn't want to see that in your eyes."

I didn't deny her words. She wasn't wrong about being a little afraid, but that's part of why I was here. I wanted to see for myself what my mother had wrought, probably in my name, despite what she'd said. "You're wrong. I'm not afraid of you, just the magic that changed you. And I do love you, still."

Her face softened at that, but the pain of loss still lingered there. "And I love you. Which is why I have to do this."

My hands slipped from my blades languidly as something brushed at the back of my thoughts, and my will to move or say anything collapsed. I felt incredibly relaxed. Boudka's blue eyes seemed to grow and expand, encompassing everything, glowing first with blue fire, then turning a deep crimson. It was like contentedly drowning in a pool of deep red water.

Her voice echoed through me, deep into my very soul. "You don't love me. You are in love with Zilyana, and I know that. *You* know that. Stop looking for me. There is no hurt. I am happy and alive, and that's all you need to care about. Now let me go."

She paused, and somewhere in the distance of my thoughts, I heard the sniff of tears. "Let me go, Skaja. In a moment, I will be gone, and you'll remember none of this, only that it's okay that I am gone. You will know that I am happy and that I am happy that you have found someone. It was just young love, and you will remember that your father told you that young love seldom turns out in the end. Do you understand?"

"Yes," I whispered mechanically.

I stayed outside my mother's cabin for some time, but Boudka never showed. At one point, I thought I caught the scent of her hair and felt the brush of her lips on mine, but it was just one of those flights of imagination. After the sun had set and the sky grew dark, I left, realizing that there was no point in being here. She was probably fine, and I had other places to be.

After that, I would catch other glimpses of her from time to time. But I never had the urge to follow her or chase her down. She was a wraith, haunting the shadows of the fort or moving about the countryside late in the evening, not really interacting with anyone, least of all me. I'd have liked to say that it left me with a stone in the pit of my stomach, but it didn't. Maybe I hadn't been as much in love with her as I thought I had. Or maybe I'd just come to realize that she was really gone. The woman that I had loved had become someone—something—else. So I continued to train, and over time, it took my mind off of things.

CHAPTER FORTY-FOUR

Aoife

My image twisted in the mirror, and my skin seemed to show off all by itself, the iridescent colors moving and shifting like the makeup on a rave girl. The only thing missing was glitter. I gently ran a hand down the flesh of my tummy and watched the shimmer move and ripple over my abs. The effect might have been cool on anyone else, maybe a skinny girl at the club. On me, though, it just looked like I'd bathed in holographic highlighter. Freaky and stupid. *No,* I reminded myself. *Just different. This is how the Kylr look. And that is me now. There's no going back.*

I ran a hand through my silver hair, which was a bit thicker than it had been. The color wasn't terrible, and it wasn't like I couldn't go to the salon and get my auburn back if I wanted. Maybe I'd get used to it. And it didn't seem to frizz as it used to, so that was good. It would also hide the modestly pointed ears, which Fiona kept pressing on, apparently watching the colors move.

"I'm an elf," I murmured to her as a nuzzled her furry face with a finger. "Like the ones out of Lothlorien in Tolkien. You know, girl?"

It was so strange seeing these changes, and yet it was still my body, my face. Even the eyes, while almost monochrome with their dark grey, almost black, irises, still looked the same. Only the color had changed. They weren't unflattering against the iridescent skin, though, very similar in nature to Déra's,

337

which were gorgeous. I'd never liked my green eyes, and neither had Cait, as I recalled. I should have been thankful for small favors, but I wasn't. I'd tried to just let myself die, and I'd even fucked that up.

I wiped a few tears from my cheeks. I knew I was feeling sorry for myself, which made it even worse. We were supposed to soldier on, weren't we?

Morgan's rough tenor echoed from the door. "How are you coping?"

I glanced at her, then sighed and swatted at a tear. "I don't know. It's strange. It looks like me, mostly. And it feels like me, though my skin feels different, like every cell is straining to capture even the lightest sensation. I can't really describe it. But it doesn't hurt anywhere if that's what you're asking. And there are these occasional phantom scents that fill my nose and mouth from time to time, burnt embers, spring grass, loamy earth, sulfur, all kinds of things. I think it's magic." I looked back at my body and then gazed back into my own eyes. "I think the strangest thing is the idea that I don't have an actual brain anymore, not in the human sense, just this mass of neurons grown from the wiggly worm that ate my noggin. Makes me wonder if I'm still me?"

More tears flowed down my cheeks unbidden, and Morgan stepped closer, reaching out a hand and placing it on my shoulder.

"It's your soul, Aoife. Bian confirmed that. You can believe her."

"I feel so bad for Déra," I said, turning and putting my arms around Morgan, resting my head against her chest.

Morgan sighed. "It's easy for me to imagine what she's going through. I was just there."

I shook my head. "It's worse for her. She's been looking for Umbrá for years."

Morgan just nodded and hugged me close. "Please don't ever do that again. I'm a vampire, Aoife. I can take the hits."

"Yeah, well, now, so can I. Kylr are nearly indestructible. We just wiggle out and grab the next body. Just the thought, though, it seems so wrong."

Morgan shrugged. "Which part? Taking over a dead body, or the fact that what you really are is a little wiggly worm."

I snorted in genuine amusement. "I am *not* a wiggly worm. The tlehos is just the repository for my soul and memories when this body dies."

Morgan chuckled and ran her hands across my shoulders, watching the iridescent color flow.

The feeling of her fingers on my bare skin was so strange. The sensation was muted in some ways and heightened in others. The coolness of her touch was still there, but it felt less like a chill and more like a slight difference. The caress of her touch, though, flowed like the softest silk I'd ever felt, shimmering across my nerve endings so pleasantly that I wanted more. Part of me wanted to strip off my sports bra and workout shorts and let her run her hands all over my exposed skin; so pleasing was the feeling. I looked up into those emerald green eyes, staring for long moments.

"What?" Her voice was soft, almost a whisper, bringing with it the copper scent of blood and a sweet, almost lyrical quality that pricked some deep part of me.

I blinked at my tears, grabbed a hand towel to wipe my now running nose, and sniffed. I continued to gaze into her face, searching for something. Because at that particular moment, I felt so much like the leftovers, like no one, ever, in my life, had ever held me as a priority, and I knew that she did. Or, at least, she had. Maybe it was just my own insecurities or self-doubt, but it didn't matter. The feeling was real. And so was my absolute inability to voice it.

I swallowed hard as Morgan put out her other arm, inviting me toward her again. I stood there for long moments, a weird part of my brain, or whatever it was, noodling on how perfectly still her arm was. Then I caved and practically fell forward into her, resting my head on her shoulder and letting it all out. I was emotionally exhausted.

Morgan pushed me back slightly, placing a hand on my cheek. "Aoife, love, what's wrong?"

"Everything," I choked out through a sob as I pressed my cheek into her palm, desperate to feel every inch of it on my skin. When she pulled away, my face tingled for a second, as if her hand had been part of me, torn away, leaving a raw spot behind.

She pulled me out of the tiny loo and over to the bed, sitting down and patting the space beside her. "Come on. Tell me what it is."

I sat down next to her, gently placed Fiona next to me, and, unable to stop myself, unloaded. "Am I still important? To you, I mean."

"What?" Her voice was full of shocked incredulity. "Of course you are. I love you. Of course, you're important. Why would you even ask?"

"I'm sorry. I've never had a decent relationship. Emily, my ex, from New York, she told me she couldn't be with me because I couldn't communicate my feelings." I snorted in mirthless amusement. "My life has been pretty much mediocre at best. Lousy sex with lousy partners." I paused at her raised eyebrow and hastily added, "Sorry, not you.

"Anyway, I had a middling, unremarkable military career where nothing notable happened. A police career where, again, nothing notable happened. And a home life that involved three people, me, myself, and I, since Donny died. Cait's fucking Wonder Woman. I can't compete with that. I don't have the skills or the courage she has. I just don't measure up. I was the spare. Just in case something happened to Cait, so I could open the gate instead. But the gate's open, and I'm not needed." I sniffed and dropped my hands in my lap, and hung my head in despair. "What do I matter? I'm useless to everyone."

Morgan was quiet for a long time, just listening to me bitch about what shite I was before she spoke, then she said, "Aoife, I think you're very special. Not because of your sister or what you are, but because of you. You are level-headed and thoughtful. You're funny and sweet. You have a genius intellect, and you're resourceful and brave. You just gave your life trying to save me from a hail of bullets. And let me tell you something you don't already know. Carlos confirmed that those bullets were made of black-steel, the same stuff that

Déra's blade is made from."

"Shadowsteel," I murmured quietly.

"Huh?"

"The correct translation is shadowsteel," I corrected again. "I know what it is."

"Really?" She raised an eyebrow.

I cracked a slight smile and sniffed away my tears. "Yeah, but it doesn't matter.   You were just about to tell me how wonderful I am. Keep going. I could use a pep-talk."

"Anyway, they could have killed me easily. So, you really did save my life. Don't mistake the lack of opportunity for the lack of ability." She paused, laying down fully on the bed, and pulled me to her shoulder. "Look at all you've done. You served in the military, spent time in Afghanistan, for which, Liz tells me, you were awarded the Medal of the British Empire."

"That doesn't matter. They hand out MBEs like candy. They can give it to anyone."

"So, every officer in Afghanistan got one?"

"Well, no, but—"

"I rest my case. So, while all that was going on, you worked your ass off for your Master's and then got a Ph.D. You did all this in a span of what, eleven years?"

"Twelve. And it's a DPhil, not a Ph.D. It's Oxford, you know."

Morgan laughed. "Of course it is. The point is, you weren't in combat. Ireland isn't a hotbed of murder and mystery, especially in Mayo, so why would you have had to do anything heroic or even interesting with the Garda? But you made the best of everything you had and more. You're a fucking genius, and it's sexy as hell.   Aoife, you are beautiful and smart and every inch the person of integrity that your sister ever was. So, now would you like to know what's really wrong? Why you're really sad?"

I laughed. She sounded like a shrink. "Okay, Dr. Kennedy, tell me. What's eating Aoife Reagan?"

"Well, Dr. Reagan, you're feeling a little lost because you've changed. It's perfectly normal. But there are some things you should know. I had a chat with Marcella. You're not the leftovers. She told you that. In a way, Cait is. You were chosen to inherit your mother's power, not her. And you weren't just fucked off to Ireland for no reason. You were the one she was protecting. You're special."

I snorted in annoyance. "So I've been told. I just wish someone had said something to me when I was younger, you know?"

She spoke softly, love and kindness in her voice without any sense of condescension or pandering. "Most of them didn't understand how special you are. And when Cait wakes up, I think you'll find she's a little afraid of you."

"Afraid of what? She's a fucking hero of legend."

"Afraid you'll take her place."

I just stared at her, dumbfounded. "What?" I whispered, unable to believe my ears.

"You did a fair approximation of doing just that. So well, in fact, that Sesi hired you into a detective role on the spot. You were an asset to the team and still are."

I chuckled. "Yeah, I guess I am."

"So, yeah, Cait is gone right now, and you took over."

"Okay. So, this may sound soon and all, but would you like to see what it's like to make love to a Kyliri woman?"

Morgan laughed. "I was just waiting for you to ask."

We both stripped and climbed into bed. We'd be late for work, but fuck it.

CHAPTER FORTY-FIVE

Skaja

With the enemy now massed on the far side of the ridge, we trained all the harder. Saya was largely absent, closeted all day in the war tent, leaving supervision to Óbin, not that she had much to do. We were always in pretty much peak form.

"You want to go spar?" Zilly asked from the edge of the bathing pool.

I lounged next to her, staring at the stars again and feeling uncharacteristically melancholy. "Not really. I'm really getting bored of constant training."

She smirked and held out her hand to me. "Well, come on. I've got a surprise for you. The rest have gone down to the village. Probably to drink and make trouble. But I just wasn't feeling it. Besides, I had something else in mind."

Intrigued, I took her hand and let her draw me from the bath, then I dried off and went to lounge on my bed, a knee propped, "Well, I doubt our sisters will make much trouble with Óbin following them around. Anyway, what's this surprise?"

She sighed in irritation at my ill mood and dropped onto the end of my bunk. A slight shiver slid down my back, and Zilly caught the flexing of my shoulder muscles as I tried to suppress it. "Do I make you nervous?"

I gave her a shaky smile, and my voice cracked. "Nervous? No. You don't make me nervous. It's just—"

Now it was her turn to grin as she slid a little further up the bed. "Just what?"

With her now sitting beside me, I was very aware of how close she was—and how beautiful. Her face, bare inches from mine, still held that crooked smirk as I battled for words.

"I, uh—"

She raised her eyebrows, her eyes gleaming with amusement. "Yes?"

I swallowed hard, feeling heat creep up my neck and into my cheeks. "There's something intimate about being a Valtárí pair, and—"

I never finished the sentence as she licked her lips and then bit the bottom one before she finally leaned in and placed a kiss on mine. I parted my lips with a soft sigh and lay back on my cot, letting her climb on top.

"Yes," she whispered, her face hovering just above my own and the heat of her breath flowing across my face. "And it's not a rare thing for relationships, even attraction and other, uh, needs to build from such closeness. Trust between Valtárí is complete and implicit in what we do. Occasionally, that blossoms," she kissed me again, "into something else."

I wrapped my arms around her and pulled her to me, feeling the press of her muscled body against me. "Goddess, you're heavy," I whispered, grinning through another kiss.

She didn't lift up, instead replying in a soft, breathy tone, also with our lips still touching, "I certainly hope you're not saying I'm fat."

I chuckled lightly. "No." I looked into her black eyes and let my gaze travel her face. "You're perfect."

With that, she pressed down again, pinning me to the cot, and kissed me once more. This time it wasn't gentle. It was hungry, full of need and desire. Her hand dug into my wet hair, and her tongue swept my mouth as I surrendered to her, wanting her, needing to give myself to her.

"Do you like this?" She whispered, her breath tickling my ear.

There was a weird sense of deja vu at that moment, as if I'd been in this position with someone else, someone close to me, another warrior, but it passed quickly as she ran a rough hand across my breast, and I gasped in a mixture of discomfort and pleasure.

Zilly paused for a moment. "Are you sure you're up to this?"

I smirked. "Are you asking because of Boudka, or are you asking because you're like twice my size?"

She grew serious and sat up, still straddling me on the small cot, basically sitting on me with her feet on the floor, which, somewhere in the back of my mind, was almost hysterical.

"I'm serious, Skaja. I don't want this to be a fling. If you're still hung up—"

I tried to make my words soft and gentle because I was afraid they might come out as callous. "I'm not. She and I weren't meant to be. So, let's not ruin the night by talking about it, okay?"

"Okay, then." She resumed her previous position and pressed my upper arms tightly to the cot, almost painfully, speaking between small kisses to my jaw and brushing her lips across mine. "What about the second question?"

"I like it."

She pressed herself to me, and her kisses turned back to hungry need as she let go of my arms. I fumbled with the belt and ties of her skirt, stripping it aside as best I could so that I could reach her more fully, running my hands up her gorgeous, well-muscled thighs and moaning amid the kisses.

Zilly forced her tongue into my mouth and roughly probed it, and I groaned with want even louder. I lifted my knees to prod her forward, grabbing the cheeks of her ass and drawing her up to me. She was more than happy to oblige, stripping off her bandeau as she did so, and I found myself wishing that it wasn't so dark so that I could just look at her, see her face as my tongue finally found her center, making slow circles around her clit. I wanted to watch her moan, see the ecstasy writ on her face.

My tongue lapped between her folds in slow, wet strokes that ended with small flicks at her clit, and I was rewarded with light spasms in the muscles of her legs. As I allowed myself to be consumed by my own lust and want, I wondered briefly how long I had wanted this. I'd certainly thought of it the first time I'd seen her in the bath. But those musings vanished as Zilly snatched a handful of my hair and pressed my face to her.

I sucked at her clit, running my tongue over it quickly, feeling her shake as she closed on her climax, the orgasm building more and more. My nails dug into her backside as I grunted with her on her way up. Then she cast her head back, moaning so loud that I was sure the entire camp heard us as she crested on a long wave of pleasure.

I tried to draw it out further, but with every flick of my tongue, she jerked slightly until she finally drew back, chest heaving. "Enough." She gasped. "Enough. Oh, Goddess, enough." Her legs trembled, but she only paused for a moment before she moved back off the end of the cot.

Kneeling on the floor, she roughly jerked me by the ankles until my butt hung over the edge and pushed two of her large fingers inside of me quickly, eliciting a grunt of pleasure from my lips. Drawing them out, slick and wet, she licked the ends.

"I had to see how you tasted, you know?" She said with a mischievous smile. Then she joked lightly, "I expected blood sausage. You eat enough of it."

I shook my head in exasperated amusement. "Really? You want to make a joke like that, now?"

She tilted her head and smiled crookedly, then she dipped her head into the darkness between my legs and went to work. I lay back and closed my eyes, feeling my brow furrow as small gasps and whimpers of pleasure escaped my lips. It was like heaven. I had been greedy and needful with her, but she was slow and deliberate, taking her time, running her tongue and lips across the insides of my thighs, and using her fingers to massage my clit gently from time to time.

She drew out my pleasure until I begged her for more. Even then, though, as I tried to rise up, her large hand came down on my chest and pressed me back to the cot.

"No," she whispered. "Just relax. I promise I'll make it worth your while."

So I lay back and let my arms dangle, occasionally bringing

them to my own hips to squeeze at the skin in delicious frustration as she kept taking her time with me, fingers inside me, moving slowly and tongue moving up and down on my clit, leaving me breathless.

My legs began to jerk and shake, and my moans became more intense as I came closer, as the pleasure built, despite how slow she was moving.

She picked up the pace, pushing her fingers in and out, hitting just the right spot, adding a third, filling me. "Oh, Goddess, Zilly." The intensity of my emotions clouded over my thoughts, and the swiftness of my rising orgasm startled me, taking me over the edge in a way I'd never felt before. My whole body shook, and I stuck my palm in my mouth, biting down to keep from screaming with abject ecstasy. I came so hard, and my mind simply ceased to function. Lights flashed in my vision. "Ungh," I almost squeaked as I finally rode the wave of pleasure downward, and she moved back.

I opened my eyes to find her hand offered out, silently waiting. I took it, and she drew me to her bed, much larger, designed for her size and then some. She lay down and drew me in next to her, spooning up behind me without a word and running a hand through my hair.

Boudka was long forgotten by this point. Later I'd have a moment of pause about that, but then I would remember something my father had told me once between his drunken benders. That childhood romances often meant little in the end.

And as Zilly finally settled up against me and her breath turned to the regular rhythm of sleep, the feelings that welled up in my chest for her blossomed, and I understood what my father had meant.

CHAPTER FORTY-SIX

Aoife

The last time I'd sat at his desk, I'd been human. They'd asked me to help find Cait's killer and I'd had nothing to lose, but now I was in love and settled in, actually happy. And through the machinations of an ancient, wily, and likely senile old lamia, I was still alive. I wasn't going to waste it.

As I noodled on the attack, I still wondered why Matt, assuming my assailant was Matt, had thought a bullet, even a shadowsteel bullet, would do the job, given that he thought Cait was a vampire. It didn't make any sense. I decided not to focus too much on the decisions of a mad person and move on.

My mother, and probably Cait, too, would remind me that he was mentally ill, not 'mad.' But I had two categories for that. Mentally ill became 'mad' when they started being a serious threat to the general public, or, in this case, yours truly. It was just my way of coping, and I wasn't going to apologize to anyone for it. This wasn't to say that I didn't feel bad for people who lost their shit like that. I just didn't feel I could be terribly sympathetic until they were caught. So until then, to me, they were nutters through and through, and I didn't care if it made me a bad person to think of them that way.

"Did you fall in a vat of industrial strength highlighter, Aoife?" A thick Boston accent asked me, pulling me from my frustrated musings.

"Fuck you, Cardozo," I said and shot him two fingers. "I just died a week ago, you asshole. I'd think you'd show more respect to someone who just came back from the fucking dead."

I couldn't understand why Cait disliked Cardozo so much. Yeah, he liked to play political games, but that wasn't uncommon in policing, and he had a good sense of humor with just my preferred level of raunchiness. Frankly, he'd been nothing but nice to me since the day I'd arrived. Of course, Carlos had my back, so it wasn't like he could really stab me in it.

Tony sat down in Maki's chair.

"Careful you don't get donut powder on Maki's stuff," I said and grinned at him.

"You fuckin' mick bitch," he responded good-heartedly. "I don't eat donuts anymore. I'm losing weight. I'm down twenty pounds."

I laughed. "Good for you. And as a reminder, I am 'The Mick Bitch,' you dumb wop; try not to forget that. Seriously though, I'm glad you're losing weight. What are you at now? About six-hundred?"

"Four-fifty," he shot back with a grin, then added, "Seriously, I just hit two-thirty, and I'm dead-lifting three-hundred. Thanks for turning me on to that Wendler stuff. It's been really helpful."

I nodded. Jim Wendler was a powerlifting trainer who had a technique for building muscle and losing weight that actually worked. I'd turned Tony onto it maybe a week after I'd started. I didn't have the heart to tell Tony that the twenty pounds was likely mostly water weight and it would get harder. He didn't need to hear that.

"Well, as you've noticed, my resurrection had some odd side effects. It'll go down pretty well at the club, though, don't you think? Some bee-gees and black lights?"

Cardozo chuckled and turned serious. "It actually looks good on you. You wear it well. How's your sister?"

"Same," I answered automatically. "Still in a coma. I just keep hoping she'll wake up."

"Well, maybe whisper in her ear that I'm taking her spot in the squad if she doesn't. That'll probably get her up and at 'em."

I gave him a wry smile. "You're probably right. So, what brings you to my neck of the woods? Besides my hot body and stellar personality, of course."

Tony sipped at his coffee. "Morgan told me to come get you. She's in the conference room. You have a call out. By the way, my girlfriend is making us pizza this weekend. I thought maybe you and Morgan might want to come over."

I gave him a sly look. "Aren't you afraid one of us might steal her away from you?"

"Cardozo!" Morgan called from the conference room. "Quit flirting with my girlfriend. She's got work to do!"

Cardozo stood up, ignoring Morgan. "Nope. We're in love."

"Wife number three, huh?" I joked as I rose and started toward the conference room.

"Maybe," Tony said as he headed back to his cube, but he shot me the finger over his shoulder.

I chuckled.

"Hey," Morgan greeted me when I entered the conference room. "We've got a full note downtown. And get this. It's the Chinese Attaché and his entire security retinue, six dead."

I raised one silver eyebrow. "You're shitting me."

"Nope. Torn apart, the lot of them, just as they were leaving. Car's wrecked, too. How much you want to bet it's our sea monster."

I shook my head in disbelief. "Please, I'm not taking that bet. Let's go."

The trip to the scene was blissfully short, given the late hour, but the small consulate office was on State Street, not far from the theater district, so partygoers were milling around, many in various states of intoxication and undress. A woman walked by, staggering along with a beer in one hand and a pair of ridiculously high platform heels in the other. Her body-con electric blue dress was one she had to have shaved to wear, and I didn't mean her legs. She looked more like a hooker from a Hollywood film than anything, but the well-kept hair and full set of teeth said otherwise.

"Wow, just—wow," I scoffed as we pushed our way through

the streets. "I suspect patrol is going to have a long night."

"Here? Not really," Morgan said, popping the sirens a few times to goose along the pedestrians. "A few bar fights, maybe some D and D, that's about it."

Drunk and disorderly was right. Everywhere I looked, I saw wasted kids in their twenties meandering around, smoking joints, cigarettes, and probably other things. It was a roaring Friday night, and the district was in full swing. I felt a momentary pang, realizing that Cait and I would likely never go out and experience this together, and it brought yet another heavy sigh to my lips for lost time. When we were kids, we'd always wanted to hang out in the theater district together, hitting the clubs and bars.

Police tape was up, and we flashed our badges as we walked in. Carlos and Maki approached from the other direction. I spied the mayor on the far side of the tape spewing her nauseating hatred for all things preternatural, just in front of the building entrance amid a gaggle of press corp. Given a challenge made by newly minted lamia, Róisín Reagan, to keep her job and move freely about the city, Kim was pushing for the federal government to step in with some new law.

That was news to me, and I made a note to ask her about it when I saw her.

"Shit," I said. "Bitchface is here."

Morgan chuckled. "That's Mayor Bitchface to you."

I shook my head. The crime scene team was putting up massive screens around the entire scene, though it was pretty much too late. Body parts lay strewn about, and the consulate limousine was a twisted wreck. Gawkers were already taking pictures and videos.

"Jaysus," I breathed as I took it all in. "What a mess." I swallowed down my rising gorge.

"Hey, ya'll, look at this," Carlos called from the far side of the scene. He was standing next to a patrolman looking at something on a tablet.

Morgan and I picked our way over and found them restarting a video they'd found online.

I frowned. This had just happened, and already it was

uploaded? Fucking kids.

Carlos hit play, and we watched in morbid fascination.

Yi and his retinue walked out of the building just as the limousine pulled up. The driver exited the vehicle, moving around to open the door.

"Wait. Pause," Maki said. "There."

We all looked at the screen and then over toward the sewer grate at the curb. Morgan made a groaning noise, and Maki just said, "fuck."

"What are you kids watching?" Freyer said, picking his way to us around the worst of the carnage.

Carlos pointed at the screen. As the men were walking down the stairs toward the limousine, a dark shape started oozing from the sewer grate. It was squashed a little flat, but we got our first real look at the Atkor Kumuy.

"Fuck," Freyer agreed. "Another fucking crawl through another fucking tunnel. I'm really getting sick of these guys. God only knows what else is down there."

"Lieutenant Ramirez!" The mayor snapped as she walked over in her smartly pressed pantsuit, pretty gold Rolex, and a black onyx pendant dangling from what looked to be an expensive braided gold necklace. She must have been doing pretty well, given that I could see the Armani label on her inside breast pocket as her suit jacket flapped in the breeze. "Where is Detective Washington? I specifically stated that all leave was canceled!"

Ramirez frowned and walked to her, staring down at her from his impressive height. "You can't do that, ma'am," he said flatly. "She has put in all the appropriate paperwork for her leave of absence, and under the law, we have to respect that. The reform act doesn't give us the authority to penalize an officer on legitimately approved leave."

The Mayor's lips were pursed so hard she looked like she'd just eaten a lemon. "Who approved that?"

Sesi stepped forward, seemingly from nowhere. "I did, Madame Mayor."

"Senator Franklin died this afternoon from an acute stroke and I've accepted an appointment as his replacement.

Councilor Cortese-Williams will be taking my place as Mayor Pro-Tem until a special election can be held."

"Oh! Well, that changes things, then," Carlos said with a broad grin. "Senator Kim, will you kindly get the fuck off my crime scene?"

Kim sputtered for a moment. Then she looked at Sesi, who just shrugged. "It's his scene, Senator, and since you have resigned as mayor by your own admission, you need to leave."

The newly minted junior senator from Massachusetts turned beet red and stalked off, her four-inch court shoes clacking away toward her waiting limo.

Sesi rolled her eyes. "I'm going to pay for that, Carlos. You know that."

He nodded. "I know. But thanks for backing me up."

She looked at him, non-plussed. "Just remember, Carlos. Shit flows downhill."

He nodded again, and she headed back over to the press corp, who were blissfully out of sight now that all the barriers were up.

"I'm gonna kill that fucking bitch one of these days," Morgan growled. "I fucking hate bigots."

"Don't we all," Freyer agreed and threw a half-hearted finger toward the retreating back of the Mayor, whom we could barely see through a gap in the screens.

CHAPTER FORTY-SEVEN

Aoife

"Do we really have to do this?" I bitched as Carlos lifted the sewer great, tearing it from the asphalt like it was old mortar.

"Yup, 'fraid so," Carlos said as he tossed the grate aside.

"I really wish you were coming with us," Maki groused as she sniffed at the hole and wrinkled her nose. "At least it's not actually the sewers this time, just a run-off tunnel. But that looks like about a six-foot drop."

"No can do, darlin'," Carlos said. "Not my job anymore. But feel free to put good detail in the report. Besides, one trip in a cramped ass tunnel was enough for me. My back is still sore."

Freyer seemed to do some maths in his head. He looked down into the tunnel, shone a light around, then looked left and right. "Shit. This is the same fucking run-off channel that crossed the Ogumo tunnel."

"Wevkrana," I corrected, then blinked.

"Sorry?" Morgan stared at me with a puzzled expression.

"They're called Wevkrana, not Ogumo. I mean, yes, that's a Japanese word for them, but there's an older name for them. It's Wevkrana."

Maki's head snapped around, and her gaze turned fierce and penetrating as if she were looking right through me. "What is with you Reagans? Do you all have weird magic floating around you?"

I raised an eyebrow. "Uh, no. I don't. It's really just Cait that's the weirdness magnet."

She squinted at me skeptically, then turned away. "I'll go first." Before any of us could stop her, she gave a cry of "Geronimo!" and jumped into the hole. A slightly pained "Oof" followed a moment later. I looked down, and she was sitting on her arse. "Watch your step down here," she called. " It's a bit slick."

I felt the usual brush of magic as she lit up her foxfire to illuminate the tunnel. I'd started calling it that, and she hadn't objected, so it stuck. "It's clear," she called from below. "It went southwest, looking at the slick of ink here."

I grabbed the lip of the manhole and lowered myself down, dropping the last few inches and almost planting on my own arse as I did so. "You weren't kidding. It's more slippery than a sly MP with a mistress."

Morgan shook her head in amusement and dropped in behind us, followed by Freyer.

"You know," Morgan whispered as she flipped on her tactical light. "And here I'd thought I'd heard every good metaphor there was from Carlos."

I smirked. "That's a simile."

Morgan gave me a lighthearted scowl. "Fucking language nerd."

"Yup, and I'm proud of it." On a whim, I slapped her on the butt.

"Hey! Not at work," Morgan protested.

I laughed.

"Knock off the grab ass, you two," Freyer snapped. "But, since you're official, Aoife, you go first."

I growled in irritation at Freyer but did as he asked. It was a little easier this time. I felt more steady than I had at the boat as I reminded myself that the monsters don't shoot back, and that Morgan and Maki were both here. Also, I was suddenly a lot tougher, and my brain wasn't about to explode. Maybe this whole Kylr thing wouldn't be so bad.

"Oh! Here." Morgan said, handing me Cait's sword. "Just don't lose that. Cait will murder you. It was a gift from Déra and a special one at that. It belonged to one of her dead friends or something."

I took it and scratched my ear as I stared at it. "I don't know how to use this."

"Yeah, that's what Cait said, and she turned out to be a pro without any training, and Liz tore the shit out of a half dozen dudes with it, too. I think there's something with the sword. It might work for you."

I raised a skeptical eyebrow. "Thanks, I guess." *Great, a magic sword,* I thought. But I strapped it on anyway, feeling it riding between my shoulder blades. I reached back, finding it an easy draw.

I hoisted my MP5 to my shoulders and pressed on down the tunnel in easy careful steps.

We had walked maybe a mile down the tunnel before the ink trail petered out. Here, there was a reasonably large pool of blood, too, red and bright, recent.

I knelt and examined the pool, noting that the blood and ink didn't mix. I shone my light backward and frowned. There was no blood further back. It would have been obvious.

"Hold," I said. "Either this thing found a person down here, or something down here wounded it."

Freyer grunted. "You smell that?"

Now that he mentioned it, amidst the brine and stale water from the run-off tunnel was something acrid and sulfurous. "What is that?"

"Ogumo," Maki said.

"Wevkrana," I corrected automatically, then cringed. "Sorry. I really don't know where that's coming from."

"Um, Aoife, can you give me a hand for a moment," Maki said from the rear.

"Sure, what is it?" I turned back, letting Morgan and Freyer move up.

"I need—" She gave me an embarrassed half-smile. "Um, I need you to cut a hole in these fatigues."

I raised my eyebrows in surprise. "Wait, you need what?"

She turned around and pointed to her rump.

"Oh!" I snickered slightly as I pulled my knife and carefully cut a slit in the ass of her pants. As soon as it was long enough, nine shimmering tails covered in beautiful white fur popped out, almost knocking me down. Then I laughed more.

"It's not funny. You try walking around with these stuffed down your pant legs. It hurts. That's my spine in there, you know."

I about sucked in half my face to suppress the guffaws building in my chest. As it was, my shoulders shook.

"Have they been stuffed down there the whole time?"

She shook her head and opened her mouth, but Freyer interrupted us.

"Contact."

I moved back up, kneeling below their line of fire. I couldn't see anything.

"Position?"

"Ahead left, eleven o'clock. There something—"

And that's as far as Freyer got before something slimy and pale slipped from a small side tunnel. Several wevkrana spilled out behind it. They seemed to be attacking the thing, but it moved like lightning, avoiding most of the strikes from the pursuing wevkrana. Then a dozen of the things suddenly broke off and charged as they noticed us.

"Is this?" I yelled as I opened up, my MP5 peppering the spidery things.

"Yeah, and they were supposed to be fucking sealed," Morgan shouted, confirming that this was the ogumo tunnel that Cait and team had traversed almost four months ago. *God, had it been four months?*

The wevkrana went down quickly, and most of the rest took off back into the tunnel from which they'd emerged. The monstrous octopoid thing now flexing to its full bulk did not.

"Fall back," Morgan called, but I was too focused on the massive thing.

It was enormous, easily the size of a mid-sized car, and slithering forward with its eight long tentacles that ended in vicious spikes. Barbed suckers covered the lower half of each wriggling arm. I unloaded a full clip from the MP5, but it kept coming. It did indeed look like a pallid, nastier version of Ursula from The Little Mermaid.

Morgan rocketed forward to yank me back, but a long angry

tentacle swept from left to right, knocking her hard against the tunnel wall and leaving a nasty crack in the concrete.

I ran over and covered her, kneeling between her and it, trying to shield her from the swinging tentacles. Morgan would survive the hit, but not if the thing tore her apart.

"Aoife! Get back!" Freyer shouted.

I jerked back as a tentacle struck out toward me. Slipping in the mud, I landed on my arse as the appendage swished just over my head. Sprawled half on top of Morgan, I put my hand up to fend off the massive clawed rope-like thing and felt the hot breath of magic course through my extremities. It flowed from all directions like an electric current, focusing through my outstretched palm. Heat flared across my skin, and a lance of bruised purple, blue, and black light shot outward. The blast took the thing in the middle of its body, burning across its skin, and then down the tunnel wall beyond.

It screeched in pain, a high-pitched squeal that damn near shattered my eardrums. Then it took off back the way it had come, sliding into the small tunnel. I only had a moment to stare at my still-glowing palm before a piece of the ceiling fell onto my head, knocking me senseless.

Distant voices filtered through my head as if my ears were filled with cotton, but they slowly resolved themselves to clarity.

"What the hell was that?" That was Freyer.

"Magic, John. Magic like I've never seen. I certainly couldn't have done that." That was Maki. Okay, so I wasn't dead—or we all were.

I opened my eyes and then squeezed them shut again as light shone into my face.

A hand pressed to the back of my neck, soothing and ice cold. "Hey," Morgan cooed. "Welcome back. You okay?"

"Yeah," I groaned. I opened my eyes again and found myself supine in the muck of the tunnel with my head in Morgan's lap. Maki and Freyer were kneeling on either side, gazing down with worried expressions. "I should have worn a helmet."

Morgan nodded, looking not at all convinced I was okay.

"How did you do that?"

"I—I don't know. I just—reacted." But I could still feel the buzzing of magic within me. And my vision was funny. Everything was all lines and twisting lights like threads of energy moving through and around Morgan, Freyer, and Maki. Maki was like a blazing star. The lines and lights within Morgan were all dark purple, blue, and deep vermillion with muted silver and green underneath somewhere shining through a black shadowy veil. Freyer's aura was a mixture of whites and greens, but absent the darker obscuring colors.

Their souls, I realized. I was seeing their souls and the magic within them. I shook my head, but the perception remained. On a whim, I let my perception drift to the little tendrils in my hand, and they moved and jerked slightly.

Freyer and Maki stood up and backed away.

"Whoa, what are you doing?" Maki asked.

I stopped focusing on the threads. "I don't know. What do you mean?"

"You're hand was glowing for a moment, in much the same way as when I call my fire."

I had to look to her left to avoid being blinded by her magic. I squeezed my eyes shut, trying to focus, then opened them again. Everything finally looked normal once more.

"I don't know. I don't know anything. I'm just a kid—"

"From Dorchester?" Morgan said wryly. "Yeah, I've heard that before. We all have."

"You're a demigod, Aoife, and, well, an alien," Maki said, her voice exasperated and tense. "It's what Carlos was trying to tell you. And you're showing far more magical aptitude than Cait ever did, even before your transformation. Though, for goodness' sake, you're about as fucking reckless. What were you thinking running over there like that?"

"I didn't want my girlfriend gobbled up by a sea monster," I said flatly and pulled myself up.

"Well, there's miles of tunnel down here," Freyer said. "We're not going to find it now. We should probably go back up."

We all agreed.

"It's only targeting people involved with its capture and transport," I said to the group as we walked back to the hole where we'd entered. "This may work to our advantage if we can figure out who it might go after next. Zhi's got private security and is holed up in a hotel room, so I think we lay low until it goes after her."

I felt something and looked to my right. In my mind's eye, in that magic place I'd seen their souls, it looked like a massive wave of gold light. Maki clearly saw it, too, because she was staring in the same direction I was with a shocked and horrified expression.

It washed over us. Morgan gasped, Freyer said nothing, but Maki and I staggered under it as if we'd been hit by a firehose or a massive breaker at the beach, and I had a fleeting image of playing a strange harp-like instrument.

"Jaysus," I said. "What the fuck was that."

Maki was doubled over, gasping for breath. "Someone opened another gate."

TV news confirmed Maki's assertion as live aerial shots showed a massive gate glowing with a pretty golden light, and beyond sat a beautiful fairytale landscape. Bethad, I surmised and shook my head. There was just too much shit going on.

"What's RTE?" Cardozo asked from the doorway.

"Irish news," I said and shushed him as I listened to the commentator. So far, there'd been no other activity from the gate, but there would be, that much I knew. Gates didn't just open by accident. But it wasn't something we could deal with right now, so we put it aside in favor of the case.

I stared at the small drawing on my pad. Two guys from Zhu Pharmaceuticals, the Chinese Attaché, and the sailors. The only person left was Zhi, and maybe that attorney from Zhu, but I doubted she had any involvement. She looked pretty lost when we'd discussed it with her. Unfortunately, there was no pattern to the attacks in terms of time or place. They were truly random. And the Akkorkamui wasn't being stealthy about it.

I looked at the others standing around the conference room.

"Maybe Zhi's not a target?" Freyer said. "I would have expected her to be one of the first."

I thought about it and frowned. "If that's the case, then we're well and truly fucked. There has to be a way to track its movements. What are we forgetting?"

"Food," Morgan said flatly. "That's what we're not tracking. When I was a kid, my dad took me hunting. If you find out where they eat, you find out where they'll be. The Akkorkamui didn't eat any of the people it murdered. Zhi as much as said that it was the mermaids that chewed on the sailors."

"Fuck," I muttered. "Of course."

"So, what does it eat?" A voice asked from the door.

I turned around to see a woman of about my height, with caramel-colored skin and pretty brown eyes standing next to Carlos.

"Everyone," Carlos announced. "I'd like to introduce you to Celeste Turner, she's a special consultant approved by Chief Williams. She'll be filling in for Doyle with the digital forensics work while Doyle's on leave." We all made introductions with Celeste and then filled her in as Carlos left and closed the door.

"Seafood," Celeste said firmly. "The answer is seafood, clams, mussels, and crustaceans, to be precise. Any large-scale seafood thefts? Warehouses, that sort of thing?"

"Hang on," Maki said, giving Celeste a skeptical glare. "And how would you know that?"

"This is so cool," she responded. "Do you really have nine tails?"

Maki glared even harder and shifted into her vulpine form, her tails fanned out behind her. The transformation of her ears was wild to watch as they basically slid up the side of her head and shifted. I had never actually seen it.

"There," Maki groused. "Happy? Now, how do you know it eats that kind of seafood."

"Oh, it's a cephalopod, right? So it probably prefers the same food as others of its kind."

None of us could argue. The logic seemed sound. "Okay," I said. "Maki, check on that. Morgan, would you get Celeste set

361

up at Doyle's desk and show her where the drives are? We need that data."

CHAPTER FORTY-EIGHT

Skaja

"Mother of Crows, mistress of battle and shadow, lend us wings," I whispered as I watched in horror. There had to be a thousand of them or more. The Fomori host flowed over the rise like a great black wave in the waning evening sunlight. So thick as to look like a carpet of shining black skin oozing down the far ridge into the valley below, broken only by the monstrous glacially deposited boulders that littered the landscape.

"You can say that again," Zilly said over my left shoulder.

Lugh stared through the Óṣeni field glasses. "What in all the burning fires of Shaddan is that."

I took them from him and stared into the mass below. "Where?"

"Coming over the far rise." He pointed off to our left, and I trained my vision in that direction.

The gargantuan beast, for there was no better description, that lumbered over the horizon was easily as wide as thirty emisai and over fifty feet tall. It crawled in long, ponderous steps on six massive legs. Dead center of its forebody lay a massive black-lidded, eye-like orb. Shining black plates of chitinous exoskeleton, etched with ancient runes I'd never seen before that flickered and changed like living fire, covered almost every inch of it like some ancient malevolent god from the abyss.

"Mother? Saya? Have you seen anything like that?"

They both shook their heads.

"No, child," my mother said, her tone grim. "I have not. I do not know what that is."

The sight of the Fomori army threatened to strip the heart from me, but Zilly placed her hand on my shoulder as if she could feel my fear. "Remember the kóṣánt. Trust your training, trust your instincts, and trust me. I've never lost a Valtárí sister in battle, do not forget that. If we go down, we do it together. Anyway, it's not ours to figure this out. We have a job to do."

Surveying the horde one more time, I took a deep breath and then looked to my mother for some kind of reassurance. But she had none to give as she took my shoulders.

"Weyna." She paused, then corrected. "Skaja, I cannot see this battle or its outcome. But do not fear for yourself or for me. There is no need. If we die on this field, it is not the end. Our souls will find each other once more."

I nodded and wrapped my arms around her. "I love you, Mother."

She returned the embrace, and a single tear slid down from her cheek to mine. "And I love you, Skaja. I am proud of the woman you have become." She pulled back, once again grasping my shoulders. "Now go. We each have our appointed duties."

I nodded, squeezed her hand, and followed Zilly from the rise, dropping down the gentle slope toward the army. I glanced back up toward the fort, where all of the people from the surrounding villages waited and watched in fear.

A few Fae archers stood with them for protection in the event that any of the enemies slipped past or dug their way under us. At one corner of the southern parapet, a pale, solitary figure in black robes stood, watching us. I sighed, silently wishing Boudka the best of luck wherever she landed.

Just before we reached the Óṣeni muster area, Zilly stopped and turned, pushing a thin strand of hair from my face. She gazed into my eyes, then kissed me passionately on the lips.

"Save that for later, maybe," she said as we broke the embrace. Then her face broke into a broad smile. "You know, we're too gorgeous a couple to die."

The scream of the battle crow echoed, vastly amplified, and my mother waved her hands, tracing large runes in the air.

I grinned back, buoyed by her confidence and the reminder that we were Valtárí, the sword dancers. There were no warriors our equal. I reminded myself that every single one of these women other than Zilly and Saya had thought I'd quit, and to most of them, I'd handed them their asses at one point or another, even Saya herself. "Let's go."

An hour later, we were in formation and waiting, Saya standing amidst the third line, and the Valtárí behind them. Periodically, I peeked my head over the phalanx of the first and second lines to watch the enemy. The emisai were out front this time, with the second rank being taken up by the scurrying wevkrana. Something seemed off about their formation. Their left flank wasn't at all reinforced as it should be. It was a colossal weakness and not one I'd expect from Mother Darkness nor the kóṣánt, a few of whom seemed to be directing the assault from behind, which also seemed weird. The more I stared at the kóṣánt at the top of the far ridge, the more they bothered me. Even more disturbing were the missing elements.

"Where are the pteraket?" I asked Zilly.

"I have a really bad feeling about this," she answered as we huddled back down.

I reminded myself that it wasn't my problem. My job was rain fucking hell on the emisai and whatever else might get close.

The ground shook with the thunder of the approaching army. I couldn't see anything, but the Fae cavalry charged in from the left, heading toward the unprotected flank of the Fomori. So far, so good.

Moments later, our time came. Zilly and I charged forth, launching off with the rest of the Valtárí just as everything went to complete shit.

We vaulted over the front line and right into strange black spheres of yawning emptiness that appeared, spilling forth the missing pteraket.

"Portals," someone screamed from below.

Zilly and I twisted in the air, avoiding the claws of two descending flyers and slicing at them, sending them spilling to the waiting swords of our Swasari sisters below. But before we landed, three of our sisters had been scooped away and torn into by the flyers. Their screams of agony and terror tore at my heart as I landed just ahead of Zilly among the sea of emisai bodies.

Horrifying cries shook the air as Macha and Badb launched their way into the sky, taking on full form, twelve feet of winged menace, calling across the battlefield, disrupting part of the enemy advance with the power of their calls and diving toward the flyers, snatching and rending them with their clawed hands and feet.

Badb screamed from the sky, bringing speed to our strikes and strength to our limbs, while the beasts of hate seemed to stumble for a moment, confused and lost.

None of us had time to consider this, though, as we were all in the fight of our lives. Down to eight pairs and an orphan, we were struggling to keep up with the constant pounding of emisai claws.

Zilly and I were holding our own, but as I spun around to take the legs from one creature swinging at Zilly's back, I spied Nisya, desperately defending herself alone to our left down the line.

"Nisya!" I shouted to Zilly and drove us in that direction, but the wevkrana arrived, and immediately it was all we could do not to be crushed by crawling bodies leaping and scrabbling over us. We focused entirely on keeping ourselves from being shredded by their claws or buried by sheer mass.

"Not another one," I growled in frustration as I sliced across with my nisís, felling the last emisai around us, then spinning about and cutting a wevkrana in two.

A barbaric scream of defiance heralded Saya's entrance to the battlefield, launching herself over the phalanx and landing next to Nisya. Saya fought like a woman possessed, her bóllom and nsís slashing through the advancing lines like a scythe through wheat, felling them before they could get close to our heavily bleeding sister. But we couldn't keep this up forever.

Before long, we'd be overrun and crushed under the weight of sheer numbers.

A horn called from our left flank, announcing the approaching Light-Fae Cavalry, and powerful thunder that rattled our armor rang from the heavens as my mother called down lightning strike after lightning strike. A rogue emisai that had been confused by Badb's call jumped, seemingly from the shadowy ether, only to explode in a blast of sunflowers as Aine destroyed it.

The fragile right flank of the enemy collapsed as the Fae struck, and at first, it seemed as if they might cut through the enemy with ease, but a glimmer of red caught my eye in the distance as a beam of red light, magic or fire, I wasn't sure, lanced across the battlefield and disintegrated everything in its path. Nuada, the silver-armed leader of the Light-Fae Cavalry, fell, the upper half of his body simply gone.

"Oh, Gods!" Zilly cried as she watched the red light dive through the Fae lines a second time, scattering the cavalry into a wild melee of small groups. The only upside was that it killed more fomori than Fae.

To their credit, the Fae didn't falter. They split their forces, maintaining smaller clusters, intent on their task and largely able to avoid repeated strikes by the beast, though many still fell with each shot.

In the meantime, we were being pushed back. Zilly and I were dangerously close to the shield wall where dead Formori were piling up like flotsam washed up by the sea, and more slipped past us, launching themselves over the first and second lines, threatening to crush the third line.

We were losing this battle. We could all feel it. Zilly and I, who no one had been able to even touch in either practice or battle for months, each had a dozen shallow cuts.

Another horn sounded, this time blown by a single horseman riding down the embankment from the fort. Lugh had left Aine behind, flying into the field with a javelin that seemed to be made of pure light in one hand. My mother dove ahead of him, her great raven black wings beating the air.

Charging down the hillside, his horse veered first left, then right, its hooves turning up the earth in massive gobbets as it dodged the strikes of the great red eye. It loosed another shot, certain to burn Lugh away like an errant patch of fog under the sun.

My mother landed between them, the twelve-foot angel of death. She struck out with a pulsing shield of blue-black energy covering both her and Lugh. The beam slammed into it perilously close to her, exploding and rocking the battlefield, driving my mother back to slide on one knee, carving a massive furrow in the ground. She skidded to a stop, dropping to all fours and heaving with effort, but still alive.

Lugh drove his stallion forward, streaking across the battlefield like lightning, and launched his weapon. Even as the beast readied another strike to destroy the lone Fae warrior and the mighty Morrigan behind him, the javelin struck it dead center of the great red eye.

In a blinding flash of light, the beast exploded with a thunderous roar, sending a plume of dirt and debris ballooning high in the night sky, filled with fire and horrid black and red lightning. The following shockwave tore through the rear of the Fomori lines and knocked the Swasari back, though we were almost a half mile away. We Valtárí were forced to our knees to hold our ground, though several wevkrana tumbled into us, scrabbling and striking with claws.

For a moment, the sounds of battle died as we all stared in shock at the massive mushroom cloud rising over the field. Another smaller cloud of dust exploded into the air as the great orb, blown off of the obliterated beast, crashed to the earth, leaving a smoking crater further down in the valley to the north.

"Oorah!!!!" We cried as we began to advance with renewed vigor, gaining ground on the Formori and beginning to push them back.

Dusty and bloody, covered in ash, the remaining Fae began pulling themselves up as Zilly and I drove forward, splitting out and coming back together, covering for a disturbing lack of defense to our left.

In a split-second lull in the onslaught, I glanced back. Saya and Nisya were nowhere to be Sean.

"Valtárí, spread and cover!" I shouted across to the twins, Ahra and Ahnut, who relayed the message down the line.

Moments later, though, I slammed to the earth, the impact rattling my bones to the marrow as a great claw struck the flat of my blade with unyielding ferocity. I found my left arm and nisís pinned to my chest, as the razor-sharp foreclaw exposed the bone of my shoulder in a cruel gash. I screamed in agony and struck out with my bóllom, taking the offending hand from the kóṣánt. It stomped its foot onto my midsection, one clawed toe digging deeply into my gut.

Fuck, I thought bitterly as the breath was stolen from my chest, and a bust of stars blurred my vision. And then, as in the aged tapestries on her walls, my mother landed, blasting the kóṣánt from me with a lance of blue-black fire that blew it to dust on the wind. Like a creature of storm and starlight, The Morrigan, in all her battle-hardened glory, straddled my beaten form striking out with magic that painted the air in violent hues of blue and red as she swept the landscape with clawed fingers.

I tried to rise, but the muscles of my abdomen, torn and bleeding, refused to answer. Zilly fought at my mother's back, fending off anything and everything that sought her flanks. Black spots swam in my vision, and I felt the world seem to spin away from me. Zilly's face appeared above me.

"Hold on, Skaja. I have you." She tore away part of her tunic and pressed it to the wound in my gut.

I couldn't get air. "Zilly," I said, my voice blowing out as a harsh breath of panic. I closed my eyes for just a second trying to squeeze away the pain. I wasn't going to make it.

Zilly struck out backhanded, cutting down an emisai that tried to reach us as another of the Morrigna landed nearby.

Badb, her body bleeding from a dozen cuts and covered in ichor, tore through the creatures one-handed, moving in our direction, intent on rescue. Under her other arm, she carried something small and golden, Mother Danu's bowl, wrought of the echoes of the first ages of Bethad and Shaddan.

Badb bent down as she reached me, speaking ancient words

in hushed tones, dipping the bowl not into water but the raw essence of existence, the dreams of lost loves, the flutters of forgotten wings over distant lands, the secret whispers between the roots of ancient trees. And from the bowl swirled forth the laughter of rivers and eon's slow melt of crystalline sorrow that fell upon me, wiping away my wounds like a hand brushing dust from a desert stone.

I blinked. And I breathed. And I stood, drawing up my blades once more as Badb took wing to the next injured soul.

Zilly and I resumed our position, fighting once more against the massive tide. We lost ourselves in the flow of the Skolmeh, the dance of the honored dead, hewing through the claws and bodies of anything that drew near. The fire of Shaddani magic coursed through my veins, flowing outward from us, flying from our fingers as I became an unwitting conduit for Zilyana, joining the power of our souls together in a bond I didn't understand. Our bóllom glowed red, and jolts of magic sparked from them, felling as many Fomori in a single pass as we had the entire battle.

Hours may have passed—I couldn't be sure—before the sounds of battle quieted from a roar to the brief noises of small skirmishes, then to the quietude of victory. In the end, Zilly and I found ourselves facing each other, heaving for breath in the light of the embers of the scorched demons about us. And there within her face, I saw the reflection of my own feelings, a bond beyond the battle or the spiraling ballet of destruction we'd wrought, a joining of souls that carved a love deeper than either of us could understand. And we were alive.

"Oye Konbom!" I shouted.

"Oye Konbom!" The others returned absent many voices.

CHAPTER FORTY-NINE

Aoife

The next day I tried yet again to read my latest trashy romance, but Fiona kept jumping up in my lap demanding attention, chittering in my ear, or otherwise being a nuisance.

"What is wrong with you, honey?" I asked her for about the thousandth time, wishing she'd just curl back up in my lap and go back to sleep, when my phone rang.

"Reagan, Homicide," I answered without looking at the number.

It was Liz. "Look, I wanted to apologize for the way I just fucked off—"

"Forget it," I interrupted before Liz could go any further. After making peace with Marcella, I just wasn't ready to deal with another deep heartfelt conversation. "It's done."

She whispered something I could barely hear, and I had to ask her to repeat it.

"I said, I'm here now."

Damnit, Liz. I sniffed and pushed back the tears with a pawing hand. "I understand. It's okay, really. Why did you call?"

"When Morgan wakes up, would you let her know that Cailleigh's things are here along with a letter from her parents? Also, Carol is here waiting. She doesn't need to rush over, as we're just catching up. But I know you two are off tonight. Is seven okay?"

Morgan sat bolt upright. "Finally. Fuck, that took forever.

What did my parents do? Send it pony express? Tell her we're on our way."

"She just woke up. She said to tell you we're coming."

There was a pause. "Yeah, I heard. That's fine. We'll be waiting."

"Yeah, sure." I went to hang up, but she said something else that I didn't catch. "I'm sorry?"

"I love you, Aoife, and I'm sorry."

I tried to fight off the tears once again, but I couldn't. "I love you too, Auntie Liz. I missed you."

Another long pause. "I'll see you soon."

I sniffed again and wiped away my tears with a handkerchief. "Yeah, we'll be there." I hung up and blew my nose.

Morgan was getting on her pants and looked at me with concern. "You okay?"

"Yeah, I think so." I sniffed again and pressed my lips together, and closed my burning eyes for long moments to hold my emotions in check. "Come on. Let's go see where Cailleigh is."

"Where she's buried, you mean."

I nodded. I wasn't going to play at the platitudes of false hope. It had been months.

I'd never actually met Carol before, or her wife Janelle. Both of them were cute and seemed perfect together. Carol's no-nonsense demeanor fit well with Janelle, a bubbly and boisterous Latin woman about my age with sharp brown eyes and an even sharper tongue.

Forty minutes after we arrived, we all sat in the kitchen. Morgan was staring at a small corrugated cardboard box in the center of the table, marked 'Fragile,' and I thought perhaps that sticker might sit just as well on Morgan's forehead, given how she looked, not that I blamed her.

Marcella sat to my left, looking almost uncomfortable, as if she wanted to say something but either wasn't sure what to say or whether it was time.

"Do you want me to open it?" I asked, placing my hand in Morgan's.

"No. I'll probably need your shoulder to cry on. Carol, do you mind?"

Carol sat across the table from Morgan, with Janelle on her left and Liz on her right. Katie sat at the bar, watching like she always seemed to. Her face was full of compassion and worry for Morgan, but there was also a hawkish nature to her gaze. She was watching every one of us, analyzing every move. Looking for tells and indications of mood. As a vampire with so few memories, that feral hunter's nature was never very far from the surface, even when she wanted to bury it. I'd say 'poor kid,' but she didn't know any other way, and I kind of envied her for that sometimes.

Carol donned latex gloves and then pulled the box and the scissors next to it closer, opening it carefully.

First, she removed a small, round porcelain music box wrapped tightly in bubble wrap. Second, she pulled out an old compact disc with the handwritten words 'Love Ya Sis' on it.

Morgan's grip on my hand tightened painfully, and I had to tap her fingers to get her to ease up.

"Sorry," she whispered. She reached for the CD, but Carol shook her head.

"Don't touch them, please," she said respectfully but firmly.

Finally, she pulled out a gold medal.

"NCAA Swimming Championships, 1650," Morgan said, looking at the medal.

Morgan's face was a patina of misery. I released her hand and pulled her close to me, wrapping my arms around her as best I could and running my hands through her hair.

She broke then, letting out every pent-up tear of the last few weeks waiting for this moment. Loud sobs shook her massive frame, and I just held on as she bunched up my shirt in her fingers.

The rest of the group waited patiently for her. Carol watched impassively. Janelle wiped at her own eyes, as did Liz. Marcella just sat there, her eyes fixed on me.

'What?' I mouthed, but she just shook her head.

Once Morgan was spent, Carol wasted no time. She removed the glove and hovered a hand over each item, first taking the CD.

"You recorded this," Carol said. "She played the first song over and over."

Morgan laughed. "It was one of her favorites. I never understood why. I'm not a big Katy Perry fan, but she was really hip on 'Roar,' for some reason."

Carol closed her eyes once more and waited. "There's nothing here." She looked at the music box but finally decided on the gold medal next. As she picked it up, she gasped, and a terrified look crossed her face.

"Men," she began. "Men with guns. They grabbed her on her way back to her dorm room. Then they put her in a van. Get the map."

While she held the medal, still with her eyes closed, she placed her hand on the map, moving her hand over to Massachusetts. "She's close. Near here."

"Is she alive?" Morgan asked, her face showing that she wasn't daring to hope, though.

Carol sat for a moment, concentrating, then she said almost imperceptibly, "No, I'm sorry, Morgan. She's not. But I know where she is."

"Well, let's go," I said and started to rise.

"No," Morgan said, taking my arm. "I want to do this on my own."

Hurt swirled in my chest as I looked at her. "Why not? I just want to be there for you."

"I know. But you have other things you need to attend to. And I was expecting this. I'll be okay."

"But Morgan, I just want to be with you. Be there for you."

She stared at me for long moments, her jaw working, before she finally sighed. "I don't want you to see me like that. If I lose it, I mean."

I marched over and cupped her face, looking straight into those emerald-green eyes. "I love you. And in this relationship, it's my responsibility and absolute fucking pleasure to comfort

374

you when you are hurting. So, I'm going. Understand?"
    She nodded.

The location Carol identified turned out to be an abandoned farmhouse just outside Framingham, dilapidated and overgrown. Morgan asked three times if this was the joint when we arrived, but Carol insisted that it was.

We drove the last few miles with lights and sirens blaring. Liz and Marcella rode behind us in a rented SUV, and Maki and Freyer had broken away from the Yi case, rounding out our little motorcade at the rear.

The property was weed-eaten and overgrown, though the gravel driveway looked freshly maintained, indicating that it had been in recent use. Both the farmhouse and the barn behind it had partially collapsed, and the whole area gave off a creepy vibe. As I scanned the surrounding grounds from the cruiser, something weird caught my eye.

"Why does a collapsed farmhouse need live electricity?" I said more than asked, pointing at an electrical junction box with a small red light attached to the building. Morgan, Liz, and Marcella got out first, making quick work of scouting the surroundings, returning moments later.

"It's clear," Morgan said. She didn't even have her weapon, which I took as a bad sign. Whoever she encountered was going to get a pissed-off vampire rather than an angry cop. I had no illusions about which was worse or how that would turn out for them.

"The rest of us got out and followed a relatively worn footpath around the house to a pair of wooden bulkhead doors." The vampires didn't even wait, yanking the doors wide. There was a nasty ping sound, but before I could shout 'grenade,' Marcella had snatched the thing from its bolting in the wall and hurled it off to explode in the trees.

This is why you don't fuck with vampires, I thought. The grenade probably wouldn't have caught us if we'd dropped quickly enough and far enough, but the speed with which

Marcella had identified the grenade and disposed of it had been blinding. I certainly didn't want to fuck with these three, that was for sure.

Morgan started to step down onto the suspiciously clean and new-looking metal staircase beyond, but I put a hand on her arm. "You know better. There could be more grenades or claymores. The stairs could be rigged."

Moments later, I was hanging upside down by the ankles and looking under each stair as we descended.

"This can't be good for my tlehos," I groaned, using a small tac light to look for any signs of explosives. My night vision was now just as good as any vampire's, but the light made it easier to see flashing reflections of metal or the shadowed line of a wire. The stairs were long, and the descent seemed to take forever, yet despite my misgivings, I wasn't even dizzy by the time we reached the bottom, and Morgan turned me right side up, lowering me gently to my feet.

At the base of the stairs, a pair of rusted and worn double doors sat slightly ajar, with a broken camera dangling above. The hinges looked oiled, though. There had been people down here at some point in the recent past. From what I read in Cait's files, probably within the last couple of months. From beneath the doors, a sliver of dim yellow light shone, casting the dirty floor in an ugly mustard hue.

We all backed up and cringed slightly as Morgan pushed through, but nothing happened, no alarms, no ping of another cheap trip wire, nil. Morgan stopped being even remotely cautious then, plowing down the short hallway that followed.

The illumination, it turned out glowed from an old fluorescent light ensconced in a yellowing cover recessed about midway down the corridor. This area was mostly clean, meaning it was free of debris or mud or dirt, though a thin layer of dust had built up over time, obscuring any footprints other than our own.

"Morgan?" I prodded as she stood under the light and stared through a door to our right. Her hand was over her mouth, and her eyes blazed with rage. She didn't look at me as I approached and peered around the jamb. "Oh, Gods," I whispered in horror.

Inside a simple ten-foot square room were three cylindrical, coffin-like structures partially canted backward. The occupants could be seen through a small porthole in each one. Two of the canisters—probably the best word for them—were cracked, and the bodies within were desiccated. In the center, though, a young woman with bright red hair rested supine, Cailleigh. Her eyes were closed in the pantomime of sleep that makes for the recently deceased. She was pale and blue, with a thin coating of frost on her face and around the edges of the porthole. A green light glowed at one corner of the exterior. It was simply marked 'Active.'

"You know," Morgan said thickly with a sniff and her voice laden with sadness. "Until this moment, I'd held out hope. I'd hoped Carol was wrong. I'd hope that whoever had her would have had some kind of humanity and maybe kept her alive. I'd hoped Reese had been lying."

"He did lie," I whispered. "I don't see any wounds."

Morgan snorted in misery. "Yeah, I guess he did." Then she turned toward me, her eyes searching mine for comfort. I furrowed my brow in sympathy and opened my arms. She stepped into them and buried her face in my shoulder, and sobbed.

One by one, our companions, even Marcella, came and placed a hand on her shoulder.

Freyer walked over and reached for the plug, but Marcella stopped him. "Don't, John. We'll move her back to Bian's lab and see if there's something we can do. I don't think there is, but I just don't know."

Morgan didn't seem to hear her, and I said nothing. I didn't want to give her any hope at all. She'd been frozen. Her cells were probably destroyed, exploded by the frozen water within them. But she was right about one thing. If we thawed her out, she would decay rapidly, and I was sure Morgan would want to see her shipped home.

"Let's go," I whispered and led Morgan back the way we came, leaving Freyer and Maki to check out the rest of the place.

CHAPTER FIFTY
Skaja

For the rest of the night, neither Zilly nor I spoke. We drew away from the others and took refuge in the spare room of my mother's home. Though it was now Boudka's room, she stalked the night once more, leaving it empty, and I felt she wouldn't begrudge us a moment's privacy and rest.

Bathed and clean, our cuts mended, we lay quietly in the empty bed. And still, neither of us spoke. I pressed my lips to hers, feeling the press of her. The coils of magic that had flowed between us still floated in the bond of our souls that had formed in the heat of the battle, filling us both with a deep sense of love and closeness neither of us would ever be able to vocalize with any adequacy. It was long hours before the shock faded, and we finally drifted off to sleep in each other's arms.

Sometime later, Boudka came through the door and roused us, her cold hands shaking our shoulders and speaking softly. "Skaja. Zilyana. Preparations are being made to march on the gate. It's time to go."

Zilly nodded, and I rose. We donned our boots and snatched our breastplates from the floor, then assisted each other in buckling fast our armor before we looked at each other once more. I gazed into her eyes and her into mine, and we knew we were locked together, tightly wound into a single being. There would be no others.

In silence born of deep emotion, we left my mother's abode, picking our way to the eastern gate and outside, beyond which sat the remnants of the army.

And we were stunned.

Of the hundred or so Bethadi Knights that had ridden forth from their station at the village, only twenty remained. Many of the rest were brought down in the blasts of what we were now calling the balor or pulled from their mounts and killed by the ground forces.

Among the Gods and Goddesses, the Bethadi and Shaddani leaders, three had fallen. Nuada had died in the field. Aunt Badb lay horribly wounded and unmoving in the infirmary, though she would likely recover. Macha had been pulled from the sky by the ptereket and had died in the field. And though she and I had never been close, I still felt her loss keenly.

However, the most painful wound for my sisters and I was the loss of twenty-five Swasari, including our beloved Saya, Semi, and Óbin, lying in repose just off to the right of the gate, laid out in a long line of honored dead, each wrapped with due care by the servants who gave us water, cleaned our bath, our barracks, and even fed us. All would be buried here beneath the stone cairns around which the rath had been constructed, graves that drew the superstitions of the locals, making them unlikely to be disturbed in the coming centuries.

One of my sisters commenced the haunting echo of an ancient Óşeni dirge. It began as a single thread of sound, weaving its way into the fabric of the gathering, only to be picked up and strengthened by the rest of us.

My eyes settled on Óbin, her worn karkariné resting over her shroud, dented and scratched from dozens of battles. She had taught me this very song on one of our magic training expeditions, and now I sang it for her, and the pain of it drove deep furrows in my soul.

Our voices twined together, their resonance spilling over the edges of our hearts. The bittersweet melody, filled with longing and valor, unfurled in the mind, painting vivid images of grandeur and conflict, of dauntless warriors caught in the merciless dance of battle.

Though the lyrics, steeped in the dialect of Óşeni, stretched lengthy and complex, the prose they gave voice to possessed an undeniable lyricism. It was the poetry of the spirit, born of warrior women in the loom of our collective experience and echoing with the voice of our hearts.

In the tapestry of twilight, where echoes of ancient ballads cradled the mourning earth, an elegy was woven for the valorous women, Daughters of the Tempest. Born of the land, kissed by the winds, and blessed by the red sun's hymn, these women warriors, with blades that sing the songs of the storm, held their vigil at the precipice where shadows breathed with ravenous hunger.

In a symphony both fierce and tender, they danced with the shadows in a battle that made the stars weep. Attended by a leader whose voice was an echo of the dawn, they became the storm itself as the heavens wept for them. They fought not as mere mortals but as spirits bound to the very soul of the world. With each brave heart that fell, a light dimmed, yet the ground itself embraced them, and the land thrummed with the power of their sacrifice.

In the memory of the world, the lives and deaths of these fallen daughters were etched into the whispering winds, the gentle blooms, and the tear-kissed rains. Óṣen did not forget; it cradled their names in every leaf and every stone. Their legacy became an eternal song, a reminder of the storm's caress and the unwavering valor that guards the fragile tapestry of the dawn.

And as our song ended, we drew ourselves together into formation, dried our tears, and ensured we were properly kitted, armed, and ready. Then we all mounted up on horseback for the ride from the gates of the Green Rath toward the portals that would lead us to Mother Darkness and the Bethadi home.

Our first day of travel led us to the burrows once held by the Fomori, nestled within a modest hillock blanketed with lush emerald grasses and dotted with fragrant heather, some ten leagues north of the erstwhile village of Omagh. I could hear the distant babble of a creek, a place I had seen in younger days, where fish leaped amidst the cascading water, and the scent of damp earth and the coolness of the lingering mist caressed our skin as we moved.

In the wake of the Fomori defeat, Omagh had already shown faint, budding signs of life—tendrils of ivy creeping over ruined stones, a few animals walking among them. The damage that Mother Darkness had done would not be lasting, and our victory had stemmed the tide of her progress.

The sun descended beyond the western horizon, painting the heavens in hues of pink, orange, and crimson and bathing the leaden clouds in fire as we elected to halt our progress in the waning twilight.

I recognized this place where the giant hawthorn tree was said to be a gateway to the Fae realms. Not so very far off stood the remains of my village, where Da had died and where my life had first started on the road to becoming something greater than all it had been. I knew that if I topped the rise to the east, I'd see its remains. It wasn't much of a walk, but I didn't. I knew there was nothing to see, and no sense of nostalgia called to me, or at least not so much that I'd want to look.

Instead, I joined the Bethadi in a thorough reconnaissance of the burrows encircling our chosen encampment. The entrances were overgrown with ferns, and the earth had a musky, primal scent. We moved quietly, our footsteps cushioned by moss and soft ground, ensuring they were shallow, unconnected, and absent of any nasty surprises. The slow work was punctuated by moments of extreme anxiety where my heart raced, and I expected an attack from wevkrana or some great worm-like beast. But none came, and we finished clearing the area without incident.

The rest of the Swasari, their robust frames swathed in their tunics and their karkariné, found the tunnels too confining for their imposing stature, so they stayed behind to raise the tents and kindle the fires.

With the tents set and the burrows cleared, we lit our campfires, and the playful flames and sparks rising to the stars winking above lightened our mood significantly.

We laughed when Zilly slyly glanced about and slowly drew out a surprise from her pack, a bottle of Bethadi spirits she'd squirreled away from the fort. We passed it around in the firelight, and its taste reminded me of smoky oak and wild honey. I looked around at my sisters. *This is my life,* I thought, and I was happy with it, despite the risks and our losses.

After a time, we began to share stories of those we had lost, our voices rising and falling with the wind. The flames flickered, casting shadows that danced with our tales. Nisya, when her turn came, wove magic in the night. She was always the best storyteller.

"So, here we are," Nisya continued as we sat. "Óbin's got this map, right? And we're in this little village, completely and hopelessly lost. Outside, as far as the eye can see, it's nothing but subtropical forest mixed in with bits of jungle-like foliage. And she spots this adorable little human woman, no more than eighteen or nineteen years. Long black hair, curvy body, brown skin, you know. And this woman is looking at us like the gods themselves have just descended on this little village."

"What did she do?" I asked, eyes intent and fixed on Nisya, just waiting.

A few of the others chuckled, and then Zilly pipes up and says, "She goes over to the girl and says in this sultry voice, at least the best she can manage, 'I'm the goddess of love. If you lay down with me, I will ensure that you have your pick of the men in the village. Also, can you point me toward Dwarka?' And she holds out the map."

Nisya picked the story back up from there. "Faster than the Summer Queen can spot bad fashion, this kid's mother appears out of nowhere, looks up at Óbin, and begins beating her with a stick, screaming, 'You are not the goddess of love! You just want to get under my daughter's sari. Now get out of my village this instant? Go west to the coast and then go south. You've passed the bloody place!'"

The entire group descended into laughter so hard that the little wooden logs we sat on shook. Tears came to our eyes, and they felt warm and tasted salty as they streamed down our cheeks and across our lips. It was good to laugh, to remember, and not be so filled with sorrow.

"You're pretty quiet, Skaja," Nisya probed, her voice honeyed and lilting as the soft tunes of a flute played over the babbling brook nearby. The air was turning crisp, and each word was accentuated by visible puffs of breath as she spoke. "What about you? Any salacious stories that we don't already know about your Valtárí partner?" The mischievous twinkle in her eye was accented by the firelight.

Zilly's skin flushed a dark gray, like a storm cloud against the silvery moon, and the fire cast shadows that danced upon her features as she tried to conceal her embarrassment.

I felt a wave of heat rush to my own face turning me a shade of crimson that rivaled the ripest berries of midsummer.

"I mean, there's not much to tell?" My voice wavered, and I grew suddenly aware of the dewy grass tickling my ankles slightly and swatted at it.

Ahra, one of the twins, almost shouted, "That's for sure. Blessed Avra, Zilyana, can you moan any louder? Makes me want to fuck Skaja just to see what's so great about it!"

The entire circle devolved into laughter once more. The campfire, enlivened by our energy, seemed to leap and flicker more passionately, casting a warm, golden glow on our faces.

I felt my face afire once more like a sun-kissed burn, and my heart pounded like tribal drums in a ritual dance. I pressed my lips together.

Zilly's eyes widened, and then she smirked, and in a moment of mad inspiration, she lunged at me and laid a fierce and passionate kiss on my lips.

Her lips were both soft and insistent, and I could taste the lingering hint of mead and the smoky tang of the campfire. My toes curled as if trying to clutch the cool grass and tiny pebbles underfoot. The sensation was electric, like the strike of a blacksmith's hammer, and I melted.

Hoots and hollers from the circle surrounded us, and we broke away, breathing heavily and creating wispy clouds in the cool air. I grinned and averted my eyes from the group, thoroughly embarrassed and totally turned on.

As the night wore on, we drank, laughed, and let the ancient land envelop us in its embrace. Our souls were on fire, just like the heavens above when the sun had set, and the bonds that were formed that night felt as ancient and eternal as the hills around us that bore witness.

CHAPTER FIFTY-ONE

Aoife

"I'm not really feeling this," Morgan said as we sat at the bar at Leslie's just over an hour later. She had started to get hungry, and we'd stopped off to make sure she was okay. It was a quiet night as if a pall had fallen over the city in the wake of our discovery. Somehow, Marcella had arranged with Carrie, one of the bartenders, to keep a stash of O-Neg around for the local vampires, and Morgan was sipping on that. I was drinking soda water since I didn't know exactly how my body would respond to alcohol, and I hadn't had the heart to ask Déra since everything had gone wrong.

"I need to feed," Morgan continued, "I can feel it rising, but I just can't bring myself to. I think I just want to go home."

I nodded and signed off on the tab that Marcella kept for us, and, despite the shitty day, I realized that I liked it here. Morgan and I had a thing going. Marcella took care of us all. Liz was trying to get back into my good graces, and I'd probably talk to her the next day to bury the hatchet once and for all with her. In the end, despite the challenges they all had, they were good people just trying to make their way. And they'd welcomed me into their hearts without much effort.

So, quietly, we left and returned home. Morgan didn't even say anything as we walked in. I knew the hunger had to be eating at her, but she just crawled into the bed and stared out the window.

I stripped and curled up with her. "Do you want to take a

little?" I asked, surprising even myself. "I know you're miserable, but you need something to take the edge off."

"You mean that?" She whispered.

"Yeah," I nodded into her back. "It's okay."

"But what if it makes me sick?" Morgan said. "I don't know if I can drink your blood."

"The blood's just a medium, Morgan. I'm sure it'll be fine."

She rolled over and looked at me, pink vampire tears streaming from her eyes.

I ran a hand across her forehead and through her hair, then gazed at her face once more. Her eyes were so beautiful, clouded even as they were by grief.

"Off or on," I said gently, as if Morgan might shatter at any second with just a word.

"Huh?" She responded absently, her voice seeming almost lost and little.

"The light," I clarified. "Do you want it off or on?"

She gave me a half smile that didn't reach her eyes. "That's up to you. I can see either way, you know."

"So can I, but I wasn't sure if it would bother you." I reached over and turned out the lamp, then returned to her side. She was ice cold, only just beginning to be warmed by the heating blanket.

In the thick darkness, Morgan was silent, but I could feel her moving, adjusting her position, and slowly, her weight descended onto me, subtle and sensitive, not at all pressing.

Her soft finger gently prodded my chin up and away to my right. I tried to keep my breathing under control and my pulse steady, but it was no use. I was nervous. She had bitten me in the throes of passion, but this was different. She was truly hungry.

"I'm sorry," Morgan said softly into my throat.

I made a puzzled expression. "For what?"

"This won't be the beautiful expression of affection that it ought to be. Between us, it should always be."

I raised an eyebrow at that, not so much confused as a little lost in the admission and the tenderness behind it. Affection. She wanted this to be special with me, something sweet. And for me, it was, just not the way she imagined.

"You have nothing to apologize for," I said finally. "I want to do this for you. And because of that, it will be sweet. And, as far as I'm concerned, that's just as important as what you're talking about."

She nodded into my neck, moved a little more, one hand rose to hold my jaw gently, and she bit down, straight into my throat.

I whimpered slightly at the piercing pain. A soft feeling of love and affection washed over me. Not the ardent sexual need that it had been before. This was a feeling of intense love. There was no scraping against my thoughts. These were my feelings, my gift. What I was feeling was genuine, and my pulse quickened further, even as Morgan began her first pull at my blood.

Gently, easily, I wrapped my left arm around her and stroked her back while my right hand played in her hair. My heart stuttered and palpitated on the next pull. But then it continued a steady rhythm, beating for this woman strong and fierce. I knew what was happening to me, and amid the joy, I felt a release then. The pent-up frustration at my transformation just melted away as I accepted that our love, which I'd thought would be short and bittersweet, now had a second chance. My transformation wasn't a fuck up. It was a gift. And I would treat it that way.

After the fourth pull, when I began to feel a touch of wooziness, Morgan lifted and placed her now warm lips to mine. Blood, both hot and raw and cool and changed, flowed into my mouth. I swallowed quietly. The taste was still coppery and salty, but there was something else, and I allowed it to linger before I swallowed. Before she could withdraw, I deepened the kiss, bringing my hands to her cheeks before letting her go.

She looked down at me with her beautiful face, cast in hues of black and white amid the dim light from outside. There was a gleam in her eyes, not of lust, but of something else, something deep and altogether differently needful.

"Thank you," she said, gently stroking the hair from my

eyes, then she stood and padded her way to the kitchen. When she returned, she wiped the remnants of the silvery blood from our faces and necks.

"No," I said softly, my words fading into the dim blackness. "Thank you for letting me give you this." Once she was done, she replaced the towel in the kitchen and curled up next to me, throwing an arm over my abdomen as she spooned in. I relaxed into her. "I'm so sorry, Morgan."

I felt and heard her nod in the movement of the pillowcase. "Yeah, me too."

She was silent for a long time before she spoke again. "I'm going to miss her. I was a lousy sister, you know?"

I patted her hand. "I doubt that."

Her voice was full of remorse and pain. "No, it's true. I never called her. She always called me. And when she wrote, I never wrote back. I always had to hear about it, though, when I did talk to her. My parents have all but disowned me, and they're blaming me for this. I don't know what to tell them, even if I felt like I could talk to them right now."

Hearing the echo of my own feelings, I rolled over, placing a hand on her cheek. "Now you listen to me, Morgan Kennedy. We all have busy lives, and we assume we have all the time in the world. We never expect our siblings to go first. But that doesn't make us lousy sisters. It makes us just what we are, busy people. That's all, nothin' else. You loved her, and she knew that. I'm sure. And I know it doesn't help much to hear it, but I'll say it anyway. You don't need to be floggin' yourself about it. You've had some shitty turns, but that's all they are. And that's all this is. We get what we get, that much I know. Now come here, put your head on my shoulder, and lament for what you've lost like a proper Irish woman."

Morgan stared at me for a second with just a hint of subdued and pained amusement, but then she did lay her head on my shoulder just as I asked, though she didn't cry. She was all dried up for the day and wasn't ready to give away more. Fiona crawled over and curled into the crook of Morgan's neck with her soft crooning, rubbing her furry face into Morgan's chin. Morgan just lay there, her eyes closed, feeling Fiona's soft fur and occasionally tapping my sternum in time with the rhythm of my heart. Which was just fine.

CHAPTER FIFTY-TWO

Skaja

In the heart of the night, as the world was cloaked in velvety darkness, Zilly and I lay entwined beneath the endless canvas of stars. Our breaths danced together, creating soft whispers that mingled with the scent of dewy grass and the remnants of our fervor. Perspiration still slid down my skin as I straddled her hips and gazed into her shining face, reveling in her bare skin on mine.

Zilly, her gray body luminous under the moon's caress, looked up at me with eyes that could quell storms. Her voice, a whisper carried on the midnight breeze, spoke, "Tomorrow we reach the Black Gate. The threshold to Shaddan."

My chest tightened. Shaddan, the desolate desert that was once the home of my mother, Nemhain, The Morrigan.

"I know," I murmured, the haunting specters of tales my mother had whispered dancing in my head. My thoughts drifted to those tales of Shaddan and the contrast to its current state. It was the land of my forebears, now a forsaken wasteland. The shadow of my lineage seemed to press down on me then—a home I'd never know, a place I would never set foot.

Zilly's hand, strong and yet tender, caressed my cheek. Her eyes bore into mine. "Whatever comes our way, we will face it together," she vowed. "If we must, we will embrace death as we live, side by side."

The certainty in her voice wrapped around me like the

warmest cloak, and at that moment, I knew I'd follow her to the ends of the world and that, yes, one day, we would die together.

We had no more time to ruminate on it, though. Both of us flew into motion from our intimate position as a scream pierced the night, shocking, raw, and primal. A scream I knew so well, and that set every nerve on edge. Badb.

My heart thundered as Zilly and I sprang to our feet.

Another scream sounded, this one quieter and more pained, a scream of agony and terror.

"Aine!" I exclaimed as recognition clawed through me. I looked at Zilly, and we needed no further words.

Snatching weapons, we raced through the darkness, Nisya joining us as we darted like naked shadows through the night.

Only a few moments later, we found Aine lying in a small copse of nearby trees, her once resplendent form marred by brutal wounds. The scent of blood mingled with the loamy aroma of the copse.

I checked her pulse and felt her injuries. They didn't seem too serious, though she was covered with cuts and rents in her skin that healed slowly, a sign of a magical weapon or goddess-born strikes. Unfortunately, they were too far healed for me to tell what made them, but their placement suggested four fingers and an opposable thumb.

Together, we lifted her delicate form and carried her back to the camp. Her breath came shallow, and I could feel the frailty of her once indomitable presence.

As we lay her by the fire near her tent and the Bethadi swarmed around us, and Aine feebly told us of her attacker. "It was Badb," she rasped, her expression haunted. "She was like a storm, and her eyes—her eyes were voids."

She paused, taking a sip of water and coughing before she continued. "She's lost her mind," Aine whispered. "The shadows have consumed her."

My blood ran cold.

As we tended to Aine, I felt Zilly's hand find mine. A silent promise bound us, and as the fire crackled and the dawn threatened to cast away the night, we knew we would face the shadows at the threshold, bound by blood, love, and a shared destiny.

My mother came running, and we relayed Aine's words. Faster than a falcon from a cliff, she was gone, winging into the air in search of her sister.

A short time later, we gathered in a semi-circle around our flickering campfire, which cast a warm yet haunting glow on our faces. The Óṣeni, my kin in blood and in arms, were all in deep contemplation. The scent of crushed herbs and balms filled the air as the medhen tended Aine. The whispers of the leaves seemed to grow louder as though the forest itself was joining our council.

"Why would Badb attack Aine?" Nisya's voice cut through the silence. Her brow furrowed, and her eyes were as sharp as the question.

Zilly spoke next. "Could Badb be tainted by the Mother Darkness? Her madness could be an affliction."

I felt my heart skip a beat. The thought that Badb could be under such influence sent chills through me. Even my mother would be hard-pressed to bring Badb down if it came to that, and I didn't know if she could do it without killing her.

"It could be something simpler?" countered Ailis, one of the older Óṣeni archers. "Badb and Aine have shared no love between them. A dozen slights, a hundred wrongs, over the years, any could be the reason."

"Yeah, but why now? That makes no sense," Nisya countered.

The night was punctuated by the crackling of the fire and the sounds of our whispers and speculation.

"Could it be a warning?" I dared to suggest. "Maybe Badb didn't want us to reach the Black Gate? She might just be in an altered state of some sort from her injuries."

Nisya's hand found my shoulder. "What could be so dire that Badb would resort to such violence?"

I shrugged. I was well aware that the suggestion was a desperate one when I'd made it and patently ridiculous on its face. But I didn't want to believe the one alternative that loomed largest.

Our voices melded into a symphony of conjecture and theories, each word a note in the song of our shared tension.

A sudden gust of wind swept through the encampment as my mother returned. Her black cloak billowed behind her as she walked, and her eyes were as deep as the night sky. The very air seemed to thicken with her presence.

"I could not find my sister," She said, her voice low and sorrowful. "The night swallowed her like a forgotten whisper."

We all fell silent, our gazes shifting towards her as she moved with the grace of shadows to where Aine lay.

After what seemed an eternity, Mother turned back to us. "It's of no matter now, however. We still have to reach the Black Gate and close it," she declared. Her eyes swept over all of us. "Now, rest. Tomorrow's journey will be long and, perhaps, fraught with perils we cannot yet foresee."

As we settled back into our sleeping places, the cool night air caressing our weary bodies, I felt Zilly's warmth beside me.

"Rest," she whispered, her breath a balm to my restless spirit, and I curled up within her grasp.

The last thing I saw before sleep claimed me was the flickering firelight, dancing like the spirits of old, and the glint of my mother's ageless eyes.

CHAPTER FIFTY-THREE

Aoife

It was three weeks before the Akkorokamui appeared again. Morgan and I had been staking out a seafood warehouse that had seen some heavy thefts recently. But it had been abject boredom. I spent some of the time going over some kind of alphanumeric code on a scrap of paper that Maki and Freyer had turned up at the warehouse, but I couldn't really make heads or tails of it. The sea monster never showed. Instead, it popped up in Cambridge again, this time outside a cafe, and it was the usual insanity when we arrived.

Cruisers surrounded the place, and a line of Cambridge police officers was keeping gawkers and onlookers from getting too close to the scene. Freyer got the lowdown since he and Maki were already dressed for success. I grabbed my fatigues and climbed into the back of the cruiser to change. It was better than getting geared up in the street, especially with the rubberneckers and arriving news vans. I didn't feel the need to be on the television in my knickers tonight.

By the time I was dressed and exiting the cruiser, Freyer had returned. "The two victims, or what's left of 'em, are Michael Lee and Nancy Willis, according to the IDs they found at the scene. One is a researcher for Zhu Pharmaceuticals. The other is their US General Counsel."

"Fuck," I muttered. I had thought she'd be safe. "We know Nancy Willis. We interviewed her on a related case. What happened?"

He gestured toward an open manhole. "It crawled out of that manhole over there, tore them apart in seconds as they were sitting having dinner at that cafe."

The storefront of the Ramen joint he indicated was completely destroyed, all shattered chairs and exploded glass windows.

Freyer pointed to two female patrol officers who both looked absolutely terrified. "Then it slid back down into the drainage system. Those two officers over there were across the street, sitting outside for a quick bite at Franklin's right after coming off shift. They were Johnny on the spot and took shots at it, but it just ignored them."

"Back in the hole?" Morgan asked, looking at the open manhole and the discarded cover.

"Cambridge is working the evidence collection, so yeah, back in the hole," Freyer confirmed. "Let's do this."

We drew our usual contingent of weapons from the trunk of the cruiser, and Morgan pulled out Cait's black sword and scabbard.

"Feyla ca Valtárí," I murmured, reading the Óşenic inscription on the blade.

Morgan eyed me suspiciously. "You can read those?"

"Yeah," I said, taking the blade and hefting it. "It means Feyla of the Death Dancers in English." I flourished it a little and hefted it again. It was incredibly light and thoroughly comfortable in my hand, but I passed it back to Morgan.

She took the blade back and sheathed it, strapping it to her back. "Truthfully, I still think the sword's magic. Or—" she eyed me with an impish grin. "Deft hands just run in the family." She waggled her eyebrows at me.

I rolled my eyes. "Really, Red?"

Freyer looked at the two of us, then leaned in and hissed at Morgan, "Jesus, Red, knock it off."

Morgan just gave him a sidelong smile. "What, you jealous, John?"

I stomped my foot. "I'm right here, you two. Stop talking about me like I'm a piece of meat, please."

"Sorry, babe," Morgan said with a snicker. "I'll try to be

more—sensitive, I guess?"

"Sure you will," I replied, shaking my head. "Maybe when the sky falls to the ground."

Finally, all geared up, we went over to the open sewer cover, and I sighed. "I'll go first."

"Nope," Morgan said. "I always go first. Those are the rules."

"I put my hand out. Not this time." Without waiting for her to argue further, I dropped onto the rungs and climbed into the blackness. My perception shifted automatically, showing me the lines and threads I'd seen earlier. Now that I had time to examine them, I realized there was order to their movement and a pattern related to my perception of their color. The green lines seemed to flow all around. There were gold threads that seemed to shift and flow from east-northeast of the city somewhere, and the blue and purple lines were moving from the southeast of us. Again, as I moved, the threads bent toward me, small bits flaking away.

On a hunch, I let my consciousness feel its way out to the lines and pull away more and more of the flakes, imagining a little ball of liquid fire like Maki used. Abruptly the threads flowed through me for just a second, causing me to squeak a bit, then the little ball of fire appeared, constructed from bits of the threads torn and spun into a slowly rotating ball, casting the tunnel in a soft blue glow.

"Holy shit," I whispered. "They're threads of magic. I can do magic!" The realization that I could really do this and that what happened in the compound wasn't just some fluke of being around her practically floored me.

"Clear!" I called and moved to the side of the ladder, bringing my weapon to bear, keeping the little ball of fire hovering over my head. It wasn't even hot.

"Um, babe?" Morgan said as she descended the ladder. "What's that?"

"I'm bloody magic!" I said. "I'm feckin' magic, do you believe that?"

"Yeah, we kind of already knew that."

"But I can control it! And it's feckin' easy!" I whispered,

trying desperately to wipe the shit-eating grin off my face. If we hadn't been on the job, I'd have hopped around.

Freyer moved down the ladder next. He didn't even acknowledge the light source until I said, "Dude! Magic!"

Freyer glanced back at me with a wry smile, then chuckled before turning away. "Yeah, yeah, I gathered. Nothing surprises me about your weird ass family."

Maki came down next. "Ooh, nicely done, Aoife," she said before dropping down the final rung. "Did you figure that out on your own?"

I nodded vigorously, ridiculously proud of myself.

"Can you change the color?"

I thought about it, visualizing the orb as a shining white rather than a light blue, and it shifted immediately, swirling into a ball of white and gold. I figured she'd be impressed, but she frowned at that and paused, closing her eyes.

"Something wrong? I can go back to blue."

"No," Maki replied. "That's Light-Fae magic. I thought you were Dark-Fae."

"Okay, so that means what?" I asked.

"Nothing important right now. But I think you should limit your magic use for a bit. You clearly have a lot of power. If you're not careful, you could do a lot of damage."

"But this is okay, right?" I asked, pointing at the little floating fireball over my shoulder.

"Yeah, but—" she walked over and took my hands. "Here, like this." She moved my hands closer and showed me how to slide the little tendrils of magic into a more cohesive ball of light, less fire, more illumination. Suddenly, the entire tunnel was filled with something akin to sunlight.

"Wow," I whispered, glancing first to the light, from which I had to shield my eyes, and then back to Maki with astonishment. "Thanks."

"No problem. Do you feel the difference?"

I nodded. "Yeah, I got it. Oh! That's a simple spherical formula coupled with a hydrodynamic tension equation. "

"Good. Now, no more than that if you can help it. You didn't get a good look at the tunnel walls from the last time. I did. You melted the concrete in a thirty-foot line, and that was on instinct. If you're not careful, you could level half the city without meaning to."

My eyes grew even wider. "What?"

"Yeah," she whispered. "So, by the Gods, don't do that again. I don't feel like getting flattened by the street collapsing from above us or vaporized because you accidentally fused a few atoms."

Freyer signaled us to move out and told us to pipe down.

I frowned. Looking around, I couldn't see any obvious signs indicating which way the creature had gone, no drag marks, no ink, no blood, nothing. "Hold up," I hissed.

Freyer turned back and looked at me, voice low. "I said move out."

"And I said, hold the fuck up, John. This is fucking stupid, okay?"

Morgan and Maki both raised their eyebrows. John looked like he was about to pop. His face burned red, and a little vein popped out on his temple.

"Just hear me out," I dimmed my light so it wasn't quite so garish, and we could all look at each other, more importantly, so everyone could look at me without squinting. "We've got three dead researchers and an attorney from Zhu Pharmaceuticals, one dead consulate employee along with his retinue, and a boatload of dead PLAN sailors. Furthermore, there's no way we can take this thing down with what we've got. I got lucky last time, and still have no idea how I did that. And frankly whatever magic I can tap into is probably more of a threat to us than the Akkorkamui."

"Okay," Freyer responded. "So, what do you suggest?"

"I think we need to go see Zhi. She was involved with this from the start. She was there when they were carting this thing around. She was there when Yi accosted her on the beach. She was the one who told us that Zhu Pharmaceuticals was supposed to take possession of it. Either she knows where it will hit next, or she'll be its next target. But we're never going to catch the thing down here anyway. And if we do, I don't like our chances."

Morgan shrugged. "She's got a point, John. The last time we saw this thing, it knocked the shit out of me, and I could kill all of you in seconds here without breaking a sweat."

"She's right," Maki agreed. "Let's get the fuck out of here and work a little smarter."

Freyer slung his weapon. "Fine. But we're going to have to figure out how to take this thing down eventually."

"Do we?" I asked as we started back toward the rungs. "I think this thing is just trying to defend itself. It's clearly intelligent. Maybe we can convince it to go elsewhere."

"Need I remind you that it's murdered dozens of people?" John retorted as he started up the ladder.

"No, you don't. But people kill other people all the time, and we don't just hunt them down and shoot them. We're not the Preternatural Termination Squad. This isn't a bunch of wevkrana or emisai. This is a living, breathing, sentient creature that may have been around for thousands of years. It's not on us to just snuff it out because some foreign government pissed it off."

Maki gave me a thumbs-up as we exited the hole behind Freyer. "I agree with Aoife, John."

"Yeah, I got that, Maki, thanks," John grumped as we started stowing our gear.

CHAPTER FIFTY-FOUR

Aoife

Zhi was staying in the lap of luxury. Marcella had rented a suite in the same hotel where Morgan and I had gone on our Valentine's date. A few of Marcella's security team were still in the lobby. One of them, a short brunette woman and obviously a vampire, nodded curtly as we strolled into the hotel, making quite the scene. Two balding gentlemen smelling of cigars quickly exited the lift when we got in. The surprised looks on their faces had been a hoot.

"Some days, I love my job," Morgan said after the doors closed.

I shook my head. "You only say that because you're carrying a suppressed submachine gun with subsonic rounds."

"Yep. And a magic sword."

"It's not magic," Maki said without inflection, leaning against the lift wall, arms crossed.

"Well, then how does Cait use it so well?"

Maki just shrugged. "Maybe the same way I have four hundred years of knowledge crammed in my skull."

"Cait's possessed by our Mameó? Too bad for her," I joked.

Morgan laughed. Maki didn't. Freyer was Freyer and shook his head as he hit the button for the twenty-fifth floor.

"Who was the vampire with Marcella's detail?" I asked.

Morgan just shrugged. "No clue. Never met her. But it's good to see we're adding a few to our dismally thin ranks."

The ride up took a minute or so, and we got to listen to one of the more popular new pop songs. Morgan and I even started bobbing our heads to the music and singing along.

"Jesus, you two. We're working," Freyer groused.

Maki responded to the complaint by joining in, making us break out in peels of laughter.

"Come on, John. Lighten up. This job's serious enough."

"You keep singing, and when we get back to the squad room, Carlos and I'll serenade you two with Hank Williams Sr."

We all stopped, but Morgan said. "Hey, I like Hank Williams."

"Divorce," I said loudly. "Grounds for divorce."

Morgan bumped me with her shoulder. "We'll see."

The door dinged, and we all stepped out into the long hallway.

"Hey guys," Freyer called to the two patrol officers as we walked up. "We need to talk to Dr. Zhi, please."

They nodded, and Maki knocked on the door. "I'll go in alone. We have a rapport."

I shrugged. That was something I couldn't deny, I'd seen it when we'd first interviewed her.

Zhi answered the door in a bathrobe, her hair in a towel. "I'm sorry, Detective Imai. I just got out of the shower. Give me a second to get dressed."

Maki nodded, and Zhi closed the door while we waited. A few minutes later, the door opened again, and Zhi, dressed in jeans and a t-shirt, invited us in.

"Uh," I said. "We'll wait out here. Maki only has a few questions."

Zhi shrugged. "Okay, Detective."

Maki went inside, and the door closed automatically before I could get my foot into it. I was about to knock again when my phone rang.

"Reagan, Preternatural," I answered automatically.

"It's Zhi!" Celeste said over the line in a panic. "It's Dr. Zhi!"

I shook my head. "Slow down, Celeste. What are you talking about? What about Dr. Zhi?"

"The Akkorowhatever, the sea monster. It's Dr. Zhi. She's the thing. I decoded the videos."

I cursed under my breath. "Okay, thanks." I hung up.

"I heard," Morgan said and kicked the door off its hinges. "Stay back, she said to the two patrol officers who moved aside as we filed in."

Maki stood in front of the bed facing the door, a surprised look on her face. Behind her, Dr. Zhi's body had already begun to expand and shift.

"Maki, lookout," I said and raised my weapon. "We don't want to hurt you," I said to Zhi, now half-transformed, her lower half sitting on eight massive tentacles, one of which snaked out and wrapped around Maki, jerking her back against Zhi's body.

"I'm not here for you," Zhi said as one of her other tentacles lifted to Maki's throat, the clawed end of it pressed to her throat. "They made me eat them. They starved me until I had no choice. I couldn't help myself. Don't you understand?"

The real gravity of her words seeped into my head, sending a spike of ice-cold horror through my veins, and a ghastly pallor washed over my face. "Oh, Gods, Victoria, I'm so sorry," I gasped. "But, we don't want to make this worse. Please, just come with us so we can sort this out."

"No!" She said sharply. "I won't go back."

In the blink of an eye, Zhi twisted and threw Maki out the window. Morgan, faster than the rest of us, dropped her MP5 and dove out the window after her, crossing right through my line of fire as Freyer and I opened up on Zhi. We might as well have been shooting blanks as Zhi slipped out the broken window and grabbed the side of the building.

I ran to the window. Even as I watched, I had to blink several times. Fog appeared, shrouding Morgan's body. Then, in an explosion of blood and gore, Morgan transformed into a huge creature, like a succubus of old, her main of long red hair flowing between two furled wings as she dove toward Maki.

"Holy shit," I breathed as I watched. I had heard Marcella could do that, but I never thought I'd see it. Regardless, what I should have been doing was looking at the extant threat on the side of the building because the next thing I knew, I was snatched around the waist by a long tentacle and hauled out of a twenty-fifth-floor window as Zhi crawled up the side of the building on suckered legs. I scrabbled at the tentacle, trying to get a firm hold on the slick skin, terrified Zhi would just drop me.

Below, Morgan caught up with Maki and snatched her out of the air, cradling her in her arms. Then unfurling her wings, Morgan arced away from the building and down to the street.

"Stop, Victoria, please," I shouted against fierce winds screaming around the building.

If she heard me, she made no indication, clearing the final two floors in seconds. She set me down as she hauled us onto the roof but kept her tentacle wrapped firmly about my midsection.

"What are you doing?" I asked, trying to maintain some level of calm in my voice.

"You're my insurance policy, Detective Reagan."

I switched to Chinese, hoping that maybe that might somehow calm her some. "Can we talk about this?"

"There is nothing to talk about. Look around you, Aoife Reagan. Yes, I know who you are. Humans are destroying everything. I'm sure you see it."

From this altitude, I could see the entire city all the way to the harbor, where pinpoints of lights from boats and ships bobbed and moved. "I know it's bad. We're all feeling it. But we're trying. What can you do by yourself?"

"Look again."

I glanced down, and my eyes widened in horror. The water in the harbor was rapidly running backward, out to sea, against the tide.

"Don't do it, please. There are others down there besides the humans. There are redcaps and lamia, and dryads. You'll drown them all." My voice had turned shrill, desperate. I'd long since dropped my accent.

"It doesn't matter. The humans will kill them anyway."

The water was still slowly receding from the harbor, dropping several ships to ground at the docks, and I closed my eyes for a moment. *There's no way out of this,* I thought. She's going to drown the city and everyone in it. As it was, even if I could stop her right then, the seaport and everything around it would be inundated.

"Please don't do this," I pleaded, unable to say anything else as her tentacle squeezed tighter around my chest, choking off my breath.

"Shut up!" She shouted.

"But, Zhi! Chinatown is right there!"

She looked at me coldly then. "You think there's a difference? Chinese, Japanese, American, British, Dutch, French, pick one. They all act the exact same way. Using whatever they can to further the destruction of the planet in the name of the survival of their own species in an insane scramble for power. And they don't care how many species or people they murder in the process. Why are you defending them?"

The tentacle loosened slightly, though. Maybe I was getting through to her.

"Yeah, for sure, I get it. They're awful. Humans are a bunch of terrified children. But we can work with them, maybe even guide them, I don't know. But there's always hope!"

She smirked. "You can't really believe that. You're not one of them, I can smell the goddess in you. Feel the power. They'll take you, too! That skin, that hair. They're already putting together a dissection table just for you! You're a fool. Better to end your suffering now."

Her tentacle squeezed tight against my chest again, and I felt my chest collapse under the pressure, my breath coming out in a whoosh. A sharp pain lanced through my side as a rib cracked, and then a second.

Out of nowhere, a dark shadow flashed down, slicing completely through the tentacle that held me, dropping me to the rooftop. The shadow dropped to the ground and stumbled slightly, spinning around. Morgan had landed, though it looked like she couldn't hold her shape as she shifted back into her more human form. In her hand, though, was Cait's shadowsteel blade.

Maki had been clutched under one arm, and she'd landed just past me, tumbling almost to the edge of the roof.

Zhi slashed out, but Morgan was like a woman possessed, slicing through the first tentacle and vaulting over the second as if she'd been born with the blade in her hand.

Another tentacle flashed out, and she dodged that, too, cutting a long gash in it. And Gods, she was fast, dodging left and right. But she only had two legs, and Zhi still had seven, with another growing rapidly in a cascade of water and goo from the stump.

Despite Morgan's deftness on her feet and her speed with Cait's sword, one of Zhi's long tentacles caught her across the midsection, finally knocking her back perilously close to the roof.

Zhi advanced on her, only to be hit in the back with a ball of fire that scorched her skin.

She whirled, slicing deep into Maki's left leg and knocking her feet out from under her. Then she turned back to Morgan and grabbed her, hoisting her into the air, spread eagle, ready to rend her limb from limb.

In a moment of total panic, I held out my palms and willed all of the magic around me to stream toward her, unsure what it might do, hoping it would just stop her.

It did. A beam of pure magic, mixed of green, gold and white, blue and purple, and vermillion braided together, shot through her midsection and off into the night, leaving a smoking hole.

Zhi turned back toward me, a dumbfounded and confused look on her face before she dropped Morgan to the rooftop and dove over the side of the building.

Below, the sounds of thousands of screams and alarms and god only knew what else crashing about echoed as the wave she'd been building slid back into the harbor and over the docks through the seaport, and the streets below us, drowning everything and everyone within a quarter mile of the harbor.

I ran over to Morgan, who was doubled over.

"Morgan! Are you okay? Where'd she hit you?"

Morgan's head snapped up, her eyes predatory and vacant.

"Oh, shit," I murmured and tried to back away, but she was on me in a flash, her teeth digging painfully into my throat.

"Oh," I gasped as the ecstasy of the bite and her glamour slid over me. I thought of using magic, but I didn't know how without killing her outright. I fought her glamour for a moment but then gave in. Fighting would only bring pain, horrible pain, and I couldn't escape. She was latched on too tightly. My last thought as the darkness began to close in around me was that she was going to kill me, and it would break her. *Oh, Gods, Morgan, I'm so sorry.*

CHAPTER FIFTY-FIVE

Skaja

After camping overnight once more a few miles from the gates, we made our final trek north, and the morning of the third day was still young as our diverse entourage of Bethadi, Shaddani, and Óșeni warriors made its way to shore.

As we crested the last hill before the shoreline, the sight that unfolded before my eyes made my heartbeat stutter. I gazed over what seemed to be an impossible creation, something that whispered of ancient, earthly magic. Never in my wildest dreams or stories heard around the fireside had I imagined anything like this. "It's unreal." My voice came out in a hushed whisper, so faint that only the winds could hear.

The land before me seemed to be woven from stone and waves. Countless hexagonal pillars, shaped with such precision that they seemed to have been chiseled by the gods themselves, rose from the earth. Each column, with its crisp hexagonal sides, fit perfectly with its brethren, forming an undulating carpet of rock that led to the sea.

The sun, rising from over our right shoulders, still low in the sky, cast ethereal hues of amber and gold upon the stone. As the waves broke against the rocks, the mist from the sea intermingled with the air, making it taste of salt and age-old tales. The very atmosphere around this place seemed to hum with an energy that spoke to my blood and soul. The stones were dark, like the night sky, with hints of glimmering minerals that mirrored the stars.

I dismounted, my feet touching the stone, and I felt an affinity, a kinship with this place. It was as if the very essence of the earth was speaking to me through the soles of my feet.

"The steps of giants, carved in stone," I whispered to myself, my eyes wide with wonder.

My mother glanced at me in amusement. "It's an ancient upwelling of molten stone crystallized into these pillars, daughter, but you're right. It is a breathtaking sight."

I ignored the pedestrian explanation, instead choosing to let my imagination work unfettered. My fingers grazed the surface of the rock. It felt cool to the touch, smooth, with an undercurrent of vibrations that resonated through me.

I felt humbled and awestruck by this place, and for a brief moment, the impending clash that lay before us felt like a mere flicker against the backdrop of eternity that this place represented. In the end, this world, these forces that created it, would endure, and we were just a speck in the grand turning of time.

Turning to Zilly, who was close by, my voice, though low, carried the weight of my emotions. "This place—it feels alive, sacred. It is like the world itself, with its endless cycles and ancient heart, laid bare before our eyes."

Zilly nodded. "Óşeni has its own stark beauty, but this world holds surprises like this at every corner, and I've still seen only a small portion." Then she dismounted and walked over to me, placing a hand on my shoulder. "And I have no desire to leave it."

I looked up at her and smiled, then back to the landscape, a carpet of stone leading out into the sea. But it wasn't just the natural splendor that gripped me; not far from the shore lay the Black and White Gates. They stood like ancient sentinels, side by side, two colossal spheres seemingly defying gravity itself. The Black Gate was ominous, and I could feel the echoes of broken Shaddan emanating from it in the streams of our magic. The White Gate seemed to offer solace, like a window into a landscape unmarred by shadows, brilliant and beautiful and filled with green trees and brightly colored flowers.

However, what lay before the Gates was a sight that sent a

shiver through us all—a host of Fomori. They were not as numerous as the swarms we'd faced in the past, but still, a force to be reckoned with, at least in the hundreds.

Nemhain, on her raven-black steed, looked upon the Fomori with eyes like twin storms. "We must attack now before they know we are here and begin to organize, or one of the little bastards runs back for reinforcements," she spoke with a voice that sent ripples through the air.

The Bethadi, their armor gleaming in the early light, nodded in agreement. Their steely gazes were fixed upon the adversaries that lay ahead.

To my utter confusion and disbelief, all eyes then turned to me, and I blinked, not comprehending.

"What say you, Commander?" Nisya said with a smirk.

"Me? I'm the least of you. Any one of you has more battle experience than I do."

"And yet, we look to you, still," Ahnut stated flatly, and her sister nodded grim-faced.

Zilly spoke then. "When a commander and her second falls, when no other is of rank to fill the role, we choose our next until others arrive. During the battle, you saw the loss of our sisters. You called to spread and cover. You gave the order that likely kept us alive." Then her mouth curved in a sardonic smile. "Before you got stabbed horribly, that is."

The others chuckled.

"So," Zilly said, watching me with those eyes that could force the stars themselves to stand and take notice. "What are your orders."

I mounted my horse and felt the weight of their gazes like a physical presence. I looked at Zilly, whose eyes offered her unyielding support. My heart raced, my hands trembled. It was as if the ancient land itself was watching, waiting.

I made my decision.

With resolve welling up inside me, I turned my horse towards the Fomori. It was as if I could feel the pulsing energy of the earth beneath us and the crackling anticipation in the air.

"String bows," I ordered, and with a whisper of sinew and wood, I breathed life into mine as the taut string sang with a test of my fingers, a hymn to the spirits of our honored dead.

The remaining Óşeni lined up behind me. My mother moved her mount to my right. Lugh moved to my left, and the Bethadi knights drew up next to my sisters in a line.

I caressed my bow one last time, feeling the tension of the string like the tension in my very soul. "For our fallen, for the lands we hold dear, and for the battle that awaits before!" My voice roared over the surf.

"CHARGE!"

Like a torrent unleashed, we descended through a narrow pass that led to the beach, reforming our lines as the landscape spread out beyond. The thundering hooves finally caught the attention of the Fomori, milling about. There were no Kosant and no pteraket, only emisai and wevkrana awaited us.

Through the winds and salt and spray that blew in from the sea across the sand, I felt connected to something greater, something ancient and timeless. I thought of my mother, of the legacy that coursed through my veins. I thought of Saya and Óbin and those who had trained me. Most of all, I thought of Zilly, who now rode at my side.

In the rush of anticipation, as the whispering winds carried the sea's songs to our ears, Zilly, I, and the other Óşeni rode in a line before the Bethadi, shoulder to shoulder, as our spirits rose in a tightly lain mosaic of purpose. With our bows raised to the heavens, we looked like avenging deities summoned from the annals of legends. The air grew electric around us, and time seemed to hang suspended like a pendulum at the peak of its arc.

In an orchestrated symphony, our hands pulled back the strings in perfect harmony. The tension thrummed through the air like the heartbeat of the earth, a deep resonance that stirred our very cores.

"RELEASE!"

A cascade of arrows flew, winged serpents soaring through the air, their path illuminated by the sun's golden embrace. The arrows danced and weaved like swallows in the dawn winds, descending upon the Fomori with the fury of storms.

The shafts found their marks by the dozen, felling the dark

Fomori with the grace and finality of leaves in autumn's descent. The haunting thud of their impact whispered of ancient battles and sacred duties fulfilled.

"BLADES!" I cried as we closed on the beasts of hate and dropped our bows.

The world seemed to pulse with the drumming of hoofbeats and the clash of steel as we, the Óşeni and Bethadi, tore into the Fomori like a tempest unleashed. My blade sang songs of both sorrow and fury, glinting in the fading light as I cleaved through the monstrous forms before me.

My mount was quickly taken from beneath me, but I rolled up, and Zilly dropped to my side in formation. My heart raced, and my breath came in gasps, but my body was ablaze with the fiery light of Óşen.

Zilly was a force of nature beside me. Her movements were poetry and devastation interwoven. The air around her seemed to shiver as she slashed through the Fomori. The other Óşeni fought with a fierceness and grace that made them seem more phantoms of death than mortal beings.

The Bethadi, clad in armor that shone like starlight, fought like the mythical beings they were. Their blades and spears flashed, each strike a thunderclap as they cut down the Fomori with an almost terrifying ferocity.

But even as we pressed on, a shadow fell upon my soul as the screams of fallen comrades tore through the air. The sand drank the blood of Óşeni and Bethadi alike, and the bodies of brave warriors fell amid the waning tide.

Amidst the harsh, dissonant music of battle, a crackle filled the air like the very heavens tearing asunder. Lightning unfurled from the sky, called forth by The Morrigan's outstretched hands as she flew above us in the rapidly intensifying tempest.

The electric tendrils twisted and coiled like ancient serpentine beasts of pure energy, blasting the Fomori to ash where they stood. Her voice was an ancient, echoing chant, her figure an avatar of the primal forces she wielded.

In the heart of the conjured storm, the Fomori faltered and then began to retreat, scrambling back through the Black Gate like shadows fleeing the dawn.

We were heroes of song. We were the army of Mother Danu. We were the victors.

When the battle ended, and we looked to our compatriots, there were but four of us left. The rest of our beloved sisters lay around us in pools of thickening blood that stained the sands and the waters.

The Bethadi had faired better, losing only a few.

The winds died, and the sky cleared as my mother returned to the earth, landing at my side.

A deep disquiet countenanced her face, and she spoke in choked words. "It is done."

Then she looked at me closely. "Remember all that you have seen here. May it serve you well. In the end, it was the only gift I had left to give. I will always love you. Find the mantle. It will save them."

Then she raised her voice, relentless and commanding, summoning my gaze. With a grace that defied the chaos of the battle now gone, she drew the gate tablets from her satchel, and her voice lifted in an incantation that made the very air shiver. The stones, the sea, and the wind all seemed to listen and bend to her will. The tablets drew into the air and exploded in a brilliant light that sang in colored tones of our homeland.

I could feel the ancient power she wielded enveloping the Black Gate, the very threads of reality twisting and folding upon themselves. The air was thick with magic as her voice bound tendrils of her power around the gate.

Three blasts knocked us down as the pressure of air, and the shudder of the land took our feet from under us. And as the final words of the incantation left her lips, there was a resounding silence, as if the world itself were holding its breath. Then, a shockwave of pure energy rippled through the air, and the Black Gate shuddered and collapsed in upon itself, sealed for all eternity. Or so we hoped.

I rose, my blade still clenched in my hand, my breath ragged, as I felt the weight of both loss and triumph. The winds carried whispers of those who had fallen and of a darkness forever locked away.

We had fought, we had sacrificed, and at the end of it all, we had reclaimed the future from the shadows. And now, we were done.

I turned to Zilly, and the world seemed blurred. I felt drawn from my body. I watched from the outside as I embraced Zilly and kissed her, and spoke to her, though I heard none of it. And the world went black as I was stolen away from myself.

"And that is how it all began for you, my lovely child," a resonant and familiar voice said from behind me. But as I turned, she was gone. I found myself staring down at my own body, swathed in a silk gown. A beautiful blonde woman lay with her head on my belly in a room of treasures, deep beneath the ground, in a city far removed from Skaja, by both distance and time.

"Liz," I whispered in recognition, my words disappearing quickly into the ethereal state in which I existed. And I was myself once more as the shrouded orb of my dark gifted soul followed a long line of silver thread into my body.

CHAPTER FIFTY-SIX

Aoife

"Where am I?" I found myself laying in a twin bed. Above me, glow-in-the-dark stars and planets decorated the ceiling in irregular patterns, and soft, muffled music played somewhere. My left arm hurt, and I realized someone had put in an IV which was feeding me blood, human blood.

"At Marcella's," a young girl's voice said from my right. It took me a moment to recognize it as Katie's.

"Is this safe?" I asked, lifting my arm weakly to indicate the IV.

Katie looked over at me, pulling out one of her earbuds. The muffled music ceased. "Yeah, Déra says your body will use blood from about anyone. You don't really have a blood type anymore, and the tlehos just mutates it into what you need. See! I pay attention." That last comment was almost petulant as if she wasn't actually speaking to me but maybe griping at Liz. I suspected there was a mother-daughter issue about thoroughness or following directions there.

"Déra's here?" I asked.

Katie shook her head. "Liz called her. Wanted to find out if it was okay to give you human blood."

"Is this your room?"

"Yup. I'm glad you're okay, Auntie Aoife. You've been in and out of it for three days. Morgan was so blood starved after that crazy transformation and the fight that she almost drained you. I'll go get her. She's downstairs and has been freaking out. She absolutely refused to leave. It's been really annoying. And I want my room back."

"How did I get here?"

Katie stood up and moved into my line of sight. "Angela called in a favor and had you snatched from the hospital almost as soon as the life-flight helicopter landed. I'll go get Auntie Red."

I scratched an itch in my ear as I tried to sit up, but my body was weak and wobbly, so I stayed put.

A few minutes later, Morgan trod in and sat down next to me. "Oh, God, honey, I'm so sorry. I couldn't help it. This is why— "

"Stop," I croaked. "I'm okay. Let it go. It wasn't your fault."

Morgan gave me a look that told me she'd feel guilty about it for a while, but she didn't keep apologizing. Instead, she said. "Well, I won't ask how you're feeling."

My chest hurt from the effort of laughing. "Ow. Yeah, that's probably best. Is Zhi—"

"Escaped," Morgan said. "Best bet is somewhere in the cape."

"That's not good, but we'll never find her out there."

"No. It's not likely. But that's someone else's problem now."

I nodded. I'd read the report, and I didn't want to think about what that monster had done. I changed the subject. "I feel bad for Zhi."

"I know. But it was a sad state of affairs. It was her or us."

I had to remind myself of who, or more importantly, what, I was talking to, as the frankness of her words left me a little cold.

"No, Red, that's not what I mean. She wasn't wrong, was she? It really is us against them, isn't it? The humans, I mean."

She looked away out the window. "I try not to think that way. It used to be gay people against the straights, remember?"

"Yes, and we're always one law, one court decision, or one stray bullet away from the worst. Look at Florida. People say it can't happen here, but it has, with the Japanese internment in World War II. Almost two-thousand people died just because of the shape of their faces and the color of their skin."

"I don't want to discuss this, Cai—sorry, Aoife."

I heard the slip, though. "You've had this conversation with my sister. She feels the same way, doesn't she?"

Morgan nodded. "She hates them. She doesn't say it often, but I can see it in her eyes."

"I know there are good humans out there, Red. What happened downtown was an abomination, but I don't know how much longer we'll be able to hold out. Cait's files said there were two-thousand preternatural creatures under Boston, and, as far as we know, that's it. She thought that having Kaja and Gretchen be the spokespersons would help because who wants to kill Princess Ariel, right? But I've seen Twitter. A lot of people want to kill Princess Ariel."

Morgan sighed, and I reached over to the nightstand to grab a bottle of water and took a sip. A protracted silence ensued until I couldn't stand it anymore. I opened my arms and practically begged her to hug me.

She straddled my legs and wrapped her arms around me.

"Easy," I groaned. "Watch the ribs."

"Sorry," she whispered and adjusted her grip before finally letting go.

Then I cleared my throat. "So, how's Maki? Is she okay? She took a hell of a hit."

Morgan stroked at my hair while she spoke. "Probably questioning her line of work, but she's fine otherwise. It turns out that Kitsune heal like we do. In other news, half the city is in ruins. The death toll is estimated in the tens of thousands and rising. I know we did our best, but it's really bad. Senator Kim is blaming this all on the preternatural creatures of Boston. She's introduced a bill to the senate to have them all rounded up and moved to a 'safe location' in Nevada. It's already in committee."

"And that's what I was talking about. Damnit. Did she draft it on a napkin, or was it already waiting somewhere?"

"My guess is she had it already stashed, waiting for something bad to happen. The way she had the camps locked down, something was bound to go wrong eventually. This just happened to be the thing."

"Or she had something to do with it," I said. "I don't really believe in coincidences. I just don't understand her game yet."

"Well," Morgan said with a sigh of despair. "The support in the house looks to be overwhelming. The Senate is split fifty-fifty with the vice president against it, so we're safe, at least for the moment."

I took in as deep a breath as I could and coughed, then I swallowed hard. "Five gets you twenty that this isn't the end. With the Vice President holding the tie vote, something else will happen—to him probably."

Morgan raised a skeptical eyebrow. "That's a little far-fetched, don't you think?"

"Despite the fact that I wasn't living here, I did pay attention to the news. First, Mayor Kim creates the PIU. Then the Liberty Hotel incident happens. Then the crackdown on the camps, which was easy because the only holdout councilman suddenly died after his home was 'randomly' invaded by ogumo. Then she was suddenly elevated to the US Senate just a few weeks ago after the current senator died from a stroke. He was fifty-five. Not too young for it to be suspicious, but still. Now she's the one calling for internment and rousing the rabble. Her rise has been a bit meteoric, don't you think?"

"Well, when you put it that way, it certainly looks suspicious, in a conspiracy theory kind of way, but think about what it would take to do all of that."

I nodded. "Maybe. Of course, she'd have to be in control of the creatures coming through the gate."

"It gets worse. The acting Mayor has ordered that the camps be cordoned off and kept under guard. He's also ordered the dismissal of the entire PIU squad. Sesi's slow-walking the camp order, but she can only do so much. Fortunately, the Mayor can't just up and fire us. He has to go through paperwork, and there's an appeal process. Also, a strange thing is going on with the City Council. They were all hip on creating the PIU at Kim's request as if they were in her pocket, but now they don't want to disband it."

"Again, I smell Kim's hand in all of this. She's fucking with us, though. I'm sure she knows he can't just dismiss us, Reform Act or no Reform Act. She'll call one of us in and threaten to expose vampires. As for why the City Council is fighting the PIU dissolution, ask Marcella. I suspect her hand in that." Morgan frowned hard at that, squinting suspiciously. Clearly, her wheels were turning.

I let that percolate. "How's John?"

Morgan snorted. "He's fine. Grumpy as ever. He was just pissed that he missed the action."

I chuckled again and was once more greeted with the soreness in my chest. "That sounds like John." I reached out a hand, and she helped me to a sitting position, piling a couple of pillows under my back. "So, now what?"

"So, now, we go about our job. We're still cops, and we're still a team. As soon as that unit is empty," she gestured to the bag of blood, "I'm taking you home to get some rest, and then we'll find Cait's would-be assassin."

"Guys," Katie said, returning to the door. "Mama's awake!"

CHAPTER FIFTY-SEVEN

Cait

My fingers slid across the hard wooden platform as my eyes fluttered open. Panic enveloped me for a moment, squeezing at my chest. "Zilly?" I whispered, my throat raw and parched, not painful, just disused. A tear of loss and grief dripped from the corner of my eye, sliding down the side of my face in the harsh lights above.

I remembered: the gunshot, the pain in my chest, the suffocation, the blood. But that memory lay shrouded in the morning mists of Boudka and Zilly and my mother. The battle at the Giant's Causeway was lost to a time in which heroes died, and no one knew. Where we'd saved the Earth, but no one would ever tell the tale. I wanted to go back. To see her again, to feel her rough calloused hands holding me once more.

"Oh, Métehr," I murmured in grief and sniffed.

I lifted my head and traced the Valtárí brand spiraling on my left breast just under my collarbone. What I had experienced wasn't some memory of a past life. *I am Skaja*, I thought.

Slowly, though I felt no urge for it, I took in a shuddering, miserable breath. I felt my stomach rise and fall, the air entering my lungs. I was alive, and the hunger prowled around at the edge of my consciousness, reminding me of what I am now. Liz lay her head on my stomach, weeping softly.

"Honey?" The words came out a little strangled, and I cleared my throat, speaking louder this time. "Honey?"

Liz lifted, turning her head slowly toward me. Her eyes were wide, her cheeks stained with faint pink streaks, and she blinked several times as if she couldn't believe what she saw.

"Liz, honey?" I inquired again.

"Cait?" Her voice was low, pained. And it took me a moment to get my bearings enough to realize that soft tears ran down her cheeks.

"I'm home," I said quietly, just in the way I might have if I'd found her just waking after I'd been on a long trip.

"Cait?" She said again, and a slow, thin smile crawled across my face.

"Yeah." The thin smile curved into a broad grin.

Before I could move any further, she jerked me roughly into her arms and began slathering my face with kisses. "Oh! Goddess! You're awake. You're back with us!" She squeezed me closer, bunching up my gown in her hands.

I wrapped my arms around her and held on, just drinking in her presence and the waft of dragon's blood. "I missed you so much." I dug my fingers into that soft scented hair I remembered something my mother had said. 'Love, my daughter, is one of the most powerful magics in all worlds. It binds others to us and us to them.'

"I missed you, too. Don't ever do that again." She sniffed loudly. "Damnit."

I smiled wryly at that. "Do what? Get shot by a sweaty, urine-soaked, and drunken madman? I think that was a one-off, dear. But I'll do my best."

Liz snorted a laugh and leaned back, capturing my eyes with her gaze. I'd never seen her so happy, so relieved.

"I'm sorry," I said, turning serious. "I'll try to be more careful. It'll be okay, though, because I know who shot me."

"Matt Reynolds," she said. "We know."

She must have seen the puzzled look on my face because she got very quiet and pressed her lips together.

"Liz?"

"Two months."

My eyes opened wide, astonishment ringing in my voice. "Two months? I was down for Two months? Holy shit." Every minute of living as Weyna, experiencing my past life, had taken only two months. As if on cue, my body ran with needles and bees under my skin, my stomach cramped, and I groaned.

"Hang on, I'll run and get you some blood," her eyes were still wet with tears, but the happy smile on her face, as she ran out of the room, filled me with joy. God, I'd missed her.

Sitting up, I dangled my legs off the table and looked around. Nothing, it seemed, had changed, at least not in this room, filling me with some comfort that some part of my life remained intact. Liz was here. Everything was clean, and there was a new journal laying on Marcella's desk, so she was still around here somewhere. Somehow, I could feel Katie. She was here, too. Everything was okay.

It was probably stupid, but I wondered about my job. How was I going to explain this to Sesi?

A familiar voice called from the door, "Cait?"

I looked up. After sixteen years, it was surreal. Looking at Aoife was like looking at a shimmering reflection, with her silver hair flowing about her shoulders and opalescent Kyliri skin. She was muscular and built, her shoulders broad from working out, just like mine.

I only had a moment to acknowledge her presence, though, before the hunger shot through me again, more intensely this time, and my thoughts became sluggish. The intense desperation for blood began to drown out even my most basic emotions.

Before I could say anything, however, Aoife ran forward and clasped me in a tight hug, pulling me to a standing position. "Gods," she said, " I'm so glad you're back."

Almost involuntarily, my own arms snapped around her, and my hands tugged at her shirt.

Mother, please, I pleaded in my thoughts as I struggled just to stay still, to keep from tearing her throat open. I wanted to pull away, but she smelled so good, like coconut shampoo, my Dior perfume, and the blood that pumped through her veins as her heartbeat percussed through me. Her blood was my blood, and mine hers.

Aoife groaned playfully and started to pull away, still not understanding. "Sis, not so hard. I can't—"

"Don't move," I growled.

"What is it?" She hissed, finally feeling the tension and seriousness of the moment.

I couldn't conjure any words, and I felt my glamour begin to slip out of control, flooding Aoife's thoughts with a desire to surrender herself to me. *I am your sister*, it whispered seductively. *I need what you have. You want to give me all that you are.*

Aoife's breathing became labored, and the heat of her flush flowed into my cheek. She pressed into me with a soft sigh.

"Cait! Stop!" Liz shouted from the doorway, but the power of her command just flowed over and around me as if it wasn't meant for me.

I'm not the same as I was. Oh no, I'm more. The thought cackled through me with wicked, wicked intent. *I'm so much more.*

Ever so slowly, my eyes cracked open, and my gaze turned to Liz over Aoife's shoulder. I licked my lips and said quietly, "No, no, no, Liz. She's mine. You can't have her."

Aoife stroked my head and spoke, and her voice held none of the dreamy quality I expected. She sounded totally lucid, not glamoured at all. But she was. I could feel her inside my thoughts. "Oh, Cait."

As Aoife's thoughts mingled further with my own, the black, wispy coils of my glamour gently pushed aside her will, digging deeply into her emotions, unleashing a pent-up love that she'd stuffed away in the pain of our separation, and filling her with a desperate need.

Even as she tilted her head back, offering her throat, a hiccupping sob burbled from her lips, and she sniffed. Her hot, wet tears slid down, pooling between our cheeks, only to slide past and fall once more.

I was going to take her. Right here, right now.

Abruptly, I was shut out. A blast of something hot and

painful lanced into my chest, and Aoife jerked roughly away, crashing into the massive orrery, where she landed with a loud oof.

Liz shot forward, handing me a bag of blood and pulling Aoife away.

Morgan launched into the room moments later, the two units of blood in her hands dropping and sliding across the floor as she flew off the stairs toward Aoife.

I sucked at the tube hungrily, taking in the salt-copper taste of the blood and slumping back against the table in relief. "Oh, Goddess, Aoife," I said after a few gulps. "I'm so sorry. Are you okay?"

She sat up and waved an arm from the floor. "Yeah, sure. I'm grand." Though she groaned and rubbed at her lower back when she stood. "No worries, but I was afraid you'd try to shag me, and then Morgan would've been fuckin' ragin'."

I barked a laugh. "I don't think that's where it was going?"

"Speak for yourself. The thoughts you were giving out were positively pornographic. Please don't ever do that again. It was gross."

If I'd had any blood in me to speak of, I'd have flushed. As it was, I looked down in absolute mortification. "I'm so sorry."

"Ah, don't worry about it. I'm just glad you're awake."

Then my brain caught up to all that had been said in the last few minutes. "Wait, what? Morgan?"

Aoife stood back up and put an arm around Morgan's waist, pulling her close. "Yeah. Not sure how you let this one get away, but she got a taste of the new and improved model and forgot all about you. She's handy with a blade, too. A right fuckin' Jedi."

Morgan looked away, embarrassed. "Honestly, I'm not sure where it came from. I really think it's the blade. It's magical or something."

Then she turned back and gave us that crooked smile she always wore, and the resemblance to Zilly drove a deep pang of sorrow into my chest. I did my best to push it away, but it was there.

"Hey! I'm right here." Liz snapped. "Cait picked me, you

wanker. I wasn't second prize."

I grabbed Liz by the arm and pulled her to me as I sipped at the blood with my other hand. "Too fucking right. Now ignore them." Somehow, just having her closer made me feel more complete and whole. As if the last puzzle piece in my world had finally fallen into place.

After a moment, I said, "How's Ma? Have you seen her?"

"Yeah, she's good. She's got the lamia working on fixing the unstable tunnel to camp two, and she asked me to help her with a book translation, but I haven't been able to make the time yet."

I raised an incredulous eyebrow. "Translation? Don't tell me you became a bookworm?"

"No," Morgan interjected. "She's a badass like you, Cait. Just smarter."

Before I could answer, though, someone else came barreling through the door with two more bags of blood in her hands. "Mama!"

Everything else fell away as Katie leaped through the air and landed in my arms.

"Oh, baby! I missed you so much!" I crowed and squeezed her to me.

She pulled away, practically jumping. "I missed you, too. I have so much to tell you. Auntie Aoife beat a real-life sea monster! With magic!"

I looked at her, then at Aoife, who shrugged, then at Morgan, who just grinned from ear to ear. "Like I said, Cait, badass. Oh, and did I mention smarter."

I gave her a look of mock distress. "Like you could tell the difference, you fucking spanner."

"Better a dumb tool than looking like a reject from a casting call of a gothic romance."

I glanced down at my gown in earnest for the first time. It was pretty sheer, made of soft linen, and my nipples poked out rather, well, pointedly. "Okay, who bloody dressed me in this gown? I look like fucking Mathilda May."

Liz leaned over. "That would be me. Do you not like it?"

I gave her an amused look. "It's fine, I guess. But why do I feel like it wasn't for me?"

She shrugged, playing innocent. "If you don't like it, we could go upstairs and find something more—I don't know—comfortable."

CHAPTER FIFTY-EIGHT

Aoife

"As of this evening," President James said, his face pained. "Given the very grave nature of the events in Boston, I have taken the steps to ensure the safety of all Americans. To ensure that no preternatural creatures leave the Boston area and threaten lives and livelihoods in other parts of the country, I have ordered the US military to place armed checkpoints at all major entry and exit points of the city. It is not without serious consideration that I take this action, given the need for relief in downtown Boston after the horrific events just last week. However, in the interests of public safety, we must protect American lives."

"Turn it off," I protested from the bed as Morgan watched.

Morgan shushed me. "We need to hear this."

"While the full extent and nature of the unprecedented tsunami that struck Boston are still as of yet not fully known, we must err on the side of caution. Vice President Camden will be making his way to Boston soon to survey the damage and address the Massachusetts General Assembly. I want to be crystal clear, we do not believe that the public outside of Boston is in any danger, nor do we expect a repeat of this event. But, given several recent reports from other countries around the world, specifically from the Strait of Messina, the mass abduction of children in Ukraine, and the total loss of contact with both the Republic of Ireland and the UK Nation of Northern Ireland, we must take extreme measures to ensure the safety of American Lives.

"In cooperation with federal, state, and local law enforcement agencies, we are asking all Americans to report any incidents of preternatural or supernatural activity in their areas. Once more, I want to be crystal clear that these actions are directed only to protect Americans from a very real and extant threat as a precaution. We do not believe that there are preternatural creatures outside of the Boston area, nor do we believe that the public at large is in any danger at this time.

"During this time of crisis, we encourage Americans to continue forward as we always have, with dignity and diligence. We will prevail against these threats and continue to make America the beacon of prosperity it has always been

"Thank you very much, and, as always, God Bless America."

"Jaysus," I whispered and sat back against the headboard, stunned. "When did we lose contact with home?"

"Late last night," Morgan said matter of factly. "The feed cut abruptly. Since then, the UK sent several drones but lost contact with them just as they crossed over the coastline, no crashes, no signals, no nothing. They just vanished. The entire island is without power as well, totally dark." She turned back to me, giving me a sad look. "I'm sorry, Aoife."

"Ten days," I murmured to myself. It had only been ten days since our battle with Zhi on the rooftop of the Sojourn, and now all of this. I pulled myself out of bed and walked over to Morgan, wrapping my arms around her. I didn't know what else to do.

She held me for a minute, kissed me, then said, "Get dressed. We need to go by Marcella's. She has some things in the armory I want to pick up. I don't want to be caught flat-footed if the shit hits the fan."

Things were subdued when we arrived at Marcella's. Cait, Liz, and the lady of the house were in the kitchen discussing the president's announcement.

"We should evacuate," Liz said as she leaned back in her chair.

Cait's eyebrows shot up. "What? This is our home as much as it ever was theirs."

"Slow down," Marcella said. "It's just a suggestion and not a terrible idea. But we don't have anywhere to go at this point."

"I'm not evacuating shit," Morgan said as she stepped into the kitchen. "I'm with Cait. This is our home."

Liz and Marcella both looked at me like I was supposed to say something. I just shrugged and jerked a thumb at Morgan. "I go where she goes."

Cait smirked and then shook her head as if something was immensely funny. I gave her a sidelong glance and narrowed my eyes. "What?"

"Nothing, really. I'm still just digesting that you two are together. Good on you both."

Morgan pulled me closer and beamed a wide smile, and I gave her a kiss on the cheek. "Yeah," I said. "I think we'll be alright."

I took the last chair around the table, and Morgan pulled a barstool around next to me before dropping into it. "So," she said. "There's no place to go, and we're surrounded by the military. Now what?"

"We still need to be prepared for the possibility," Liz commented. "This could get ugly."

"It already has," Cait said.

I just listened for a while, waiting for someone to state the obvious, but no one did. So, after about ten minutes, I finally raised my hand. "Can I ask a question?"

Marcella turned to me, an eyebrow raised.

"How many Fae creatures are there here in Boston?" I asked.

"Fae creatures?" Marcella grimaced. "I'm not sure exactly. Maybe twelve-hundred. Most of the preternatural people here. Why?"

"And they're all Light-Fae?" I asked and watched as Cait's face lit up with understanding.

"The gate in Ireland."

I waggled my eyebrows. "There's a passageway to Bethad sitting right across the pond if they want to go. We would just have to find a way to get them there."

"There is a way," Cait said flatly. "Short-distance portals are possible. Mother Darkness used them against the Sidhe army."

"How short?" I asked, immediately considering the possibilities.

Cait shook her head. "I don't know. Magic's not my area. I really wish Boudka was—" She stopped cold, a slow realization crossing her face. "The queen," she said softly, looking at Marcella.

"You know who she is," Marcella responded. It wasn't a question.

Cait nodded. "I do. And I have an idea where she's buried. She would know how to do it. But she's like us. She can't perform magic anymore."

"But I can," I responded. "If we could find her. If she's still alive, she could show me how."

"But would they want to go?" Morgan asked, raising the point we'd all been ignoring.

"I think I can persuade—" Marcella said, but we were interrupted by the slamming of the front door.

"I quit!" Schaefer fumed as she stormed into the house.

Marcella got up and strode into the foyer. "Wait, you quit? As in, you quit the Bureau?"

"I tendered my resignation an hour ago and was walked out. My shit's in my car. I told the new SAC he could take his fascist assignment and shove it up his ass and that I wouldn't be a party to this, whatever it is. You have no idea what they wanted me to do." Angela pawed at her eyes and sniffed. "I used to fucking love my job, you know?"

Marcella gave Schaeffer a hug and tugged at her arms. "Come in the sitting room, dear, and tell me what happened."

Schaeffer balked, still red-faced and furious. "I just told you what happened. I explained to that asshole, DeMille, what happened on top of the Sojourn. I gave him Cait—I mean Aoife's report, and Morgan's, and Detective Imai's. And you know what he said?"

Marcella waited, still holding Schaeffer's arms.

"He said," Angela continued. "We have orders. I told him. No, we're not the fucking military. We don't take orders. We get instructions from DC, and we execute them with discretion. He, as the SAC, could fight those instructions, but he said—and get this—he said, 'It wouldn't be a good political decision for either of our careers to fight it.' So I told him to take his politics and go fuck himself with them. Then I quit. His ass had me walked out right then, just barely giving me time to collect my shit."

"Damn," Morgan whispered. "Good on you, sister. You know she shot me once."

I rolled my eyes. "Yeah, I know. Now shush. They're having a moment."

Morgan looked at me, then back at Marcella, who was now ushering Angela into the sitting room, then back at me as reality dawned on her. "Angela? I thought she was straight. Doesn't she have a daughter?"

I shook my head. "Lots of women do. You really are clueless sometimes, you big lunk."

I got up and went to the kitchen doorway so I could hear what was being said.

Angela kept talking, her voice turning a little more subdued. "I'm tired, Marcella. I can't be one of them anymore. They're small and petty and awful. You've shown me that, and you promised me."

"Angela, I don't want you to make a rash decision— "

"Rash?" She retorted, but there was no heat in it. "What's rash about it? I've been thinking about this for months now."

"Okay, okay," Marcella responded softly. "But not here. Let's go talk about this and make sure it's what you really want."

I scurried back to my seat to give the two of them some semblance of privacy just as they left the sitting room, stopping Morgan just as she was going to the door herself.

"I really wanted to hear the rest of that," Morgan hissed.

I glared at her until I no longer heard their footsteps. "Let's just give them some privacy, yeah? Besides, didn't you want to grab some stuff from the armory?"

Morgan pouted. "Yeah. I'll be right back." She left and headed downstairs.

"So," Cait murmured without looking at me. "How are you two getting on?"

"Just fine," I smirked, but didn't say more, waiting for my sister to ask the question that I could see was just killing her.

"I guess you two are in love, then?"

I knew my sister so well. "Just like you and Liz," I replied.

Cait looked up. For a moment, I thought she looked disappointed, but then her face split into a wide grin. "Good. You both deserve to be happy."

I smiled back at her. "We're right for each other, Cait. Turns out Marcella's a pretty good matchmaker. So, I'm sure we'll be together for a long time to come. Now. Tell me about this Aine person."

Morgan returned a short while later as Cait explained some of what she'd experienced. Apparently, the only person she'd told the whole story to was Liz, so we just sat around listening attentively. And when she was done, we were at a loss for words.

"So," Morgan said, finally breaking the silence. "With one of these portals, all of the Light-Fae could go home. Great for them. But what about the rest of us?"

"We fight," I said softly but firmly.

CHAPTER FIFTY-NINE

Aoife

The hair on the back of my neck stood up as we stepped out of Marcella's a few hours later.

"Get down!" Morgan shouted and pushed me roughly to the concrete behind Schaefer's Honda. A shot rang out, and Morgan staggered back, blood leaking from her chest. I hadn't even seen where the shot came from.

"Morgan!" I cried as I started to rise.

"I'm fine," she hissed. "Stay down. I saw him." She scuttled down the length of the car and then disappeared into the darkness behind another vehicle.

"Come on out, little vampire! I know you're behind that car!" It was a man's voice, gruff and taut as if he were straining to speak, not at all matching his taunting words.

I found I no longer had to shift my perception to focus on the magic around me. It was just there when I wanted to see it. I didn't know if I was getting better at perceiving it or what, but the man, if I could call him that, looked strange. Most humans I'd seen so far were wreathed in the greens and turquoises of earth magic that seemed to move upward from the ground and swirl all around their bodies, some brighter, some dimmer. A few were shot through with strange gold strands as well. But this man was all wonky. The green of his body was twisted and gnarled through on one side as if something were invading it, something black and purple.

He strode across the Park toward me. Obscured visually by

the car, the man's aura was all I could see. But from the way he held himself, he appeared to be carrying a rifle.

I watched the angle of his head as he stopped and shifted, looking around. "I'm gonna get that hot bitch vampire girlfriend of yours, too." He shouted.

"Not bloody likely!" I called. I wanted to keep his attention on me. I didn't know what Morgan had planned, but I knew she was stalking him. He started walking my way again. *Good motherfucker*, I thought. *Just keep coming.*

"Y—y—you know, Cait. I killed that bitch wife of his! Now I'm going to get you, too!"

I edged toward the backside of the Honda just as my vision went blurry, losing the perception of magic. The man, wearing a threadbare brown overcoat and carrying a .380 semi-automatic rifle, moved around the other end of the car, aiming at me. "Die you—"

"Hey," a quiet voice said behind him. "The vampire bitch is over here." Morgan whacked him over the back of the head before he could finish raising the weapon, knocking him to the ground, unconscious.

I closed my eyes and took a deep breath, shifting my perception again by force of will, feeling the threads around my head chaotic and loose. Something was wrong. I had a vision of Déra smiling down at me in a huge marble room filled with sculptures and artwork.

"No," I growled, grinding the threads into a stable form, steady and frozen, but the threads of dark magic wormed against the bulwark. I remembered a three-dimensional graphic I'd seen of carbon crystalline structure. I coaxed and pulled at threads of my magic and drew them into a tight cubic matrix.

My focus snapped taut, and I instantly relaxed. When I opened my eyes, my vision was clear. I felt like I'd just moved a freight train.

"Hey, you alright?" Morgan asked, kneeling down next to me. Her shoulder was still bleeding badly. It should have healed by now.

I nodded and swallowed, letting out a relieved breath I

hadn't realized I'd been holding. "Yeah, I'm alright, I think. What's with your shoulder? The wound isn't closing?"

She looked down. "Shadowsteel. It's a through-and-through, though, so it'll close up soon enough. Hang on."

Morgan dashed to the cruiser and returned in latex gloves with cuffs dangling from one hand. As she went to restrain him, though, she jerked away in surprise. "Holy shit!"

"What? What is it?" I asked, slowly pulling myself up onto my feet and following Morgan's gaze to the man's arm. "Fuck," I swore. His left arm was covered in black goo that seemed to pulse and ooze. "Gross."

"Yeah, I had a hunch, but it's still awful to look at. That's the shit we were trying to tell you about back at the ship."

Liz and Marcella poked their heads out a moment later. Seeing Reynold's on the ground, Liz launched herself out the door, knocking Morgan aside.

"You're a right dead man, you cunt!" She shouted as she hoisted him off the ground. "I'm going to flay the fucking skin from your bones."

"Slow down, Liz," Morgan said, grabbing the hand that was reaching for his throat. "He's possessed somehow with that black shit we saw at the hotel. I don't think it's his fault."

"Take him to Bian's," Marcella ordered. "I want her to have a look at him."

"But M.," Liz argued. "He shot Cait."

"Yes, and I want to know how we can reverse this if it happens to someone we actually care about. So he goes to Bian. That's final."

Cait stepped out of the doorway and put a hand on Liz's shoulder. "It's okay, Liz. Let him go. If Mother Darkness has infected him, he's a dead man anyway. Besides, he's not worth the time."

I stared at her for a moment, listening to the cool confidence of her tone and the simple emotionless assessment. Cait had changed. She seemed tougher, more put together, more self-possessed than I'd ever seen. If I were still in the army, I'd have called her officer material. In our last conversation, she'd been wrecked and angry, almost destructive, now she was calm and, well, in command. It wasn't that I had a ton of experience with her lately, but even compared to the brief discussions we'd had and what everyone else had said, I could see a stark contrast.

Liz glanced at Cait and then back at Reynolds, hate filling her eyes. But she released him, letting him drop like a sack of wet flour to the ground.

***

"In here," Bian said as Morgan and I brought Reynolds into the lab wrapped in a blanket, directing us to place him on a small operating table in the corner cell. "I've been waiting for this chance."

He hadn't moved or woken since Morgan had knocked him out. Once we set him down and got him unwrapped, Bian placed her hand on his chest and then pulled it back moments later, slipping on some gloves and cutting open his shirt. The black ooze was all over him, covering his torso up to his collarbone and all down one arm and parts of both legs.

"Jesus Christ," Morgan said in horror.

I felt a shiver of revulsion run through me. "Good Gods."

Bian pulled in a magnifying lamp and cut a sample from the goo, placing it in a Petri dish.

I shifted my perspective once more. The black goo wasn't quite totally black. Dark purple threads of magic coursed through it as it pulsed, growing very slowly. I reach out with my will and tugged at one, and the stuff just pulsed faster, sucking in the threads of my magic, so I pulled away with a shiver. "I can't fix this or do anything with it. It feeds on my magic."

Bian looked up. "What magic?"

We took a minute to go through what had happened in the sewer. I was just about to talk about the fight on top of the Sojourn when Reynolds' arm snapped out, and he grabbed me.

I jerked back, pulling him from the table to the floor, just losing his grip.

"She's coming," he said, his voice raspy and frantic. "She's coming."

I knelt down in front of him.

"Careful, Aoife," Morgan warned, but I held up a hand.

I looked into his eyes. "Mother Darkness?"

He nodded vigorously in confirmation.

"Did Cait cause you to kill your family?"

He shook his head. "No, *she* did. She put something on me, this stuff. I didn't know it at the time. But she infected me with something." He screwed up his face in pain. "Kill me. Burn the body. I don't want to be one of those things."

"Who? Who put this on you?"

He gave a groan, of effort or agony, I couldn't tell. His eyes rolled up in his head, then they snapped back down, turning feral, and he swiped at me. I fell backward as Morgan bent down and snapped his neck in one fluid motion before pulling me out, followed by Bian, who closed the door and locked it.

While we watched, the goo began to advance faster, crawling over Reynolds' skin. His head snapped back into position from the weird canted angle Morgan had left it in and swiveled to look at me. Then he launched himself at the containment unit wall. Fortunately, it held fast. After a few minutes of banging at it, the thing moved into the corner and began to watch us out of Reynolds' deep blue eyes.

"Fuck, me," I said and covered my mouth with my hand.

Bian moved up next to us, speaking quietly. "Go back to Marcella's and let her know what he said. We have a real problem if she's coming in force. Cait said there were thousands of creatures beyond the gate."

"Sure. . ." I began, but I couldn't focus as a wave of dizziness crept over me.

Morgan caught me just before I fell over. "Hey, what's wrong?"

"I—I don't know. I—Ugh." I grabbed my head as a spike of pain erupted behind my right eye, shooting backward. I felt like something was stabbing into it.

"Aoife?"

An overwhelming and vast pool of memories opened up, and I fell into them as one might fall into a pit. They mixed with—no, that wasn't right. They mixed with her memories. The one they called Aoife. *My...no...her...* My head began to keen again, and the dagger-like pain returned, stabbing deep into my brain. I doubled over, nauseated.

"Make it—presht—presht. Oh, Avra and Mother Darkness, it hurts!" The words spilled from my mouth. *I said them. Did I? I don't know.*

Sights and wonders filled my mind, all familiar and yet foreign: tall brilliant spires of black rock and lightning, the obelisk just outside the house, and the smoldering and fuming passages of a dark and beautiful planet. It was all there. Home.

"Morgan?" I called out, feeling arms around me. *Who? No, not that one.* "Déra..." I gagged as I jerked from Morgan's grasp and dropped to my knees, vomiting onto the floor.

Each experience was my own and not. Nothing felt like me, as if I were a visitor in my own body.

"Kwis díri?" The question just spilled from me. "I am Aoife," I tried to say in response, but two names tumbled together and crashed out unintelligible. I opened my eyes, looking into the face of the woman who loved me.

"Aoife! Aoife!" Morgan shouted, face painted with worry. I knew her. She was Aoife's lover, *my* lover.

The pain began to subside again, and I pulled back as if stung by Morgan's hands. "Get away! I love you. I—" My hands clawed at my hair, and I didn't know whose they were. Mine? Or hers! *No, she can't have them.*

"I am Aoife. No...I am Umbrá." I spat. A war raged in my mind with me on both sides, and I didn't know who was supposed to win.

"Oh, Goddess—no," I uttered in horror. "I'm...I'm inside someone...alive. No!" The sin of it was devastating, an abomination. "Who...?" *Who what?* I tried to draw myself together, piecing together my own memories. But which were mine? "Déra...Morgan, help me. I can't find me." I sounded like a child scrambling in search of a lost doll.

Stop! A voice shouted in my skull, high-pitched and ringing. The agony in my head started anew. A scream erupted from my mouth. It was my voice. I grabbed a hold of that sound. It was my voice. I was the physical body. A warmth descended on my thoughts, comforting and intimate.

"Please talk to me, baby," Morgan said. I was in her arms, but her voice faded into the background, leaving me alone in the darkness with just the other one. Everything was gone. I could feel nothing, no body, no life, nothing at all. It was like having my consciousness stuffed into a gaping hole and left to rot.

Umbrá spoke. "We cannot survive like this. You must leave."

"No, Umbrá," I whispered in my thoughts. "This is my body. I will not give it up without a fight."

"Then we cease to exist."

Something akin to a wicked smile formed in my thoughts. There was no physicality to it, just an emotion, but it was very real. "I have already died. I'm not afraid. Are you?"

Epilogue

"I don't understand this," Bian said after she'd finished her examination of Aoife. "There was no sense of a second soul when I examined her after we applied the tlehos."

We were all gathered at Bian's lab, the entire unit, even Freyer and Celeste, plus Marcella, Liz, Nastasia, and Doyle.

I narrowed my eyes at Bian. "So, both Umbrá and Aoife are in there." My narrowed eyes turned to a full scowl. "You should have known better, Bian, after what happened to me." I thought about the dreams and visions I'd had when the tlehos had been inside me, memories that didn't belong there. It seemed like another lifetime ago.

"That was different," Bian said. "I had no idea that this would happen. And I am tired of being accused of either incompetence or malfeasance. This was simply unforeseen."

I gave her a disappointed look but backed off, instead drawing in a breath and letting it out to give the appearance of settling down. "For the future," I said as gently as I could. "Shaddani souls cling to their bodies. Now two souls are in one body. No human, no Shaddani, no Kyliri can survive in such a state for long. Best case, Aoife destroys Umbrá and recovers."

Déra gasped, "No. You can't let that happen."

I held up my hand. "We won't. Worst case, their souls unravel, and they vanish into the fabric and weave of magic around us. This was foolish. And yes, Mother Lamia knew what would happen. She was trying to preserve Aoife's life because she thinks she's the fucking next messiah or whatever,

439

I'm sure."

Liz stared at me but said not a word. I could see it in her eyes, though. She was wondering just how changed I was. A million flickering thoughts lay there, twisting through those beautiful green eyes. Does she still love me? Do I still know her? Will we be the same?

I would set aside her worries later. For now, we all had a larger problem, namely how to save my sister, let her have her body back, and preserve Umbrá's soul.

I sighed. "If I had a soulstone and enough power, I could probably fix this." I frowned in concentration, trying to remember what, if anything, my mother had said about the soulstone we had used for Boudka. I couldn't remember where she put it, and Mother's Waters only knew where it was now.

"Déra, have you ever seen one of these?" I asked as I drew a fair approximation of the soulstone.

She nodded, glancing at the paper. "A karanite crystal? Sure. They're used as decoration in Ishir."

"Where do you get them?"

"It's forbidden to tell anyone," she replied, a stern fixity to her features.

I didn't press her, but I thought about everything I'd learned from Óbin and Nemhain, and then it hit me. "You've been mining in Shaddan!" It was the only thing that made sense. It's why the Óşeni kept their gate to Shaddan open despite the dangers. They could have closed it—no, they should have closed it. The tablets were relatively easy to make, and to power them, they had the Mens-Dhe engines.

Déra said nothing, crossing her arms defiantly. "It is forbidden to discuss."

"Even with Valtárí?" I asked.

Déra raised an eyebrow at that. "Are you claiming my heritage now, too? What is it your people call it? Stolen honor?"

I slid back the left collar of my shirt, revealing the spiral soul brand over my left breast. "No," I answered in flawless, crisp Óşeni. "I am claiming my right by induction and brand."

Déra still looked skeptical, but she couldn't deny the soul

brand. The magic of it was unique.

"To the Valtárí, my name is Skaja." I gave her a brief explanation of what I'd experienced while I'd been down, at least the Reader's Digest version. If she was in any way impressed, she didn't show it. But I expected no less. Óşeni warriors were women of action. In combat was where I'd make my mark with her.

Déra shook her head. "It doesn't matter, karanite crystals are far rarer than your diamonds, and you'd only find one by luck."

I slammed my hand down on the steel countertop, leaving a modest print. "That's not helpful. The Óşeni gate is in flux and can't be opened. Our chances of digging a karanite crystal out and shaping it in time are next to nil—" I paused, a thought forming. "There is one here on earth. It was last seen in Ireland about two thousand years ago."

"Maybe the Bethadi have one," Doyle said softly, her voice sounding almost tiny.

I turned back to look at her. "Huh?"

"Maki said that the gate in Ireland is Bethadi. Maybe we could ask them."

"All roads lead to Aine," I muttered. "That'll be fun. I guess we're off to Ireland."

Join Cait Reagan
In
Dark Sisters: A Cait Reagan Novel
Coming 2024 - Wherever Books are Sold

GLOSSARY

Ánámensí - (os. Ah-nah-men-si) Matron of one of the remaining thirty-seven high houses of the city of Işir on the world of Oşen.

Centrus - (unk. Sen-truss) City that serves as a hub for the currently open inter-dimensional gates, including, most notably, the Kaushkari, Oşeni, and Niatamo gates.

Déra - (os. Day-rah) Uncommon Oşeni female name. Most famously, the appellation of a former guard captain of Işir, who vanished following the defeat of Avra in the Cycle of Our Lady 6998.

Emisai - (os. Em-is-eye) Construct of Mother Darkness, this creature is bipedal but has no head or obvious sensing organs. Only black-steel as constructed by the Oşeni scholars of Mens-Dhe can harm them. Other metals without magical construction will leave no long-term injury.

Işir - (os. Ish-eer) Primary city of the world of Óşen. The city is ruled by a matriarchal priestess caste. Males are considered second-class citizens having fewer rights.

Koşant - (os. Kō-shant) Bipedal demon-like creature with razor-sharp claws, roughly man-shaped and covered in mottled insectile chitin. It has a triangular, mantis-like face, with a beak-like mouth.

Kylr - (ky. Kī-ler) Single sex, bipedal humanoid species that is the dominant life form of the world known only as the Kylr Plain. They are characterized by iridescent white skin, silver hair, and black eyes. Most notable and interesting is their reproductive cycle. At death, the corpse of the dead Kyliri transforms into a second stage, a worm-like creature that carries a smaller parasitic animal in which the life and memories of the dead Kylr are preserved until introduced to a new host, at which point the parasite consumes the brain of the host, preserving the memories and adding it to its own as it assumes control of the host body.

Óşen - (os. Ō-shen) One of the ten known worlds containing gates to Centrus, the core city of the ancients who constructed the first gates. It is populated by a dioecious species known locally as the Oşeni.

Óşeni - (os. Ō-shen-ee) Bipedal humanoid species populating the world of Oşen. They are concentrated in a single city on the world's surface known as Işir. The species is dioecious (having two sexes, male and female) and typically stands between 2 and 2.1 meters in height. They are characterized by lustrous gray skin, thick silver hair, and muscular frames. It is believed by some scholars that this group may have been the inspiration for certain depictions of elves because of their pointed ears.

Xharpras - (os. ħarp-rahs) A stringed instrument of the Oşeni similar to a harp. The black-steel strings and unusual tunings create secondary thematic elements in music, such as the sounds of waves crashing on rocks or wind blowing through trees. It is considered one of the most difficult instruments to play in the ten known worlds.

Umbrá - (os. Um-brah) Uncommon Oşeni female name. Most famously, the appellation of a Kyliri slave who was responsible for the downfall of Avra following the Dark Invasion in the Cycle of Our Lady 6998.

ABOUT THE AUTHOR

Aoibh Wood lives in New England with her wife and their wonderful orange Tabby, who may or may not resemble an intergalactic gangster of some notoriety. She enjoys writing, playing guitar, and the occasional game or two.

BLOOD RITUALS BY AOIBH WOOD

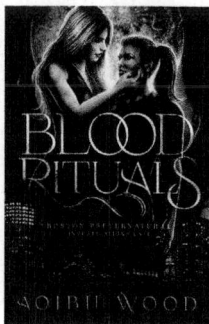

Available wherever books are sold.

Boston Homicide Detective, Caitlin Reagan, walks a razor's edge, propping up her life on emotional constructs designed to help her manage grueling PTSD. She keeps her mother, boyfriend, and work separated and controlled, all in service to one horrible, tragic act she committed amid the Iraq war.

But when the murder of a charity worker brings her face to face with the beautiful and charismatic philanthropist, Marcella Carson, Cait is unable to deny the attraction and finds everything she thought she knew about her world, her life, and her very identity called into question as Marcella draws Cait into her dark world.

Sliding inexorably into an unsuspected Boston subculture, where creatures of myth and nightmare struggle to survive in a world of fading magic and proliferating public surveillance, Cait must face down her inner demons, rediscover her lost past, and catch an undead serial killer.

BLACK MIRROR BY AOIBH WOOD

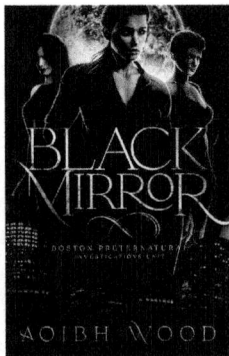

Available wherever books are sold.

Detective Cait Reagan, forever changed by her relationship with Marcella Carson, has survived the opening of the black gate and the vampire curse. Now, seemingly cured, Cait has a new lease on her mortal life, but difficulties beset her at every turn. Cait's mother, Róisín, is neurologically devastated, unable to function without constant supervision. Her reunion with Morgan Kennedy, the first woman she ever loved, is downright awkward. In the meantime, Cait struggles to raise Katie, the sixteen-year-old vampire she turned in a desperate bid to save her life. Once Cait's enemy, Elizabeth is helping with Katie, but Cait's relationship with Liz is tenuous and strange. And eight-hundred-year-old vampire Nastasia Volkova, the acting head of the vampire council, seems to have her eye on Cait, refusing to remove her from the roll of known vampires.

As if all of this turmoil wasn't enough for one woman to handle, Marcella is missing, and someone is murdering the remaining vampires who survived the battle of the Black Gate. Nastasia has made it crystal clear that she wants the culprits found and brought to her brand of justice. Meanwhile, something sinister stalks from the black gate deep beneath Boston.

Cait must juggle her increasingly complicated personal life with the needs of her job, Nastasia's strange fixation, and the whirlwind of her own desperate search for self as she grasps for answers to the question, 'What is true evil?'

Printed in Great Britain
by Amazon